CHEZ CORDELIA

CHEZ CORDELIA

Kitty Burns Florey

SEAVIEW BOOKS

NEW YORK

Manufactured in the United States of America.

FIRST EDITION

Designed by Tere LoPrete

Library of Congress Cataloging in Publication Data

Florey, Kitty Burns.
    Chez Cordelia.

      I. Title.
PZ4.F6329Ch   [PS3556.L588] 813'.54   80-5194
ISBN 0-87223-623-4

"Preparation is everything."

JULIA CHILD

For Ken and Kate

CHEZ CORDELIA

Chapter One

THE CHAMBER OF HORRORS

I make lists. Not just shopping lists and lists of "Things I Must Do Next Tuesday," but lists designed to organize my life. I make a list when I need to get things straight—what's straighter than a list? Nice and neat, with all the nonessentials pruned away. I would like my life to be like that.

I'm writing this account of my life out of necessity, because I need to make sense out of it and lists aren't enough. I doubt that this will be enough, either. I'm a talker, not a writer. I don't put much faith in the adequacy of the written word, and this is a labor not of love or of faith but of pure anguish. All my life, I've been at war with words put down on paper, and now I'm waging the war in earnest. I have to do it because my honor is at stake. In that respect, it's like any war, and I suppose it will be just as futile, producing—after all the napalm burns and bombed-out cities—only a temporary peace, or an illusion of peace. But I push on, each page its own lonely battlefield.

I suppose writing is painful for me because reading is. From the time I learned to read, I disliked it. I learned late. Instinctively, I put it off as long as possible. I didn't really read with fluency until third grade, and I'll tell you one reason why: I had a mother, a father, two older sisters, and a brother to read to me, and they read so well, with such drama, assuming with such magical ease and accuracy the roles of Flopsy Bunny and Mrs. Piggle-Wiggle and Freddy the Pig, that the printed words, the mere letters marching in dull rows across the page, were hopelessly insipid by comparison.

But that's not all of it. I resisted reading because books were the family trade, the family obsession. My parents and my siblings read and write as gracefully and as necessarily as they breathe. With me the genes for that sort of thing must have been used up or gone stale or refused to cooperate. From the time I was a child, I was the maverick, the little oddball who hated books.

Books, for me, were never the key to the pleasures of plot and character and language that my anxious mother, during our unproductive talks, claimed them to be (her face subtly horrified at her mutant daughter, the afterthought, supposed to be the joy and comfort of her middle age, apparently no relation—at least spiritually—to her or my father or their other three children, who at tender ages had been reading Dickens and the comedies of Shakespeare). Books were simply a vehicle for getting my family to pay some attention to me, and if that implies that they stopped paying attention to me when I learned to read for myself, it's supposed to. That's just what happened, as I sensed it would, though my parents, who in their own way are conscientious about their children, would wince at my thinking so.

But the truth was that they didn't find me and my oddity very interesting. In fact, they seldom acknowledged its existence. My happy illiteracy was glossed over for years as if it wasn't there, like some minor flaw I'd probably grow out of with a little help—a lisp, or baby fat. My father always gave me books for Christmas and birthdays, beautifully inscribed in his distinctive handwriting (of course, on top of everything else, the whole family has distinctive handwriting): "To

Cordelia, from her loving father," and the date. I still have all of them (the illustrated *David Copperfield* he gave me for my fourth birthday makes an excellent place for pressing wildflowers), but I've still never read them. Whenever I open one and read "Your loving father," I think: if he really loved me he would never have given me these books.

It wasn't just my parents. My brother and sisters were in on it, too—the conspiracy to entice me into the world of books, and the polite refusal to acknowledge my lack of enthusiasm. Books were waved before me like doughnuts before a dieter, but I can't remember being very tempted. I think back to Juliet squealing her affected squeal, when I was five and she ten, over *The Mill on the Floss.* "You are going to love this in a couple of years, Cordelia. Here—" She tossed it in my lap. "Give it a try," she said, and gave me a sisterly hug before she floated off somewhere to begin on something else. Blast her, she knew I could no more give *The Mill on the Floss* a try than I could fly up the chimney, but that was her way of teaching me to read. "That's how *I* learned," she used to say to me in the earnest voice she used when she wanted to cover up bragging. "Just by doing it, Cordelia. Start at the beginning and sound out the words, don't worry if you don't know what they mean, just keep going on . . ."

Her voice kept going on. I was her project, and if I could have flown up the chimney I would have. What an escape, what an event it would have been. "Good-bye forever, Jule," I would have said, and swooshed up the chimney like a skinny little Santa Claus. But no. I used to sit there with those heavy books on my lap, feeling deadened by them, their weight, the immense bulk of the millions and millions of ABC's in them. Once I told Juliet I didn't much want to learn to read, and she giggled as at a naughty joke. "Of course you do," she said, and returned to her book.

All of them—they couldn't wait until I got tangled in the web of the printed word. They just couldn't understand what was taking me so long.

"Why do you resist it?" my mother asked me finally when, at six, I brought home my U in first-grade reading. (The U was for Unsatisfactory, which was severely understating the case, but there was no lower grade than U in my positive-thinking, sunny-side-up school.) My mother's face was almost unlined—she was in her late thirties then—except for two furrows between her eyebrows, the result of all those years of frowning over books. When she looked at my report card the lines deepened, and I could see the hint of more coming, lines that would get sharper the more I brought home lousy report cards. I felt bloated with guilt, my stomach began to hurt, I had to go to the bathroom.

"Why don't you like reading?" she asked me in despair. "With all this around you?" She gestured widely, and indeed the walls (though we were in the kitchen) were lined with books, and through the door into the living room we could see Juliet slumped in a chair, chewing her hair and getting her print fix. On the table before us lay the book my mother had been reading when I got home from school, face down to mark the place.

She waited patiently for an answer. "It's too hard," I said, not knowing what else to say. I looked down at the book on the table. If pressed, I would have deciphered the title as *Silly Wimps*. That couldn't have been it, of course, but that's how bad a reader I was—or maybe I was projecting.

My mother sighed. At least I hadn't confessed the total antipathy she feared. "It'll get easier," she said, squeezing my hand. "You'll work at it, won't you, Cordelia?" She gazed intently at me, as if my face were a book.

I nodded with enthusiasm, and was rewarded for my fib by seeing the lines smooth out a bit. She gave me a little bowl of salty black olives and a glass of milk. Before I'd finished my first olive she was deep in her book again.

I remember eating olives and feeling lonely, feeling like an alien invader of another planet. The lie I'd just told bothered me—I knew perfectly well I wasn't going to *work at* reading.

6

I saw that little evasion as the first in a long string of them; already, at age six, I'd learned how to sneak and compromise in order to get along in hostile territory. My mother was far away in *Silly Wimps*, though she raised her head once or twice to smile dimly at me. Juliet chewed her long hair and read and read like an enchanted princess. The others weren't home from school yet. My father was up in his third-floor study. It was raining outside. I'd gotten a U on my report card. Dinner was hours away. I finished all the olives. I began to bang my feet against the rungs of my chair and cry.

It ended with Juliet reading to me. "She's upset about her report card," my mother said softly to Juliet, and I yelled, "I am not! I don't care!" I banged my feet harder. My sister and my mother exchanged a look: "That just shows how much she *does* care." I kept muttering "I don't care" until Juliet offered to read to me. "This always calms her down," she said to my mother in the prissy, grown-up voice she had adopted when she began getting poems published on the children's page of the newspaper.

We curled up on the sofa together with one of the Freddy the Pig books I was addicted to. My mother beamed at us. Such traditional family scenes always abstractly touched her; Juliet even had one arm around my shoulder. I sniffled a few more times and burrowed closer to her. Juliet was the best reader of all, better even than my father. She had a real dramatic gift, which was what probably made her, later, a good fashion model; and when she put on her brave, squeaky voice for Freddy and her high, snooty one for awful Mrs. Underdunk, I giggled with delight, looking resolutely at the pictures and not at the words.

This was what I wanted—someone to snuggle with, someone to pay attention to me, the sound of a human voice. The stories were only a welcome adjunct to these other pleasures. It was the solitariness of reading that turned me off, the deadly grown-up-ness of it. I saw learning to read, and I still believe rightly, as the end of childhood.

And I suppose, put simply, I preferred people to books—not such a bizarre preference, it seems to me. But in my family it was. In my family the eccentricities of characters in novels were lovable, and the eccentricities of the youngest child were unacceptable. It's *that* that I thought I could never forgive them for.

But of course I did, finally, learn to read. The full force of family pressure came down on me, abetted by my teachers, when I was in the third grade and still reading at first-grade level, still getting U's. When I read aloud in the classroom there were sighs of impatience and occasional groans, and I'd see the cold marble face of Sister Victoria Marie close up in silent prayer while I broke out in a sweat over words like *surprise* and *neighbor*. I was a whiz at arithmetic, at the head of the class without effort, and my parents had hopes (slightly appalled ones, considering the family talents) that I would distinguish myself in numbers if not in letters. My promise faded with adolescence when I discovered the stigma attached to girls who got A's in math, but at eight I was a natural, and for that reason I was not held back a grade and was, in fact, considered bright enough—although I had heard my parents more than once discuss the possibility that I was one of those idiots savants who babble and dribble through life until presented with a column of figures, which they promptly add up in their heads, square, and translate into metric feet.

"If she can multiply, she can read," they said to each other—illogically and without much hope but, it turned out, truly. My parents got after the school, and the school got the Reading Specialist after me.

Her name was Mrs. Meek (so much for the power of words), and she bullied me into it. She had a will of iron, I had as yet no discernible will at all, and by the time I was nine I was spewing out whole chapters of the red-covered First Reader. What a dull book it was, too—what a reward for all my pains: *Neighborhood Friends*, starring Ted and Nancy and their dog Spot. After I finished it and went sloppily through its accompanying workbook, I pushed on to the Second Reader, *This Wide World*, in which Ted and Nancy take up basketball, travel to the big city, build a playhouse, and get a new puppy (Skippy, an Airedale), never letting on what happened to faithful Spot or mourning the old boy for a minute.

But in the end, no matter how glibly I rattled off the adventures of Ted and Nancy and their doomed mutts, I knew my parents were disappointed in me. The fact that I'd had to work so hard at reading, and, worse yet, didn't enjoy it at all, was a grievous blow to them. There was Juliet, in the eighth grade, winning the Junior Scholastic short story contest for the third year in a row and regularly contributing to the children's page. And Miranda, in tenth grade, editor of the school paper, honor student, spelling bee veteran. And Horatio, in his senior year, a Merit scholar finishing up his first novel and ready to head for Harvard. And me . . . an unpromising third-grader who read simpleminded texts not for pleasure but because I was browbeaten into it by Mrs. Meek. I never told them I was bribed into it, too, with candy. A worse ignominy than not to read at all: to read for Hershey bars.

I look back on my sessions with Mrs. Meek—that calculated breaking of my will, the first hard assault on my spirit—as the point at which I said to myself, "No more. Never again," and resolved to go my own way. It's the search for that way that I've had to build my life on, and it's because of my parents and my siblings and Mrs. Meek that I sit, today, at this particular table, with this particular pencil in my hand and this particular view (trees, banks of flowers, quiet blue lake) before me.

There was another third-grade failure taken on by Mrs. Meek, along with me—Danny Frontenac. Three times a week Danny and I met with Mrs. Meek in her little room with the bright green tables and chairs and yellow walls and red square of carpet, a room so deliberately cheery that even third-graders noticed and resented it. There were always animal cutouts stuck up on the walls with tape, the kind of thing we were far too old to relish—duckies wearing boots and carrying umbrellas, black cats popping out of jack-o'-lanterns, that sort of nonsense. There was a permanent one on the door, under the sign JUNE MEEK, READING SPECIALIST (which for months I deciphered as JUNIOR MEEK, READING SPACEMAN)—a white kitten with glassy green eyes and a ballon coming out of its mouth saying, "Please Come In!"

In we went, every Monday, Wednesday, and Friday before lunch, and I recall that for some reason we went hand in hand, like Hansel and Gretel into the forest, perhaps because children in St. Agatha's Catholic Academy were made to travel in pairs, on the grounds that idle hands are the devil's playground and linked hands are therefore at least half spoken for. But I can't remember if our hand-holding was officially sanctioned school policy, or if it was a symbol of our unity. For we were united, Danny and I, not in friendship but in fear. Terror of Mrs. Meek was what we had in common. Otherwise we disliked each other heartily, as all third-grade boys and girls who have been ruthlessly segregated since kindergarten dislike each other. But for those three half-hours a week we were bound by ties of hate and fear, and by our clutched hands, which kept their white-knuckled grip on each other down the corridor to the stairs, up the stairs, down half another corridor, and into a cul-de-sac which contained the nurse's office on the right, the nuns' bathroom (hee hee hee!) on the left, and straight ahead Mrs. Meek's chamber of horrors inviting us in. There our sweaty hands parted, reluctantly, and took up pencils and workbooks and chocolates.

The horrors in the chamber were the words, our enemies—books full of them, and flash cards which Mrs. Meek could snap in our faces like a magician doing some evil card trick, and stories with questions to go with them that were designed to trip us up and humiliate us. And there was Mrs. Meek herself.

She terrified us, though it's hard now to say why. She was tall and broad, middle-aged, with short blond hair, and she always wore dark blazers and skirts. "She looks like a daddy," Danny said once, shuddering, but while I saw his point—there *was* something of the female impersonator about her—I didn't agree. For one thing, my daddy had a long black beard. I thought she looked like an off-duty nun, out of uniform.

She had a way of looking swiftly stunned (eyes popping, lips parted, nostrils pinched) and then pained (eyebrows angled down, teeth bared to the canines, eyes squinted half shut) at our mistakes, before the forbearing nunlike smile appeared again and the encouraging nods commenced. She filed her nails short, in points, and painted them red. Her eyes were pale blue with brown streaks in them. She must have worn a powerful girdle under her dark straight skirts, because I once jostled her and she felt exactly like a piece of furniture—the unyielding back of our sofa, maybe, stuffed with horsehair and covered tightly with fabric. She always seemed to both of us like a fraud, a witch disguised as a nice lady. She smiled a lot, showing plenty of crimson gum line and sharp white teeth, and she always spoke gently, and she rewarded us with candy, and she was always patient, but the whole performance, no matter how well acted, reminded me of the witch in Hansel and Gretel—sweet as pie until she had the children where she wanted them, and then *wham!* The door slammed shut, the oven was lighted, the fiendish cackles were released at last . . .

I had to hold off Mrs. Meek, and the only way to do it was to resist reading, resist the words she sent flying at me, fight the workbook with its trick questions. And I did fight; so did Danny. My weapon was inattention, his a slowness of mind I thought well feigned. Together we drove her crazy, drove her to superhuman patience and weekly more terrible smiles and bags and bags of Hershey kisses. (Even then a practical child, I used to wonder who paid for the candy, Mrs. Meek or the nuns?) She used to say, "That's better, Cordelia, really much better, it's coming nicely," after I stumbled through the tale of the spotted dog and the mud puddle; translated, her words meant "You little beast, how much longer will this go on?" (I could hardly read English, but I could read Mrs. Meek.) Once—only once—when my absentminded stammerings drove her to some kind of brink, she raised her hand as if to slap me, and there was an awful pause, an eternal three seconds that lasted until she deflected her hand to the candy bag. The smile remained frozen on her face, no less grim than the creepy leer of the cat-sprouting jack-o'-lantern on the wall, and she pushed a piece of candy at me and watched me eat it, showing her sharp teeth, her sharp claws reaching for another one. I ate all she gave me, hungrily; it was not for nothing that our remedial sessions were held just before lunch. But the candy wasn't candy: it was reading medicine, and all three of us knew it. I would have resisted that, too, along with the other witch-blandishments, but though I knew it was medicine as surely as Robitussin and Kaopectate were medicine, it tasted just like candy, and I bolted it.

It worked. Gradually I learned to read, against my will. My will, as I said, was no match for Mrs. Meek's. I sat at her knee and prattled off the little stories, stumbling still but, if I went slowly and kept my mind on it, getting through them passably, at least as well as Vinnie DeLuca, who was the worst reader in the third grade except for Danny and me.

Danny learned, too, though even more slowly than I did. He was always a Problem Reader, all through elementary school, sullenly collecting U's and 43's and "Disgraceful!"s on his spelling tests and book reports. I remember once, in sixth grade, I sat across the aisle from him, and we had to correct each other's English tests. In an exercise requiring us to class a list of sentences as simple or compound, Danny got two out of ten right, obviously by hit-or-miss, and he spelled *simple* and *compound*, consistently, as *smiple* and *compond*, two words I came to like very much by the end of the test. (I had four wrong myself, but Danny caught only one of them.)

When I graduated out of the remedial class, Mrs. Meek gave me a giant Hershey bar, tied with a red ribbon, which I ate sitting on a toilet in the girls' bathroom before I returned to the third grade. Candy was one of the many aspects of what I considered normal life that were forbidden by my parents, and even though the eight-ounce slab of Hershey chocolate was my diploma certifying passage into the world of letters, I knew it was best to devour it and destroy the evidence. I flushed the wrappers down the toilet along with the red ribbon, wiped my mouth on a paper towel, and marched, slightly sick, down the hall to the third-grade classroom, where Sister Victoria Maria gave me a cold smile and the Third Reader, *Earth and Sky*, in which I laboriously wrote my name. I leafed through it before lunch (which I gave to Billy Arp in exchange for being allowed into the kickball game at recess) in hopes of finding Ted and Nancy replaced at last by more interesting children. But there they were, lumpishly smiling, visiting Uncle Bill's farm and learning about weather and romping with yet another dog, a collie named Sport. And I could read it all. I felt no triumph, only a sort of drab, betrayed gloom and a vivid, precocious resolution never to let such a thing happen to me again.

I had mastered reading, after a fashion, as I had learned to make my bed, and I put it in that category: "Boring Chores." But I did it when I had to, and I ascribe to the fanged, creepy witchiness of Mrs. Meek the fact that the only kind of books I really like to read, to this day, are mysteries—and, come to think of it, that, I suppose, is what I'm writing.

Chapter Two

MY FATHER'S HOUSE

My brother, Horatio, writes real mysteries—or, rather, *not-real* ones, fictional ones. He began as a professor specializing in Chaucer, but in the donnish tradition of academics who turn to crime writing as a sideline, he produced (one summer when it was too hot, he explained, for Middle English) his first murder mystery, *Pride, Prejudice, and Poison,* in which Jane Austen tracks down the "spa poisoner" who is mixing strychnine with the healthful waters of Bath. It was such a success, winning the Edgar award and selling half a million copies, that, at the expense of his book on Chaucer, Horatio turned out another the following summer: *Deep in the Madding Crowd,* with Thomas Hardy as the amateur detective who exposes a mass murderer. And when that too hit the best-seller lists he abandoned forever Chaucer, his associate professorship, and the hopes of my parents which he'd filled so faithfully all his life, and became a full-time writer of lurid literary detective stories: *Death on the Mississippi* (starring Mark Twain), *Remembrance of Crimes Past* (in which Proust solves the crime without leaving his cork-lined bedroom), and his latest, *The Canterbury Deaths* (because he got homesick for Chaucer).

My parents always tolerated Horatio's degeneration into popular culture because he made so much money at it. My father is a poet, and like all poets he has spent most of his adult life grubbing after cash—grants, fellowships, chairs, residencies, readings, publishers' advances—and he respects the stuff with a respect bordering on dementia, but he'd never admit it, any more than he'd admit he looked down on Horatio and considered him a sellout and a crass materialist. Money, according to my parents, is no good unless it's been grubbed after in some arty way, and achieved in bits. The cash that flowed into Horatio's bank account (and promptly out again, I should say) they considered tainted money.

Juliet did a little better: she was perpetually hard-up but intellectually respectable, writing verse dramas no one would produce and sonnet sequences no one would publish. For years, she flitted around the earth living on grants at various universities where she studied Greek. In her spare time, she poured out her soul into her verse epic, *The Labyrinth*, which dealt with herself in relation to Greek mythology. She'd been working on it for nine years, and the end was not in sight— which was just as well, because although my father (who managed to remain wildly excited by the project for all those nine years) promised to get Juliet a publisher, I had a feeling that this time his vast network of connections would break down and no one would touch it. I had seen the thing: it was thicker than *David Copperfield* and it was partly in Greek. Juliet used to bring my parents all the new bits, and they read them and beamed ecstatically and hugged her, as if she'd presented them with grandchildren.

My other sister, Miranda, was married to a man named Gilbert Sullivan (I kid you not) and had her own printing press, on which she and Gilbert published, chiefly their own works. (Miranda wrote novels about tormented women in analysis; Gilbert wrote art criticism.) Miranda is shaped like a hatpin—tall and thin, with piled-up hair. She used to play basketball. Both my sisters, in fact, went through periods of what my parents considered frivolity in connection with their height: Miranda, as "Ready Randy" Miller, put herself through college on basketball scholarships, and Juliet was briefly a fashion model. But Daddy went to Miranda's games, and Mom bought the magazines in which Juliet was featured, just as they both read Horatio's books. Their disapproval of Miranda's and Juliet's and Horatio's strayings from the fold was always touched with amusement, and that's because the three of them are relentlessly literary types, whatever their peccadilloes. Juliet with her epic, Miranda with her little press, even Horatio with his abandoned professorship and vulgar success: they all sit smack in the middle of various literary pies. Small wonder that I, by contrast, am the family disappointment: short to their tall, discreet to their flashy, sense to their sensibility. What they liked to do when we all got together was play Botticelli or Scrabble, or read Juliet's verse epic aloud. What I liked to do was watch *Hawaii Five-O* or play blackjack.

My father is Jeremiah Miller, "a household word the way Tennyson was," my mother likes to say when she sums up his career. There used to be a picture of Tennyson in the guest room (where all the odds and ends went), and he did remind me of my father—the beard, the melancholy brown eyes, the look of celebrity about him. But my father seems rougher, heartier, and I doubt Tennyson would want to have anything to do with him.

My father is, officially, an old-fashioned family man. He can be flamboyantly paternal. "These are my best poems," he would say when we were small, gathering us to his bosom where the soft black beard flowed. "My masterpieces," he sometimes continued. "My *chefs d'oeuvres*, my *Don Juan*, my *Canterbury Tales*, my *Four Quartets*—" His I-don't-know-whats. It's always been clear that he loves us—*adores* us—although it was also clear to me, from my earliest youth, that he loved us best when we were quiet, that children should be as unobtrusive as books on a shelf except when they were taken down for inspection, for inspiration, for amusement—sometimes for annotation. He loved us best when we were the children he had designed in his head.

I was never one of those children, and I learned early to stay out of his way, to avoid in particular his attic study (where Horatio had put a sign on the door: HALLOWED GROUND—characteristically, my father didn't remove it when the joke was over) and the window beneath it. I learned silence. I tried to stay out of the house all I could. For one thing, I got more dirty work than any of my siblings. They caught on early that, at our house, you could effectively shirk chores if you whined out, "I'm *reading!*" or "Can't I just finish this chapter?" So it was I, little Cinderella ("Here, Cordelia, you're not doing anything—take out the garbage"), who became, by default, mother's helper. At six, at seven, I was drying dishes, emptying garbage, setting the table, while Horatio and Juliet and Miranda slouched around lapping up pages of print. It made me mad, but it didn't make me read. The truth was, I preferred to empty the garbage.

I wasn't allowed to bring most of my friends home. My parents hardly ever approved of them. But I became adept at wangling invitations to their houses. They were mostly non-readers like me, kids whose parents would have admonished them if they had done much reading, "Don't sit around all day with your nose in a book. You'll ruin your eyes! Go out and play!" At their homes, no one ever said, "Hush! Daddy's working!" because their daddies didn't work at home. I used to long for a regular daddy who left the house in the morning and arrived home at dinnertime. Sandy Schutz (my best friend) had a daddy who got home at 6:30 and played kickball with her and her brother until dinner and then watched TV with them. I drooled over such normal living. My father's poetry writing was like an illness, our house the house of an invalid who was confined to his room all day and emerged only in the evening. His poems come hard to him, he always tells interviewers, and in order to write them he needs long stretches of quiet. But in the evenings he wanted us to be there, confirming his success as a father, and what he liked best was for all of us to be in the same room, reading, with someone occasionally reading something aloud, or being struck by some idea, or proposing some word game. It was okay to interrupt as long as it was a literary or otherwise intellectual interruption; they would all look up, fingers keeping their places, and join in; then, interruption disposed of, down they'd dive again. I was a talkative kid, but gradually within the bosom of the family I developed a reputation for taciturnity—though it was really the stark knowledge that my interruptions would be met with patient smiles and small response. I sometimes thought living, for them, was little more than a break in their reading or their writing, and to me the silence that surrounded them was oppressive, alien, and hateful.

I, of course, during those jolly family evenings, was seldom reading. Not *never*: I was required as a schoolchild to do a certain amount. At the weekly compulsory trip to the school library I picked out a book along with everyone else, and occasionally even read it, if it was about animals and had plenty of pictures. Sometimes I was forced to read it. My fourth-grade teacher, Sister Caroline, used to make us write a weekly book report, and Sister Joseph Edward, in fifth grade, used to quiz me (and Danny and Vinnie and one or two other reading-resisters) about our library books. (I still remember, at the age of ten, trying to get away with *How the Grinch Stole Christmas*.)

But on most of those long evenings in our messy living room, I had to find other occupations for myself. What I wanted to do plenty of times was scream, throw apple cores, smash something, grab someone's book and stuff pages in my mouth, and gabble horrible noises at them all. But I did none of these things, though it comforted me to imagine them, and worse. After I finished my homework I usually looked at my coins.

When I was eleven, my Aunt Phoebe gave me my grand-father's coin collection, and I fell in love with it. At first my parents were thrilled because it was a faintly intellectual inter-est. "You'll pick up some history, at least," they said en-couragingly. But as time went on my passion for the coins puzzled and even faintly disgusted them. They couldn't understand how I could just keep looking at them, lying on the floor turning the pages of my coin albums as if they were—well, books. They gave me books on numismatics, but I didn't read them, though I liked looking at the pictures. I preferred to learn about coins from Gene at the East Shore Stamp and Coin Shop. And in my spare time I coin-gazed, simply because I liked my coins—the way they looked, the aura they carried of many hands and many transactions and many people, and the fact that they were mine, all mine. And I liked adding up their value (accurately, in my head) and planning what coins I would add to my collection when I grew up and became rich. And I liked puzzling my parents perhaps best of all.

Why haven't I said much about my mother? Maybe be-cause I loved her most, or because she bugged me least. I think she was always quietly motherly as my father, for all his show, wasn't really fatherly. Not that the family disease didn't infect her as much as any of them. She writes biographies, short ones, of obscure literary figures. I used to think maybe I would read one or two of them, they're so short; also, they're inviting books. They're published by Owl & Bantling, Ltd., of London, a firm that publishes Anglican liturgical works, treatises on gardening, and my mother's biographies, and they treat my mother well. Her books are printed on creamy thick paper with the ragged edges that are hard to turn, and they all have rose-colored covers with a white spine and gold letters . . . thin, pretty books by my thin, pretty mother. I opened one once (waiting until no one was home, lest they get their hopes up), the thinnest one (82 pp.), called *The Fire's Path: A Life of Hywel ab Owain Gwynedd*. It was about a twelfth-century Welsh warrior poet. I made out that his mother's name was

Pyfog and that his fame rests on eight poems and a good deal of Norman-bashing, but the story was so clogged with words I could hardly read it. I admit I didn't try for long—I was afraid she'd come in and find me at it, and I'd have to confess I found it dull and incomprehensible—it was Welsh to me, har har har. My mother's work is apparently a critical and scholarly success, though not—needless to say—a popular one. But Owl & Bantling don't expect their authors to write best-sellers, they'd probably drop her if she did, and they write my mother affectionate letters, in ink. "Caviar to the general," my father always said about her stuff, and this expression of her failure seemed curiously satisfying to both my parents. But though I've been acquainted with caviar since I was a baby and used to practice my small-motor skills on it, eating it black pearl by black pearl, no one ever told me who the general is; I was expected to know.

She was always at it, my mother. Unlike Daddy, she always did her work in the midst of the family, and I used to find her at the kitchen table when I got home from school, drinking Jackson's Coronation Tea and, say, writing out lists of Anglo-Saxon verbs. Languages are her specialty; I think she knows all of them, particularly the ones which are dead, obsolete, or spoken only by one small tribe living on the banks of a tributary of some minor Australian river—that sort of thing. It depresses me, all that mental energy going for zilch. Not to be disrespectful of my mother. But I can see learning French if you're going on vacation in France. I can even understand learning Latin or Old English so you can read the books written in it if that's your inclination. But the Jeshoba dialect of the Murai? I ask you. In fact, I have asked her: she says she does it for fun, and I must admit my mother has always seemed to me a singularly happy woman. I once asked Juliet, though, and she said something else: "She does it to keep sane. Because of Daddy." I am still absorbing this blasphemy.

When we were kids, our parents' lives revolved around the family and my father's work. We had plenty of company because my father needed to show off. His poet friends would come for interminable weekends of poetry reading and whiskey drinking. Juliet and I used to sneak out of bed at night to listen to the uproar. "Why do you have to be drunk all the time to be a poet?" I asked her once. "I'm a poet," she said loftily, "and I'm not drunk."

There was one man in particular, Theodore Low (jokingly called "The Dentist Poet" because he had briefly, in his youth, gone to dental school), who used to fascinate us. He became violent when he was drunk enough, and he was nearly always drunk enough. He came to visit perhaps twice a year, and I always looked forward to his coming—the way I looked forward to other natural disasters, like blizzards. For one thing, he liked me. I was the only dark-haired one in a houseful of blonde women, and he used to call me his little chocolate cream and sneak me expensive candies from New York. Once he brought me a white fur muff. Another time—not so pleasant a memory, though then it seemed like fun—when he was very drunk, he picked me up, threw me on the sofa, and began tickling me, both of us giggling ecstatically until my mother came in and he suddenly stopped. I remember his pungent breath and my mother's set face. Ted Low also broke windows, pulled the phone out of the wall, smashed whiskey bottles, once set fire to his bed, and made passes at my mother. But my father said he had a great gift, so he kept coming—a short, fat man with a face the color of the suet we put out for the birds. He died in an asylum when I was seventeen, and I cried so hard I had to be kept home from school.

During the time my father was teaching (at Wesleyan for a while, then at Yale), there would be intense students hanging around with sheaves of poems, usually small squares of words typed in the middle of a big sheet of paper (a silly waste, I thought; why couldn't they type two or three to a page?). They idolized my parents, fell in love with our big, book-messy house, and publicly envied us kids our terrific life. And there I was, the little malcontent, huddled over my gold and silver coins like a cavewoman over her fire, to keep off the ravening beasts: books, and book talk, and college boys trying to buddy up to me in order to make a good impression on my father.

For years, though, my war with the printed word never penetrated my father's consciousness—not really. My mother and I used to discuss it, briefly but regularly over the years, discussions ending in sad sighs all around, but no matter how many U's and notes from my teachers and picture-ridden library books I brought home, my father kept giving me absurdly inappropriate books for presents, and couching his affection for me in literary terms. What did it mean to me to be told I was his masterpiece, his *Hamlet*? Or to be thrust, helpless, into his poems? Or to be asked, every time I sulked, " 'So young and so untender?' " I didn't want to be my father's inspiration, I didn't want to be a damned literary allusion, I just wanted to be his daughter. I wanted him to accept my differences, but his attitude toward me was always expectant: one of these days I'd take to books, just as one of these days I'd grow tall.

These hopes weren't unreasonable when I was little, but they persisted into my adulthood. The truth is, my father is a snob; he couldn't let a book-resistant offspring into the clan. But I was his daughter, he was the poet of family life, he couldn't very well expel me. So he refused to admit my failings were final. He applied faith, hope, and charity to my case. And he waited for the baby of the family to grow up, to settle down, to become the person he expected.

The waiting hasn't aged him; he doesn't seem to have changed much from his early pictures—the series of snapshots, for instance, he and my mother took of each other on their honeymoon (a walking tour through England) in 1941. My father today hasn't one white hair, his cheeks are rosy, his vision is 20-20, his belly curves out over his belt to exactly the same degree it did when he was twenty-five. If all his hair turned white, he'd look like Santa Claus, but for the moment he is a large, hearty man who looks more like a lumberjack than a poet. You'd never peg him as someone who sits around writing and reading all day. His poems, by contrast, are apparently polished and classical—and "accessible," I'm told, in spite of his turning me into a red maple in one of them. They achieve, according to *Time* magazine, "the difficult combination of readability and profundity." His fourth book, *Where the Children Go*, is in paperback at the drugstore in town: "America's best-loved poet," the cover blurb says. (I saw it in the rack the other day when I was in there and blushed scarlet, remembering that it's the volume that contains the poem about my getting my period: "Meditation on a Daughter's Menses.") The two-part TV special about him and his family (I refused to appear) set a record for audience response on the public broadcasting station. My mother smiles and murmurs about Browning, Frost . . . There are times when Tennyson isn't enough for her.

It may be partly my father's large, picturesque hairiness, and our big old house in the Connecticut woods, that have endeared him to the public at a time when bushy beards and wood stoves (we have four of them) and ten acres of birch forest and meadow and close family ties are dear to the hearts of Americans. Or it may be, as they said on the TV special, that "Americans are ready for poetry again," and specifically for Jeremiah Miller's brand of poetry.

But it's my theory that he simply knows how to market himself. He has always made sure that he and his beard and his stoves and acres and kids are visible. Even before the TV special, he let us all be used in a *Time* photo essay: "The Poet and His Family." I was too young to protest: there I am, "Cordelia, youngest of the Miller brood," sitting up in the apple tree. I'm even quoted: "Says Daughter Cordelia, 12, with the devastating honesty of her namesake, 'What's all the fuss about? He's just my dad,'" words I never uttered. (They could make me sit for the damned photographers, but they couldn't make me talk; and even at the age of twelve I knew that, whatever my father was, he was surely not just my dad.)

Then, besides *Time*, there were women's magazine articles on my mother: "Elizabeth Miller, devoted mother, first-class cook, nature buff, linguist, biographer, and—last but by no means least—wife to America's unofficial Poet Laureate." One magazine even featured some of my mother's bizarre, extravagant, impetuous recipes, and another was keen to make her over with a haircut and eyeshadow and a string of pearls until my father put his foot down. Daddy has appeared on the Dick Cavett show twice, and he writes articles for the *Times* Op-Ed page, usually about the old-fashioned virtues of this and that and the other thing. He got his publishers to put into print Horatio's autobiographical novel (written before he left for Harvard). He even got in on Juliet's modeling career: *Vogue* did a series called "The Renaissance of the Family" that included a four-page spread on Juliet (in Ralph Lauren) and her pop (in flannel shirt and dungarees he'd had since the 1940s), and along with it a poem he composed for the occasion called "Daughter," which compared Juliet to (I think) a loaf of rising bread.

It tires me to think of it, the lengths he's gone to for the purpose of cramming literature down the throats of his countrymen. On them, it works. People write him letters saying he's changed their lives. They send him gifts, usually handmade. He's always giving readings—college students love him, so do senior citizens. Dick Cavett calls him up. Yale wants him back. He's been to the White House four times. Only with his youngest daughter has he failed.

I once made a list—I suppose I was about thirteen—of my differences from the rest of the family. It's in my List Notebook, the same one I've been using all these years, so tidy are my habits, so tiny my handwriting. What it actually is, is a dark blue Old Honesty Composition Book, the kind with the boy and the dog on the front cover and Useful Tables on the back. I bought it when I was in the fifth grade, at the suggestion of Sister Joseph Edward, to keep a list of difficult spelling words, but I never went beyond the first five: *lavender, sheriff, radiator, fiendish, humble.* That was one list that could have gone on indefinitely, but I quit there, perhaps from the hopelessness of it, more probably from sheer boredom. I devoted the rest of the book to more interesting lists. "Friends," for example (six names: Danny Frontenac and Billy Arp plus Sandy Schutz and three other girls in my class) and "Coins" (I can date this list precisely: the night of the day—my eleventh birthday—when my aunt gave me Grandpa Cole's collection).

This particular list is on the fourth or fifth page of my List Notebook, and it's headed "Differences":

1. Don't like reading or writting
2. left-handed
3. short
4. scallop-ear
5.

Number five is left blank not because I could think of only four but because there were so many—such vastness that was not covered in those four superficial items. The profound difference between the others and me was undefinable, unlistable. To this day I haven't been able to fill in number five, but I still see the rightness of that extra number and the blank space after it.

The differences I did list, though, are not really all that trivial—even my left-handedness. How I came to be the only left-handed person in a family of righties I don't know. Grandpa Cole, the coin collector, was left-handed. He's the only one anybody knows of. He died when I was a baby, and I've always wondered if he was as left-handed as I am: my right hand is practically useless for any movement more delicate than simply picking something up. I couldn't hold a fork properly with my right hand if my life depended on it, and when kids used to fool around by scrawling their names with their opposite hand, I was a sensation, hardly able to hold a pencil, much less write, even a scribble. My whole right side, in fact, I've always thought of as my vulnerable side; it's my right ear, too, that has the queer, deeply scalloped lobe. When I was married, I insisted on wearing my ring on my right hand, mostly so it wouldn't get in the way, though eventually I decided it added strength and stability to my bad hand. And when I was obliged to remove it my hand was always uneasy, less defended than ever . . .

I'm beginning to be bothered by my lack of organization here. Written-down words have a way of wandering off, and you can't organize them with a gesture or an inflection or a touch on the hand the way you can speech. You set them down neatly (in your tiny, slanting backhand), and before you know it they march off, forming odd links, hauling in other words, clogging together in ideas you never intended. I keep wanting to supply headings to hold them in: "My Left Hand" and "Lists" and, before that, "Learning to Read" and "My Father's Poems." I would still prefer, probably, merely to list instead of write. But listing does have its limitations, even I can see that. It could never deal adequately with the tale I have to tell; I know I have to write it out. If I'm going to deal with it at all, I have to do it with words.

Whenever I read my father's poems, I always think: why doesn't he just come out and *say* it? I know this is the philistine's approach, I know I'm condemning myself as an inferior form of humanity even to admit to it—my father, after all, is Jeremiah Miller—but I still can't understand why a poem about me (at least it's called "Of Cordelia, Small Daughter") should go on for thirty lines about a red maple tree. I always come out and *say* it. I believe experience can be explained and understood, and I'm here to do it, taking my pencil in my strong left hand and setting down word after laborious word. But I resent all the way the necessity of doing so, of succumbing at last to the family fetish—*me* writing a book! It's another victory for the forces of Mrs. Meek. And this time, if I'm rewarded with a ribbon-tied Hershey bar, I won't be able to eat it, not even secretly in the bathroom, because candy bars are on my list of "Forbidden Foods." But I don't need anything tied up in ribbon. The setting-down of this story, the labor of this writing, is its own reward—like virtue.

There won't be much virtue in this tale, though. It's a story of crime, punishment, prison, adultery, deceit . . .

There. I've whipped up interest right at the beginning, just as Horatio did in *Pride, Prejudice, and Poison.*

Chapter Three

HECTOR'S MARKET

As you might expect, I left my father's house as soon as I could. I did it by getting married to Danny Frontenac when I was nineteen.

Danny was one of the friends I fled to after school and on weekends, as often as I could escape, while my parents and siblings swam in books. Our real friendship—not the Meek-inspired, morally supportive, hand-holding third-grade bond—began when Danny discovered sex. At least, that was when he began to notice me. I already liked him a lot, and I began hanging around him when we were in the sixth grade. He barely tolerated me and hardly ever spoke to me, but he never made me go away, and he and his friend Billy Arp and I became a sort of trio. We hung around the East Shore Stamp and Coin Shop looking at double eagles, and we went fishing together down at Billy's. I considered them my dearest friends, not counting Sandy Schutz, though I knew full well that Danny and Billy didn't reciprocate my feeling.

Billy Arp lived in a house that stood on stilts above the water. His father was an amateur architect and was building the house himself. During the whole time I knew Billy his father was still building it, but it never seemed to change much. It had a glassed-in living room that looked out over the water, a compact kitchen—all gadgets—like the galley on a boat, and an elaborate redwood deck; the rest of the house was half done and chaotic. Billy's bedroom was never insulated, and in the winter the winds whipping across Long Island Sound would find every crack, so that Billy and Danny and I sat up there playing Monopoly in jackets and mittens. Sometimes we spent long afternoons leaning on the redwood railings of the deck looking out over the water, not doing anything else, just looking at sea, sky, gulls, boats. "If damn Long Island wasn't in the way," Billy said once, "we could see all the way to England."

"Cut it out," Danny said, always the skeptic.

"We could, it's right across from us," Billy insisted, as if the ocean were Main Street.

"Bull," Danny said. "It's too far, you couldn't see a thing, you can't even see Long Island from here." He snickered. "He thinks you can look across the ocean from his back yard and see the queen in her girdle." (We were perhaps twelve, and this was the kind of remark Danny was beginning to direct toward me: slightly risqué acknowledgments of the existence of sex. I noted each one carefully, but never answered, some code requiring that I turn away with a prissy smirk tempered with barely visible amused admiration for his ribald wit.)

Danny and Billy used to argue a lot—ignorant, theoretical disagreements that did nothing to disturb their friendship. I seldom joined in; in fact, I can't recall ever doing so in those preadolescent days except once, when Danny announced he had life and death figured out.

"I read in the paper that the universe came from one big explosion—right?" This was obviously a new concept for Billy, but he nodded readily enough, wanting to be up-to-date. "And that the whole process may be reversing itself—right?" Danny pursued. "And that Mars'll come slamming into Con-

necticut again one of these days—right? Right?" He punched
Billy in the biceps because Billy was guffawing over Mars
slamming into Connecticut. "Come on, I'm serious, Arp.
Come on, you guys." (That included me, though I wasn't
laughing.) "Well, I figure it keeps happening over and over,"
Danny went on. "Same explosion, same history of the world,
over and over again, same things happening to us over the
same billions of years, over and over—"

"Wow," Billy said softly, no longer laughing.

"Get it? It's like immortality," Danny said with reverence.
"I mean, it explains a lot of things."

My head swam, and for some reason I was angry. I heard
myself—the silent consort—shouting at them. "That's stupid,
that's just stupid!" They looked at me, startled. "First of all,
the same explosion over and over is crazy, it would take some
higher intelligence, but an insane higher intelligence, which
is ridiculous—" I stopped, all choked up. The boys looked
embarrassed, and gazed out over the Sound as if I didn't exist.
Billy fiddled with his portable radio. I went on. "Besides, what
kind of thrill is it, a theory like that? I mean, it could never
be proved—right?" Consciously, I aped Danny's locutions.
"We don't remember sitting out here billions and billions of
years ago at four o'clock in the afternoon eating Cheez-Its and
listening to the Beatles—do we?" I began to cry. "What's the
use of something like that? Who needs it?" I sobbed a little,
as quietly as I could, ashamed of my outburst and at the same
time angry that they ignored it. The worst of it was the affection I had for the two of them, affection that had no outlet.
I wanted to put my arms around them and hug them to me
for comfort. I would have held off Mars with my bare hands
if it came anywhere near us. I was overcome with despair at
the uselessness of my love.

"What's the use? What's the use?" I blubbered. The boys
looked intently out to sea, toward England. The Beatles sang
"A Hard Day's Night." Some time passed. Billy threw a
Cheez-It to the beach below, and a gull caught it in midair,

and he and Danny laughed and began to talk about gulls, leaving me to recover myself. I did, and I watched the gulls as nonchalantly as either of them after that, but even today Danny's Perpetual Big Bang theory fills me with rage and frustration. I suppose it's the grim impersonality of it that bothers me—and the inevitability.

I like to think I'm in charge of my life. In the beginning, I was the controlling force in my affair with Danny. I was the leader and the instigator, so what happened to me as a result of that affair is my own fault—and that's as it should be. Sitting across the aisle from him in the sixth grade, I used to admire Danny out of the corner of my eye. I didn't dare look at him directly, but secretly I checked out his shiny red hair, and his wrists (he has marvelous wrists and forearms, pale brown and nearly hairless, slender and strong and curiously flat, like sword blades).

I used to watch, furtively, the bones of his arm and hand moving as he doodled in the margins of his English book. His doodles were complex and artistic, the doodles of a potentially profound personality; they tended toward spiral shapes, whirl-pool constructions of astonishing symmetry which seemed to tremble on the page, but he also did a lot of interconnected cubes, partly shaded in, that looked like housing developments on some unimaginably wacky planet. He always worked in pencil, and he kept a good supply of sharp yellow number twos in his desk. Every couple of days he spent several minutes at the pencil sharpener, honing his tools for the doodles ahead.

I wouldn't say I actually fell in love with Danny that awkward sixth-grade year when I sat across the aisle and mooned over his wrists and exchanged appalling English papers with him. I was busy being in love with John Lennon and trying to keep my passion a secret from my parents, who sanctioned preadolescent imaginary love affairs only if they were with dead writers. I had a black-and-white glossy picture of my idol, procured for me by Sandy Schutz, hidden in Volume Ten of the Book of Knowledge, which I was attempting, with the aid of a pad of tracing paper, to copy; what impulse prompted this I don't know, unless I was drawing John Lennon the way conscientious art students sit in museums copying Rembrandts—to feel my way, to learn from my ideal, to assimilate my notion of perfection, drawing it into my bones and blood. I studied John Lennon to prepare myself for Danny Frontenac.

It wasn't Danny I fell in love with that year I was eleven, though: it was his house. It wasn't far from ours. For all our acres, we lived less than half a mile from the center of town, where the Frontenacs lived. They lived as smack in the center as you could get without pitching a tent on the Green. They lived over Hector's Market.

Hector's was the heart of the town, and Danny's father ran it. The Green there is flanked with important and distinguished buildings, all wearing plaques put up by the Historical Society: the Town Hall (1737), the Congregational Church (1803), the Library (1889), the Christian Science Reading Room set up in the Jared Pitch House (1684), the Village Gallery of Fine Arts in a 1668 saltbox, the Village Apothecary (1855), the Oyster Inne (1825), and the huge Squire Blodgett mansion, which houses, discreetly, a card shop called The Purple Parrot, a liquor store, Francine's House of Beauty, and the East Shore Stamp and Coin Shop.

In the midst of all this New England stateliness, between the Apothecary and the Library, once bloomed Hector's Market. It was not without historical interest. Danny's grandfather built it on the site of the old general store when that burned down in 1900, and it was a grand old building in the lovely, fanciful late-Victorian style, covered with peeling ivory paint, with trim around the crenelated windows that was exactly the rich color of mud. There were people in the village who sneered at it, especially at its cute Gothic dipped gables and diamond-paned upstairs windows, but I loved it.

George Frontenac, Danny's father, never tried to make anyone love it—in fact, he did his best to turn it into a supermarket. But, short of gutting the place and starting over, the task was impossible. He tried to light it up as brightly as the Stop & Shop, but the fluorescent lights were defeated to a large degree by the sheer quantity of stuff in there and the scarcity of the space to accommodate it. The aisles were narrow, barely letting a shopping cart pass, and jammed with articles that couldn't be made to fit on the shelves. If two shopping carts headed down the same aisle, one simply had to retreat (a feat in itself). And the shelves rose so high the light was cut off in places; this dimness made even Purina Dog Chow and Campbell's Chicken Consommé look mysterious and appealing. Why this should be, I don't know, but I do know that buying Campbell's Chicken Consommé at Hector's was a wholly different experience from buying it at the Stop & Shop on Route 1, and that town shoppers (who of course did their main shopping at the Stop & Shop) running into Hector's for a can of tomatoes and a pound of butter invariably ended up buying more than that. The dark and the clutter cast a better spell than Muzak; people bought at Hector's because it was an adventure, however much they sneered at the architecture.

The Frontenacs lived upstairs under the pointed gables. George once had the mad idea of expanding the market upward, but Claire, his wife, talked him out of it: "Whoever heard of a supermarket with a second floor? How would people get their carts up and down?" George brooded about it for a long time: two airy, uncluttered floors, with maybe a curved ramp leading from one to another, the basics downstairs, the luxury items upstairs. ("Who's going to decide what's basic and what's luxury in a town like this?") But it never came to anything. "He's a visionary!" Claire said (not without pride). "We would have had to move!" Danny said (not without horror).

He loved living over Hector's, and I envied him his abode. It was right in the middle of everything, it was noisy, it was on Main Street, where, night and day, there was always something

33

going on. I used to hang out there, first in the store, where I bagged groceries for nothing (but I carried them home for people for tips), then upstairs when I got friendly with Snowball, the Frontenacs' cat. Claire used to let me take Snowball upstairs and feed him when he got hungry. I'll never forget the first time this happened; it was one of the six or seven high points in my life.

The store was busy, late on a Friday afternoon. George and Claire were at the checkout counters (no matter how George schemed, there was room for only two), Danny was bagging along with Billy Arp, and I was petting Snowball on the floor under the cigarette display. Snowball was obviously hungry: you could tell because he was so affectionate, with a purr that vibrated above the babble of the cash registers, and he kept sidling away from me and hopping to the counter where Claire was checking out groceries. The customers didn't like that, of course—a big, dusty white cat jumping on their broccoli and rubbing his head against their cornflake boxes.

"Delia, honey, could you take him up and feed him?" Claire asked me at last. The scarf she tied her hair up in was askew, her face shone with sweat; she looked especially desperate. "There's a can open upstairs in the fridge—go right up the back stairs, his dish is on the floor beside the broom closet . . ."

I was thrilled. I grabbed Snowball and hurried before Danny could say, "I'll go, Ma," or the customers slack off suddenly and leave Claire free. The back stairs smelled of food and cat. The door at the head was unlocked, and inside was the Frontenac kitchen. I'd been there before—trick-or-treating every year, and once when I'd gone with Juliet to collect money for the United Way—but only as far as the door. This time I went right in, as if it were my own house. I released Snowball, who meowed loudly and began to rub fondly against the refrigerator, and I got out the food and scooped some into his dish, an old pink-flowered soup bowl. Then I looked around.

The late afternoon sun was pouring through the tiny diamond panes; you wouldn't think they'd let so much light in.

There was a chrome dinette set in the middle of the floor, upholstered in red and gray plastic. I fell in love with it, though I knew it was cheap and tacky; it reminded me of the diner Aunt Phoebe sometimes took me to after the movies, called the Little Gem, where I was allowed to consume two orders of French fries, two Cokes, and a hot fudge sundae. My aunt called it the Little Germ, but that was a joke; she ate glazed doughnuts and drank cup after cup of coffee. (I think she had something on with the cook, a tall thin black man with a toothbrush moustache and a chef's hat that said "Whit" on it. He used to call me "Cookie" and my aunt "Gloria," I never knew why, and he used to say, "Two orders of fries à la French coming up," in a funny accent he put on for my benefit.)

While Snowball audibly chomped his Puss & Boots, I inspected the cookie jar set in the middle of the gray Formica table; it was a jolly monk in a brown robe. Remove his head and shoulders, and there was a monkful of Oreo cookies. It was wonderful to me, the idea of owning a store and being able to pick your cookies from the shelves, whatever you wanted. (At our house, snacks tended to be things like olives, anchovy paste on melba toast, and creamed herring.)

I fell for the monk, and for the gritty taste of the cookie I shamelessly ate. I was enraptured by the whole room, every detail. There was a spice rack on the wall, twelve bottles with ground-glass stoppers and neat labels; I thought they were adorable. There was a row of graduated-size tin canisters, each with a large cabbage-rose decal; I admired them wholeheartedly. The sounds from the store below rose up, a muted rumble with its own rhythm; I longed to live with such a noise. There was a wooden plaque over the door that said EAST WEST, HOME IS BEST, and I had to agree, if this was home. In the cupboards were all my favorite foods: Sugar Pops, Nestlé's Chocolate Morsels, Campbell's Pork & Beans, packs of Dentine, canned spaghetti sauce, brownie mix. There were no bookshelves, no books, not even a cookbook, that I could see.

I began to have the oddest feeling: for the first time, I perceived—really perceived, with all my senses—the largeness and strangeness and wonderfulness of the world. (List of "Senses and What They Perceived":

> Sight: absence of printed matter
> Hearing: store noises
> Smell: cat
> Touch: plastic upholstery
> Taste: Oreo)

Hardly any of the things I admired in the Frontenacs' flat were allowed in my house. Our kitchen was large and oppressively old-fashioned, with a wood stove for heat and a fireplace for atmosphere and a huge English stove called an Aga for cooking. Our cupboards contained wild rice, dried Chinese mushrooms, glacé fruit, pine nuts, soy sauce, and six kinds of olives. We couldn't have pets because Miranda and Juliet were allergic. The trees around our house sheltered it from noise and sun. And it was crammed with books. The books would drive out the people if they could. We had books the way the Frontenacs had Oreos. But as I stood there in the Frontenac kitchen eating cookies, it came to me with the brilliance of sunlight through diamond panes that it didn't have to be that way, the way I grew up with. I could choose something else for myself; I could take control of my own life. And for the first time I became impatient to be an adult.

I peeked with longing in the direction of the rooms beyond the kitchen, and got a tantalizing glimpse of a sofa covered in gold brocade with a red pillow tossed in each corner; my heart lurched as if I beheld John Lennon (and I had no doubt his sofa was similar). But I dared go no further. The kitchen was enough for the moment.

I don't know how long I remained, looking around and poking gingerly into cupboards—long enough to eat six cookies and for Snowball to finish his meal and begin washing up in a patch of sun. I left him there, finally, and with the greatest reluctance I'd ever known went back downstairs. I'd had my vision. When Claire (momentarily respited) grinned at me, whisked the white cat hairs and the crumbs off my T-shirt, and said, "Thanks, honey—I'm glad you helped yourself to a cookie," I was too charmed to be embarrassed.

"I love your apartment, Mrs. Frontenac," I breathed.

She turned, smiling, to wait on a customer, but Danny, setting up a bag, threw me a speculative look.

Spiritually speaking, I suppose I left my father's house that afternoon. I know that, ever after, I looked at things differently, as if I'd acquired a pair of special glasses. I watched carefully for places and people I felt comfortable and happy with. My Aunt Phoebe was one, and after my moment of vision I inspected her more closely to find out why.

She was my mother's sister, and very like her: tall, fragile, frizzy-haired, blue-eyed, booky. But there were important differences, and I made a list of them in my List Notebook:

Mom	Aunt P.
1. reads all day	1. runs orchurd
2. only likes exoctic food	2. likes all food
3. hates movies	3. loves movies

Aunt Phoebe, I understood, was a failure in my parents' eyes because she'd once had literary ambitions and talents and had never fulfilled them. My mother, Elizabeth, and her younger sister, Phoebe, were the only children of apple farmers, Grandma and Grandpa Cole, who both died when I was little. I imagine my grandfather up on a ladder, briskly picking apples with his left hand; I feel his lively genes in me. Grandma was a poetess; she wrote verses about nature (birds, trees, and flowers, mostly; occasionally bees, cats, and clouds). She had three names—Helen Harper Cole—and she brought her daughters up to be literary women. She and my grandfather had hoped for a son to work the farm while the daughters read books and wrote poetry, but one didn't come along.

When my grandfather died, and Grandma became too feeble to do anything with an apple but eat it sauced, Aunt Phoebe married an apple picker named Jack Appleman, and they ran the orchard together. Grandma Cole didn't like it, her daughter picking apples instead of writing poems about them, but what could she do? She died, with her hopes for her younger daughter blasted, and my aunt (remorsefully?) collected Grandma's best poems and had them printed in a little volume she paid for herself. It's called *From the Orchard*, by Helen Harper Cole, and it has a pale green cover decorated with golden apples, designed by my aunt. I have a copy here, and if I were ever forced at knifepoint to read a book of poems, I'd probably choose this one. They all seem to rhyme, and a couple of them sound like you could jump rope to them.

My aunt confided to me one day at the Little Germ that she married Jack Appleman for his name and his moustache. Aunt Phoebe liked moustaches, and in those days no one had one except my father and Clark Gable and Jack Appleman. Jack shaved his off around the time President Kennedy was shot, and they got divorced, and since then my aunt has run the orchard herself. She has a Ph.D. in English literature, seven unpublished novels she's never shown anyone, and piles of books all over the house, but you'd never have known it. To me, she was just my aunt, Phoebe Appleman, who lived in an orchard, took me to movies, and flirted with moustachioed men—a sensible woman.

I used to complain to her about the family vice. "Isn't there something wrong with people who read all the time?" I asked her once.

She thought for a minute and then said, "Possibly." That concession alone meant a lot to me (my own family wouldn't have deigned even to answer, would probably not have looked up from their books), but she went on: "I think too many books can make people dissatisfied with life. It seems so messy by comparison." She sighed. "I like reading a lot, Delia, but I like living, too." (By "living," I took it she meant the Little Germ and all its ramifications.)

I told her that life's messiness was one of the things that made it interesting to me. "I like the way you have to keep neatening it up."

She gave me a look of mild incredulity. "You like *what?*"

"I like trying to make sense out of it," I elaborated. I did. I went through life like a housewife with a neatness obsession (I have that, too), sorting and arranging and eliminating until it suited me. "*You* know," I said, and hit on one of my father's phrases: "Order out of chaos, Aunt Phoebe."

"Delia, honey, that's what writers do!"

We had a good laugh over that one. It was after this conversation that she showed me what is probably the only interesting thing about books I have ever learned: the "Note on the Type" a lot of them have in the back. I was fascinated, and I spent a wholly satisfying afternoon going through her books comparing Granjon and Electra and 12-point Romanee (my favorite).

Aunt Phoebe changed when she got divorced. I was ten, and I remember how she was when Uncle Jack lived with her. She chain-smoked, she came over to our house and cried, she wore matching sweaters and skirts, and she wrote her seven novels while Jack managed the orchard. Then he moved back to the state of Washington (he's still an apple picker out there, and he writes us every couple of years to say that the Washington apples make the Cole Orchard apples look like gumballs), and Aunt Phoebe pulled herself together. She still looked fragile, but her fragility had something useful about it, like that of a spiderweb, or a tissue. She got going. She put her long hair into a frizzy braid, and she took to hiking, to arguing with people, to shrugging her shoulders a lot, and to sitting on the floor with her chin sticking out and her head against the wall—a meditating posture except for her bright, expectant eyes. She went out and picked her own apples and worked at the stand. She instituted guided tours of the orchard for school groups. She got up on a ladder and painted her house—which had been stark white with black shutters since my grandfather's day—the color of a greening, and the shutters dark red. She gave me Grandpa Cole's coin albums for my birthday, told me (in confidence) that I was her favorite niece, and began taking me to the movies on slow winter afternoons when there was no action at the orchard.

I doubt she ever wrote another word. My parents admitted that she seemed happier, but they said it ruefully, as though she shouldn't be, or as though happiness wasn't the point. "Everyone's got one crazy relative," my father said (making me wonder if Horatio and Miranda and Juliet would say the same thing about me when we all grew up).

She never seemed the least bit crazy to me. There were times when I lived from movie to movie, when the postponement of an afternoon with my aunt was a tragedy even Hector's Market couldn't assuage. I loved my aunt and her orchard, and I loved the orchard in all its seasons: spring, all blossoms and bees; summer, when the apples blew up like balloons, it seemed overnight; fall, and the taste of the first Spartans; and even winter, when the trees went rough and black, but with tiny buds, if you looked closely. It all seemed far less crazy than sticking in the house getting endless ink transfusions.

My aunt and I went to New Haven one Saturday afternoon, to see a revival of A Taste of Honey. (We both liked English movies—the more outlandish the accent, the better.) I cried so hard she let me have a cup of coffee, with cream and four sugars, at the Little Germ afterward. Whit brought it over to our table personally, and put his skinny dark hand on my head, and said, "She's the spitting image of you, Gloria."

"Go on," said my aunt. "She doesn't look a bit like me."

"Around the eyes—look here." He turned my head like a doorknob under his hand. "Look at those gorgeous eyes—that perky little nose—just like yours."

"Bull," said my aunt.

I went to the ladies' room and checked my eyes in the mirror. Except for looking pinkish around the edges, they were the same as ever, narrow and brown like my father's instead of round and blue like my aunt's and my mother's. My perky little nose was red and running. But I hoped, possibly even prayed, that the resemblance was there, and I toyed with the agreeable notion that I was my aunt's secret child, born under an apple tree. When I went back Whit was still there, examining my aunt's eyes intently.

"Feeling better, Cookie?" he asked me. "Ready to order?" He was a handsome man, with a moustache that seemed to bristle out of his nose, and he took my order back to the kitchen (the usual: fries and a sundae) with a spring in his step. My aunt watched him fondly, and so did I.

Sometimes I stayed overnight in my aunt's little apple-colored house. She let me watch TV, and one April she actually allowed me to sleep outside under the apple blossoms. She had a fat, playful, apple-eating hound dog named Bounce, whom I loved with a pure and joyful passion similar to my passion for John Lennon. I hugged and romped with Bounce as I would have hugged and romped with John Lennon, given the chance.

Aunt Phoebe had the great gift of acceptance. I'm convinced it's a gift, something you're born with, the ability to take people as they are, to let them take whatever shape they will, and never try to change it. I can't remember my aunt ever, *ever* trying to get me to read a book.

I decided that Aunt Phoebe, and the Frontenacs, lived as close to the way I wanted to live as anyone I could think of, and some nights while I was poring over my coin albums I used to lay plans for becoming more like them. It was on one of those nights that I decided to marry Danny. What a shortcut! To marry right into the family! I was overcome with chuckles at my cleverness, but even if they hadn't been in the middle of a game of Botticelli I couldn't, of course, have told my family.

I had become a regular at the Frontenacs' by then. I loved it there, especially in their apartment, where the TV was on every night after the store closed, and where there was no one watching everything I said, ready to pounce on every grammatical error with some witty riposte, and where there didn't seem to be any books except the Bible, *TV Guide,* and *Modern Grocer.* As I got older, my parents let me go out in the evenings, and I was always at the Frontenacs', eating dinner and watching TV and playing poker with them, stalking Danny.

He and I used to stretch out on the floor on our stomachs, leaning on our elbows, and watch *Star Trek* and *The Dick Van Dyke Show* and *The Wonderful World of Disney.* There was always a bag of Cheez-Its or Fig Newtons between us. His parents didn't care what we ate, or how much we ate, as long as we didn't get crumbs on the gold wall-to-wall. We munched with paper napkins spread out under our chins. We used to feed Cheez-Its to Snowball, who crunched obediently over his own napkin. Claire and George would often sit on the sofa behind us; they seemed endlessly amiable, boundlessly kind, superhumanly patient with Danny and me and our lame adolescent jokes, uncomplaining when our raucous teasing of each other drowned out the TV—for that was the form our friendship took when it first got off the ground: teasing and insults. Claire would ask Danny to pass her a couple of Cheez-Its, Danny would reply yeah if I can get them away from El Piggo here, I would say who's calling who a pig, look at him, his mouth is full and both hands too, Danny would interrupt oh yeah Fatty? well all I can say is when we were out in Billy's boat the other day it wasn't *my* end that sank down like a rock, and I'd give him a punch on the arm, and he'd say my father always told me never to hit a lady but that doesn't apply to you, and he'd punch me back, and Claire would say where's my Cheez-Its? and we'd hand her the bag and start giggling and punching each other again while Starship Enterprise shot through space toward impossible dangers.

I had watched Danny's attitude toward me slowly change. We still didn't talk much, except to fool around. I could see in the punches we exchanged, in the teasing, and in his broody brown eyes the dawn of something even I didn't fully comprehend (though I comprehended it better than he did). I thought he was the handsomest boy in town, like a tree in autumn (a red maple!), with his flaming hair and brown wrists and long bones. Sandy Schutz didn't agree; she didn't like his freckles. "I'll bet he's even got freckles—you know—all over," she said with a simulated shiver. I hadn't thought of that, but I began to, often. By this time I was over John Lennon. I was fourteen or so, about the age Miranda got over Byron. I was ready for a more local, less speculative and pure passion.

Danny was it. It took a couple of more years of following him around and letting him punch me, but by the time we were sixteen we were going steady. I don't know what finally did it—hormones, probably—and I can't recall how I advanced from silent companion to girlfriend. I do remember the first time he kissed me. We were fishing off the pier down by Billy Arp's, and Billy went inside for something to eat, and I baited Danny's hook for him (I always did; he was squeamish), and he flung his line out and then he kissed me—crookedly, without preamble or embrace, and fast, before Billy came back. It wasn't so much a kiss as a coded message: things will be different between us now, there's more to come. Then a fish tugged on his line, and Billy returned, and the shock and thrill of being kissed became irrelevant, and disappeared. There was just the fish and the sea and Billy with a bag of pretzels. But the message lingered on, and from then on things *were* different between us; and there *was* more to come.

It was the typical adolescent pilgrimage along the paths of love and sex, starting with kisses, then better kisses, gropings, then better gropings, and all the rest of it. We made love the first time in Danny's living room, in front of the TV, while George and Claire were at a bowling banquet. It was late spring, the windows were wide open, and there was a warm breeze bringing in all the Saturday-night sounds of Main Street. On the TV, the Yankees were creaming the Red Sox.

And when Danny and I rolled apart at last, and he told me over and over again that he loved me, the secure, serene happiness I felt was something new to me. I had never been happy in quite that miraculous way before, and in spite of all my years of practical dreaming I had never expected—not really—that my long dream would, quite precisely and literally, come true.

After that, besides making love every chance we got, we began to talk to each other, telling each other what we had never told anyone, even Sandy Schutz and Billy Arp. Danny was a talker. That's one of the things I liked about him, he talked about things instead of reading about them. But Danny (unlike me) was naturally reticent about himself. By diligent attention during my years of being his silent shadow, I had learned certain things about him. I knew he wanted eventually to fit into the slot his father had designed for him, the takeover of Hector's, and a wonderful thing I thought that, the passing on from parent to child of something as vital and tangible as Hector's. It was like Aunt Phoebe and her orchard, and I pictured Danny and me growing strong and wise among the cans and boxes the way my aunt had among the apple trees.

But I knew, too, that Danny wanted to do something on his own first. He and Billy had talked a little about that, letting me humbly listen. Billy wanted nothing more than to go right from high school to the navy, and he talked about basic training the way most seventeen-year-olds talk about the senior prom. He was a boat nut, and he figured on a hitch in the navy followed by college on the GI Bill and a degree in naval architecture, and then he'd go out to the West Coast and build boats. Danny and I listened respectfully to these hopes, but it was a relief to me when Danny let me drag it out of him, once our relationship had progressed to that stage, that he didn't share them. Billy looked forward to going to Vietnam; Danny spent his whole senior year sweating over the prospect of his number coming up, and I sweated with him. We talked of escaping to Canada; the Frontenacs had relatives in Quebec. I began to wonder if, after all, I should learn French. We carried signs to Hartford during Anti-Draft Week in March and lugged them around the capitol buildings, chanting.

The day it was discovered that Danny had a small heart murmur, he cried from relief with his head in my lap. He said he'd rather drop dead of a heart attack in the middle of a basketball game than have to shoot at people and drop bombs. I loved it that he was afraid to go to war and that he had confessed it to me, and as I stroked his bright hair I dropped my own joyful tears on it. It seemed to me that anyone in his right mind should be afraid to go to war, and I couldn't see why there were so many wars, when so many people were afraid to fight in them. I had to blame it on the generals and the presidents and the Billy Arps, but Billy was such a nice, amiable, extroverted kid, who liked messing around in boats and whacking fish on the head, that it made me wonder about the other warmongers. But I picketed with Danny, and wept with him when his own scare was over.

Freed from it, he decided he'd get a job in New Haven and live there for a year or two before he committed himself to me or to Hector's—to see the world a bit, but on his own modest terms. New Haven was enough of the world for him, at least at that point. This minuscule ambition, too, was something he confessed only to me, keeping it from Billy (who wanted someday to hitchhike to Alaska) and from his parents (who would have preferred that he stay in the village, gliding smoothly from the graduation ceremonies to Hector's produce department). I understood it perfectly, the funny mix of claustrophobia and affection a small town can generate when you've lived in it all your life. We both wanted to live out our days in the village; we were both small-town people; but we wanted to stand back for a while and get a new perspective on it.

At least, that's the way Danny saw it; to be honest, I didn't want a perspective any different from the one I had. Hadn't I, all these years, been standing back from my family and what they represented? Hadn't I been born distanced? School was the only blight on my life. Once I was out, the town would be my oyster. And someday I'd be mistress of Hector's Market, the rock that anchored the town. It seemed the ideal combination: to live in the town I'd always lived in, but on my own, in my own way, with sunshine and fresh air coming in through diamond-paned windows, with my husband. I liked the place, I was comfortable there.

Danny, of course, was part of my comfort. I understood his need for some breathing space, away from the town, Hector's, his parents, me. But I worried about losing him. I was, after all, the initiator of our romance; I was his pursuer, and I'd caught him, and now that I had him it seemed the way to keep him was to let him go. He was beginning to snap at me for bossing him. "Quit nagging me," he sometimes said. He sounded like a disillusioned husband, and it frightened me.

So I agreed, with my old calculated humility, playing him like a fish, that a separation from each other would be only practical. We would wait a year or two—see other people—get away on our own—blah blah blah. Then we'd get married and pitch in at Hector's as planned. "After all," Danny said, "we were childhood sweethearts, we've been together practically all our lives!" This touched and charmed me; it threw a veil of such romantic and dogged devotion over the long, vague, tentative friendship that began with our hands linked against Mrs. Meek and her books.

My parents had never said much about our courtship. I'm sure they didn't know that was what it was. They liked Danny, and they knew he was a "nice boy" (which he was, though not in the way they thought). They liked and respected his parents, who represented small-town virtues and old-fashioned values and special-ordered bean curd and Jackson's Coronation Tea for my mother. So they didn't mind my hanging around the Frontenacs', though they were puzzled sometimes that I didn't bring Danny home more often—forgetting, once I became a determinedly social teenager, the long tradition of discouraging me from having my low, noisy friends over. But

I could just see it—everyone sitting around reading after dinner, and Danny with his boxing magazine.

Danny's parents liked me, and encouraged me to come around, even if I did snitch cookies. I was, in fact, given carte blanche with the cookie jar, and when I was sixteen I became a paid, part-time bagger and stock girl at Hector's. I worked after school and got a dollar fifty an hour. I never spent a dime of it. I opened a savings account and faithfully made a deposit every week. "Save it for college," my parents said hopefully. They were proud of my resourcefulness. None of my siblings had ever had a job; they were too busy reading. But I wasn't saving up for college; I wouldn't have gone to college even if I'd been able to get into one. I was getting my dowry together. By the time I graduated from high school, I had over two thousand dollars saved.

I didn't graduate until I was nineteen. I flunked senior English. Even I was humiliated by this. I had never flunked anything before. I'd always prided myself on getting through St. Agatha's on the strength of my natural intelligence and gift of bull, without cracking many books. But I was tripped up, finally, by Shakespeare.

I couldn't read *Macbeth*. It wasn't true, as Sister Charles Ann insisted, that I wasn't trying. I tried, dozens of times, but I never got beyond the witches. My mind closed up at that point, it refused to function, it ground to a halt, and the words on the page turned into mere squiggles, mere designs, and not very interesting ones. It was like being back in elementary school, pre-Meek. I tried reading it aloud, I tried getting Danny and Billy and Sandy to read it to me, I even tried rewarding myself with candy. But nothing helped. I couldn't make it out, or make out what I was supposed to do with it. Every time I went near that paperback book, with Lady Macbeth looking gory and sinister on the cover, little teeth of pain began to nibble at the insides of my head.

I tried to get through the final exam, which featured large helpings of *Macbeth*, on the strength of the class discussions, but my mind had closed up on those, too, and I couldn't even get the plot right. I could hardly tell Macbeth from Macduff, and I was never sure who killed the king, Mr. or Mrs. I wrote one sentence (which I would reproduce here to illustrate my helplessness had it not passed mercifully from my memory) and went home.

"Of course, we can't pass this," Sister Charles said to my parents. There was a special conference the afternoon of report-card day. I wasn't present, but I can imagine their reactions. By the time they got home, they were pretty well under control, but my father's eyes were more dolefully Tennysonian than ever, and there were new pouches under my mother's eyes, perhaps from crying. I'd hoped they could talk Sister Charles into passing me. I was revolted at the idea of repeating a course that had been agony the first time around. Besides, I wanted to get out into the real world. I'd been half promised a job at the animal shelter in Madison, and I had dreams of my own little studio apartment full of cute things I liked. I had my eye on a huge cookie jar at Bradlee's that looked just like Bounce—take off his hound-dog head and inside find a million Oreos.

"You'll have to repeat twelfth grade," my father said, more in sorrow than in anger. Horatio was a professor at Harvard, Miranda had started up her little press, Juliet was working on her Ph.D. in Greek literature, and I had flunked twelfth grade because I couldn't get through *Macbeth.*

It takes a lot to get me down. It took *that,* my first tragedy, my first setback. I saw myself as a practical and determined person set firmly upon a certain kind of course in life (still blurry as to details but with powerfully distinct general outlines), and here I was brought up short by Literature, downed by the enemy, as much a victim of the Macbeths as old Duncan.

My parents were very kind. Neither of them read a book or wrote a line that day. We sat in the kitchen eating macadamia nuts and drinking sherry (mine cut drastically with orange juice) while they listened to me talk about myself. I can't recall this ever happening before, but it did that day. They listened with something like respect. It was, in a way, a feat to have flunked English. For the first time they woke up to the extent of my difference from them, and they listened with the flattering attention they might pay to a European visitor talking of life in a remote Alpine village.

My first, practical reaction was that I should take the course over again in summer school. But my parents didn't think I should simply repeat senior English. It wasn't only my failing grade on the final exam in English that got to them. I had a 75 in religion, 78 in trigonometry, and 89 in typing (my best subject), but I had barely scraped through history (66) and biology (67). Better to repeat the whole mess, they felt, hoping (though they wouldn't say so) I'd raise my grades high enough to get into college.

"Why didn't you take courses that were—well—easier?" my father asked.

"More suited to your talents?" my mother reworded it.

"There are no easy courses at St. Agatha's," I told them. I worked up resentment, and wailed, "Why couldn't I have gone to public school? At Shoreline High I could have taken art and shop and business math—" I saw my parents shudder delicately, or maybe I only imagined it. They were trying to be open-minded. "I don't see that I got anything much out of twelve years at St. Agatha's that I wouldn't get at Shoreline. A lot less, if you ask me."

Nobody ever had, but it was true. My parents, lapsed Catholics, had sent the four of us to parochial school for the "old-fashioned values" and for the "culture." They seemed to think it was important for us to say "Yes, ma'am," and to know how to sing the "Dies Irae" and what Rogation Days were and St. Anselm's argument for the existence of God and what Cain said to Abel. Horatio and Miranda and Juliet picked up all this stuff effortlessly, of course. I didn't. For one thing, the Church reformed when I was in the fourth grade.

The "Dies Irae" was out and "Amazing Grace" was in. By the time I was in high school, the religion course consisted mainly of debates about birth control and acted-out stories from the New Bible, complete with costumes and props and music. Independent thinking and creative self-expression instead of the Baltimore Catechism and inflexible dogmas and the long fasts of my parents' (and siblings') day. In fact, I liked the religion course, and considering that I didn't do much of the reading, I considered my final grade of 75 brilliant.

"If I'd gone to Shoreline, I wouldn't have had any trouble graduating," I whimpered. I realized I had a grievance. I had asked them, once or twice, if I could transfer to the public high school. The requests had been halfhearted—I really hadn't wanted to leave Danny and my friends, even for shop and business courses—but none of us remembered that. "I'm just not cut out for Shakespeare and foreign languages and that stuff," I pressed on. "I can't help it. Why couldn't I have gone someplace that would teach me something useful?"

My parents were visibly chagrined. They looked guiltily at each other. I rubbed it in. "I might have been really good at something if I'd had the training." I wept with indignation. I drained my sherry and o.j. at a gulp and slammed down the glass.

"What do you want to do, Cordelia?" my father asked me at last.

I clammed up. I couldn't say it: marry Danny Frontenac and run the cash register at Hector's. Not yet. "I really don't know," I said. I lost a bit of ground there. I should have had a secret passion for carpentry or lobstering up my sleeve. "Something practical," I fumbled on. I was feeling the sherry. "Something . . ." I had to resort to gestures—sweeps of my hand that took in the dim corners of Hector's, the village, the great world—flapping gestures that tumbled away the bookcases and elevated me up over the trees to I know not what. Possibly toward where I am now. Possibly there was something inevitable in all this: if I hadn't flunked twelfth grade, Danny might not have gotten around to marrying me, and if I hadn't married Danny I might never etc. etc. etc. Who knows? Who wants to? I leave inevitability to the Macbeths.

Well, we compromised. I repeated twelfth grade at Shoreline High. I got into the English course for subliterates and didn't have to read *Macbeth*. I did have to read some of Shakespeare's sonnets (my father helped me make my painful way through them), but we were never tested on them. I got a 74 in English! I also got 93 in business math, 92 in advanced typing, 90 in art and design. And in shop I made—of all things—a bookcase. It was that or a revolving TV table (an interesting choice, I thought). I would have preferred, naturally, to make the table, but since we didn't have a TV, it seemed pointless. And as it turned out, the bookcase has been useful; it's before me now, between the windows, containing all the books my father has optimistically bestowed on me over the years, along with Horatio's murder mysteries and my grandmother's poetry book. I keep my TV on top. In a place as small as this one, the last thing I need is a revolving TV table.

My repeating the twelfth grade gave my romance with Danny a huge boost. Danny had a job in New Haven, and an apartment. He was lonesome. All of a sudden a year or two on his own seemed too long. Danny wanted us to get married the day after my graduation from Shoreline, as people did in rock 'n' roll songs of the fifties. I think my failure in school made it clear that he was the leader, not me. True, I'd pursued him, I'd baited his hooks (and my own), I'd let him cry in my arms. I think maybe all this had unmanned him in some way, even though I always kept my math grades low to match his. But my flunking English changed things. There I was, a schoolgirl sweating over homework, while he was pulling down $4.72 an hour at the shirt factory in New Haven. The Macbeths brought us together.

It was a funny thing, but those Macbeths and their strange, bloody deeds hadn't thrown Danny at all; he got an 81 on the final exam, an achievement that continues to amaze me. ("*Macbeth* is not a smiple play," I imagine him writing.) I sprang Danny's final-exam grade on my parents as one of the arguments in favor of marrying him. They were not impressed by it any more than they were by his shirt-factory job or the prospect of his inheriting Hector's.

When I graduated from Shoreline High, I was nineteen years old and I had $2,127 in the bank. My parents thought I should take a year to think it over. Going steady with a nice boy like Danny was okay; marrying him was something else. They offered to double my savings so I could take a long jaunt to Europe. A walking tour through England with some wholesome youth group, they suggested, thinking back to their honeymoon. Or a couple of months in Greece with Juliet?

"I don't speak Greek!" I said. "I don't know any wholesome youth groups!" They thought I should be more like Miranda, who had lived with a French family for a year. Or Juliet, my mother's pride, who could speak six languages at the age of twenty-four. By the family standards, I barely knew English, and my idea of traveling was to drive down I-95 and see the West Haven Yankees. I didn't want to see the world or sow any oats. I just wanted to live with Danny and stave off life's messiness by arranging it in patterns that pleased me. If I was the black sheep of the family, I wanted my own cozy pen, and my red-headed shepherd.

"Cordelia, you're throwing your life away!"

"Mom! Daddy! I love him!" I said this over and over again, earnestly and sincerely.

"It's not love," my mother patiently explained. "It's physical attraction and habit."

Juliet, obviously urged, wrote me a silly letter from Greece advising me to have my "fling" with Danny to get him out of my system. She wrote, "You don't have to make an honest husband out of every man you sleep with." (She was going through her brittle, sophisticated phase.)

"I love him," I kept insisting. It was so unfair! All my

father's poem-writing and my mother's vast reading and Juliet's studying, all the books and poems and ideas they'd filled their heads with, should have told them the difference between true love and having a fling. "I love him," I kept saying, and they acted as if I'd just learned an obscure language which, incredibly, none of them spoke. Love: those sonnets of Shakespeare's had been riddled with it, and my father had painstakingly picked it out for me; it was as clear as diamonds to him as long as it was centuries old. In this nineteen-year-old daughter it was something else.

"It's the juices of youth!" he said to me. "Cordelia—think! Do you want to spend your life as a grocer's wife?"

"I don't see why not," I said.

> To spend my life
> As a grocer's wife . . .

It was the only poem of my father's I ever liked. I thought he and my mother were insensitive snobs, and I refused to say what I'd been about to say—my trump card—when Danny's English-exam grade had failed to move them: that Danny was in line to become supervisor of the night shift—after working there only one year! "He has great leadership potential," I was going to point out with pride, figuring the phrase *leadership potential* would get to them. But when I saw how they felt, I said not a word. Danny's promotion would provoke only more veiled sneers. I was ashamed for them. What did they think I should marry, a college professor? The mind boggles, as Miranda used to say before she found out everyone else said it.

My parents had glimpsed their daughter Cordelia briefly that afternoon in the kitchen (a thin, brown-eyed girl with a scalloped earlobe who drank her sherry and o.j. left-handed and didn't understand Shakespeare), but the vision hadn't lasted. When the question of marriage came up, I became again their dream-daughter, the late bloomer, the one who'd surprise us all yet—and marrying Danny Frontenac would put the lid on that lovely surprise for good. Clang! And I'd be stuck with the rabble.

I married him anyway, of course. Thanks to Shakespeare, I had spent my year seeing the world not from my own little apartment but from Shoreline High, but it had been plenty. I'd seen life long enough without Danny, and I knew I preferred it with him. And the longer I slogged through that wasted year at Shoreline, the stubborner I got. And finally, after a summer of arguing, my parents gave in. What else could they do? As I've said, they tried to be good parents; they honestly loved me in their way.

My father's way was to hand me over to Danny officially at a nuptial mass, but not without the recital of an epithalamium he wrote for us, comparing us to (I think) emerging butterflies. ("We might as well do it gracefully, since it looks like we've got to do it," I heard him say grimly to my mother a few days before the wedding.) My mother's way was to give us the $2,127 matching funds for a wedding present, to show no grudge was held. At the wedding reception, she ran her hand through Danny's bright hair and sighed, "At least you'll have beautiful children."

Both my parents cried, and my mother and Claire Frontenac sniffled noisily together over the loss of, respectively, their youngest and their only. George and my father got drunk together. Sandy Schutz and Miranda and Juliet were bridesmaids. Juliet, back from Greece with her hair in braids, tried to look tragic and world-weary, but the champagne got to her, and she danced all evening with one of Danny's Quebec cousins, dazzling him with her French. Miranda retired into a corner with her husband, Gilbert Sullivan, and our uncle, Oliver Miller, who is a professor of philology, and they had an animated discussion of structural linguistics. Sandy Schutz caught my bouquet and, sure enough, got engaged a couple of months later to a medical student she met during her nurse's training. Danny and I went to Boston for a honeymoon and spent the weekend going to movies and eating huge meals, and plotting our future.

And little did any of us know that within two years Hector's Market would be transformed into Uncle Jody's Country Crackerbarrel, and our future . . .

Enough of these hints! Enough whipping-up of interest! Out with it, Delia! Danny's in Sommers State Prison, serving a life sentence for murder, and I—? I've found, I think, my proper task, which is to get it all straight in my mind, reduce it to mere words, and so be finished with it. And go on from there.

Chapter Four

COLONIAL TOWERS

For one year, Danny and I lived together in perfect happiness. All my life, whenever I inspect my existence and rate it, I'll hold up those months with Danny as my happiness standard, and when I make lists of my satisfactions I'll make that time number one.

It was, I suppose, the happiness of adolescents freed from the restrictions of family. But there was nothing wanton, or wild, or even rebellious about Danny and me. We were as sober and respectable as fifty-year-olds—as our parents. Our lives were blameless, pure, even regular. But the regulation of them was our own doing. That was the happiness—that and the fusing of our two fussy, meticulous lives. Released from the enchantment of childhood, we cast spells on each other, on our apartment, on everything we owned.

We moved into a three-room apartment on the tenth floor of a New Haven high rise, the kind of building that is usually called faceless, impersonal, dehumanizing. It wasn't like that; it was downright homey, and we approved of it all, from the stainless-steel elevator whose buttons lit at a touch (our "10" with a special, intimate glow) to the grove of striated snake plants which flourished in the lobby (fed and watered by Mrs. Smolover, the super's wife).

Our apartment was perfect. In the month before our wedding we had devoted our free time to fixing it up. Mr. Smolover gave us the paint, and we colored each room a different pastel, painting meticulously, with love. In the blue bedroom was our king-size bed and nothing else. Nothing else would fit, so that we had to keep our big dresser in the living room. But neither of us minded that. In fact, we liked the polished cherry wood of that dresser so much that it seemed only sensible to keep it out where people could see it. It was the color of Danny's hair, and it had fancy brass drawer pulls that thudded like door knockers when you let them go. It had four drawers—two little, two big—and a giant mirror as clear and silvery as all the mirrors in my parents' house were murky and old. I felt I never saw myself properly until I stood with Danny, his arm around my waist, before the new mirror we had bought and paid for ourselves. We stood like that often, admiring ourselves as a couple: tall, bright Danny, small, dark Delia, each smiling at the other's image in the mirror.

There was a tiny kitchenette, all-electric, all-Formica. It wasn't big enough for a table, so we ate in the living room. The table was a round one topped with fake marble, and we had four white-wire ice cream parlor chairs with red seats. We set these up just outside the kitchenette on their own area rug, to create a little dining nook. We used to keep the dog cookie jar precisely in the middle, and I filled it with cookies just as the Frontenacs used to. When I looked at this grouping— table, chairs, rug, cookie jar—I felt a pang of perfect joy, and the thought would come to me: this is just right.

The rest of the living-room space was taken by our tweed sofa and the two matching chairs and the TV. My little book-case, stuffed with its undefiled books, stood by the front door and held the phone. Here and there we displayed a wedding present. Our gifts had been mostly silver, which we stored in boxes under the bed, but we hung up the kitchen clock from Sandy, a cat with a pendulum tail. Miranda actually gave us a blender, which I used to make pudding. Horatio gave us a large rubber plant in a ceramic tub; we kept it in the sun, in front of the double balcony doors, where it was dreadfully in the way, but it thrived and we became fond of it. On one wall hung our best coins framed against velvet, including the double eagles Aunt Phoebe gave us for a wedding present. On the dresser was what Juliet had brought us from Greece, the plaster head of a woman with braids bound up with leaves. We got to like it, as we did the rubber plant, though Danny sometimes hung his ski cap on it, tilted over one of its staring eyes.

Danny and I loved our cozy apartment, and I tended it faithfully. After living in my parents' messy house all those years—only my bedroom was neat—I took a special pleasure in cleaning. My mother never used to clean; she was always reading. Once every couple of months she'd have Mrs. Fox from the village come in and vacuum and wash the floors and do the huge pile of ironing that had accumulated. But our house was generally a wreck—and everyone in the family took pride in it except me: it meant we were intellectuals and artists with other things on our mind than dust and bathtub rings.

But the bringing of order out of chaos was what I took pride in, and I was a rabid cleaner. I could clean the whole kitchen with a sponge and a few squirts of spray cleaner. I did that every couple of days, and I vacuumed the rugs with our new Hoover, and mopped the square of kitchen floor with Mop & Glo. And I put bleach in the toilet. And twice a week I took all the stale crumbs out of the dog cookie jar and refilled it. I loved to see Danny head straight for it when he got home from work and have a couple of cookies with a glass of chocolate milk—the way some men would have martinis. I loved rituals—any kind except the bookish ones my family favored—

and so did Danny. We loved doing the same things over and over, in the same way: going to the laundromat on Saturday mornings, having bagels at the deli while the clothes washed, picking up groceries while the clothes dried, and then, together, folding our warm underwear and towels. We had our special TV shows, our favorite meals, an unvarying place for everything. The apartment took shape around us, and accommodated itself to us, finally, like an old and beloved garment. I suppose it was largely my creation—Danny, I think, could have lived anywhere—but he said that after his dreary bachelor place (one room, furnished with junky, dusty old castoffs) moving into our apartment was like moving into heaven.

Whenever I was outside our building, my eyes, if I looked up, went instantly to our small balcony with its green chairs and Danny's old bike and the hibachi—unmistakably our own. We thought it was a handsome building, not impersonal at all. Each apartment, in fact, was utterly unique. I found it wonderfully exciting to enter anyone else's apartment for the first time—so like ours (kitchenette, living room with glass doors to the balcony, corridor with bedroom and bathroom off it) yet so utterly different. True, to passersby it was just that urban blight, Colonial Towers, an offensive high rise stuck with identical windows and 6' x 9' balconies, but to those of us who lived in it it was our village. It didn't feel much different, to Danny and me, from the village we had left behind.

There was, on the first floor, the deli where we used to get bagels, and our dentist, and the doctor who treated Danny's ear infection, and the drugstore where we bought rubbers and beer and soda. When "EW & PD—tru luv 4-ever" was scratched on the stairwell by our incinerator, we knew that EW was Elisa Wandrel from down the hall, and PD was her boyfriend, Peter Davies. We met Elisa through Mr. Blenka, the agoraphobe at the end of the hall, who needed to have his groceries brought to him; Elisa and I and Jeff Thalman, the paperboy, were his chief suppliers. We got to know Miss Harper, the aged ex-flutist across the hall, during an elevator failure, when we helped her down the nine flights of stairs to the front door. And when the Liebermanns asked me, through Elisa, to baby-sit for Jennifer and Joey, our list was complete: we knew everyone on our floor.

Most of all, we got to know each other. We found that all our years of school-fellowship, our years of courting, countless hours spent together watching TV, talking, eating, making love, hadn't been nearly enough. What a risk we took (we said to each other, scared), embarking on the awesome dailiness of marriage with no more preparation than that! We returned from our weekend honeymoon, unpacked our suitcases, stared at each other across our new king-size bed, and let it hit us: *we're married.*

We clung to each other all that evening—forgetting *Gunsmoke*—and confessed all our fears. The fact of marriage was, suddenly, frightful. We were only nineteen, too young. We were homesick, he for his drab bachelor pad, I for my father's house; though I'd left it in spirit years before, I'd never actually been away from home. We were scared to death.

Gradually, we grew calm. The sound of our voices was a comfort, that night and on future nights. So was the order of our apartment, the familiar objects we had arranged with so much care. The cookie jar soothed us, and the rug, the green-and-gold towels, the fruit magnets on the refrigerator. We grew calm, we settled down, we took each other's quirks for granted like regular married people.

But it was funny in some ways, being married to Danny. I had assumed I knew him thoroughly. Certainly, we had spent those long hours and years together. Certainly, we had talked. But sometimes it seemed to me, after we moved into our apartment together, that I must have done most of the talking. If the subject was baseball or fishing or the sociological pros and cons of small-town life or the oddities of our teachers, Danny was voluble. But it must have been I who did the heavy critical analyses of our families, our relationship, ourselves. It must have been, because in some ways I obviously didn't know Danny at all, had never tried to know him, had assumed I must know him well because I'd known him so long.

I hate to admit this, it makes me sound like one of my sisters, but I truly didn't think there was much to know. I didn't love Danny for his complexity or his brilliance or his brains, I loved him because he was steady, predictable, sincere, kind, good-looking, and the inheritor of a way of life that appealed to me. That's the bald, unpleasant truth.

What made me wonder about this was that now and then Danny surprised me. Each surprise was double: the surprise itself, and the fact that it was happening. For instance, I assumed he never read a book, but one day he came home with a bag from the drugstore downstairs, and inside it was the second volume of the *Lord of the Rings* books. He'd read the first one in high school, he said, and thought he'd try the second. "I like to read in bed sometimes," he told me. I'd never seen him read anything but sports magazines and textbooks. I was stunned, and the fact that he read only about a third of the book made no difference. And then one day he referred to Hector's, with a sigh, as "the old trapdoor," and he didn't laugh when he said it. And Spiro Agnew—I would have expected Danny to approve Agnew's sneers against intellectuals and agitators. Danny had hated the war, but chiefly (as Agnew always implied) because he was afraid to fight in it. Now he was calling Nixon and Agnew fascists and killers, sometimes even tuning in the news to feed his disgust.

I don't mean to say they weren't all right, these surprises. I don't mean they put any dents in my happiness. I see now that they should have, of course. I should have paid attention to them, and probably to other things as well: those complex doodles of his, and the need to get off by himself for that year, and the tears he shed over the war, even the babyish, resentful look he threw at me back in third grade when I graduated out of the remedial class before he did . . . O God, I was condescending in my way, as bad as the rest of the family. I deserved everything I got.

Well, we settled down. Danny worked hard at the shirt factory; in the evenings we watched TV and played cards and invited people over; and on good-weather afternoons, after I'd done my cleaning, I sometimes walked the streets of New Haven.

I walked up George Street to Howe, and down to the corner of Chapel, where after dark the real streetwalkers hung out. There was an ice cream parlor where I usually bought a cone, before I proceeded down Howe to the buildings of Yale. Sometimes I went into one of the college courtyards, mentally lording it over the lounging students because I was married, with a husband and a home of my own—I don't think I ever doubted for a minute that, if they knew, they would envy me.

I would walk down Elm to Church to Whitney and out past the old mansions turned computer places or doctors' offices. I walked miles, sometimes as far out as Edgerton Park, where I drew an unexpected satisfaction from being among trees that reminded me of my father's woods. And here I must admit something else: I walked because I didn't know what else to do. I loved cleaning and straightening and fixing up our apartment, but I was so efficient it didn't take much of my time. When I was done, there I was: drinking a cup of coffee, alone, staring through the balcony doors at the people moving past. So I went out and joined them, walking until I was so tired it was an effort to walk back—and when I got home I was glad to rest, to sit with my coffee and wait for Danny. But at times I felt the same empty day stretch out before me like the well-worn path on the board of some dull kids' game. I'd thought the cleaning, the cooking, the being in love with my husband, would be enough for me, and the emptiness of my days was another surprise of married life. I knew that as soon as Danny and I were properly "settled," I must look for a job, I must get out among the people—but with a purpose. Sometimes I read the want ads. That animal shelter job I'd had to give up nagged at me: that was the job I wanted, and nothing else appealed to me. I waited, suspended, for something to turn up and inspire me.

Meanwhile, I cleaned, I walked, I ran errands for Mr. Blenka.

Of all our friends, it was Mr. Blenka, the agoraphobe, who intrigued me most, aside from Ray Royal. Mr. Blenka didn't come to our place, of course; he never left home, even to go down the hall. But I got to know him well from dropping off his groceries. His apartment was full of birds and plants. He raised parakeets, which he called "budgies" because, though he was (I believe) Polish—his first name was Taddei—Mr. Blenka had been raised in England. He opened his door and it was all green and twittering, a jungle. He had the budgie seed delivered in twenty-pound sacks.

Mr. Blenka was a fat man, with breasts. "He's got bigger boobies than I do," Elisa used to giggle. She thought Mr. Blenka and his phobia were hilarious. Even the budgies could get her giggling. I was three years older than Elisa, and although Mr. Blenka amused me, too, I could see that in a way his life made perfect sense. He had adapted, the way a particolored lizard in a real jungle would adapt. Even his fatness made sense: his fat was an extra layer of protection, and food had replaced normal, human loves. Mr. Blenka was too timid for these, but food filled him up just as well. And food had to be brought to him—that had a function, too: we, his neighbors, his food bringers, were another substitute. I wouldn't call him lonely. He was, in fact, self-sufficient. He said he was always busy, and had never in his life been bored. He devoured the newspapers, clipping out stories that touched his sentimental side, like one he showed me about a cat mothering an orphaned baby mouse. These he would put up on a bulletin board in the kitchenette until they crumbled and yellowed. "You see," he used to say, as if to himself, gazing at those clippings while the bag of groceries waited on the tiny table to be put away. "There is good in life, there is some good." And he would beam his fat, sudden, angelic smile at me.

He liked me to come in and talk. He wanted to hear the most minute details of everyday life. Trivia that would bore anyone else was exotic to him: how much the laundromat cost, and what the man at the meat counter said. Once he asked me if I got dressed before breakfast or after. He intrigued me because, behind his phobia and his huge body, he was both wholly independent and wholly dependent. I sometimes felt a peculiar attraction toward his phobia—toward its safe, enclosing quality. I had the same feeling once when I traveled with my parents and Juliet to Ephrata, Pennsylvania, to the cloisters there. I said to Juliet, "I wouldn't mind living in a cloister," and she found that funny (or "highly amusing," as she put it), thinking I suppose that only booky people lived in cloisters. But I meant it—and pondering it now I think of those long, quiet evenings with my coin albums, when I seemed to enter a world made of bits of gold and silver where, though I was alone, I felt perfectly at home.

I suspected Mr. Blenka of being more than he seemed, and if it had been suddenly revealed that he was a famous novelist, or Howard Hughes, or in communication with another planet, I wouldn't have been much surprised. His apartment was dirty and shabby, but I knew he had plenty of money. He insisted on paying Elisa and me for doing his errands—by check, of course—and he was sometimes extravagant with us. He was especially fond of a hard-crusted French peasant bread, available only at a market on Orange Street. Sometimes I used to walk over and get him a couple of loaves, and when I brought it back he always tipped me hugely and then he offered me a piece: he insisted it had to be broken off in chunks and eaten without butter. Once, on my birthday, he gave me ten dollars for getting him a hot pastrami on rye from the deli.

Danny thought Mr. Blenka was weird, but I liked him. He was so cheerful all the time, except when he thought he might have to go out and the look of horror and panic came over his fat, saggy face. There was the time he needed a tooth pulled, for example, and when I persuaded the dentist downstairs to come up and take care of him in his apartment, he collapsed on his old green sofa, laughing in huge sobs with relief. Danny was convinced his phobia didn't exist, and that Mr. Blenka simply liked being waited on. If it was true, it was okay with me. He paid generously for his whims. I admired the ingenuity with which he'd set up his life to suit him.

I was glad I never told my parents about Danny's coming promotion. He didn't get it because soon after our marriage he switched from the night shift to the day shift. He did it for me—I couldn't bear sleeping in the daytime—but the price was that he lost his chance of becoming a supervisor. It was in the lonely nights that men were needed, that hard workers like Danny, however low on the ladder, could make their way up. On the day shift there was no shortage of candidates for supervisor. But it didn't matter. We had Hector's before us. George was beginning to talk vaguely of giving up the business and taking his arthritis to Florida. And we had each other.

We were also very sociable. There were a lot of people we liked. It wasn't that either of us was particularly close to any of them—we were still getting close to each other, still preoccupied with that—but we loved being around people as, I think, another way of defining ourselves to ourselves. There are more mirrors thrown up by six people playing cards at a table than by two alone. And, in an odd way, we were shy with each other. Our marriage was like an especially valuable present, achieved at long last after ages of coveting; it takes time to accept it as one of the family, to use it without self-consciousness. Our friends helped us over that breaking-in period, the way Billy Arp had in the first days of our teenage romance.

For the first time in my life I could invite my friends over to my house without embarrassment or constraint. It got so that there was a regular small parade of people, and Danny and I would say how we really had to quit being so sociable for the sake of our beer-and-potato-chip bills, and then the phone or the doorbell would ring, and we would grin at each other and shrug. We liked the parade.

We saw a lot of Sandy and her fiancé, Harvey Sanderson.

Sandy was in nurse's training at Yale–New Haven hospital. I never told Sandy this, but if I ever found myself in a hospital with her for a nurse I'd rather go home and die of my illness. Well, I exaggerate, but it's true she wasn't the nurse type; she was nervous, dippy, overweight, a chain-smoker, a worrier. I was very fond of her, she was a good friend, but she must have been a terrible nurse.

Nor would I have let Harvey Sanderson, who was planning to be a surgeon, cut me open. There was something sadistic about his relish for his profession. Sandy thought he was a scream, but the enthusiasm with which he talked of organs and cadavers made me queasy. It was the flowing of blood that seemed to spur him, the sheer love of getting his hands into it—a gory Macbeth of a man. He said once that he regretted the invention of surgical gloves. He looked at us as if we were simply a collection of organs, potentially diseased or malfunctioning, as if he longed to get his hands in us. I couldn't imagine going to bed with someone like that, but I knew Sandy was, and I must admit Harvey was handsome enough, one of those large, smooth, muscular guys—blond, with square teeth and a big jaw. He and Sandy were always pawing each other, and when I once saw him take her earlobe between his teeth, I had to look away.

Thank God she never did marry him. For months they were inseparable; then, suddenly, Jack the Ripper was gone, replaced by Carl Keyes, whom she did finally marry. She moved to California with him shortly after Danny's and my first anniversary—moving out of my life at a time when I needed a friend most.

During that year, Sandy and Harvey, and then Sandy and Carl, were often at our apartment, and so was Danny's friend Ray Royal. Ray worked at the shirt factory; Danny met him on the day shift. I considered him the oddest person I had ever met. He had gone to Yale, he was black, and he was living in sin with a woman old enough to be his mother. After he graduated from Yale, he began work at the factory because he wanted to get in touch with real people—that's what he said. Danny was apparently one of the real people, because Ray took to him right away. Ray was very handsome, with skin precisely the color and (so it looked to me) texture of a Hershey bar, and he had a vast nest of frizzy black hair exploding around his head; he used to pull strands of it out straight when he talked and then let it twang back again. He had a mournful face, everything turned down—eyes, lips, the sides of his nose. Even his smile was lugubrious. Only when he honked out his abrupt laugh (showing big, perfect teeth like Chiclets) did he ever seem truly cheerful.

He claimed to come from a wealthy black family in New Orleans who had made their money after the Civil War by assassinating influential Southern whites for enormous sums; their specialty was nasty, slow death made to look accidental. He told us this with his wily, liver-colored eyes glittering, and he told us the terrible details, too. Harvey listened open-mouthed, licking his bottom lip slowly across and back. He and Danny believed everything Ray said; Sandy and I rolled our eyes at each other behind their backs. Danny would have believed Ray if he claimed to have been raised by wolves.

I liked Ray, but he scared me a little, and I didn't really trust him. Yale was true, though; he had a diploma and a Co-op number. And May was true—his fifty-three-year-old mistress. We never met her, but she used to call him at our place, asking for "Raymond" in a soft whiskey voice, and once or twice she picked him up at work—a tall, statuesque black woman, Danny reported, with a head of thick, straight white hair that tumbled over her shoulders. "It could be his mother," I said to Danny, but he shook his head. "She's no mother," he said, impressed.

Danny's susceptibility to Ray Royal made me keep my own gullible nature reined in. It was odd that Danny trusted Ray and I didn't. I was the truster, not Danny. He was always wary with people, almost suspicious, until he got to know them well. He expected people to laugh at him, though he wasn't laughable. Even in school, it wasn't Danny who got jeered at for stumbling through *Neighborhood Friends*; it was me. Danny has a natural dignity, possibly only because of the harsh planes of his face; he looks like Sir Walter Raleigh on the 1937 Roanoke Island commemorative half dollar, and his normal facial expression is serious to the point of severity in spite of the freckles. I, on the other hand, seemed to invite ridicule. Partly, I courted it; I could always clown to good effect, and ridicule never bothered me. After all, I was used to being the family anomaly, the butt of a ridicule that was tacit and affectionate but nonetheless there. I liked attention, nearly any kind. And except for Mrs. Meek and a few nuns, I trusted individuals, and from there went on to trust mankind. (Unlike Danny, for example, I was never afraid to go out at night in New Haven.) With Mr. Blenka, I believed in the goodness of people. I became aware of this in myself only because I saw its opposite in Danny.

But he trusted Ray Royal, all right. He believed every word Ray ever uttered. And when Ray used to come over after work and sit at our table and tell us his preposterous tales (like the one about his great-uncle, who learned scalping from the Indians and personally massacred a whole Tara full of whites with an axe), Danny used to listen closely, with his head cocked to one side and his eyes shining, and murmur, "No shit, Ray." His own ancestors were all French-Canadian shopkeepers and domestics.

It was funny about Ray Royal. I didn't believe half of his crazy stories, and I didn't consider him a good influence on Danny—I don't know why; I kept expecting him to peddle us dope, I suppose. But I did like him. I couldn't help it. He was bright without being bookish, for one thing. And he liked to hear other people talk as well as himself. He liked to hear about my father, whom he considered a comic character right up there with Archie Bunker. He howled when I told him about the poetry journals in the bathroom, the *Vogue* piece, the wood stoves, the kippers for breakfast. Sometimes I played my father for laughs, but at other times I couldn't always see what was so funny. Ray heard Daddy speak once at Yale, and every time he recalled it he collapsed in tenor giggles. "That big black beard!" he sputtered. "That big booming voice! That flannel shirt! Oo, man! What an act!" The giggles erupted out of him while I got more and more solemn. That wasn't what was funny about my father—his appearance. And that, at least, was no act: he'd been born on a New England farm; he'd always dressed that way, and his father before him. But maybe I was reluctant to discuss with Ray the really funny things, whatever they were. Maybe I didn't altogether like his ridicule.

Ray had some amazing ideas. Once he said, "You know, I think it's very odd how people go to sleep every night. Just sink into unconsciousness like that without a protest. You know, Delia? Dan?" (He had a way of using your name a lot, and of seeking confirmation from his audience as he talked. Mostly we just nodded, Danny and I, but I think Ray would have liked it better if we threw up our hands and cried, "Yes, Lord, I hear you!") "Do you know what I mean? I think it must be designed to make death easier, don't you? To give us something to compare it to, something familiar. Now I call that real consideration on the part of the Almighty. Just imagine if there was no such thing as sleep, Dan. I mean, death would be weird, man, don't you think so?"

"I think it's weird anyway," Danny said. (That's what I mean about our friends acting as mirrors.)

And then Ray said what was to me a startling thing, which I've never forgotten: "I think it's going to be an adventure unlike anything else." He had a velvety voice, pitched high, with traces of a Southern accent left in it in spite of Yale and a lot of effort; and he spoke, when he was in these reflective moods, with a peculiar distinctness. "Think of it!" he said, letting go one of the springy strands of his hair. "Everybody who's ever lived has done it, and everybody's going to do it! It's waiting there somewhere for all of us! And we don't know one goddamned thing about it!" He tipped his chair back on two white-wire legs and took a swig of beer. "Now that is what I call something damned exciting to look forward to!"

Then the phone rang. It was May wanting Ray home, so he left in a hurry, as he always did when she called, as if she really were his mother.

The conversation agitated Danny. That's one reason I remember it so well. I always thought Ray's words had some bearing on Danny's disappearance, though I have no reason to think so except that he used to bring it up during those odd months before he left.

"Remember all that stuff Ray said about death that time?" he used to ask me, out of the blue. "The big adventure?" And then he'd pause, and his face would get sterner and bonier before my eyes, and then he'd say, with all the irony leached out of his voice, "I don't know, Delia. I just don't know." And I would look back at him helplessly, not knowing what to say. When he left me, that October morning (a year and a month after our wedding), I thought at first he'd gone somewhere to die, until I realized that a dead person can't disappear with the thoroughness Danny had.

We had a year, though, before the oddness began which culminated in Danny's exit. But I'm beginning to dislike, now, the way this story rambles, the way it can only approximate what is to me so clear. Why all these friends and neighbors? Why put them in? Because they were so important to me, I suppose, and to give an idea of the life we led—the normality of it. Mr. and Mrs. John Q. Average, that was us—with our friends, our happy home, our hot dogs and Coca-Cola and Budweiser, the Vanish in our toilet, the Lux under our sink. I had no idea the friends we cultivated would sound so eccentric, become on paper such characters. It's the evil power of words again, with their false magic. Day to day, these people weren't peculiar, except maybe for Mr. Blenka, but even he—except for his phobia—was bland enough, a fat man, optimistic about human nature, generous with his cash, addicted to French bread, enamored of budgies. Even Harvey Sanderson was only a smart-mouthed young medical student with a grotesque sense of humor. And Danny—ah, my dear, lost Danny. On my twentieth birthday he gave me a pretty little gold wristwatch; on the back it was engraved, "For Delia, my dearly beloved wife—DHF, 1973." It made me cry; it was so old-fashioned, so sincere, so sweet and typical, and far too extravagant. We were happy; the watch proves it. I wear it still. It keeps perfect time. I think of Danny, in Sommers State Prison, keeping time by bells. The watch is like our good year together, gentle and regular and somehow delicate—easily shattered.

Well, I ramble on. Let me get to the parents, and the shattering. Danny's mother and father were proud of us, thought we had done very well for ourselves. They often came to dinner on Sundays, when the market was closed. Claire especially liked the ice-cream-parlor chairs, and George used to stretch out on the tweed sofa after dinner and take a nap. "He feels right at home," Claire said over her knitting the first couple of times he did it. "It's that kind of apartment," she sometimes added, and I saw Danny, who pretended he didn't care about his parents' approval, beam.

Mine were another story. I could tell the apartment pained them deeply. They came over less often than the Frontenacs—every month or two, perhaps—and while they were there my father was in a state of perpetual wince. He never said anything to me, but he seemed to sit gingerly in the big armchair, unable to believe in the reality of any furniture but shabby old antiques. Once, when I was in the kitchenette, I overheard him say to my mother, "This is *living?*"—as if he were Jewish.

Another time, Ray Royal came in with a couple of guys from the shirt factory while my mother was visiting. It was summer, and Danny took them out on the balcony to drink beer and play poker. "Quite a little salon you have here," my mother murmured to me. It was one of the few sarcastic things I ever heard her say. It disconcerted me, not so much because my mother disapproved of my life—*that* I expected—but because her view of it was false and would never get put right, no matter what anyone said or did. It was as if I was some intractable biography she'd been working on for twenty years. I *irritated* her. The howling beer drinkers on the balcony, the cheap new furniture, the baloney on white bread for lunch, the canned iced tea, the cat clock—all of it was wrong, if you were my mother. She would have liked to rip it up and start over. And still we loved each other. Mother and daughter, we looked at each other in mutual, affectionate, silent disappointment over the remains of the lunch, and when she left we hugged tighter than ever. But each on her own side of the door breathed with relief.

We used to visit the parents, too. Mine liked us to come for brunch. My mother's cooking was either negligent (once we had sardines, wholemeal biscuits, and imported brandy-soaked cherries for dinner) or elaborate, and for these brunches she used to outdo herself with kipper-stuffed crêpes and sausages flown over from England and odd bits of fish in sauce. Setting me an example, I suppose, of civilized entertaining. Danny couldn't get over my mothers' cooking. He ate it—he ate anything—but every time she brought out a slab of smelly Camembert for dessert he gaped.

Then we would go into town to the Frontenacs' for a large dinner, usually spaghetti and meatballs with lettuce salad and Italian bread, or pot roast, or turkey and gravy and mashed potatoes, with a regular dessert like a Sara Lee chocolate cake and chocolate chip ice cream. It was at one of those dinners, that summer we were both twenty, that George and Claire broke it to us about Hector's.

They had been talking retirement for years, and especially since Danny and I got married. George wanted to live in Florida, in the sun. Claire used to say, "I'm fifty years old, and I've worked every day of my life since I was seventeen." It was true: she had quit school when her father died, and become a waitress. At twenty she married George and went to work at Hector's. "Enough is enough," Claire said. It was always assumed that Danny would take over the store. In fact, he and I had talked tentatively of moving back into the village, maybe in the spring, and easing ourselves into Hector's. We'd planned to discuss this with his parents one Sunday soon. But that summer day, over the pot roast and boiled potatoes and Le Sueur baby peas, George told us he'd sold Hector's.

It is absolutely accurate to say Danny and I were stunned. I felt as if someone had taken a baseball bat to my head. Our lives, all we'd planned, spilled out on the table before us. There was nothing left. And our year of perfect happiness was up.

George elaborated. Hector's was no longer a money-making enterprise. The competition from the supermarket chains was doing in the mom-and-pop operations like Hector's.

"Hector's is a luxury," George said. He'd had several drinks before dinner. His eyes pleaded with us (Don't hate me, don't hate me) as he recited his obviously well-rehearsed lines. "It would never support the two of you, Dan. Delia. It's in the red now and it'll only get worse." His own red eyes sank to his plate.

They had had a substantial offer from a man who wanted to open an old-time general store there. "Herbs and spices in barrels, penny candy, tea cozies—all that junk," George said bitterly. Claire put her hand over his, and all of a sudden I saw my father-in-law for what he was—a loser and a failure, a disappointed man. "I should have had the balls to get out years ago," he said to Claire, confirming my impression, and his tone was briefly savage. I wondered if he blamed Claire for snuffing out, over the years, all the bright ideas that might have saved him—the remodeling, the expansion, the ramps. I didn't envy my in-laws their retirement years in Florida, with George's wounds bleeding in the sun and Claire trying to bind them up.

I pitied the two of them, but I was angry, too. They could

have told us. They could have given us a chance to buy the store; we might have managed it. Danny said all this, and the reply infuriated him. "We didn't want to wish it on you kids, we didn't want to saddle you with it."

Danny insisted we get up right then and leave, and of course I had no choice, though I felt awful leaving the Frontenacs there at the table with George's fifth drink before him and the roast sitting in its juice. I called Claire later that night. I had calmed down by then, but Danny stayed mad. He was hurt and he had been insulted. "They treat us like kids," he kept saying. We *are* kids, I thought, but I didn't say anything. Part of the conflict was none of my business. It was between Danny and his parents, and it involved the long years of Hector's Market, of the tiny apartment upstairs with its diamond-paned windows, of only-childhood, of promises spoken and unspoken and now broken. I sympathized with everyone. I was on both sides at once. I could see that the Frontenacs were right, and also that Danny was right to feel cheated. And I was miserable; for me, the loss involved not pride but visions: of sunlight through diamond panes, of the warm, dim dustiness of the store with its plenty, of living my life as a grocer's wife. I'll never be able to explain the strange appeal of that poem.

The weeks went by, and in the fall George and Claire left. They had bought a condominium in Sarasota, Florida. They brought us boxes and boxes of groceries before they went— peace offerings, tokens of their love, bribes, bonds. Danny, stony-faced, helped carry the stuff in, all our favorites—canned pork and beans, Campbell's soup, Dinty Moore stews, Lipton onion soup mix, boxes of spaghetti and elbow macaroni, all kinds of cookies. Danny never said a word of thanks, and every night at dinner, he'd ask, "Any of this stuff from the market?" And when I said, "Yes, the peas," or the corn or the steak sauce, his lips would wrinkle up in disgust. It was the first time he had ever really irked me. Sitting across from him and his prissy anger, I thought, if it offends you so much, why did you accept it? Finally I said as much, and the vehemence of his answer scared me: "They owe us this, and plenty more."

He told Ray about the groceries one night when we were all eating a Hector's meal, and Ray just laughed. He slapped Danny on the shoulder and said in an exaggerated Southern accent, "When it rains corn pone, baby, hold out your dish." Danny didn't laugh. When he gets angry his ears burn red, and they were flaming. But he kept on eating his pork and beans.

He never got over it. All that summer and fall he did nothing but go to work and, when he was home, sit out on the balcony, brooding until it got dark. Then he slumped in front of the TV. He didn't care what he watched. He just sat there, half watching, and making his angular doodles in the margins of *TV Guide*, until he got sleepy.

People stopped coming over, except for Ray once in a while. I still had coffee or Cokes with Lois Liebermann or Mrs. Smolover or Elisa or Mr. Blenka during the day. They never bothered me when Danny was home. I didn't tell any of them my troubles, although once in a while someone, usually Mr. Blenka, asked me if anything was wrong. I believe Mrs. Smolover thought I was pregnant, and then, when I didn't get bigger, that I had had an abortion and was depressed about it. She used to lean across the table and pat my hand and say, with a heavy sigh, "It's not an easy life, is it, honey?"

Danny put in a lot of overtime and often worked Saturdays. He asked me once if I'd mind if he went back on the night shift. I did mind, and I said so: our being together was more important than the extra money, the possible promotion. Not that we were together much any more. He avoided me as he avoided everyone. Only in bed at night, from time to time, was he tender and human; I kept expecting him to cry in my arms as he had over the war, and I wished he would, so that, comforting him, I could get a little comfort for myself. But he never did. And we never discussed the future. I didn't press him. I thought it would come, in time.

What came, though, was that October morning when I awoke, early, alone in our giant bed. It seems to me I was dreaming about when Danny used to work nights and I sometimes slept alone. What woke me, I don't know—pehaps the sudden chill of his absence, perhaps a noise. I called out, but there was no answer. I got out of bed and went over the whole apartment—bathroom, kitchen, and living room, even the closets. I opened the door into the hall and looked in both directions. In a panic of apprehension I ran to the balcony doors, opened them, went to the railing, and looked down.

I was just in time. A black Volkswagen pulled up in front of the building, and Danny, who had been standing on the curb, went right up to it, as if he had been waiting. He opened the door on the passenger side, and I saw him exchange a few words with the driver. Ten stories up I couldn't see who it was or hear what they said. There was a row of puny new maple trees planted between the sidewalk and the road. They were shedding their leaves, and as Danny stood there a light gust of wind swirled a jumble of red leaves around him. Then he got in and slammed the door, and the car drove away. He was in his pajamas, maroon-and-white-striped ones. His feet were bare. He carried a paper bag.

I stood on the balcony, shivering in my nightgown, for a long time, watching for Danny's return. The sun finished rising, revealing a gentle October morning—blue sky, red leaves. The cars on the street looked shiny, and the brick hospital buildings over across George Street to the south looked bright and clean, like a postcard.

Danny didn't return. A lot of black Volkswagens went by, but none of them stopped to let out a man in striped pajamas. Eventually I went inside and waited there. I didn't know what else to do. The apartment was unfamiliar and impersonal, the way a place can look when you've just come back from a long vacation. The cherry dresser looked dull, the ice-cream chairs tinny, the dog cookie jar corny. My reflection in the mirror had something missing from it, and it wasn't just Danny with his arm around me; it was part of me, gone away with him.

I wandered into the bedroom and made the bed, thinking how unnecessarily huge and silly-looking it was in that tiny room. I got dressed, in any old thing. In the kitchen the cat clock said 8:20 and made its whirring noise. I suppose I ate breakfast. Now and then there were voices in the hall—Elisa going out, the Liebermann kids leaving for school, Jeff dropping *Journal-Couriers* on doormats. These familiar noises comforted me until I remembered, and snapped back into my misery and confusion. I kept going to the terrace to look down at the street. I don't know what I expected. Some version of Danny's Perpetual Big Bang theory, perhaps: Danny would back out of the car, walk backward across the parking lot and come upstairs in the elevator, and our door would open behind him and he'd get into bed—and outside, the black Volkswagen would be backing down George Street and the sun would lower itself in the sky and the leaves fly back up to the trees . . .

I tried to pull myself together and work it out sanely, but my mind dragged, as if in shock, and I could only suppose his going out in pajamas before dawn suggested an emergency, a secret emergency involving a friend in trouble. This train suggested Ray Royal, and I thought of kidnap: Ray had lured Danny away . . . My mind would go no further. I couldn't imagine why Ray would want to kidnap Danny, but I couldn't turn the idea loose. Then Danny's musings on death as the great adventure took hold of me, and I got scared. When I caught myself walking in circles around the sofa, bent over, hugging myself and moaning, I decided I had better take action.

It occurred to me, finally, to call the factory and ask for Danny; failing Danny, I'd ask for Ray. And if they were both missing I would call the police.

The voice of Joe, the day supervisor, gave me back my confidence. If Danny hadn't come in he wouldn't sound so like himself.

"Is Danny around, Joe? Could I speak to him?"

There was a grunt and then a pause, in which my confidence disappeared again. I heard Joe breathe.

"Joe?"

"Delia—I don't know how to say this but Danny quit on me a week ago. Now I don't know why he hasn't told you this, I'm sure he has his reasons, that's between you and him, but he give me notice on October third and his last day was Friday the seventeenth. I haven't seen him since."

Just the way they do on TV, I shut my eyes and sank into a chair, weak-kneed. Not only hadn't he told me, but he'd gone off to work every morning with his lunch in a brown bag. I felt another fit of moaning coming on, and I suppressed it.

"What about Ray, Joe?" I managed. "Is he there?"

"Sure, Delia, I'll put him on. Look, honey, if Danny's in some kind of trouble—"

"No, Joe. No trouble. Put Ray on."

"Okay, honey. Will do."

I heard him bellow for Ray, and then Ray said, "Hello, baby—what's up now?"

"Ray, Danny's gone."

"Now what exactly do you mean—gone?" he asked.

The mixture of concern and skepticism and a touch of jaunty amusement were just right. I knew he had nothing to do with it, and the void gaped wider. I began to cry.

"He sneaked out of bed at quarter to five and got in a car down on George Street in his pajamas and somebody drove him away."

I blubbered as I said this, and Ray made me repeat it and asked questions: who was driving? did Danny have anything with him? did I recognize the car? did he leave a note? I pulled myself together and answered them all. I could see that the interrogation was designed to calm me down, but I hoped Ray had a theory he was trying to fit the facts to as well.

"He's been acting really strange, Ray—for weeks, ever since we lost the market. He never told me he quit the factory. He went to work every morning. Where was he all those days, Ray? Where is he now?"

I began to cry again. Ray said not to worry, it was probably just one of Danny's crazy schemes.

"Danny doesn't *get* crazy schemes, Ray," I said, finally losing all hope. "That's why I married him. He's left me—that's all. Why would he just go off like that? And where? He must have another woman someplace."

Even as I said this, though, I didn't believe it. I said it because I felt it was what I was expected to say. I had no good reason for not believing it—I just didn't, and Ray didn't either.

"Bull*shit*," he said, giving *shit* the full, two-syllable Southern treatment. "I'll tell you what, Delia. I admit this is pretty weird. But it may not be all that weird. Let me make a couple of phone calls. I'll call everybody who knows Danny. I'll talk to the guys here and try to get a lead. I'll pick my brain for ideas. And I'll call you back. Okay? You relax—hell, he might be home any minute. And you could—you know—look around for—what? a note? some kind of clue? okay? Just relax, don't worry, take it nice and easy, let old Uncle Ray take over. Eat protein. I'll call you later. You call me if our man Dan turns up."

He hung up. I had no faith in Ray's methods for finding Danny. I knew in my soul that his disapearance *was* weird, incomprehensible, impossible. I got my list notebook out of my underwear drawer and prepared to make a list. Never had I needed so desperately to organize my life. I intended it to be a list of possibilities followed by a list of practical actions: where Danny might be, and what I must do to either get him back or get along without him. But I sat there listening to the clock whirr and marking the premature sag of the sofa cushions, unable to write a word. All I could think was: we're out of tunafish, and that spurred me to make a grocery list, not in my List Notebook but on a piece from the roll of grocery-list paper that unreeled from a varnished pine holder on the wall.

79

Carefully, I penciled down: *tunafish, hot dogs, Oreos, 2 qt. ginger ale.* I sat looking at it until I heard Elisa come home, and then I gave it to her so she could bring my groceries when she brought Mr. Blenka's.

For three days I sat in the apartment eating tuna salad and hot dogs, drinking ginger ale, eating Oreos. I wandered from the sofa to the balcony and back again until I fell asleep each night on the rough tweed. I never changed my clothes or brushed my teeth. I never turned on the radio or the TV; for some reason I was afraid to make a noise, afraid I'd miss something, maybe—the sound of Danny climbing up the balcony, of his key in the lock, of a whispered message from the dog cookie jar, the cat clock, the plaster head from Greece. I saw no one but Elisa. I told her Danny had gone to Florida because his father was sick, and that I had a cold. My mother called and I said I had a cold and would call her back. I spoke to Ray Royal on the phone every day; he was "making inquiries," but they came to nothing, whatever they were.

I didn't tell anyone else Danny had gone. Ray half suggested I report his disappearance to the police, but I felt I had no right. I'd seen him leave, he'd gone freely. My husband had left me: that was the plain fact. The incomprehensibility of it turned me around. I'd never wanted anything more than for life to be open and undisguised and honest. That was the kind of life I had created for myself—that, at least, was how I saw it—fighting my way out of the jungle of verbiage and ambiguity and downright falsehood in which I'd been raised, to the clean air where I could breathe. And here I was, with the vines closing over me again. Nothing made any sense. Life was as crazy as a dream or a poem. Unable to make a pattern out of it, my mind wandered random paths, conjuring these disjointed images: Danny and I in the mirror, the sounds Danny made in bed, the freckled skin on the backs of his hands, his blue eyes against blue sky on Billy Arp's pier, the precise look of his feet, his wrists, his pained face when he had the ear infection, his mouth pursed over the leavings of Hector's . . . Puzzle pieces. He had gone and left me with them. It was the mystery that disturbed me most. I can't stand mysteries, except in books like Horatio's. I can't stand *not knowing*.

It was as if Danny wanted to get at me and knew me well enough to pick out the most effective way—knew me, finally, better than I ever, ever knew him. "Puzzle her, mystify her," I imagined him cackling to himself, rubbing his hands. But why? The Danny I knew would not torment me that way. Therefore, the Danny who left me was not the Danny I knew. Therefore, why mourn him?

This was the way I instructed myself, but it didn't keep me from mourning. Nor did it erase that horrifying final impression of a carefree Danny jumping lightheartedly into a strange car and driving off without a backward glance. He hadn't been light of heart for months. In my last glimpse of him, he had looked—no doubt about it—like a man who'd just been released.

I told this to Ray. He couldn't figure it out. I'd stopped expecting him to, but his failure seemed to surprise him. "I'd put old Dan down as a model husband out of the *Reader's Digest*," he said. "I can't understand it." He thought maybe Danny had indeed gone to Florida to have it out with his parents, but he couldn't explain the secrecy or the pajamas. I thought privately that Danny had gone to Florida to murder his parents. It was hard for me to see Danny as a murderer, recalling his despair over the war and having to kill, but the loss of Hector's could have unhinged his mind—and those mass murderers were always described as gentle, kindly people, the last ones on earth you'd expect to—

This theory got hold of me so hard that I became afraid for George and Claire and wondered if I should call them in Sarasota to warn them Danny was on his way with a gun in a paper bag. I couldn't bring myself to do it. I called my Aunt Phoebe, instead, on the fourth day, and poured everything out. She came and got me and took me up to her house in Middletown.

I stayed there a month, moping around and helping with

the apple picking. There was no word of Danny. The police were informed. And my parents. I wouldn't talk to them on the phone, anticipating satisfaction in their voices. Finally my mother came to see me, and though I scrutinized her sympathy closely, I found it pure. The delicate lines around her eyes were wet with tears. I collapsed weeping in her arms, and then I pulled myself together, and my poor life, too, as well as I was able.

I couldn't go back to Colonial Towers. My mother closed up the apartment for me and disposed of my things. I imagined—again, maybe unjustly—the glee with which she turned our furniture over to the Salvation Army. I pictured her hurling the cookie jar down the incinerator, tossing the cat clock from the balcony, breaking the mirror with a can of Dinty Moore stew. I wept for my treasures, but I had stopped by the time my mother returned. She brought me my clothes and my coins and my list notebook and the bookcase full of books. She stored the silver wedding presents in the attic. The rest—neighbors, furniture, rituals, all my loves—disappeared into a void just as Danny did.

My mother called Claire and George, who were alive and thrown into a panic by Danny's disappearance. I believe they hired a private detective, but nothing ever came of it, or of anything. I became, eventually, an official Abandoned Woman, and though I didn't do it then, I'll make my list now.

How an Abandoned Woman Feels

1. lonesome
2. bored
3. depressed
4. pissed off

That just about covers the weeks I spent at my aunt's. My parents wanted me to try college. My aunt wanted me to stay on and work at the orchard. Various modes of therapy were suggested. The trip abroad was revived. What I wanted was to stay by myself in my aunt's little white guest room looking out the window at the apples on the trees. I felt that all my energy must go into my anger and puzzlement and anxiety. There was nothing left over for ordinary life—which had proved so unreliable and uncontrollable anyway that I wanted no part of it.

I was forced back into it, though, by my kind aunt's kindness. She couldn't help it. I looked like the same old Cordelia—how can I blame her for treating me like the old Cordelia? She cosseted me. She tried to jolly me out of it. She was always trying to get me to go places, to abandon my nice cold quiet bedroom. It was her busiest season, but she even took me to the movies. We saw *Paper Moon* and *The Sting* and *A New Leaf*. (She thought only cheerful movies were suitable.) After *The Sting*, we went to the Little Germ. Whit was gone by then—out of my aunt's life too, as far as I knew—and we were served our coffee and doughnuts by a blond woman who reminded me immediately of Claire. I sat across from my aunt and tried to look happier, but she said, "You'll be back on your feet in no time if you just work at it a little bit," so I knew I must still look as detached from earth as I felt—unable to put my feet firmly down and get going.

She began to talk about her dearest scheme, that I stay on as her helper at the orchard: what fun we could have, going to movies, working the new cider press; she wanted me to help her shingle the roof in the spring, she'd learned to tap-dance out of a book and she'd teach me. I smiled and made suitable faces, as if she were a child. Her trump card was the nice college boys who picked apples for her during the season. She pimped for them shamelessly. I'd met the current pickers, a shifty-eyed boy named Mike who looked as if what he wanted to do was get off in a corner somewhere and masturbate, and a plump-hipped boy named Johnny who, presumably to impress me, had chug-a-lugged the contents of a pint jar of honey.

"I know Johnny would like to take you out," said my aunt, and I almost gagged on my coffee, thinking of the honey dribbling down his jowls. My aunt put her hand over mine; she had tiny pink fingernails, clipped short, and she wore a garnet ring. (The ring was new, probably a gift from her new Whit.)

"What's wrong, Delia?" she asked me in her gentle voice.

"I'm still married, you know." It seemed incredible that Danny was gone, forgotten, discounted in such a short time.

"Oh—married," she said. "Technically, I suppose you are." There she would have left it, but I wouldn't. "It's only been six weeks."

"How long do you plan to give him?"

I didn't know. A year? Another week? Forever? Would I be any more inclined to accept a date with some Johnny in six years than in six weeks? I had no answer.

"You can't carry the torch forever, honey," my aunt answered for me.

"I'm not carrying the torch!" I burst out angrily. "I just— don't—know—what's—happened to him!" The words came out choked. For once, there was something I didn't want to talk about. Why couldn't my good, perceptive aunt see that? "He could be in trouble, he could be dead, he could be anything. I can't just abandon him!"

She took that up, of course. "Even though he abandoned you."

"I don't *know* that." It was the not knowing, the mystery, the puzzle. I had no desire to explain this to my aunt, and for the first time in my life I saw her as part of *them*, the other side, a branch of the family conspiracy that not only didn't understand me but didn't want to.

"Aren't you even angry with him? Conditionally?" she pursued.

I hate him, I said to myself in surprise, but aloud I said rudely, "That's not your business."

"I know. I'm sorry," she said after a pause, and withdrew her hand after a last soft squeeze.

"Oh, don't listen to me," I said with contrition, wishing for her hand back. My poor right hand lay there useless, fiddling with a sugar packet. "I don't know what I'm saying," I went on. "I don't know how I feel." I hate him, I said to myself, trying it out; but I didn't cry, and I suspect my aunt thought me cold. She kept her hands wrapped around her coffee cup. Her garnet ring looked reproachful.

We went home, and that night I started reading the help-wanted ads, which is how I got the job at Madox Hardware, in the town of Hoskins. They wanted a counter girl and cashier, with experience: that was me. The store was halfway between my father's house and my aunt's, so that I could have lived at either one—and after they got used to what was considered yet another bizarre act on my part (Why a hardware store instead of the orchard? instead of college? instead of England?), they tried to get me to board with one or the other. But I wanted to get off on my own, and finally I persuaded my aunt that it would be for the best, and she convinced my parents. She compared it to the way she felt after she split up with Jack Appleman. There were some superficial similarities, I suppose; items 1 and 2 on my Abandoned Woman list would apply equally well to a woman who has kicked her husband out and one whose husband has taken off, at dawn, in his pajamas. But it wasn't an apt comparison. I let it stand, of course, since it served as well as anything as my passport to a one-room apartment in Hoskins.

This time I didn't even try. I accepted castoffs from my parents' attic—an iron cot, an old gateleg table, a couple of press-back chairs that had been my grandmother's. I dragged my bookcase and books and coins along. I cooked on a hot plate and an electric skillet, the latter a retrieved wedding present. I let the stained and peeling walls stain and peel. And I kept cookies in the bags they came in. I didn't care. I ate and slept and watched TV and went to work.

My job was supposed to be temporary, for the Christmas season, but that was okay with me. I didn't suppose I wanted to spend my life in a hardware store—it didn't rhyme, for one thing. But since I had no idea how I did want to spend it, it was okay with me, too, when Mr. Madox said the job could become permanent. He said "could" with such sly caginess that I knew the point was that I'd be on probation until after Christmas. That was also okay. All I wanted was to be left alone to find peace among the brooms, bolts, and buckets.

Chapter Five

MADOX HARDWARE

The winter I went to work at Madox Hardware was a particularly dreary, snowless winter made of gray light with a cold, dead look to it that exactly suited my mood. The hardware store was on a windy corner on the main street of Hoskins. I had to walk there every morning from the corner of Main and Woodlawn, where, over the veterinarian's offices, my room was located; and I had to walk back every evening after work. So I became a reluctant expert on the weather, especially the wind, which, no matter in which direction I was walking, always blew in my face.

I used to wake up around 6:30, without benefit of alarm clock, when the first hint of light appeared around the edges of the cold green windowshades. I would get out of bed into the cold (Dr. Epstein, the vet downstairs, turned on the heat when he arrived) and shuffle in my bed socks over to the back window, the one that looked out on the dog runs. Snow, bits of browned grass, my plastic garbage can, and beyond the parking lot Woodlawn Street, with its shabby frame houses where I imagined people waking up, cursing, to wet babies, burnt toast, morning cartoon shows. Life: bleak outside, bleak inside, whatever the weather. I would crawl back into bed and get dressed under the covers.

It was the only messy period of my life. My cot remained a jumble of blankets all day; just before bed I pulled them smooth. Whole platoons of dust kittens assembled around the room's perimeter, and there were webs of dust from ceiling to wall. The trash basket overflowed, the toilet bowl went from white to deep beige, the dirty dishes stayed stacked up for days. It wasn't that I was too depressed to notice: I noticed all right, and took perverted pleasure in the muddle. I, who had always prided myself on keeping disorder at bay— I surveyed my household anarchies with satisfaction: all right (I said silently to whatever god of chaos was listening), all right, if that's the way you want it . . .

I slept on the cot my parents donated, hidden behind a folding screen from the same source—hidden from whom, I don't know, since I hardly ever had visitors, but my genteel mother insisted I couldn't have an undisguised bed in my living room. (I suppose she thought I would be entertaining gentlemen callers who would, at the sight of a bed, be overcome with lust and insist on having their way with me.)

The building was pre–World War I, two-story, red brick, corniced, gloomy, high-ceilinged. My upstairs room was large, and easily accommodated my screened-off "bedroom" in one of its drafty corners. In another, my mother improvised a wee kitchen around a three-foot fridge and a metal cabinet with a hot plate on it. The toilet and shower stall were indecently housed behind a single fiberboard partition without a door. My mother put up a heavy curtain on brass rings over the opening, and from somewhere a draft jangled it at intervals, so that I lived with the wind-chime music of the rings. But I took for my text "Who cares?" and quickly got used to the noise, as I got used to the drafts and the drabness.

But there was worse: the plangent howls of the dogs downstairs in Dr. Epstein's kennel. One dog in particular, a big spotted spaniel named Jake who boarded there a whole month while his owners were in Florida, used to howl a most unspaniely howl, like a soul in torment. I think he was afraid of the dark (perhaps at home he'd slept with a night-light), for at dusk his howls began. The worst of the noise was that it was irregular. If the poor thing had howled steadily all night I might have hardened myself to it, but his horrible protests came at erratic intervals—a good strong one, inevitably, for openers, then perhaps two in a row, a bout of whimpering, then tense silence, in which I feared he'd died of grief, then an agonized, prolonged scream and a couple of indignant yelps before the unreliable quiet again briefly descended. It never failed to disconcert me if I was awake, and wake me up if I was asleep. "Who cares?" wasn't convincing; I cared, that's who. My heart overflowed with it: poor doggie, poor thing, poor old Jakey. There were times I mingled my own moans (I had taken to moaning in earnest, at night on my cold cot) with Jake's. Though I could never match his volume and variety, I felt we were kindred damned souls, exiled from our proper kingdoms, pining for the heaven of home.

I stopped in to see Dr. Epstein one day with a bright idea. He always seemed glad to see me. In fact, he offered me a job when Dee, his receptionist and kennel cleaner, quit to get married, but by then I was hooked on the hardware store. I'd come up with my bright idea after several nights of listening to Jake's laments: why didn't the dog come up and sleep in my apartment at night? He might be less homesick and quiet down—and so might I, I didn't tell Dr. Epstein, with a nice floppy pup snoring on the floor by my bed.

It took me a whole week to persuade him, a week of stopping by after work and helping him hose out cages and wash water bowls. He was reluctant: it wasn't orthodox, it probably wasn't even legal, he couldn't take the responsibility. Blah, blah, he fingered his moustache and avoided my eyes. I finally blew up at him. "It's easy for you! You go home every night to your quiet little house! You don't have to listen to that poor animal suffer!" And so on and so on (or "ect., ect.," as Danny used to write it). I was not really angry. I knew Dr. Epstein wasn't heartless or inhuman—he was such a good vet that I wished sometimes I were a sick pup so he would care for me. I was only playing my cards. I wanted that dog.

I got him. Dr. Epstein must have seen that it was for my benefit as much as Jake's—and, vet or no vet, it was human suffering, not canine, that finally moved him. That night he delivered a waggy, bouncing Jake to my door. Before I de- livered him back on my way to work the next morning, Jake drank the water in the toilet, chewed up a leather belt and part of the rug, and piddled in all four corners of the room. But he didn't howl once and neither did I.

Three days later his owners returned early from Florida and took him home. I missed him sorely. I kept finding white dog hairs around the place, and felt lonesomer than ever. I couldn't help seeing the loss of Jake as an omen: all I loved would be taken from me, even a homesick dog.

In an attempt to forestall the workings of fate, I asked Chuck D'Amato, who ran the Blue Bell Diner and rented me the apartment, if I could get a dog. For answer, he dug out a copy of my lease and pointed silently to the "no pets" clause. No, he couldn't make an exception. No, not even a tiny cat. No, not even a budgie, whatever that was. I gave up. Who cares? Let fate take its course. I was destined to be a loner. The signs had always been there: my isolation in my own family, and then the loss of Hector's, of Danny, of my possessions. You'd think I would have learned, and I thought I had. I brooded alone in my room. I avoided my family. I didn't even have a phone. I resolved to give up hope, to want for nothing, no one. It seemed to me I worked hard and profitably at this new life, and became as cold and hard as a stone.

But I never did learn. Every dog on the street, every cat and squirrel, drew me. I yearned toward half-heard bits of conversa- tion, toward people's worn, interesting faces, toward the lighted windows I passed on my way home in the wind. I became friendly with Dr. Epstein and his dogs, with Greta the counter woman at the Blue Bell, with the regular customers at the store—not intimate, but friendly, so that I looked forward to these human encounters no matter how often I instructed myself in the habits of stones. When Dr. Epstein talked to me about heartworm, or Greta told me to have a nice day, or I managed to locate in a carton in the storeroom just the outdated plumbing gizmo someone needed, I felt myself warming and softening, nourished back to life. But the process was slow, and I was weary.

I threw myself into the job at the store. Against my will, I became fond of the place, the way I had been of Hector's Market. It reminded me of Hector's; it was badly lit and overcrowded, its ancient shelves stocked with items which, in that atmosphere, seemed exotic and special. Best of all was the tiny Shoe Repair Shop tucked into a corner at the back: a half-door with a linoleum counter set into it, a venerable sewing machine with its ice-pick needle, a shelf full of spicy leather shoes. Only good shoes were brought in for repair. As Mr. Madox said, "Most of today's shoes, you might as well throw 'em out as get 'em repaired. That's all they're good for." He had a similar disdain for Timex watches, paperback books, Bic pens, and Kleenex. "Look at these shoes," he'd say, picking up a pair of brown-and-white ladies' spectators or old men's shoes with a fringed vamp. "Made to last a hundred years." (They looked as if they'd already lasted at least half that.) "Now that's what I call workmanship," he'd say, and make me inspect the soles, the uppers, the pungent arch supports, the stitching. He always intended to teach me to repair shoes, but he never got beyond his instructive chats, which could be grouped under the general heading "Things were better in the old days."

I got to love Mr. Madox. After a couple of weeks, he quit watching me to see that I didn't waste time, rob the till, or chew gum on the job, and we got along fine. He was a handsome, courtly man of about sixty, with a dust allergy. He was always honking into one of his spotless white handkerchiefs. His wife was dead; he ironed them himself. He lived a mile outside of town in a split-level, with his son who was away at college. He told me his whole back yard was planted with flowers and vegetables in the summer; he spent every Labor Day weekend canning his own tomatoes. He loved Italian food, and lived all winter on pasta and homemade tomato sauce. He used to bring me pint jars of it, heavy on the oregano.

I found myself wishing he were my father. He was exactly the kind of father I would have liked, a simple man who was really simple—not pretending to be. Mr. Madox told me that when his wife was alive they used to play a lot of Monopoly; sometimes the games would last a week, his wife would do anything for Park Place and Boardwalk, he himself craved railroads and utilities, his wife always used the cannon while he liked the dog. He related these details misty-eyed, and they gripped me. Why couldn't I have been their daughter? How could I have sprung from two such alien beings as my parents, and not from Monopoly players like the Madoxes? My old theory that I was adopted came back to haunt me, a possibility which I had loved as a child but which in my maturity I recognized as absurd, terrifying, unacceptable—but no less haunting, for all that.

Oddly enough, it was at this period—isolated as I was, resolved to go it alone, inviting my old foster-child fantasies—that my mother drew closer to me than she had been in years. She used to come and see me, perhaps twice a week, on the pretext of bringing me a little gift—a new shower curtain, a jar of chutney, some homey touch, or a little hint, like a dust mop or Windex. Sometimes she brought only family gossip (the tale, for instance, as it developed between Horatio and that woman novelist who let herself get pregnant because she wanted to experience motherhood so she could write about it, and then hit Horatio with outrageous child support—which he gladly paid, making her accuse him of condescending to her, rubbing it in that his trashy thrillers sold millions while her novels barely sold at all, so that she had to move to the south of France to escape his insults—where she still lives on Horatio's money with the child, my only nephew, whose name is Tacitus). Sometimes she brought dinner, or a letter from Miranda or Juliet, or a clipping about my father.

"I don't want you to cut yourself off from the family," she would say.

"It's only temporary," I assured her. "I'm pulling myself together."

At which she would frown delicately, as she always did whenever I alluded, however obliquely, to my position as abandoned woman. "Still . . ." she would murmur.

I finally figured out that my mother was coming to see me because she missed me. She was lonely, with her children gone and my father writing poetry all day. She was very tender and loving with me, just as she used to be at intervals when I was younger. But now, visiting me on my own turf, she didn't have a book to go back to when she had had enough of mothering (though I fancied I saw her eyes foam the bare walls of my room restlessly), so the mothering was constant. She was prodigal with her quick bony embraces and her unexpected confidences. She confessed to me that her own work was going badly, that she had in fact lost the desire to write exquisite lives of the obscure. What she really wanted to do (and she told me this with a blush that made her look astonishingly young and pretty) was write a cookbook, and she was working on the project—in secret, I understood. (Though it was a proper literary cookbook, with recipes for famous meals from novels, I could see that she would want to spring it on my father gradually, a cookbook being in the same class as Horatio's murder mysteries: parasites on the body of literature.) The dinners she brought over were taste tests. I suppose she wanted the philistine opinion of her daringly seasoned, eccentrically combined dishes. I ate them greedily, whether I liked them or not. They tasted of mother love, and I was hungry. My mother sat across from me, not eating much herself but beaming at me the smile of a madonna. For the first time in years (since the blessed days before I learned my letters, when my mother read me a chapter of *Mrs. Piggle-Wiggle* every night before bed), I spent time alone with my mother without feeling guilty or inadequate, without a stomachache.

But she wouldn't talk about me, not with anything like seriousness. Incredibly, after her first sympathetic reaction, she treated Danny's desertion of me as a mild joke. One of her speculations on his departure was "Maybe he went to a pajama party?" My father, of course, was even worse. It was obvious he was glad that Danny was gone. His attitude made me feel sick—like the day I was hanging out at Hector's after school, the day after Bobby Kennedy's assassination, and one of the customers said, "He deserved it." Three men and Claire had to hold George back, and that's how it was when I saw my father smirk over Danny. "I've got my baby back," he liked to say, hugging me with undisguised satisfaction.

I knew my father was writing a poem about his abandoned daughter: I knew without anyone telling me because he wrote a poem about my first menstrual period and about Miranda's wedding night and about my mother's miscarriage between Miranda and Juliet. He had no feelings. He fed off his family gluttonously, never once wondering if we could take it. Not a broken arm, not a bicycle or vacation or family crisis could be allowed to go by without his memorializing it—telling lies about us with words. Through it all, my mother stood by, abetting him with her pride and approval. Tennyson! I'll bet Tennyson never wrote a poem about his daughter's uterus, never immortalized her broken heart with smirking symbols. Oh, he loved us: that's nearly all he talked and wrote about, and it was this noisy father-love that brought home to me the profound meaning of the old warning that actions speak louder than words.

But my mother was nearly as bad. She didn't write poems about me, but she never thought of my feelings. If she had, she could not have talked blithely about how Danny "flew the coop," or implied that such irresponsible behavior was only to be expected from a nobody, a nothing, a nonperson like Danny, someone who used double negatives and watched too much television. She was relieved that it happened, and she—like my aunt—seemed to feel that Danny's departure annulled the marriage. It had never been real to her anyway. How could her daughter be in love with a nonperson?

I tried to understand my mother's callousness. I supposed motherhood must be difficult—to see your hopes for your child repeatedly dashed by the child's own orneriness. But I gave up trying to make her understand me. I never told her my heart was broken, or that I aspired to become a stone. She wouldn't have listened. She would have smiled, made a little joke, and compared the situation, unprofitably, to Horatio's for the purpose of cheering me up. Once I was properly cheered up we could get somewhere. To my mother, Danny's bizarre exit put me back where I'd started. Removed from this pernicious influence, I was transformed into pure possibility again—virgin soil in which the seeds of culture could still be planted.

My mother began this agricultral task slowly—so gently and tactfully, in fact, that I couldn't help but suspect that her visits, her empty-nest syndrome, her confidences, her mother love were designed as part of a gradual buildup of obligation. Behind every kindness there began to be a demand. For Christmas she gave me a quilt for my bed—the puffy nylon kind, not a motheaten antique patchwork like the quilts I grew up with. Was I wrong to distrust this uncharacteristic capitulation to my taste when it was accompanied by a book called *The Secret Agent*, which she said was a mystery but wasn't? Along with food and gossip, she brought me her old *New Yorkers* and *Atlantics*, the former for the cartoons (to cheer me up), the latter because it once featured an article on coin collecting, which I had actually read. And along with the little domestic gifts, she planted my apartment with college catalogues intended to produce her lushest crop: my college education.

I resisted. ("Who cares?" didn't apply to college any more

than to howling dogs.) She patiently pressed on: colleges are different nowadays, they're fun (here I saw her suppress a grimace), the requirements are so loose you can go through four years taking only what interests you, there are all kinds of unbookish areas to major in, business for example, you did so well in your business courses at Shoreline, or counseling you like working with people, math you could be a math teacher you'd spend most of your time student-teaching instead of studying, you like children Cordelia you have a way with them, or phys. ed. Cordelia honey didn't you always like kickball or was it soccer . . .

The effort made her sweat. Her glasses misted over with her ambition for me. Total resistance was clearly impossible; it would have been the Shoreline High girls' softball team versus the Yankees. But I saw a way out, and I pursued it shamelessly. I was scheduled to take the college boards in January; I would simply mark as many wrong answers as I could.

I was no novice at such reverse cheating. All through high school I had deliberately kept my math grades down below Danny's. This took some doing, because math was not, to say the least, his best subject. (Religion was, once he figured out that you could get away with just about anything on exams if it sounded pious enough.) I became adept at fudging math answers so that I seemed not merely careless (you were sometimes given credit if the answer was wrong so long as the process was right) but dimwitted. Compared with my labors to this end in algebra and trigonometry, the college board examination would be a piece of cake.

And, on the math section, it was. While a roomful of callow high school seniors sweated and groaned all about me, the right answers came to me almost instantly. All I had to do was fill in the wrong boxes. I actually enjoyed it; some of the problems were interesting, and it was an odd exhilaration to see my old math prowess, so long suppressed, come when it was called. The fact that I couldn't advertise it, that I had to find the right answer only so I could mark down the wrong, didn't bother me at all. My performance, as far as I was concerned, was brilliant.

But the English half was another story. It wasn't easy to mark the wrong answer when I didn't know the right one. The funny thing was that half the time I thought I did have the right answer, but I could never be sure. The right answer would wobble toward me, then away, and another answer would surface, just as right in its way as the first. The imprecision drove me wild: why couldn't letters be more like numbers? They reminded me of my father, who tended to answer a question with a question.

It was almost all guesswork. I considered leaving the answer sheet blank, but I was afraid the examiners would think I'd misunderstood, and make me take it again. I would have marked the answer sheet at random, but I remembered hearing once that such a system resulted in a high percentage of right answers. So I struggled over each question. I did my best to screw up. And the result was that, thanks to my vacillations and uncertainties, I got a respectable English score, well within the entrance requirements of the kind of third-rate school my mother (realistic, for once) was trying to talk me into.

My math score, however, was almost as low as it's possible to get, far too low for admission to anywhere but the sleaziest community college. To be honest, I felt a mild attraction toward one such institution, which offered a para-veterinary program, but the requirements incomprehensibly included Freshman Composition, a course Sandy Schutz had described to me in horrifying detail when she had been forced to take it as part of the nursing program. I knew I couldn't endure a course that was all reading and writing to order ("Define love," one of Sandy's assignments had been), and I never so much as hinted to my mother that the veterinary program interested me. It would only have pained her, anyway. She was of the opinion that community colleges were for juvenile delinquents and retarded people. They weren't on her list of schools to push, however debased that list became in her efforts to find fun colleges.

So the idea was abandoned at last. By this time, my father had finagled a term as writer-in-residence at Berkeley, and he and my mother were spending the spring and summer in California. She gave up her cookbook idea (I think now it was only part of the plot to get me into college) and went to work on a biography of an eighth-century Anglo-Saxon poet who wrote a series of verse riddles which may or may not have been an allegory of Christ's life and death. Her letters to me dealt almost exclusively with this dreary-sounding book, and with my father's progress on a book of sea poems. Her tone was self-absorbed and detached. I know I disappointed her grievously—so we were even.

Soon after Christmas, I encountered Mr. Madox's magnificently handsome lout of a son, Malcolm, a student in hotel management at one of the undiscriminating colleges my mother had pushed. Malcolm Madox was a specimen of the kind of perfectly constructed young man said to drive women wild. He left me unmoved. There was something inhuman about his perfection. His blue eyes were heavy-lidded and intense, but they were cold eyes all the same. His sensual mouth and small, straight teeth could have been man-made, of plastic and rubber; his yellow hair, of polyester filament. He wasn't very tall—it was his one defect—and he reminded me of a boy doll, of the little groom on a wedding cake. Malcolm worked at the store during his winter vacation, his version of work being to sit on the high stool behind the counter and watch me wait on customers. He was willing to do the macho stuff, like hauling down gallon cans of paint from the shelves. Otherwise, he observed, waiting for a chance to impress me. When I wasn't waiting on customers, he liked to talk to me so that I would look at him; he liked to be looked at. He smiled a lot, a lavish repertoire of smiles that had obviously been perfected in a mirror. He went all the way to Hartford to get his hair cut and styled, and he wore skin-tight, penis-glorifying jeans.

He was as boring as he was handsome—the Mr. America of

boredom. He talked endlessly about school. I heard all about his courses (things like Advanced Catering and The Economics of Tourism). And about his teachers, who were stupid, aesthetically unappealing, and unappreciative of his finer qualities, whatever they were. And about his physical-fitness program: his hundred push-ups and hundred sit-ups and five-mile run every morning. And about his girl friend Diane who worked in a bank and studied sociology at night. Malcolm was in all the theatrical offerings at the college, and he told me how he'd have had the part of Hamlet if Claude Kratzer didn't give Mr. Charnik, the director, a blow job every night in the men's room, and how he'd considered playing Laertes to be a gross humiliation at first but how he'd found a way to make it work for him by playing it shirtless and got a standing ovation opening night.

Mr. Madox inevitably heard of this (though Malcolm saved the blow-job story for when his father went up to the Blue Bell for his coffee break—also the description of what he called "pussy exercises," which Diane did to improve her grip), and used to stand beaming at his handsome by-product. He bristled at the insensitive teachers, commiserated over the academic difficulties, chuckled at the nasty cracks which, with Malcolm, passed for wit. He was infatuated with his son. Worse, he loved him. Malcolm was the great joy in his life, more wonderful to Mr. Madox than tomatoes, or hardware, or the memory of his dead wife.

Malcolm gave me a pain. I admit to some jealousy. Mr. Madox was obviously satisfied with his obnoxious offspring, and entertained no fantasies of foster-fatherhood on my behalf. But I also found Malcolm personally loathsome. He might have been deformed and leprous for all I cared. My smiles at his dull and and/or spiteful anecdotes were solely to hide my yawns. I knew I had to be nice to him, as I used to have to be nice to the sullen, snotty offspring of my parents' poet friends—because if I wasn't I'd catch it later. For the sake of my friendship with Mr. Madox, I put up with Malcolm passively and painfully. His vacation went on so long I wondered if he'd been thrown out of school. Everyday he hoisted his rippling muscles onto the stool and let me bask in his presence. But finally, at the end of January, he was gone, and Mr. Madox and I were left to our dusty routines.

One of my own personal routines, which no one's niceness nor the appeal of the store nor my minor satisfactions could throw out of whack, was misery. I missed Danny so I could hardly stand it at times. I missed wifehood, missed belonging to someone who belonged to me, and I was hungry for someone to hold, and kiss, and hug at night in bed. I was tormented by my old life with Danny. When I lay on my cot at night and moaned softly under my quilt, the very texture and smell of those days seemed to come back to me: the dog cookie jar, the rough tweed of the sofa, the urine-smelling elevator, Ray Royal drinking beer at the table, Mrs. Smolover's thick brown stockings wrinkling into her orthopedic shoes, Mr. Blenka's little breasts like snouts under his shirt, Sandy and Harvey necking in the kitchenette, Elisa Wandrel's dyed blond curls, Danny and me in the mirror . . .

All this, once so familiar, became something abstract that I had to believe in, like the God of the nuns at St. Agatha's. I remembered from religion class that the chief torment of the damned was their separation from the Divine Presence of God. My separation from all I had loved was my hellfire, and making it fiercer was my perpetual puzzle: why was I condemned? Why was I here shivering alone in my cold hell on a lumpy cot? My memories, my visions of Paradise, were my only hope of survival. I clutched them to my poor soul.

I dwell on these torments as extenuating circumstances. What I am about to write pains and humiliates me. But I've filled these pages with the crimes of others against me—why not my own?

I began to steal. From my dear old Mr. Madox, among others. But first from Mr. Madox, first a ceramic flowerpot.

I coveted this pot unreasonably, without even a plant to put in it. It was painted with yellow flowers and green leaves, bright and crude, and reminiscent of the large pot that had held Horatio's rubber plant. This was a small pot, six inches across, and it cost eight dollars. I wanted it, but even with my employee discount of 20 percent it cost too much. (I was trying to rebuild my old savings account, which Danny and I had diminished somewhat on furniture and entertaining.) But I wanted the pot. I saw it brightening up my apartment like sunshine. Spring was coming. I would get a cutting from my aunt for the pot—something flowering: begonia, impatiens, African violet.

I see now that my savings account was unhealthy, that it was absurd for a twenty-one-year-old hardware store clerk working for minimum wage to bank a third of her take-home pay every week. And I see that someone with over two thousand dollars in the bank doesn't need to steal an eight-dollar flower pot. But it wasn't only that I didn't feel I could afford it (this is the humiliating part), it wasn't only the money: I *wanted* to steal it. I wanted to get away with it, in secret, to spirit that pot off to my dingy room, which it would brighten better than any beam of sunshine. To steal it would be to make it more mine, more a part of me, than merely purchasing it. I wanted it directly—does that make sense?—without the intervention of money. Money was for the bank; the pot was for me.

For weeks, I watched it, stalking it as I used to stalk Danny. There were three of the pots on display near the potting soil and plant food: small, medium, and large, with three more of each size in the stockroom. It was the medium-size pot (I considered this carefully) that seemed to me most well proportioned, that glowed with the most perfect yellow and green radiance. I lived with it in the store all that time, sold it twice over and replaced it from stock, eyeing it, fondling it, imagining it filled with the shiny leaves and succulent stems of impatiens. I took my time, I wanted to be sure. And one day I walked out with it, in a bag under my arm.

This method came naturally to me. A thief must be bold,

must act with matter-of-fact confidence, as if she has a right to her spoils. It's even better if she believes she does have a right—as I did.

And I had the advantage that Mr. Madox was a little slow, a little shuffling, vague, out of it. I'd have had to walk out with the cash register for him to notice my theft.

I stole the pot on the last day of February; and I was right, it did bring spring into my apartment. It even inspired me to dust and sweep, so bright and homey did it look on my window-sill. My mother had given me yellow curtains with a ruffle; the yellow leaped from curtain to pot and back again with a liveliness that filled me with, if not joy, then a memory of joy, maybe even a belief in its continued possibility. And the secretiveness with which I had taken the pot unto myself was part of the joy.

The pot stayed empty, though. I kept forgetting to ask my aunt for a cutting. When I did see her, maybe once a month, we went to the movies, but it wasn't the same. We saw a string of terrible movies, for one thing; and the old talks were strained because of Danny. He hovered over us like the germs of a dread disease neither of us dared speak of. Our afternoons began to depress us both, I think. Something we had valued was slowly dying. I felt very, very old, older than my aunt or my mother or Mr. Madox, old as a coin. Maybe my long, affectionate friendship with my aunt depended on my being a child who needed a substitute for a mother who loved books more than me. One thing was sure, the child in me was fluttering away, finding life in a nest scratchy and confining. Aunt Phoebe talked a lot about fat Johnny, who continued to work for her on weekends. Maybe he became her child. I didn't know and almost didn't care. I only knew I didn't want to be anyone's child; even my Mr. Madox fantasy was fading away.

So the pot became a repository for old rubber bands, stamps, safety pins, bottle stoppers. Gradually it lost its radiance, and in March I stole, one by one, a glass juice carafe, a roll basket, a Teflon-lined egg poacher, and a dish towel with cardinals on it. And I stole a loofah from Mulhauser's drugstore, also a bottle of hand lotion. I bought a melon at the supermarket and stole a melon baller to go with it. And from the 5 & 10 I stole a card of six buttons shaped like daisies, a package of green grosgrain ribbon, and a tiny gold windup alarm clock.

That makes my confession complete, I think. I never made a list of my thefts, but each one, and the circumstances surrounding its taking, is burned into me somewhere. That's all of them, except for the trivet. The trivet was the last. Up to the trivet, my spoils gave me great pleasure. I felt no apprehension or guilt or shame. I saw the things I stole as mine. I became obsessed with them before I stole them.

I browsed through the stores on Main Street for the purpose of becoming obsessed, waiting for something to strike me just right, and when it did the imaginative leap would come at once: I would see it as mine, in my apartment, where it brightened my life like an indestructible ray of sun. The three-yard length of ribbon, for example: I saw it draped over my mirror, its emerald green looped down on either side when I looked at my blank face. I saw it as a life bringer, as nourishing to me as the groceries I used to bring to Mr. Blenka. It made me happy to see my face framed in green—and to pour orange juice from a handsome glass carafe, to live by the cheery ticks of my gold clock, to eat my melons globe by globe, to sew a daisy button to each curtain tieback. Each bit of brightness wore off and had to be superseded, but each one did its bit. Gradually the longing for the old days—my religion—was wearing off. I was becoming an agnostic who no longer believed so surely in the value of the past.

It must have been around this time that I removed my wedding ring. It went into my all-purpose pot with the rubber bands. It has since been lost—transmuted to that limbo where all the relics go: the things that seem important for a time, lose their luster, disappear. Without the ring, my right hand felt bereft and naked, shocked as if by an amputation, and then one morning—the process didn't take long—I woke up feeling freed, as if what had been amputated was a superfluous digit: a deformity.

April arrived, and I had my eye on a trivet. I wasn't sure about it, it wasn't love at first sight, but it interested me. Mr. Madox had ordered a dozen for Christmas, but they came late. The one I liked was a square tile set into a wrought-iron rack with handles, and painted in the center of the tile was the head of a collie dog. The trouble was that I didn't care for the metal rack it sat in. I just wanted the tile with the dog. But if I stole the tile and left the holder, it would look odd and might even give me away. If I took the whole thing I'd have to throw away the holder, and that struck me as sinful. But the two parts of the thing clashed. I saw the tile easily enough on my little old table, ready for a hot dish (my favorite tuna casserole, made with cream of celery soup and crushed potato chips), but the metal holder was superfluous, and it made me uneasy. I pondered it. (It would sound absurd to tell how important the whole question was to me, so I'll write merely that I pondered it.) I tried to reconcile myself to the holder, I tried to talk myself out of the tile, and the more I pondered the brighter the spark leaped between the painted tile and me. I was at this impasse when Malcolm Madox came to work in the store again during his spring vacation.

I didn't like him any better in the spring than I had in the winter. But he liked me, that became immediately clear. He had broken up with Diane, and he was visibly horny. He sent me smoldering looks from the corners of his blue eyes, and he stared at me with the blue half-hidden by oval lids; he arranged a deliberating smile on his full red lips. He was coquettish, like a little tart, brushing up against me every chance he got (and in that crowded store there were plenty of chances). If I spoke to him he raised one eyebrow and let his gaze roam absently to my breasts.

His performance was both boring and amusing. I would have enjoyed his ludicrous vanity more if I'd had someone to giggle about it with. But all I had was Mr. Madox, who gazed appreciatively at his son while his son leered lecherously at me. When Malcolm was in residence, Mr. Madox came in late and took long lunch hours and left early, so that Malcolm and I were thrown together. Malcolm used to get takeout from the Blue Bell at noon, but to save money I brought my lunch and ate it in the stockroom. Malcolm would join me there and talk, loving his own voice, trusting to the bell on the front door to herald customers. (Though when it sounded it was I, in the middle of my sandwich, who had to run out to wait on them—never Prince Malcolm.)

He got on my nerves and in my way, but I tried to overcome my dislike for Mr. Madox's sake. On Malcolm's last day, I came to work in a good mood, elated by the imminent return of the bland, cozy, Malcolmless days when Mr. Madox and I could bustle around the store together like an old married couple. After I ate my lunch, I decided it was the right day to steal the trivet. I'd made my decision: yes, I wanted it, I'd use the tile and put the metal holder in my junk box under the bed until I could think of a use for it.

While Mr. Madox was out to lunch and Malcolm at the bank, I carried my handbag (a large canvas thief's handbag) from its hook in the stockroom to the pile of trivets in the front of the store. I remember smiling with relief at the end of my long debate, with delight at the realism of the collie painting— and popping the trivet into my purse. And there was Malcolm Madox smiling at me over a display of flower seeds.

I know that I blushed scarlet. Confronted by that blue-eyed leer, I lost all my professional pirate's calm.

"I suppose you were going to pay for it," said Malcolm, coming out from behind the flower seeds.

"Of course," I sputtered, and actually felt gratitude to him for giving me the out. "I just wanted to put it aside before someone bought it."

"Mm-hmm," said Malcolm, sweeping away my gratitude with the tone of his voice. We walked together to the counter, where, watched by the menace of Malcolm, I took my wallet from my purse and extracted a five-dollar bill (the trivet was $3.50). I'd brazen it out. No matter what he thought, he could never prove I intended to steal it.

He took the five from me and tucked it back into my wallet. "Here. Keep it. After all, you didn't pay for that juice thingie, did you? Or the basket?"

I looked at him in horror. "How did you know?" I whispered, giving myself away. Isn't that what criminals always do?

His triumphant smirk dropped to my chest and back up. "Two plus two makes four, in my book." He paused, just perfectly long enough that I suspected he might, after all, be a passable actor. "My dad said there were some things missing." He inspected me, calculating what kind of knife to use for the twist. Then he thrust it in: "He said you were the one person he'd never suspect." He turned it: "He loves you like a daughter, he told me that."

I moaned. Malcolm held out his hand. "Let's have it, baby." I reached into my purse and took out the trivet. While he walked jauntily, like a policeman on the beat, to the front of the store with it, I went back to the storeroom. I felt sick— literally, I wanted to throw up. I sat down in the old easy chair where I always ate lunch and put my head in my hands. I could still get away with it, there was no proof—only my apartment full of plunder. Ah, my little flowerpot, glowing in the window. What if Malcolm insisted I take his father to my place right now, to prove my innocence? What could I do? My stomach heaved, and I gagged; I could taste my tuna sandwich in the back of my throat.

Malcolm came in and stood before me. "I'm not planning to tell him," he said. I raised my head, unable to believe it, but it looked true. My eyes filled, and for the second time gratitude consumed me. I felt a momentary impulse to grovel, sniveling, at his feet.

"If," he said. "If. If. If."

When I just looked puzzled, he said, "Stand up." I stood. He pulled me closer to him, put one arm around me, and unzipped his jeans with the other hand. "Come on," he said, and guided my hand to his crotch. "Come on." He spoke in an urgent whisper. "Gimme a hand job."

"What?" I pulled away. I thought I had misunderstood him, it had all happened so fast. But there it was, pink and stiff, hanging out of his open jeans. He smiled at me and pulled me back. "Come on, it'll only take a minute." He put my hand back among the golden hairs, and closed it around the smooth pink flesh, sighing. "Ah, that's it. Now come on, baby." He reached under my T-shirt, grabbed breast, and caressed my nipple with his thumb. "Come on, don't be shy, that's it, nice, nice . . ."

I did it. While he panted harder and harder, in high-pitched gulps, I pumped his penis. He pulled at my nipple convulsively, matching the rhythm, and I felt it in my own crotch, but I gritted my teeth and set myself against the sensation: no, not Malcolm Madox the pig, the loathsome swine . . .

A cry, and slimy semen all over my hand. He was right, it hadn't taken long, I broke away and ran to the bathroom behind the Shoe Repair, pulling down my T-shirt with my clean hand. In the bathroom I threw up.

I heard the bell ring as I was washing my hands. Let Malcolm wait on them, the pig, the stupid bastard. But the voices came over the transom: it was Mr. Madox. I had to go see if Malcolm told him. I looked at my face in the mirror over the sink: waxy and still, like a dead person's.

Malcolm and his father were chattering about Greta at the Blue Bell. "Second prettiest girl in Hoskins," said Mr. Madox, who loved me like a daughter, and winked in my direction. Malcolm looked at me and slowly licked his lips back and forth with his fat pink tongue.

"I don't feel very well, Mr. Madox," I said. "I wonder if I could go home early today."

Mr. Madox bustled and brooded around me like a hen with a sick chick, but he finally let me go. "Get right to bed," he said. "Take some aspirin. You got aspirin? Take two. Take some juice." Malcolm silently smirked. "Don't eat, let your stomach settle. If you don't feel better Monday, stay on home. Hear me, Delia? Take care, now."

I walked home slowly. I had never been so tired. The wind blew at me all the way, drying the sweat on my forehead. When I got home I moaned on my cot, and then I slept. I spent the weekend alone, tramping the streets of Hoskins until it got dark, staring blankly at the TV at night. I expected the police any minute, or at least Mr. Madox (his kind old eyes misted with disappointment: "You were the one person I never suspected, Delia"). I wouldn't let myself dispose of the evidence. I left everything where it was. I even made myself shower with the loofah, mix up a batch of orange juice, poach myself an egg, wind my clock before bed, as usual. And I waited for the heavy boots on the stairs, the *bam-bam* at the door.

Nothing happened. Trembling, I confronted Mr. Madox on Monday morning. He inquired after my health. He reported Malcolm's uneventful return to his classes. He showed me how he wanted to rearrange the light bulb display. He deplored violence in the local junior high school. Incredibly, Malcolm hadn't told. This didn't make me hate him less, but it calmed me. My heart still dropped like a rock when I thought of my narrow escape, but by the next day it seemed dreamlike: the nausea and fear, Malcolm behind the flower seeds, his fingers at my breast—the vague stuff of a horrible but long-ago nightmare. And my impulse to steal disappeared. I went up on purpose and forced myself to look at the trivet. I saw immediately that it was cheap and tacky, the tile chipped around the edges, the grin of the collie a grimace, the metal rack worse even than I'd thought. I was glad I hadn't been able to steal it after all (here my heart dropped like a rock), and I was relieved the whole thing was over, I was cured. No harm done—and gradually, a dollar or two a week, unobtrusively, I put money in the till to make up for what I'd taken. This act of compensation filled me with a joy more profound than any of my spoils had given.

I became fond of Mr. Madox to the point of idolatry. We began to play Monopoly on the card table in the stockroom, an ongoing game we played all through May when there were a few minutes free. I listened patiently to all Mr. Madox's yarns about the good old days and laments for the decline of conservatism, murmuring and nodding like a wife. And I marveled at the making of Malcolm from the genes of this good man.

Spring flourished. I bought myself a little impatiens plant from Hoskins Nursery. I cleaned out my stolen pot, and the plant grew rapidly toward the sun. The display of flower seeds dwindled, as did the boxes of grass seed, the rakes and trowels, the weedkiller, the fertilizer. We were kept busy re-ordering. Every morning I wheeled a couple of power mowers out to the front of the store, under the awning, and set up the small display of tomato and pepper flats. Sometimes I took my lunch to the park, where a circle of tulips surrounded a plaque listing the Hoskins war dead. My aunt was busy with tree spraying, but I had a phone put in, and we talked once in a while about Johnny (who had grown a moustache), or apples, or Mr. Madox, or family gossip. My mother's communications dwindled to pretty postcards, of orange groves and pounding surf, urging me to visit in California. Every couple of weeks she telephoned. Miranda and Gilbert were there, Horatio was expected, I could go surfing and pick oranges. I decided my father must be running out of material. The ocean hadn't been enough. The clan was gathering. But not me, no thanks. I ignored the postcards, and told my mother over the phone that I was a working woman, and that I certainly couldn't just take off for California when I pleased. My mother's exasperated little sighs reached clear across the continent.

I thought spring might bring Danny back, but as the weather warmed up I stopped wanting him so furiously. I quit worrying if he was all right, if he was happy, if his ear infection had come back. I began to wonder what I would say to him if he did show up. For the first time, reproaches sprang to my lips, and sometimes I thought if I ever saw him again I would fly at him and tear him to bits with my fingernails. I began, slowly, to want no part of the past. It beckoned to me (the look of our balcony from the street, Ray Royal scattering poker chips, the cookie jar, Danny and I giggling over TV in our vast bed), it called, wanting to draw me back, but I went resolutely forward into the new, blank life I'd become fond of. I went from agnostic to atheist: I would never go back now, any more than the tulips in the park would shrink back down into their bulbs in the earth.

The hardware store was my life. I began to work Monday and Wednesday nights for a few hours, and my bank account grew. Occasionally, in the evenings, I assisted Dr. Epstein in his surgery, helping him give shots to and extract urine from the sick dogs and cats in his care. I loved the trembling, whimpering animals and could never cultivate the proper detachment: a good thing I'd never tried the para-veterinary course. A bulldog's ripped and broken leg hurt me, too. A cat with a tumor in its throat raised a lump in mine. But the yowlings and growlings no longer seemed reflections of my own anguish. I no longer moaned on my cot. And my sympathy with the sick animals was simple sentimental humanitarianism aggravated by loneliness.

For I was still lonely. I remained friendless, though I was on joking terms with the inhabitants of every Main Street establishment. People talked to me, sensing need. Greta told me about her boyfriends, Mr. Mulhauser about inflation, Dr. Epstein about the clinic he hoped to start in Hoskins, Mr. Madox about the decline of Western civilization. I didn't talk much in return, I'd lost my gift of gab. Always a good listener, I became pure ear: it became my function to take in other people's opinions and experiences. I did so gladly; it was better than nothing. When Greta told me she was engaged to Bert D'Amato, Chuck's oldest son, my heart leaped as if it were

I who had found true love at last, and I realized with that sympathetic jolt that love was what I wanted, still. I had simply been sidetracked from it temporarily. I began to think of Danny, optimistically, as my first husband.

Then, at the end of May, Malcolm Madox returned for the summer. He would spend three days a week at the store, three days at Blackstone Pond, where he was a lifeguard.

Mr. Madox's excitement was depressing. He liked to talk about Malcolm almost as much as Malcolm liked to talk about himself, hashing over his son's final-exam woes, his swimming prowess, his acting ability, with bottomless enthusiasm. His heart must have snapped when his heir chose hotel management over hardware store management, but he gave no sign. There was a hardware chain panting to buy him out for a while, and he intended to capitulate one day—"but not yet," he cackled, looking hale and indestructible. When the chain lost patience and built a place out on the highway, Mr. Madox remained confident that he would find a successor in the business. And it was true that Chuck D'Amato ("the Howard Hughes of Hoskins," Mr. Madox called him, not without respect) occasionally showed an interest on behalf of his son, Bert.

"Wheels within wheels," Mr. Madox would say, relishing big-business intrigue which only he, perhaps, took seriously. Personally, I saw the future of Madox Hardware as identical with the future of Hector's Market.

I don't doubt that Malcolm disappointed Mr. Madox as grievously as Nixon had. But his devotion to his son never flagged. (Nixon he loathed profoundly and implacably, and he enjoyed dwelling on his infamies as much as he did on Malcolm's virtues.) His inability to see Malcolm as the epitome of all he despised eventually ceased to confound me. That was parenthood, that blind love—except in the case of my own parents, whose love was blind to everything but my failures. Eventually I stopped resenting Mr. Madox's love for his foul son, even stopped being jealous of it, and began to see it as pathetic. I didn't want my devotion to Mr. Madox to turn to pity, but what other proper emotion could I feel for a good and decent man who rested all his earthly hopes on an evil twerp like Malcolm?

I viewed Malcolm's summer advent with equanimity. He and I were square. I need have nothing more to do with him. I would avoid him, work hard, encourage him to leave early to go to the beach. He wouldn't need much prodding: "Work? I love it, I could watch it all day"—that, among other things, was Malcolm Madox.

He walked into the store on a May morning while I was taking my break (a cup of coffee and a Scooter Pie) in the stockroom. Mr. Madox was down at the diner. I heard the bell and knew it was Malcolm. He'd been expected all morning, and the jangle of the bell was uniquely insolent, Malcolmish. I heard him putter around for a bit, and then he came in. I began gulping my coffee, the sooner to get away from him and back to the batch of orders I was working on.

"Oh, it's you," he greeted me, and displayed himself in the armchair. "Don't you know that every cup of that stuff kills off like ten million brain cells?"

"I can spare them," I said—a mistake. This was the sort of remark Malcolm considered brilliant wit, and he looked at me admiringly. I finished my coffee and prepared to depart.

"Did you know Rice-a-Roni is twelve percent weevils?" he asked. He got up and picked my Scooter Pie wrapper out of the trash can. "The number of insect parts and rodent hairs in this crap is unbelievable." He waited for a smart rejoinder, and when I simply stood waiting for him to get out of the way, he looked at me with the old tarty smolder. "But you don't care, do you? Little Delia doesn't care if she's poisoning her little self." His gaze dropped to the writing on my T-shirt ("Animals are People Too—Support Your Local Humane Society"), then back (leering) to my face. He said, "Get any good stuff lately?"

The look, the double meaning, the menace brought back all the fear and disgust, and the coffee and Scooter Pie churned in my stomach. I pushed past him to the safety of bug sprays and garden hose.

For a while I warded it off—the evil. There was a flurry of customers, and when Mr. Madox returned I chattered at him, taking advantage of his joy in Malcolm's presence to vamp him a bit. "Tell Malcolm about Mrs. Waller's latest," I prodded, gagging on his son's name, knowing the story was a long one. (Mrs. Waller, at the bakery, had her cap set—as he put it—for Mr. Madox, but in vain, and her efforts were one of the few jokes the three of us had in common.) I played that story and others for far more than they were worth, but as the hot afternoon doldrums wore on Mr. Madox yawned, stretched, and announced that he'd take the rest of the day off to tend to his tomato plants. My heart sank. I stared into his bright blue eyes (so like Malcolm's except for the look in them) with naked desperation: "What about those orders?"

Mr. Madox took it as zeal, and chuckled. "In the morning," he said. "Take it easy, girl. Don't work so hard, it's siesta weather." He gave Malcolm a wink. "Not that I want my employees to sleep on the job. You watch this young lady, Mal."

"Oh, I will," bleated his son, and I couldn't prevent the old man from going out the door (jangling keys, whistling "Mañana") and leaving me to my fate.

Which was the stockroom. "I want to talk to you," said Malcolm, herding me back there. I went. He pushed me gently into the chair so that I had to look up at him or straight ahead at his zipper. I closed my eyes. "Look at me." I did. "I think we can come to an arrangement," he said.

"I thought we already came to an arrangement."

"Mm-hmm." His eyes narrowed and his tongue came briefly between his lips. "We did. I just want to see that it like continues."

"Oh, no." I got up. "No, thanks. I've got better things to do."

"You think I won't still tell him?" I sat down again: the

old humiliating fear. "Oh, I'm sure you've mended your ways," he went on. "I'm sure you've been a good girl."

"I've paid back every penny into the till," I forced myself to say.

"Oh! Good!" said Malcolm, watching me. "Then when I tell the old man he won't mind at all. I mean, you've like paid your dues, man. Right? He'll think that's really great."

"Shut up." I rose again and made for the door. "You're not going to tell him, you have nothing to tell, you make me sick, get out of my way."

"Oh, but I am going to tell him," he said softly, taking my arm. "And if you don't think he'll believe me, you don't know my dad." He backed me into a corner.

It was a repeat of the first time—the warm, stiff flesh, the clutchings at my nipple, the high panting culminating quickly in a yelp—except that I didn't throw up. I ran into the bathroom and cried instead, on my knees, laying my head against the cool sink and letting the tears drop through my fingers to the floor. I stayed in there until he knocked on the door. "I'm gonna split, babes. See you Wednesday."

I didn't answer; he didn't wait. I heard the bell, but I hesitated in case he had tricked me and was still lurking in the store. But when I came out he was gone.

All the next day, blissfully Malcolm-free, I tried to make myself confess to Mr. Madox. I would tell him, he would forgive, Malcom's power would be broken. I must have looked distraught (though the mirror showed me only that waxen, dead face), because Mr. Madox twice asked me gently what was wrong. Both times I almost told him, and failed. Malcolm apparently could let his father down without a qualm; I couldn't. And he was beginning to give me greater responsibilities. I often went to the bank for him now, and I had access to the petty cash. My confession, however nice about it he might be (and I never doubted his niceness), would change everything. The Mr. Madox who hired me on a probationary basis would be the only Mr. Madox I would henceforth know—the suspicious, disillusioned Mr. Madox who believed the world was going to the dogs, who had loved me like a daughter until I betrayed his trust. I had no choice but to continue my personal cover-up, my Watergate. I hated myself and suffered, but better my hate and suffering than Mr. Madox's.

On Wednesday Malcolm grabbed me as soon as his father left for his coffee break. The bell rang while I was jerking him off. "Ignore it," he hissed through clenched teeth. I worked him harder than ever to get it quickly over, imagining someone coming in on us, but it seemed to take hours of his panting and my pumping, while the pair of customers poked around the store discussing paint colors. At last he gave his satisfied "Ah," like a belch after a monstrous meal, and zipped up. "I'll go, sweetie pie," he said, rolling his eyes at me and smirking worse than usual, and swaggered out front while I ran to the bathroom.

It may seem incredible that Malcolm relished a rapid, reluctant hand job every couple of days from someone who clearly loathed him, but he did. He couldn't get enough. He was always ready. One frightful day we did it twice (the second time I fumbled through my tears, and it took forever). He never let me off. On every one of his so-called workdays, sooner or later the moment came when we were alone and he would leer and beckon.

The worst of our slimy, degrading backroom encounters was that I began to—there must be a word, there is no word, words fail me again and again—I began to enjoy them. No, not enjoy: they began to excite me. I hated Malcolm. I despised him, too. But after a while when he pulled me into the stockroom and pushed up my T-shirt and unzipped, I began to throb with lust. I stopped resisting it. Disgust and lust, I felt them both; one enhanced the other, and their duet had a sordid fascination.

He knew what was happening to me, and began to do little things to turn me on. Occasionally he dipped his mouth to my breasts and put his tongue to work; if I couldn't hold back a small moan of pleasure he instantly stopped. Now and then he treated me to a long French kiss. On one memorable occasion (which I try not to remember), he put his hand under my skirt, between my thighs: I thought I would faint. But his penis and my hand were his major interests, and he was stingy with his gifts. Once when I rubbed against him and nuzzled a little (begging for a kiss, a feel, anything), he held me off and said, "Slow down, babes—you're forgetting the point of all this."

It was shortly after that day when, during one of our frustrating embraces, I felt myself detach from myself—my soul from my body? again, there are no words—and I looked down at us as at a scene in hell, at Delia, me, my only self, with her hand plunged into the pubic hair of a sweating swine like Malcolm Madox—I couldn't look. I fled in revulsion, leaving with his zipper gaping, leaving him in his own hands. I went into the bathroom, locked the door, and cried and cried for poor Delia.

I stayed in there for an hour and a quarter, impervious to Malcolm's threats and to the bell, until I heard the voice of Mr. Madox, returned from lunch. At which I ran out and confessed my crimes. I made no excuses, I didn't reveal my recompenses, I didn't mention Malcolm (who stood by with smirk frozen on). I just let my thefts pour out of me one by one before the horrified face of my employer. Horrified, yes, and disgusted, disappointed, all I had predicted. He tried to be kind, but his face stayed hurt and angry. In the eyes of Mr. Madox I acquired jowls and a business suit, I turned into Richard Nixon. He fired me.

Chapter Six

GRAND'MÈRE

I'm always at my best in small spaces, but at that time in particular one room just suited me. So I made the transition easily enough from my one big room at Main and Woodlawn in Hoskins, to one small room in Juliet's apartment in New Haven.

I turned to Juliet almost by accident. On the night of the day Mr. Madox kicked me out, when I was cowering on my cot, afraid to show my face on the streets of Hoskins and wondering where on earth to go and what to do, Juliet called me up.

"Mother says you never write," she dutifully began. "And when she talks to you on the phone you answer in monosyllables. She's very upset about it. Now what in hell's the matter, Cordelia?"

"Nothing's the matter," I snapped automatically, and then my eyes lit on my little impatiens plant in its purloined pot: it was drooping, dead, unwatered all those miserable Malcolm-weeks. I burst into tears—not exactly against my will, but out of some well of reserve that made the sobbing hurt my throat.

"Oh, Juliet, I've been fired from my job for shoplifting."

She either didn't hear me or couldn't believe it, because she made me repeat it twice. By the time she understood, I was back in control. "Shoplifting," I enunciated clearly.

"You poor thing!" Juliet said. She put her hand partly over the receiver and I heard her muffled voice tell someone what I'd said. "Alan says it's no wonder, after what happened," she said into the phone. "He says it's a perfectly normal adaptive reaction."

Alan was (as my mother put it, sweetly sighing) Juliet's "latest." She was living in New Haven for the summer, with a grant to study Greek metrics at Yale, and she had moved in with Alan. He was a former psychoanalyst who had dropped out of his profession to do volunteer counseling at a clinic and write plays in his spare time. Between his unproduced plays and Juliet's unpublished verse epic, the two of them were barely making ends meet. They lived on Juliet's tiny grant. This I had heard from my mother, long-distance from California; my monosyllabic comments on the situation were directly prompted by her implication that, however hard up Juliet might be, her failures were respectable ones, infinitely preferable to my squalid bit of respectability, my job as a clerk, my dogged little bank account.

"Alan says *what?*"

"Honey, you've got problems. Listen, you got married at nineteen and a year later the bastard walked out on you. What kind of history is that for a twenty-one-year-old kid?"

You don't know the half of it, I thought, but I kept quiet because Juliet was continuing: how can I convey the pleasure I felt in hearing a member of my own family take my sorrows seriously?

"You ought to get right down here and talk to Alan," she went on. "Cordelia, he is the most insightful person. He's helped me put the damned family into perspective in a way I never—"

The damned family? Was Juliet then my ally? I closed my

eyes and pressed the receiver to my ear, taking in her voice like music.

"—can see what Daddy's crazy expectations have done to you, Cordelia. I mean, we've all spent our lives trying to escape, but your way was the only one Daddy couldn't rationalize into his scheme of things. Alan says—"

"Juliet," I broke in urgently. "Can I come and see you? I'd like to stay for a while if I could. I can pay room and board, I've got money saved. I really need to get out of here."

The muffled voice had a lengthy consultation with Alan, whose distant tones began to sound to me like those of a savior. *Daddy's crazy expectations*—the phrase lit up my life, and I blinked in the light. And the idea of all of us trying to escape—I was staggered by the possibilities of it. Oh, I needed Alan, I needed Juliet . . .

"Cordelia? Alan wants to know what you had to eat today."

"*What?*"

"Breakfast—what'd you eat for breakfast? Don't argue, this is long-distance, just tell."

I decided Alan was vaguely loony, like Mr. Blenka (who used to ask me such things), but I obligingly laid out my menus: coffee for breakfast with a raspberry pop-up toastie; coffee and a Scooter Pie on my break; a baloney sandwich, a handful of Chiparoos, and an orange soda for lunch; and I'd been too sick and depressed to eat dinner.

Juliet repeated this to Alan, and then said to me, "He's dying to meet you. And, Cordelia? I'll tell you, honey, we really could use a litle help with the rent. It's killing us!" (In the background I heard Alan's saintly, apologetic laugh.) "We'd love to have you just come visit, but we're so hard up at this point—"

I repeated my willingness to pay my way. "Twenty-five a week, Jule? Would that be enough?"

"It would be terrific," Juliet breathed out.

"Make it thirty," I said, reckless with gratitude.

"I can't wait till you get here!" Juliet cried, out of the same impulse.

Now what do I do? Do I describe the further travels of my shop-project bookcase and its unread books? Do I explain that Aunt Phoebe's newly moustached Johnny backed the apple truck up to my door and transported my possessions back to the ancestral home? And do I reveal that carting the cot and the table and the bookcase and the cardboard boxes full of my things, stolen and otherwise, through my parents' silent, dusty, echoing, surprisingly shabby house—where the rows of books for once didn't glower down at me from the shelves but managed to look merely dull and impersonal, like books in a public library—moved me to a bewildered compassion for my absent parents, who had lived their lives so much between those stiff covers, and whose children had, according to my amazing sister, put all their energy into escape? Or am I letting these floods of words drown me in their tyranny and lead me out of control, into irrelevance? But is anything irrelevant in the story of a life? The trick, I suppose, is to decide what *isn't*. Order out of chaos: my father's words, my goal.

But does it contribute to order or chaos to add that Johnny tried to kiss me up in the attic after we had dragged in the last cartons, tickling my neck with his silly moustache? And that I performed one of the few—I hope—cruel acts of my life: I laughed at him and told him to cut it out.

Well, I press on—not knowing what else to do—trusting to my brain, famous for its orderliness, to sort things out right.

The next morning, I slunk down to Main Street to the bank and took out my money. I met none of my old cronies, though through the window of the Blue Bell Diner I saw Greta sail by with a tray. Madox Hardware looked smaller, ordinary, as if I'd been away a year instead of a day. I hurried by, on the other side of the street, with my head down. And later that day, I packed my suitcase and crept down the stairs so Dr. Epstein wouldn't catch me. A dog whimpered behind his door, then quieted. I walked the half mile to the bus terminal and got on the afternoon bus to New Haven.

I was grateful that Juliet's address was nowhere near Colonial Towers—scene of the crime, I kept thinking, though whose crime, or what crime, I wasn't sure. I knew I wasn't ready yet to face my old neighborhood; I'd rather confront Danny himself, I thought, with all his menacing mysteries, than the dear face of Colonial Towers, and our tenth-floor balcony, crowded now with alien hibachi, bicycles, flowerpots. Facing Juliet with my failures would be trauma enough.

Though Juliet was the sibling I was closest to (she was five years older than I, Miranda seven, Horatio almost ten), I hadn't seen her since my wedding. All my life I had had her beautiful, brilliant, scholarly image before me, speeding off ahead to some new triumph. She had always been kindest to me, aside from a tendency to lecture and to correct my grammar. (Once, describing Danny's performance in a softball game, I said that he flied out, and Juliet looked at me sternly and said, "*Flew* out, surely?") She also, from her five-year head start, assumed she knew far better than I what was best for me, and had recommended books, suggested courses of action, and opposed my marriage with the familial disregard for my preferences that was intensified by a reverent regard for her own. I hadn't missed her all this time, and had made no effort to see her. I was fond of her, I was glad to go to her, but as I rode in a taxi through the streets of New Haven there was room among the various dreads I felt for a fear of Juliet's scorn.

She and Alan lived out on the west side, on the top floor of an aged brick apartment house with a dried-up fountain and a few dead azalea bushes in its shabby courtyard. Going up the four flights to their apartment, I was so apprehensive I hardly noticed the climb; only when I reached the fifth floor did I realize I was hot and panting and my suitcase was filled with concrete blocks. Juliet appeared in a doorway. "Cordeeeelia!"

she squealed, and ran toward me with a hug ready. Her braids were gone, and she wore her hair short, as boys did when I was in grade school. It felt like dog fur against my cheek.

"God, you're sweaty," Juliet said, and let me into 5-B. "Alan will be home in a minute, dinner's almost ready, you look as if you need a glass of something cold."

I let her overwhelm me with fuss—Juliet had always fussed— and accepted some cold herb tea, a chair at the table, and a platter of carrots and feta cheese that reminded me of my mother. Juliet bustled around the overheated kitchen while I watched, munching. The kitchen was painted all over with big stenciled labels: DOOR on the pantry, and OUT on the door to the fire escape, and FRIDGE in a row of letters forming an arch around the refrigerator, stabs at order that were undercut by the grubby linoleum, the jumble of utensils I glimpsed in half-open drawers, a roach corpse Juliet crushed under her sandal.

It wasn't only the boniness and the disorder and the cheese; my sister looked so much like my mother at first that it overwhelmed me. I felt spied on. But it passed soon enough, and she began to look like herself, the unmistakable Juliet. Even in red running shorts and a torn yellow T-shirt, she had the chic, Vogue-y look she was born with. She still moved with the same languid, purposeful gestures, and there was the inevitable book face down on the table, at the ready. I began to feel strangely at home, and waited with equanimity for her to boss me.

Alan came in with a string bag of fresh vegetables. He was tall and thin like Juliet, he also wore running shorts and T-shirt, and his hair was cut just like hers, giving him a Martian pinhead. I watched their graceful maneuvers around the tiny kitchen: a handsome couple, both of them thin and austere with (but I didn't see this until later) matching fanatical lights in their eyes.

Alan complained to Juliet that the health food store was out of organic artichokes, and then enfolded me in a brotherly

hug. My head came to his Adam's apple, which was promi-
nent. He fixed a penetrating stare on me. "Let me see your
tongue." I opened up obediently; after all, he was a doctor.
"Bad news," he said. "What'd you have for breakfast—
Twinkies?" As a matter of fact, I had, with a root beer; it was
all I'd had in the house. Alan looked at me for a while with his
eyes narrowed. Then he said, "Uh-huh," and began reflectively to make a salad.

Juliet gave a last slow stir to something on the stove and
thought to show me my room. It was at the end of the short,
dark hall beyond the kitchen, and it was obviously storeroom
as well as guest room. Boxes were stacked in one corner,
Juliet's well-traveled suitcases in another; tennis rackets up on
wall hooks, coats on a rack, two chests, one atop the other. By
the window was a single bed built on a platform over two
drawers.

"I'm afraid that's it," Juliet said apologetically. She pulled
up the window shade: a view of a supermarket parking lot and
the brick and windows of another angle of the building.
"That's New Haven, what the hell." She went to pull the
shade down again, but I made her stop. It wasn't the bright,
new, high-rise New Haven Danny and I had inhabited, and
that pleased me.

"I like the light," I told her.

I did like it, and I liked the way the room contained me.
The sun at that hour made the walls amber, the air hazy with
dust motes, like an old photograph. I saw myself becoming
fond of the room. Juliet apologized for all the stuff in the way,
but I didn't mind living in the midst of other people's things.
I was cleaned out, empty, possessionless myself; there was
something consoling about an alien mess.

I spent a lot of time there in the next few weeks, especially
in the evenings, when the others were hunched over their
books and manuscripts. "You're certainly snug in here," Alan
used to say, coming to lean on the doorjamb when he needed
a break. His play was going badly.

Snug I was—too snug at times in that summer heat. "Leave your door open at night for cross-ventilation," Alan suggested. I tried it, but the door, which could open only to a right angle because of a stack of boxes behind it, blocked the passage of any air that might have drifted in. Also, hearing Juliet and Alan at night, talking, toilet-flushing, love-making, made me grit my teeth with loneliness. So I kept my door shut, and lay spread out naked across my bed in the warm, gritty breeze, remembering a record Ray Royal brought over and played for us once: Bessie Smith singing "Empty Bed Blues."

But I settled in with comparative ease, considering that I stayed lonely, and that Alan insisted on regulating what I ate. That first dinner, for example: a steaming soup of bean curd and broth which brought back to me the time I'd been sick in Billy Arp's sailboat; bean sprouts; and a loaf of brown bread with small, hard tan bits in it. I ate all of it stoutly enough while they watched me. Alan explained that I was poisoning myself with junk food. He reminded me of Malcolm Madox and his peevish strictures against my lunches: the mercury in tunafish, the rodent hairs in packaged cookies, the lethal chemicals in Coke. "Drop a tooth in a bottle of Coke, leave it overnight, and in the morning it'll be gone," Malcolm told me. And potato chips stay plastered to your stomach wall forever, stuck there in layers like papier-mâché. And the preservatives in Wonder Bread are made of the same stuff oven cleaner is.

I was willing to go along with Alan's nuttiness because he took me seriously. His bright eyes were as full of kindness as Jake the dog's, and he and Juliet bent their thin faces toward me, looking like twin missionaries determined to convert a particularly stubborn but lovable heathen. According to them, stress plus Twinkies had made me steal, and it was Coca-Cola and canned vegetables as much as anything else that had put me in such a funk when Danny left me.

"On the right food supplements you would have bounced right back," Alan said. "I'll put you on a regimen and within a week you'll be back to normal."

He helped me make a list of "Absolutely Forbidden Foods," which I still have in my List Notebook. It reads:

1. candy bars
2. potato chips
3. Twinkies
4. Coke
5. white bread

"It could go on forever," Alan said. "But let's start with those five."

"Five of my favorite foods," I mourned.

"Just try it, Cordelia," Juliet urged me. "You won't know yourself."

I told her I barely knew myself any more as it was. Juliet looked at Alan, who studied me in slit-eyed silence. "Brewer's yeast," he said finally. "Bone meal. Vitamin C. Selenium."

Juliet smiled brilliantly, as if a party menu had just been decided.

It was only logical that I take over the cooking. I was, after all, home all day with nothing to do. I was considered a domestic type because I had, for a year, been married and "run a household" (as Alan grandiosely put it, while I thought guiltily of the cans of baked beans and chocolate pudding and Spaghetti-O's with which I had run my household). So I began right away to cook up our soybean and wheatberry messes, and strangely enough I came to enjoy it. God knows, it was something to do: the all-natural meals Juliet and Alan smacked their lips over required hours of soaking and grinding and steaming and mashing and chopping to make the stuff edible. I found I could follow recipes with ease (it's all math), and that I enjoyed translating a printed recipe (from *The Vegetable Life*, the only cookbook Juliet and Alan would allow in the house) and a pile of unpromising legumes and herbs into . . . well, edibility is all I'll claim for my labors, but that was the cookbook's fault, not mine. (And what I consumed alone in my room and what wrappers I flushed down the toilet were nobody's business but my own.)

I also did the cleaning. No one ever suggested it, but Juliet must have known the mess would drive me to it. I don't know what Alan's apartment looked like before Juliet moved in, but her habits were no neater than they had been when she was a teenager, and her bedroom was ankle-deep in clothes and books. Cleaning the place up became my obsession. While the soybeans were soaking or the cracked wheat bread was rising, I took on major projects, organizing and reorganizing, putting books on their shelves and clothes in their closets. I scrubbed the kitchen floor on my knees, and bought roach powder and ant traps. "If you think these are bad," Juliet boasted, "you should see the bugs in Greece. This is nothing! Forget it!" But I persisted. I had to keep busy. I washed windows that hadn't been washed since World War II. I lined shelves and bleached the toilet. I rented a carpet shampooer and did the rugs.

Once I began, it was silently assumed I would perform these chores regularly. I was reminded of my childhood, when I was forced into housework because the others were reading. I knew Juliet and Alan were pushing me around, and had acquired a live-in maid and cook who paid them for the privilege, but I let it happen. I needed a family; more than that, I needed an occupation.

In return, I got Alan's counseling. We discussed my problems after dinner; he and Juliet drank herb teas, I drank a chicory-and-beetroot coffee substitute and tried not to think of coffee and dessert. Alan talked to me about my basic conflicts. There were times I thought I would pour my beetroot-and-chicory on him if he said the word *basic* once more, and it seemed to me that my most basic conflict was with Alan: he wanted to talk about my eating habits, I wanted to talk about my marriage.

"It's all in the balance of B vitamins," he sometimes said. At other times the secret lay in the oxygenating properties of vitamin E and selenium. Whichever, I didn't think it was very instructive to view my relationship with Danny as a simple vitamin deficiency.

"That can't be *all?* If I'd eaten more sunflower seeds I wouldn't have married him?"

"Oh well," Alan conceded wearily, "that and the usual basic adolescent rebellion."

"Some rebellion," I said. "Marriage. Why didn't I go out to the West Coast and drop acid?"

"Ah, you're subtler than that. Cordelia," he said, warming to it. "You chose the route they couldn't really reproach you for: bourgeois respectability." He chewed the skin around his thumb, which he had gnawed raw, and smiled. "A brilliant maneuver."

"And there's a lot more of Mother and Daddy in you than you're willing to admit, Cordelia," Juliet added, looking up from her rose hip tea and speaking in the schoolteacher voice she'd been using on me for twenty years. "In a way, you got brainwashed just as thoroughly as we did."

"You're not respectable, though—you're living in sin," I pointed out, because I knew she was proud of it.

"Yes, but I write poetry."

"But you *like* writing poetry."

She gave me the old exasperated look. "*Liking* has nothing to do with it."

It would be at points like this that she would get up and float in her graceful way off to the bathroom; difficult though it was to imagine in anyone so ethereal, she was always constipated.

Along with everyone else, Alan and Juliet didn't say much about Danny. Alan dismissed him as a symbol. Once he said, "The important thing is not the worth of the loved one but the depth of the love, and what you learn from it about yourself."

"Proust," said Juliet.

"Bull," I said, and went on to protest, "Besides, Danny had

a lot of worth!"—although I had passed from hurt through anger to indifference and no longer remembered the worthy details. Mostly, I remembered his red hair and his striped pajamas. "Danny's a real person, you know, Alan. It was a real person I fell in love with, not a symbol of rebellion."

"That's not the point," Alan said gently, but it certainly seemed like the point to me, and if it wasn't, what was? Alan didn't tell me. I married Danny because of my parents and a B-vitamin deficiency. I stole from Mr. Madox because my life was empty and I lacked selenium. Alan and Juliet drained their mugs and got up from the table and went to their books, leaving me with the dishes.

I didn't find it as thrilling as I'd expected to discuss things with Alan and Juliet. But an outburst of Juliet's fascinates me yet. "You were always the baby," she said suddenly one night over dinner, in a fit of impatience. I think she was tired of hearing Alan talk about me. She may even have been just plain tired of me: Juliet and I, for all our renewed sisterliness, were not exactly soul mates, and never would be. "You were always the little pet," she went on. "God, the things they let you get away with! Hanging around in town—and your rotten grades! Me they took for granted, good old Julie, following in the family footsteps. You they kept poking and prodding like some rare species. You were the different one, the challenge!"

She made a face at me—eyes bulging, teeth bared. I stared in amazement, chewing and chewing on the same tough hunk of endive. Alan said mildly, "Well, it probably worked both ways, Juliet. It usually does."

Unappeased, she tore a piece of bread in two, then in four. I sat there mechanically eating, with the sensation that the earth had opened before me and shown me some crazy new world in which Juliet was Cinderella and I a wicked stepsister. I watched, bemused, as she crumbled her bread into brown crumbs. How was it possible for two such separate, secret views of the same thing to exist side by side? I asked Alan, and he laughed. "Not only two, but—how many? Ask Miranda, ask Horatio, ask your mother and your father and the family dog—"

"Alan, we never had a family dog, you're forgetting my allergy," Juliet said irritably.

"Every one of them will have a different story. And they're all true."

"This is not something I can take in all at once," I said.

Alan drummed softly with his fork on the table, oblivious. "If only I could get that multiplicity into my play," he said to himself. His small eyes crossed slightly when he was concentrating, and he chewed his thumb.

"It was always Cordelia, Cordelia, Cordelia," Juliet muttered.

I felt I must speak to her so she'd eat. She was painfully thin, and she always took the tiniest portions and ate only half of them. "I'd say I'm sorry, Jule, but I don't know what to be sorry for."

"Oh, the hell with it," she said, but she pulled her salad toward her and took a forkful of sprouts.

Juliet's outburst, which occurred when I had been there about a month, marked the end of the honeymoon. I had run out of big cleaning projects, and I felt I had exhausted the possibilities of tofu and brown rice.

I was beginning to worry, during those hot late August days, that I might become a hard and solitary spinster. I couldn't get along with anyone. Juliet and her constipated digs at me, Alan's nutritional evangelism, my mother's subtly reproachful letters from California—all of them irritated me to the point of frenzy. I'd had high hopes for a new, mature relationship with my sister, but now all my ancient grudges were coming back: the hamster incident, the paint on the sweater, the borrowed binoculars, the tattling. I saw she was suffering— perhaps she saw I was—but we were unable to approach each other. The old walls between us, dissolved by time and distance, went up brick by brick the closer we got. Daily life, with its opposition of habits and tastes, had thickened between

us until we could hardly see each other. I saw a snappish, ego-
tistical tyrant; she saw—most likely—a pesky, moody loser.
And Alan . . . I had sensed he was uneasy at my being alone in
the apartment all day, and one night before I shut my door
I heard him say to Juliet, "It's not good for her to mope
around here."

He's afraid I'll steal from him, I immediately thought. He's
afraid one of my basic conflicts will come to a head here,
among the health foods and vitamin supplements and poetry
journals and Juliet's Greek grammars. I was tempted to yell
out to him, "Don't worry, Alan, there's nothing here I want."

I misjudged him, though. It wasn't my kleptomania that
bothered him. He was too saintly not to overlook it, and
would—I realized when I got to know him better—share his
last crumb, his last dime, with me if necessary (with me, or
with any down-and-out dope fiend at his clinic). Also, he was
sure my morning heap of vitamin pills would keep the urge
away. No, what bothered Alan was my social life. Juliet put it
bluntly. "Maybe you should get out a little more, Cordelia,"
she said. "You're never going to meet anyone if you just hang
about in here all day."

(It was one of the ways Juliet always managed to irritate
me: she said *about* instead of *around*, as they do in English
movies.)

I said, though it was a lie, "I don't want to meet anyone,"
and I said it as sullenly as I could.

"It would give you something to do," Juliet said.

"It's not good to be alone so much," Alan added in his
generalizing way. I knew from the unavoidable nighttime
sounds that Alan believed an energetic sex life was part of a
healthy regimen. I assumed also that he and Juliet probably
wanted to get rid of me and have some time to themselves, so
I did as I was told. I went out on the streets of New Haven
the next afternoon and took a walk downtown.

I left late in the day deliberately so Juliet and Alan would
have to get their own dinner (though some chick-pea patties

and a batch of tofu-tamari dressing were waiting in the FRIDGE).
I started out lonely, and the more I walked the lonelier I got.
The air was cooler for once; the streets were full of people.
No one walked alone, it was all couples or noisy groups, people
coming out of work, all of them laughing and cheerful, as if
the jobs they'd just left were in Paradise. I imagined them all
going home to eat tofuless dinners with people who didn't
criticize or analyze or pore over books. I remembered the long
walks I used to take in the city, when my biggest problem was
deciding between Mr. Clean and Top Job, and when I got
some sort of sustenance from those crowded streets. Now I
had to go only a block or two to learn that what the crowds
had to offer was just another kind of solitude. The laughing
faces were, finally, too much for me, and I walked with my eyes
down, searching the gum-dotted sidewalks, the shoes and the
pantlegs that strode by, for a clue to the puzzle my life had
become. I found no clue, of course. The passersby and the
hard-used streets were only scattered parts of the confusion.
I knew no one, I had no place, no one wanted me, there was
nothing to replace the degradation I'd brought with me from
Hoskins. The old neat plaid life I'd led was raveled hopelessly,
beginning with the loss of Danny—no, of Hector's—no, even
before that, when *Macbeth* and I entered combat and I lost.
Or was it before any of these things? And could it ever have
been, really, the neatly-squared-off life I imagined, with Juliet's
splotched, purple passions on its fringes? And Danny's . . . ?
I went back down the old dead-end road: *why* had he left me?
Why had *he* left *me?* What had happened, those long, sweet,
dull days on George Street, to lead him out the door and into
that black car?

I half expected to run into Danny in New Haven. He wasn't
any more adventurous than I was; New Haven had always
been the limit of his world. I half looked for his brown
sandals and long, freckled toes. If I saw him I would snub
him—walk right by with a faraway smile on my face, as if
life was bliss and rapture without him. And if he ran after me

and pulled at my arm, I'd look blank for a minute, then say, "Oh, *Danny!* Well, how *are* you? Long time no see!"

I had developed a trick of sealing off my thoughts by counting my footsteps. I plodded along, counting, reached a thousand, and closed my eyes. *If your life is empty, fill it up*: I opened my eyes. People were passing me, parting ranks to get by, unsurprised, continuing their conversations around me. I was on Chapel Street, way downtown—not six blocks from Colonial Towers. I was standing in front of a little basement restaurant that hadn't been there in the old days. The name of it, "Grand'mère," was scrawled in brown across a white signboard. There was an ornate wrought-iron fence—brown-and-white-checked curtains—a smell of food when the door opened.

Also a sign in the window: SALAD PERSON WANTED. I half thought I would apply for the job. After four vegetarian weeks with Juliet, salad making was one thing I knew well. But it was the smell of the food that drew me off the street. Dinner with Alan and Juliet awaited me at home (green salad made of the limp organic oddities from the health food store, the tofu-tamari dressing, chick-pea patties, and beetroot coffee), but I was desperate suddenly for a piece of meat, a dessert, maybe even a glass of wine. I didn't debate long. I hurried down the stairs and inside, as if by instinct, ready to sin.

I knew by the accent mark in Grand'mère that this was a French restaurant, and I felt pleasantly daring. My mother had rustled up plenty of vaguely French food over the years (all of it touched with her bizarre individuality—*à la maman*, Horatio always appended to her creations), but I had never been in a real French restaurant before. Without hesitation, I ordered stuffed mushrooms, boeuf en daube, and a carafe of red wine. No salad. And for dessert I'd have a big fat piece of pastry. I saw a selection of them gleaming on a wheeled cart—flaky, fruity, glazed, gorgeous.

While I waited for my food I looked around. At that time, I thought it was one of the oddest restaurants I'd ever seen. I was used to bright, antiseptic eating places. I never knew there were dim, aromatic little ones like this, outside of the movies. The ceiling was low and hung with brass lanterns. The chairs were mismatched, with caned seats, the tables tiny and topped with brown-and-white-checkered cloths. I could imagine Cary Grant or Audrey Hepburn sitting at one of them. There was a polished mahogany bar off to one side, and a woman behind it singing softly to herself while she shined a glass; when I looked at her she winked at me. The waitress was a short, fat blond girl with a deep tan, wearing a long skirt, a low-necked peasant blouse, and a checked apron. The place was half full of people digging without guilt into their unwholesome food, and the two sounds predominating were a low hum and a continual subdued clink: talk and food. Nourishing, no matter what Alan might say.

That morning I had made a list. "Jobs," it was headed. Time to be practical, time to go beyond my unofficial job of unpaid housekeeper. Time, in fact, to separate myself from Juliet and Alan, where I stuck out among the books and the nuts like a circus act in the Yale library. I had sharpened a pencil and sat up straight at the kitchen table while I wrote:

1. store clerk?
2. dogs?
3. food

I had written it quickly, and then stared at it awhile, analyzing. Clerking in a store was my obvious first choice: New Haven was full of stores, I had plenty of experience, and I was good at being a clerk—clever with money, friendly with people, and willing to work hard. But it scared me: I was afraid I would steal (was my life any less empty than it had been in Hoskins?), afraid some object would pick me out and I wouldn't rest until it was safely lodged in the spare room. The mere thought of it made the beetroot turn uneasily in my stomach. And then how was I to explain away my lack of a reference from my previous employer?

I thought more and more about some kind of job involving

animals, dogs especially. Maybe a job in a pet shop. The thought of all those fat, warm puppies in my care was inexpressibly cheering. A puppy would be hard to steal, and I knew I couldn't have one at Juliet's. A pet shop would be safe. It might also be depressing, like zoos, like anything caged against its will. What if there were certain puppies no one loved enough to buy? Whimpering puppies? Puppies who got so attached to me they cried when they were taken away? Sick puppies? And would I go berserk and shoo all the animals out the door to freedom one day when their litle paws against their cages broke my heart? I didn't know any longer what to expect from myself.

I don't know why I put down food—and why I put it down without a question mark—except that I was sick of my new regimen, lonesome for meat and butter and sweet things. Alan praised my cooking and kept asking me how I liked this and that, wasn't this delicious, never know it was good for you, would you? I didn't tell him I thought mung bean sprouts looked like little humanoids, and tofu tasted like cuticle, and that I dreamed about Big Macs and jelly doughnuts and potato chips.

Once Juliet and Alan had caught me eating a chocolate bar, a Hershey with almonds. "There's good protein in almonds," I had said, licking my fingers. They smiled, shook their heads indulgently, even joked about it from time to time, but there had been politely reined-in disgust on their faces that made me feel worse than weak and errant: loathsome. I saw then that food was a moral issue with them; my missionary comparison hadn't been far off.

It was true that I felt better than I used to. I found it easier to get up in the mornings, and two chronic chin pimples had disappeared. But I'd never admit it. Alan used to say, "You're looking terrific, Cordelia. Terrific. How do you feel? Better? More energy? More cheerful?"

"I dunno, Alan," I used to say, making my face go slack. "I get these headaches . . ." Or numbness in my fingers. Or heart palpitations. Anything to suggest that the Faith hadn't taken hold in me yet.

"It's the heat," he'd say. "Step up the brewer's yeast. But look, Julie. Don't her eyes look brighter? Doesn't her hair look great?"

I thought constantly of food—real food, as I began to call it. I imagine people in prison dream not of leading a reformed life when they get out but of returning to a life of crime. Hardened criminals, anyway (and here I deliberately don't think of Danny). I was a hardened eater, and my vice sent me straight into Grand'mère, the arms of the devil.

It was a delicious meal. It even included a large oblong hard roll that reminded me of Mr. Blenka's special French bread. The roll was made entirely of white flour. Juliet and Alan would have considered it contaminated. I consumed it ecstatically, with plenty of butter.

"I haven't eaten in a month," I said to the waitress when I finished my apricot tart and coffee.

She looked startled.

"I mean, eaten *well*," I said, and she smiled with pride, as if she had done the cooking herself.

While she was clearing away (and I was having a second cup of coffee), I asked her about the job.

"Experience?" she asked with a sharp look, flattered that I consulted her.

"I've made a lot of salads lately."

"Where?"

"My sister's kitchen."

She snickered and shrugged. "You can try," she said, ending on a dubious, musical falling note, and advised me to return the following day at four.

I was prompt, and I walked from Juliet's all the way downtown with a spring in my step that didn't come from brewer's yeast. The restaurant was empty, and I went through it unhesitatingly to the kitchen at the back. It was small, hot, and quiet. The chef was sitting at a counter spearing little pasta-looking things on the end of a knife and eating them. He was fat, with many chins and a big belly, he wore torn jeans and a torn white undershirt under a clean apron, and he had a tattoo on one arm that said "Malibu 1963" enclosed in a blue heart. A short, sandy-haired man sat on a stool listlessly chopping onions; a cigarette hung from his lip, and I pictured ash in the soupe à l'oignon until when he stuck the cigarette behind one ear I saw it wasn't lit.

The chef, whose name was Humphrey Ebbets, introduced himself and Archie the chopper and held out the knife. "Have a quenelle," he said. I had no idea what a quenelle was—my mother's repertoire hadn't included them—but I took a bite with a studied lack of hesitation. "What do you think of it?" he asked me, and Archie stopped chopping and waited for my answer. I chewed thoughtfully. It was delicious, but I decided I'd better carp. French-food eaters, I knew, were always carping. "Chewy," I said.

The chef made no comment, but asked me to chop an onion. Languidly, Archie removed himself from his stool, and I chopped, left-handed. Humphrey watched, saying, "m-hm, m-hm, yeah, yeah," as if it were a phone conversation, and then he waddled over and took the knife from me with a sigh. "Here," he said. "I'll show you how to chop an onion."

He hired me. I never found out why. He used to smile and nod and say, "I knew you'd be good at it," and once he added, "You got salad hands." I didn't believe in salad hands; I think he hired me because he was amused by the meals I was cooking at Juliet's. That's what we talked about during my interview—not, thank God, my previous occupation. I remember his saying "I think tofu has a lot of possibilities," and my disagreeing with such violence that he laughed and got the hiccups (for which he took a swig of vinegar—my mother's cure). I think, too, he had a knack for staffing his kitchen on insight alone. I turned out, after all, to be a good salad maker.

I liked watching my competence increase. I liked to see my hands at their work, one so quick, the other its slow and

cautious handmaiden. I'm not saying that salad making re-
quires a lot of skill. It's mostly a matter of cutting vegetables
up neatly and arranging them artfully on their plates. You
have to be finicky and dextrous and have a good memory, and
there was a lot of fast footwork, too—from my wooden table
to the refrigerator behind it. I also had to steam artichokes, to
make aspics and marinades and vinaigrette and mayonnaise
and the aromatic broths for the vegetables à la grecque. These
tasks I performed in the morning when I got in, at eight
o'clock. (I was the day salad person.) There was a machine
for the mayo, with huge balloon beaters that whipped up
the egg yolks while I dribbled in the oil. I loved it, at first.
I also loved the artichokes, with their good hearts like fairy-
tale princesses imprisoned in all those tight, thorny leaves.
"Hey, man, that's like poetry," Archie murmured when I
ventured this inane whimsy.

"Crap," I said from embarrassment.

"Do *not* say *crap* in my kitchen, Delia," Humphrey ordered
from the stove. "And do *not* deprecate flights of fancy. I have
known good food to inspire poetical thoughts on many an
occasion—many." Dreamily, he stirred his sauce. "Let it go, let
it flow, we're all one big happy family here."

Humphrey was given to such vague, benign utterances: he
was from California. He had gone to chef school there, and had
come East after having a dream that the Atlantic Seaboard
was sunk in depravity and needed good people to migrate there
and save it. Humph considered himself a good person and a
great chef (he was right on both counts), so off he went, by
bus, eating his way across the country. He was disappointed at
first to find the East wasn't all that depraved, but the restaurants consoled him. He went to New York and ate for three
months straight. (That's when he became, as he put it,
"stout.") Since then, he had cooked all over the East, and he
was utterly contented. Cooking was his life. I never saw him—
truly, in all the time I knew him—when he wasn't either cooking or eating. "I got a job to do, and I do it the best I can," he

used to say rhythmically, playing his big black stove like a musical instrument. "I got good food here, and I got good helpers. I got good friends, and we all get along fine."

He had begun shaving his head when a customer found a hair in the soup, and his head was fat and shiny under the white chef's hat. His eyes were sunk back deep under thick, golden eyebrows. "You must have had nice hair, Humph," I said to him once, and he glared at me.

"Food before looks," he said.

I worked from eight to five, when a chubby Puerto Rican woman named Maria came to relieve me. As soon as she took over, I was free to have dinner. Lunch was part of my wages, which were minimum, but I bought myself dinner there three or four nights a week. The kitchen staff thought I was crazy. "So expensive!" cried Maria, grasping her head in her hands and rolling it around. I explained about the meals at home. "Go to the deli," I was counseled. "Get takeout Chinese. Get a pizza." I did, sometimes, but I got an enormous kick out of removing my apron, washing up, changing my shoes, and sitting out front in the near-empty restaurant, at my special table in the corner. "She wants to meet men," Maria stage-whispered, raising her eyebrows and waggling her hips.

Maybe I did, though the only bachelor who ever seemed to penetrate the ranks of couples who ate there was old Mr. Sawyer, who wore a beret, a long handlebar moustache, and a maroon velvet jacket. But it was mostly that I liked the atmosphere of the dining room, with its brown and white checks and its warm, dim light. It was clean and quiet and orderly there. Coming out of the kitchen, it was like entering the room reserved for company, like the white-and-gold parlor at my old pal Sandy Schutz's house. And the service was sublime.

Once when I was sitting there eating, a woman at the next table began to complain. She spoke in the general direction of the kitchen, and what she said, in a tone just louder than conversational, was that her friend Edna had recommended this restaurant but the food was a disappointment.

Humphrey emerged, spatula in hand and apron filthy, and asked her what the matter was. The woman pointed to her plate. I craned my neck over: it looked like the fish stew. "What's this?" she demanded, flicking her finger at a little bit of something. Humphrey leaned to look. "And this? This here? She says to me, try one of their stews, she says. What kind of stew? I asked her. I'm not sure I like stew. She says, anything—just try it, you'll like it. But I can't eat this!" She pushed the plate away, almost in tears. "I don't know what these are! I saved up all month—I'm on a fixed income, you know—my husband passed away two years ago—I save all month so I can go out for a nice meal at the end of it—but I can't eat this!" Her voice rose, and Humph sat down and patted her arm. "And this place is not cheap, if you'd like to know!" she finished shrilly.

Humphrey picked up a spare fork and speared a little brown bit. "Is this what's troubling you?" he asked gently. "I'm the chef," he said. "I made this stew myself. This is a lardon—a little piece of pork." He spoke very gently and slowly. "I'll tell you what I do. I fry up a lot of these little guys in the big pan I'm going to make the stew in—along with the onions? You know? And I find—now this is not just my own idea, this is a classic technique of French cooking—I find that they add just that extra touch of—" He rolled his eyes to the ceiling and waggled his head, to indicate ecstasy.

"Even in a fish stew?" said the woman—meaning, I could tell, to disguise sheer ignorance as mild doubt.

"Well—yes," Humph said judiciously. "Now. What I want to say is that if you really don't like my little meurette, I'll be glad to bring you something else. I know better than anybody, believe me, what an expense it is to eat in a restaurant . . ."

He went on, and when he was done she was practically eating her stew out of his hand. She became, needless to say, a regular.

I was a regular myself. Eating at Grand'mère was always an adventure. But I also ate there because I wanted to put off going home to Juliet and Alan. They had become rather social as Juliet got to know her fellow students at Yale, and there tended to be groups of them sitting around the living room at night, eating nuts and drinking apple cider and being, I suppose, clever and profound. Even the potheads and pushers Alan towed home from his clinic were well-read. Sometimes they all played those infernal word games my siblings had so loved in their youth. They invited me to play, of course, but I never did, though sometimes I sat with them, nibbling nuts. I liked Juliet's professor, Mr. Oliver, a small man with a goatee who used to affect a Pakistani accent. He was a coin collector, and we sometimes talked about the price of gold, or about some fabulous auction. He also drew cartoons and sent them in to *The New Yorker*. They were never printed, and I never got the jokes, but I laughed dutifully and admired the drawings, which were done in a series of minute black dots.

But mostly, I avoided Juliet and Alan and their friends. I sat alone in my room listening to the radio in the evenings, comfortably full of Humphrey's cooking. I cursed my wasted life, all the years of Twinkies and hot dogs (though I missed them, too). It wasn't soybean curd I needed, it was crêpes d'épinards, it was aubergine en pistouille, it was salmon mousse with a ribbon of my own mayonnaise across it.

"U-R-KA-RA-ZEE!" Crystal, the fat tanned waitress, scrawled across my bill once. I suppose I must have looked it, eating with my eyes closed and curling my tongue around each little flavor. I was as happy eating Humph's quenelles at Grand' mère as I had been years before eating the Frontenacs' Oreos in the kitchen above Hector's.

Another reason I liked to eat there was to give my feet a rest before I started home. I cut my fingers up a bit during my first couple of weeks (before I learned to keep my weak right hand away from the knife), but the greatest casualties were my feet. After being stood upon for eight hours straight, they were swollen and painful. I had a stool to sit on, but it wasn't really tall enough for me. I did a better job standing up, and if I stood

I didn't have to keep jumping off the stool to go to the refrigerator. The first week, I barely made it to the bus stop, and when I got home I had to soak my feet in Epsom salts. Juliet and Alan were no help. Predictably, they thought my job was vile; my swollen feet weren't the worst of it.

"When are you going to take your life seriously, Cordelia?" Juliet asked me, while Alan's disappointed face hovered over her gaunt shoulder. "A salad girl!"

"Salad person,'" I corrected.

"And then the food! The junk you deal with!"

"But they use all fresh vegetables!" I told them. I described vegetables done à la grecque, figuring that would soften my Grecophile sister.

"Why do they have to junk everything up?" she demanded petulantly.

"They use eggs fresh from the chicken, fish right off the boat, pure butter." By that time I knew I was talking poison—cholesterol, hormones, mercury, insecticides. I wasn't really trying to convince them, I just wanted to see their faces. Revolted tremors passed from Juliet to Alan and back, but neither said anything. I think it was then that they officially gave up on me. I was lost, a hopeless heathen.

And it was then that I began to worry a little about Juliet. I feared she was going beyond the bounds of harmless eccentricity. She had always been judgmental, but now she was rigid, and a sense of humor no longer softened her. She even stood stiffly, perhaps because of her bowel troubles, and her lips seemed thinned out. She was as skinny, as pale and languid, as a bean sprout. She seemed to have no breasts, no superfluous flesh at all, and bones showed sharply in the oddest places: above her eyes, behind her ears, along her shoulders. She ate almost nothing, as far as I could see. It was she Alan always looked approvingly at when he said to me, "Eat as little as possible, eat just enough to keep your body functioning." Sometimes he would stroke Juliet's smooth, bony arm or her knobby knee appraisingly, as if she were a statue he was working on. I thought of that old movie about Svengali and poor Trilby.

But my concern couldn't reach her. I see now that I should have tried harder. I should have taken my intuitions more seriously. But she held me off. Most of the time we avoided each other, mutually willing. And though I felt guilt and inadequacy cling to me like the odor of beef and wine and butter, I kept thinking, I need to be with *my own kind.*

Grand'mère was my only refuge. I would gladly have moved into the hot, friendly kitchen with its good smells and its constant activity. And people I could talk to. I talked all the time, so much that Humph had to remind me once in a while, "Food before conversation, Delia." I talked to Crystal and Anne, the waitresses. I talked to Cynthia, the elegant bartender, who was sleeping with Humph. I talked to Archie, whose function in the kitchen I never did find out—he did a little of everything, but mostly he sat somewhere with the unlit weed between his lips, silent and smiling, and his fingers would tap out convulsive rhythms along the sides of his pantlegs. When I talked to him, he would nod and his smile would widen. I used to wonder if he was perhaps retarded until I later discovered he was a gifted classical pianist. I found this, literally, unbelievable, I was so used to thinking of Archie as practically an inanimate object, like the refrigerator, only not so useful. But eventually I heard him play, and became convinced.

That was after I met Nina. I went to work one day, and there was this beautiful, overweight, auburn-haired person out in the kitchen in a Grand'mère waitress uniform. She was listening closely to Humphrey, frowning as he talked. A new waitress, I thought, and then I noticed she was writing in a notebook spread out on the counter. An overconscientious new waitress, I was amending, with disgust (that's how Juliet would approach it, taking notes), when Humphrey called me over.

"Delia Miller," he said. "Nina Treat. Nina's a reporter for

the *Nickel Bag*. She's going to fill in for Crystal this week."

The *Nickel Bag* was a local weekly, it only cost a nickel, and it prided itself on being a muckraking alternative to the regular newspaper. Juliet and Alan sometimes had it around, so I knew what it was, though I'd never read it. I couldn't imagine why one of its reporters should be waitressing at Grand'mère.

"I'm doing a piece," Nina said. She had the most beautiful dark blue eyes and long black lashes I'd ever seen. She looked like Brenda Starr, plus about thirty-five pounds. "On waitressing," she added when I just looked at her. "I'm being a waitress for a week so I can write about it."

"Wouldn't it be easier just to ask the waitresses what it's like?" I asked. "I mean, you're probably not going to enjoy it much. It's even harder on the feet than salad making."

She turned to her notebook and wrote this down—or I assumed she did. At any rate, she scrawled.

"Wouldn't it be easier?" I persisted.

"The *Nickel* likes first-person, true-life tales," said Nina.

"Nina's trip is investigative reporting," Humphrey added. "Like Woodstein and Berwitz."

"She'll still hate it," I said, slipping my shoes off. I put on the soft slippers I kept there to wear while I stood. Nina looked at them.

"Feet," she said, and bent over her notebook again. "I see my angle."

I found out shortly after, when Archie came in and she grabbed him and gave him a passionate kiss, that Nina was Archie's girlfriend, and it was because Archie was Humph's best friend and right-hand man that Crystal had a week off with pay so Nina could step in and take notes on us all.

Nina worked harder than I did. She stayed there all day, watching everything and writing and helping out in the kitchen, and at five o'clock she started waiting tables as if she'd been born with a tray in her hand. I watched her admiringly; I like competent, practical people. Humphrey told me she was the *Nickel's* star reporter.

"That girl is worth her weight in gold to that crummy little paper," he said, licking a saucepan with a spoon. "She ought to go on to better things, she ought to shoot right to the top, she ought to be in New York or California standing them on their ear, but she stays here because of Archie." He crooked his neck fondly in Archie's direction. Archie was standing at the stove, stirring something in his out-of-it way, the cigarette between his lips.

"Archie," I said.

"He's a dear boy," Humphrey said with a sigh. "He's my best friend. I love that little guy like a brother, and you know I mean that, Delia. But Nina—" He shook his head, his California rhapsodies unable to do justice to the superlative Nina.

Though I admired her, I didn't like her at first—her crazy devotion to Archie, her note taking, her questions, the silliness of her project got to me. But we became friends. She used to wait on me when I ate dinner at my corner table, and when things were slow she'd come and talk to me. At first I thought she just wanted information, the inside dope on salad making (her article had expanded from waitressing to the whole operation), but instead she got me talking about Juliet and Alan and my life in general, and she talked about Archie.

"I'm a slave to that man," she told me, tossing back her flaming hair and looking dreamily off into the distance. "I'm a slave to his talent. I feel it's my duty to mankind to bring him out. Do you know, he won't play for anyone but a few friends? I'm trying to help him."

I still hadn't heard Archie play, still thought of him as a defective kitchen appliance. "Then you're in love with his piano playing?" I asked Nina, trying to understand.

Nina blushed. "It's not only that. I'm a prisoner of sex. Archie is so . . ." She rolled her eyes, and then closed them briefly, and then got up to go take an order.

It was harder to think of Archie as a sex object than as a musical genius, but if someone like Nina was enslaved and imprisoned by him, there must, I supposed, be something in it.

Becoming friends with Nina was like a passport to the social life of the Grand'mère crowd. Once in a while on Mondays, when the restaurant was closed, Humph would invite Archie and Nina and some of the rest of us to his place. The invitation, it was understood, was an honor. Humph would cook up something good, there would be wine, and the happy atmosphere of the restaurant kitchen would be there in Humph's cluttered rooms as if he concocted it on his stove. And once or twice, when I was there, Archie was persuaded to play Humph's battered old upright piano. I expected him to become a different person at the keyboard, but he looked exactly the same: half asleep, the cigarette behind his ear, and his fingers flashing over the beige and broken keys the way they moved up and down his pantlegs. But the music was gorgeous, lush and brightly colored, more like Nina than Archie. It awed me, the way it suggested the bottomlessness of people, their secret depths and delights, and it made me believe in Archie's sexual prowess. I envied Nina her passion—her enslavement and imprisonment.

I must admit I was desperately frustrated by the absence of any sex life at all. I was surrounded by couples. I'd never noticed how paired-off the world was—Nina and Archie, Juliet and Alan, Humph and Cynthia, Crystal and Anne with nice (I had no doubt they were nice) husbands at home, and all the happy couples surrounding me while I ate my Grand'mère dinners—a regular Noah's ark, and I was left behind, alone, drowning.

But I was happier than I'd been since Danny left. I liked having Nina to pal around with. Archie spent long hours practicing, and Nina worked erratically, sometimes swamped with assignments, sometimes idle for days. "I'm on retainer for the *Nickel*," she explained with pride. This meant they paid her regularly whether they had a job for her that week or not, and it was, for a journalist, a sign of success.

Nina and I used to sit around her maniacally messy apartment talking and drinking coffee in the evenings. Living with

Juliet and Alan, where after my first torrential outpourings I had become mostly silent, I needed talk the way I needed meat, and Nina was an ideal listener. She was sympathetic and, better yet, truly interested, and not because she wanted to reform me. She just wanted to hear it.

"Why?" I asked her.

"Because you're my friend, Delia!" she replied, and I almost wept.

In between my confessions, she told me her own life story. She was older than I, and had been a radical in the late sixties. She was thinner then, she told me, in better shape for dodging billy clubs. "I was at Columbia," she said. "I was in Chicago. I stuck daffodils into police rifles. I marched in New York and Washington. I lit matches for draft-card burners in Boston. I threw a rotten tomato at Nixon in Hartford."

Danny and I had probably seen her on television, those long, lovely evenings in the living room above Hector's.

"I was looking for a cause," Nina said. I remember exactly how she sat, barefoot, on her old corduroy sofa as she said this, because it impressed me so much. She held a coffee cup in one hand, and with the other she dug the dirt from between her fat toes. "And now I've found it. Archie."

The envy poured out of me in waves. I could almost see it, a dull, leaden green. It wasn't Archie I envied her, it was the simplicity of a li'e that had a purpose controlling it.

"What about your work?" I asked her.

"Oh—my work," she said absently, dismissing it, thinking of Archie. But I was impressed by her articles. After her piece on the restaurant business and Grand'mère ("FEET: Soft Shoes for a Hard Job," and a photograph of my very own feet in my slippers), Humph personally sawed down the legs on my wooden stool so I could sit and chop instead of standing, and he was considering some sort of wheeled contraption so I could scoot back and forth to the refrigerator without getting up.

It was wonderful to have a friend. Until I met Nina, I had had to consider Juliet my confidante, and it made me uneasy to be forced into cahoots with a member of my family. And then, Juliet had gone from welcoming sisterliness, to her old criticisms, to lethargy and withdrawal, as if she were in pursuit of some goal invisible to the naked eye and unintelligible to anyone except, possibly, Alan.

Sometimes, if only to escape Juliet and Alan's place, I went with Nina on her assignments for the *Nickel Bag*, which is how I happened to go to the street fair where my life took another turn.

Nina was covering the fair for the *Nickel*, which meant, I discovered, that she wandered around looking dazed, an experience from which she later would write a lively, funny, and precisely accurate reconstruction of the event, complete with quotes from participants—though she often made those up. "People aren't authentic enough," she said. "And they hardly ever talk in sentences."

We drove there in her aged blue MGB convertible with its IM NINA license plate and GOD IS MY CO-PILOT bumper sticker (Nina's talisman against accidents, of which she had a morbid fear). She explained her journalistic methods to me on the way, and asked me if I'd mind if we separated for a while when we got there; otherwise she'd get talking and be distracted.

"I'll meet you at ten by the chili-dog booth," she said as we parted. "And if you overhear anything good, try to remember it, even if you have to make it up." I pondered this as I watched her go toward the Ferris wheel, head high and nose up, the better to sniff it in.

I wandered, not much pleased—though I didn't tell Nina— to be by myself. I was sick of being alone, and I had little heart for the ring toss or the candy apples. I half thought I might meet some nice man who would win me a turquoise-blue stuffed bear, and in fact, twice men approached me, one of them quite nice-looking, but—as always in these encounters— it was like my old shoplifting compulsion: I was waiting for someone to touch me at some secret level deep in my bones— like the collie dog on the trivet. I wanted someone I couldn't possibly live without. So I always smiled and turned away, waiting for just the right face.

I bought myself a slab of pizza and ate it on the Ferris wheel. The Ferris wheel was full of couples, mostly necking, and my seat creaked, and I couldn't wait to get off. As I did, a tall skinny person with a red beard and long, scraggly hair put his hand on my arm. I expected him to say, "Any spare change?" but he said, "Delia. Delia, honey. I've found you."

It was Danny. He was eating an orange ice, in a paper cone, and he sucked at it, expressionless but for a faint grin, while I gaped. What stunned me most was not seeing him, so suddenly and after so long, but his appearance. He looked sick— every kind of sick: physical, mental, sick at heart, sick unto death. He looked like he needed a bath, a bed, a nurse, and about a million brewer's yeast tablets. He kept his free hand around my arm; it was like a claw, and his fingernails were long, longer than mine, and yellow, and dirty. And there was a little parade of pimples across his cheeks. And he wore a filthy old rag of a sweatshirt that read PUNK across the front.

I said, "Danny," and found it was all I could say. I had known him since I was in first grade. I had fed his cat and eaten his cookies and coveted his life and baited his hooks and told him my dreams and made love with him and packed his lunch, but he was a complete stranger to me, and I could think of nothing to say to him.

And there was nothing I wanted to say to him—not to this dirty, scrawny man with the long hair and the (it seemed to me) wild eyes. There was something dangerous and desperate about his eyes. He just ate his ice and watched me and I looked back at him. Neither of us spoke again until he'd sucked all the orange from the ice and thrown the rest of it on the ground. Then he said, "Let's have a ride."

We got on the Ferris wheel when it stopped, and he took my hand and smiled at me, and it was—just for that little second—the old Danny.

When he began to talk, the new Danny took over. The new

Danny was brasher, aggressive, domineering. My Danny had been, above all, gentle—too gentle to hurt a worm with a hook, too gentle to fight in a war. And he had let me boss him; I never realized that until I saw how he'd changed. There would be no bossing this Danny—no controlling him at all. I looked into his wild eyes and saw what you might expect to see in the eyes of those horses who run wild on the western plains: desperation, a touch of craziness, and a powerful determination not to be broken to the saddle.

That's not what he said, though. He held my hand and talked, talked, talked. He was sorry he'd left me, he wanted us to be back together, he wanted to settle down, he was ready now, he'd had his little time—that was how he put it: "I've had my little time, Delia, but it's over now, I'm back, and I want to start again."

I made him answer my questions, though in a way I no longer wanted to know those answers, having pondered them so long. He told me everything readily.

"What was in the paper bag?"

He had to think, then he remembered. "My lunch, of course." The lunch I'd packed for him to take to work. I'd never thought of that, and I felt silly that it had been so unmysterious, and that I'd thought bombs, cash, a gun, dope.

The rest of his explanations were equally reasonable. He'd left in his pajamas because he didn't want to wake me by getting dressed. That had been the main thing on his mind, to leave without disturbing me, without having to face me and explain. He was half crazy, he said (and now he's the other half, I thought to myself), he had to get away, he had to go off and think and pull his life together. His parents' betrayal had unhinged him, he said, and I—I hadn't helped. It was I who'd pushed him into that groove, I who'd forced the idea of Hector's on him when he knew as well as his father did that the place had gone stale. It was I who'd kept him from getting ahead at the factory, who wouldn't let him work nights, wouldn't let him commit himself, wouldn't let him give up the dream of owning the store, wouldn't help him pull out from under his parents' thumbs . . .

I listened, stunned, while he made his flat explanations, analyzing himself and me and our marriage with the glibness of an Alan with a grudge. I kept wondering where he got it all—from some dropout therapist somewhere, some nut with a mission to bring psychotherapy to the downtrodden. The Ferris wheel carried us creakily up over the fair and down again and up. The sun was setting off in the distance behind West Rock, and the sky was orange and pink and purple, blazing. Down below I saw one of the men who'd offered to buy me a beer, the nice-looking one, with another girl. I saw Nina stop in her spacey wandering and scribble in her notebook. I took all this in, I felt my mind turn toward the scene— sun, sky, crowd, Nina—and away from the new Danny and his awful words. For—new and strange though he might be— the words, I saw, had truth in them. I'd forced him into that car that October morning. It was because of me that he wore this old sweat shirt, and let his hair get long and greasy, and had the look of a wild horse in his eyes.

Later—days and weeks later—I thought over what he said to me and rejected it—or, at least, amended it (why had he *let* me run him? why hadn't he talked to me about it? and what about our happiness? that wasn't something I'd bossed him into, and it was real). But up on the Ferris wheel, with Danny's grip on my hand and the seat swaying and squeaking, and the sun setting behind West Rock, and his voice going on and on and on, I drowned in the truth of it. His side of the story—like Juliet's at the dinner table—rose up and grabbed me and pulled me under. The immensity of things scared me (crowds, sky, words), and I gasped out, as if the details were what mattered, "But who was driving the car?"

Danny chuckled. "Oh, that was May."

"May?"

"May Wyeth. You know. Ray Royal's old girlfriend."

"*May?*"

"Sure. May. I knew she was planning to split, so I asked her if I could hitch a ride to Texas."

"*Texas?*"

"I figured Texas was about as far away as I could get."

Of course: Texas, where the wild horses were. And I had pictured Danny in, maybe, Meriden or Hartford. The Ferris wheel slowed and stopped. Danny bought us two more tickets and we went up again.

"Ray never told me," I said, remembering my instinctive distrust of him.

"Why should he?" asked the new Danny.

"Did Ray know you went with her?"

"Are you kidding? Besides, I didn't go *with* her. I just hitched a ride. She went with a guy named Whit."

Whit? "Tall, thin guy with a moustache? Black?"

Danny laughed. "Hell, no. Whit's just a little guy, with a bald head. And Irish."

Was he lying? Could all this be true? Had Danny been in Florida with his parents these ten months? In California with my parents? Working for the CIA? I felt for a moment like the hero of one of those movies who's caught unwittingly in a web of conspiracy and can't trust anyone.

"May and Whit left me off in North Carolina. I decided I didn't want to go all the way to Texas. North Carolina already seemed pretty far."

"And what did you do in North Carolina?"

He became evasive for the first time—raised his eyebrows, turned down his mouth, and bobbed his head from side to side in a gesture that was new to me. "I managed."

"What do you mean, you *managed?*"

But it was all he would say. He loosened his hold on my arm and stared out over the fair. His profile was the same—freckled and beautiful—and I wondered why I felt no tenderness for him.

"Danny, you were gone almost a year," I said finally. "What were you doing all that time?"

"Getting along," he said cryptically. "Same as anyone."

We were quiet while the Ferris wheel carried us up and over and down. The sky was dimming, the colors getting smoky. It was nearly dark.

"What are you going to do now?" I asked as we stopped again.

"I want to talk to you some more." We got off and started to walk around. "I want to hear about you. I want to talk about getting back together. I'm different now. Things would be different now." I saw that. "Better," he added. I doubted it. I was glad to get my feet on the ground, to be down where the sky was less visible, where humanity pressed in on all sides. I felt safer there—though safe from what I couldn't tell you—until I glimpsed Juliet and Alan at the ring-toss booth. Juliet looked glum, as if she'd been crying recently. Alan looked determinedly cheerful; he often said how he liked to get out and mix with the people, he felt it helped him in his work.

I backed Danny away and around a corner. The last people I wanted to see just then were Juliet and Alan.

"Let's get out of here and go someplace else to talk," I said. I had in mind a bar or a coffee shop. I spotted Nina and caught her arm. Danny lurked behind me. "Nina, I've run into an old friend—" I spoke low, lest Danny come up and indignantly insist on being properly identified. "We're going out for a quick beer—is that okay with you? I'll come back later and meet you?"

"I think I'll split anyhow," she said. "I've watched it enough. Now I feel like writing it." She grinned at me. "Any good quotes? Hear anything meaningful?"

"Not really," I said. "The sunset from the Ferris wheel—"

"Yeah, I got that, thanks." She had her writing gleam in her eye. I knew she would go home and make it all up on the typewriter, and it would be more like the street fair than the street fair itself. "Have fun," she said, and then she leaned close to me and whispered, "Little did our heroine know when she left the fair early to have a drink with an old friend, that her life would be irrevocably changed from that moment," and giggled. Nina was always saying things that began, "Little did our heroine know . . ." or "Who could have foretold . . ." —as if life were some sleazy book. I never liked her doing it— sometimes what Nina called wit I called plain silliness—but now her words made cold dread sit on me. My head began to ache, and as I watched her walk away toward where her car was parked I was actually on the verge of calling her back, of asking her to join us, to lend her safe, good nuttiness to the coming encounter between Danny and me. But of course I didn't.

"That's my friend Nina," I said sorrowfully to Danny.

"Nice ass," he said, silencing me. For a moment or two I debated seriously whether he could be some crude, filthy man impersonating my sweet Danny.

He had a car, which surprised me, and we drove to Juliet's apartment. It was his idea, but, thinking it over, I decided it would be best. I didn't want to be seen with him—not without shame, I admitted this to myself. And I wanted to be on my own ground, where I could kick him out if necessary. If we went to a bar he could strand me there. I foresaw our talk as a battle that would end with one of us walking out on the other.

It wasn't quite like that. The first thing Danny wanted to do was take me to bed. I should have known that was on his mind, but it was so far from mine that he took me completely by surprise when he held me around the waist as soon as we got upstairs and said (panting from the four flights), "Where's your bedroom?"

I didn't try to dissuade him. He scared me, and I pitied him, and he was my husband, once beloved. It seemed enough.

But our coming-together was bad. Danny couldn't get an erection—he was so nervous he whimpered. And when he did get one finally, with my help, he couldn't keep it. He got just inside me and then slipped out again, limp, and during these clumsy and humiliating preliminaries, in spite of the fact that he needed a bath and that I no longer loved him, I found myself getting excited. I remembered Malcolm Madox and worried: have I sunk so low I can respond only to men who disgust me? Tears ran down my cheeks. I took his soft, cheesy penis between my palms and wept.

"Come on, come on," Danny kept saying, though whether he was instructing it to perform or me to do something about it, I don't know. At any rate, I tried. I petted and coaxed and stroked. The only thing I wouldn't do was take it in my mouth. I suppose that's what he wanted, but I balked. (He smelled so bad, and Malcolm Madox had soured me on penises in general.) I was remembering, as if it were a previous incarnation (so misty and remote it seemed), the old days when Danny and I had approached, joyfully, all possible parts of each other from every possible angle.

"Maybe we should just forget the whole thing," I said finally, careful to keep the tears out of my voice. I suppose I said this at the wrong time. The words moved Danny to a frenzy of passion or fury, I wasn't sure which. He pressed his naked body to mine violently, digging into me with his long nails, and thrust his poor penis between my legs, where, miraculously, it got hard enough to function. He worked it into me, frantically and with difficulty—our bodies were such strangers to each other. He pounded against me for a few seconds, and it was over. He sighed deeply and collapsed on my chest and then reached down to his pants pocket on the floor and dug out his cigarettes.

My tears hadn't stopped, not once, but I kept them silent. He was not the Danny I'd loved since I was a kid. I thought as we lay there, with the cigarette smoke drifting around us, that maybe *that* Danny had never existed anyway, except in my head. Maybe the old Danny had been this one all along, and my parents and my sisters and my aunt had seen him plainly. But I put the thought away in some mental closet and I have never taken it out again until now. It hurt me too much—it still does hurt me.

Danny smoked and asked me questions. What had I been doing? What had I lived on? Did I still have my coin collection? Had I had any lovers since he left? Why was I with Juliet?

I wiped my eyes on the pillowcase and told him everything, all except where I worked. I said I was unemployed, blushing and trembling in the dark at the lie. But I told him the truth about my descent into depression after he left, and my mother's attempts to get me to go to college, and my job at Madox Hardware, and my kleptomania, and Malcolm's blackmail, and my being fired. I told him about Alan's health foods and Juliet's oddness, but he interrupted me.

"You're not working now?" He sounded suspicious, and I wondered if he'd tracked me to Grand'mère, but I stuck to it. I told him I was living on my savings and looking for a job.

He was silent for a while, and so was I. I pulled the sheet up over myself, and he pulled it down again, smiling in the dim light. I was afraid he had plans for more . . . I can't call it lovemaking—more of what we'd just been doing, but he said only, "You don't have to cover up. I'm your husband."

"I was just cold," I murmured, edging the sheet up again.

He let it stay. "Delia—" He inhaled enormously, and I wondered where he got the wind for it, after his ragged breathing at Juliet's door; and, watching him lower the cigarette over the side of the bed (where he flicked the ashes on the floor), I saw what looked like sores and scratches on the inside of his arm, and my stomach dropped sickly. Needle tracks? I didn't know, I'd never seen needle tracks. I tried to think: had his eyes been bright? pupils dilated? I didn't even know what to look for. And I couldn't ask him. I was afraid to. But it was a measure of his change, the new capabilities I sensed in him, that the idea of dope leaped instantly into my mind.

"This guy Madox, the son—you never went to bed with him?"

"Never!" I said indignantly—though, if I'd been pressed, I would have had to admit that the horrible Malcolm appealed to me only slightly less than Danny did at that moment.

"You just jerked him off?"

"Yes—please, Danny, I don't want to talk about it."

"What does this son of a bitch do, work for his father or what?"

"He goes to college and works there on vacations."

"Damn college boys," Danny said bitterly, and I wondered what in his ten months away had happened to inspire such vehemence. He used to idolize Ray, who'd gone to Yale. "And you never had anybody else?" he persisted. "No other guys?"

"I told you, no," I said. I wanted to get up and wash myself. I wanted him to leave before Juliet and Alan got back. I suppose I sounded impatient.

"Don't snap at me."

"Sorry," I said shortly. To my horror, he began to cry. He lay on his back and sobbed, screwing up his face, and I could do nothing. I just watched him. His dreadful beard shook. I told myself: hold him, Delia, put your arms around him, let him cry on you. I remembered him crying over the prospect of having to kill people in the war. I made myself say, again, "I'm sorry, Danny," and at the sound of my voice he stopped, sniffed long, and got out of bed with his cigarette.

"I've got to go to the john."

I heard the cigarette hiss in the toilet, and then I heard him urinate. When he came back he began putting on his clothes, talking rapidly, with an odd cheeriness. "You don't seem too anxious to get back together with me, Delia. Honey. But I'm ready to settle down, I've got a few projects on. I'm going to get in touch with my parents, make everything up, I hold no grudges. And I'm going to get a job, get some decent clothes—" He laughed, holding out his ragged sweatshirt before he slipped it over his head. "I'm going to start fresh." He'd developed an arrogant little toss of his head, almost a tic. "The next time you see me I'll be a new man."

"You're a new man now," I said. I got up and went down the hall to the bathroom.

His voice followed me. "You wait," he said. "You're not

going to believe it, Delia. I'm going to come and get you and you'll be so impressed—you'll be impressed out of your *mind*. Wait and see."

I took a clean washcloth and soaped it and washed myself, and then I brushed my teeth and splashed cold water on my face. "Just go—*go!*" I kept saying softly. The running water drowned out his voice. Juliet's bathrobe was hanging from a hook, and as I put it on I heard the apartment door slam.

"Juliet!" I thought in a panic, but when I went out it was Danny: gone. Relief flowed into me with such force I had to sit down, and then I felt ashamed. What had he done, really, that I should exult in his departure? My husband had returned, dirty and down-and-out and probably unwell, had come home with me and made love to me—could he help it if he was nervous and a little brutal? After ten months, in his condition. I thought of the needle tracks—if they *were* needle tracks. Maybe they were flea bites. I thought of his tears, his accusations, his boasting, his childish promises, and I would have broken down and wept again, have writhed on the floor in an agony of grief and guilt, if I hadn't noticed just then my purse hanging open from the doorknob. My wallet stuck out. I opened it. There had been a twenty and a five and some ones and a little change, and all of it was gone, even the pennies.

Later, in bed (on clean sheets), I would say to myself: he got you where it hurts, Delia—right in the old pocketbook. It was my attempt to make light of the theft, to put it out of my mind. But when I found my wallet empty, I was overwhelmingly angry: at his betrayal of my trust, at the lowness to which he had stooped, and at myself for bringing him home with me and letting him violate my body and my bed and my feelings and my purse.

What disturbed me more than anything, I think—and it was this that sent me running to the toilet in the middle of that sleepless night to vomit up the pizza and Coke I'd consumed at the fair—was the fact that Danny was a thief. I had been a thief. The fear that we were birds of a feather, that we belonged with each other, and that when he returned for me I'd be ready for him, burned in me for many days.

When, two days later, Nina called me at work to tell me she had seen in the paper that Malcolm Madox had been shot and killed at the hardware store by an armed robber, I didn't connect it with Danny.

"Shot through the heart," Nina said. "They found the killer sitting in a chair near the body holding a gun." Must have been the armchair in the back room, I thought, where I used to eat my lunch. "They found a stolen car parked around the corner. The guy wouldn't give his name, apparently won't say a word. They sent him up to Connecticut Valley state loony bin for observation. Wow, I wish I could interview him! Can't you just see it? We'd sit and look at each other. Neither one of us would say a word! I could do a fabulous story on this guy!" She paused, maybe because I'd said nothing. "Hey, Delia? How do you feel about it, anyway? That a creep like Malcolm Madox is dead? I mean, are you . . . glad about it?"

That was what I was trying to think about. The Grand' mère kitchen was going full blast at 9:00 A.M., sizzling with cooking sounds. Fat Humph was dancing at his burners (softly singing "I Get a Kick Out of You"), Archie was snapping beans, Ernesto, the busboy and odd-job man, was scrubbing a pot, and I was in the middle of a garlic mayo. I couldn't think at all. I felt completely stunned, the way you always do when someone you know dies—here one day, and the next . . . no one, nothing. And I felt awful for Mr. Madox. The light gone out of his life. But I didn't feel any sorrow on Malcolm's behalf. I told this to Nina.

She said, "Frankly, I think you should thank 'white male, six foot one, age about thirty, brown hair and eyes, slender build' from the bottom of your heart. Malcolm Madox got what he deserved."

On my lunch hour I went out and sent flowers to Mr. Madox, with a note of condolence that was one hundred percent sincere. For, though I hated his wretched son, I had once loved Mr. Madox dearly, and his agonies at Malcolm's death were not something I could easily contemplate. At least he was spared the string of disappointments a son like Malcolm was bound to inflict. I imagined how poor Mr. Madox would glorify his dead son—shot, probably, in the act of defending the store from an intruder—and I felt sick.

I never once thought of Danny. He wasn't thirty, for one thing. He wasn't brown-haired. And the road from stealing twenty-odd dollars from your wife to murdering for cash was a long one for Danny to travel in just two days. So I sent off the lilies and tried to put the whole thing out of my mind. I couldn't entirely, of course, but in the days that followed I began to feel curiously free of a misery which I had come to take for granted and which had been manifesting itself in occasional sleepless nights, bad dreams, and the degrading memories that could overtake me out of the blue (like the first time I used the melon baller at Grand'mère—a model that happened to be exactly like my stolen one). I felt cleaner with Malcolm dead—not that I wouldn't rather feel filthy and defiled again and have Malcolm alive for his father's sake, but the lifting of that burden was a relief to me, and I can't deny it.

It was at about this time that I began to want to get out of New Haven. My heart sank at the prospect of moving again. I was starting to feel like one of those lonesome hobos in a song, a rolling stone who's gotta travel on down the road, drift along with the tumbling tumbleweed, etc., etc. But I felt vulnerable in the city after Danny's threat to return. Malcolm's death had freed me from one foul curse on my life, but I still felt dirty and doomed from my encounter with Danny. If he was my destiny, I'd do my best to outwit it.

I also faced certain practical problems. Grand'mère, dearly though I loved the place, was one. I didn't especially love salad making once I'd mastered it. What's to love? Making the mayo and the marinades was incidental; mainly, I chopped and tore and sliced. But I found I liked cooking very much. The idea had lodged in my mind that Humphrey would teach me how to cook, maybe because he'd shown me the proper way to chop onions that first day. But when I asked him once if he'd teach me some things (like cooking with wine—and sauce making! I longed to master those fragrant brown and white sauces he was forever turning out), he said, "You're fabulous with salads, Delia. You're a salad genius. Don't throw that talent out of whack, kid, and we'll all get along fine."

When I asked him again—more insistently—he said, without a smile and with all the kindness temporarily drained out of his voice, "Don't lay that trip on me, Delia. I said what I said. Don't bug me," and he sizzled butter in a big black pan. I stared helplessly at it as it turned dark yellow and then brown, and wondered what the difference was between brown butter and burned butter, but I knew he would never tell me. Humphrey was king of the kitchen. He'd entrust salads to me, and pastries to his pastry lady (Mrs. Moore, a spry, ancient widow with a light touch and a quick wrist, who turned out our mille-feuilles and jalousies and truffes au chocolat), and certain menial tasks of chopping and whisking to whoever was available, but he was as jealous as a magician of his secrets. He wouldn't even consider spilling the beans in a cookbook. Nina had once suggested she ghostwrite one with him, and he said, "There's hundreds of cookbooks in this world, but only one Humphrey Ebbets."

I was grateful to Humphrey, and to my summer at Grand' mère, for a number of things. Humphrey had given me a refuge when I sorely needed one. I had found friends there. And I had eaten well—Humphrey's cooking could fill a void as no other food could. I had been stumbling, and Grand'mère set me on my feet. The very smell of the place got my blood running again and my brain working.

I know it was mean of me to develop a grudge against Humphrey for not teaching me a few things, but I must record that I did develop one. And once I was convinced that he would teach me nothing, I became obsessed with the idea: to cook. I had always loved food. I felt that all my life I'd been a caterpillar in a cocoon, waiting to emerge as a butterfly in a tall white hat. I felt I needed to cook the way the rest of my family needed to read. But Grand'mère wasn't the place to learn to do it, and I started to think about giving notice.

And then, I had to find a place to live. Juliet's term at Yale was over, and she was due to leave for Greece with Alan on September 15. It was already the first week in September. I couldn't very well stay on in the apartment—too expensive, unless I blew my savings on rent, and that is not the kind of thing I do. I could have gone to my parents' place—they'd be back from California later in the month—but I wanted to advance, not to retreat. For this reason, too, I rejected the idea of sponging off my aunt.

But not only couldn't I afford to live alone, I wasn't ready for it either. The idea terrified me. The very thought of it brought back my cold room over the vet in Hoskins, and my lonely agonies there—a chilling reminder of the old oppressions. I would have moved in with Nina. I thought wistfully of getting in on the high drama of her life, of sharing her messy, overstuffed flat. I saw myself moving into the cozy back room where she kept the broken-down antiques she picked up at auctions and intended to fix up some far-off, well-organized day.

But she never suggested it, and before I could come right out and ask her, the course of my life was altered again. Another niche opened up and I popped into it, as if it had been made for me.

It was through Nina I found it. She had to do a story on a country bookshop for the *Nickel*. "Country *anything* is ultra-super-big right now," she said, not without scorn. Nina hated the country. "Everybody's dead outside polluted areas," she told me, with that air of being my instructor that reminded me of my sisters but in Nina didn't irritate me. "There must be something in the crud we breathe that keeps us alert." People who live in the country, according to Nina, go to bed at 8:00 P.M., eat cornmeal mush three times a day, and would rather chop wood than anything. "All the men wear hats with the names of tractor companies on them," she said. "All the women wear flannel shirts."

"We never ate cornmeal mush," I told her. "My mother wears cashmere sweaters."

"Oh Delia, that's not *country*, down on the shore. That's classy *suburbia*. This bookstore is in the country—wait and see."

The drive out there was a fairly long one, and Nina didn't want to go alone—it was one of her odd, improbable terrors that her car would break down on a lonely rural road where she'd be a prey to Things. So I went with her.

We left one evening after my salad shift, bringing subs and cans of Tab for dinner on the way. It was only a week or so after I'd seen Danny, and, though I hadn't meant to, I told Nina everything. She was already familiar with the background. Nina was one of the few people outside the family who knew about Danny's dawn desertion; in fact, the night she got that bit of information out of me—in the nearly wordless way she adopted for interviews—bit by bit over spanakopeta and a bottle of wine at Basel's, I realized the true extent of her talents as an investigative reporter.

Her reaction to Danny's latest appearance was characteristic. "You've got to get away from here, Delia. You've got to *move!*" I had already come to that conclusion, but, as she said it, I was sure it was not only true but urgent, and, miserably, I agreed. But my misery was an automatic association with all my other hopeful, ill-starred moves, and under it was a thin pulse of excitement that both Nina and I were aware of.

"I feel like doing something"—I breathed quickly in—"different!" I felt giddy, actually discussing my future with a sympathetic soul instead of plotting it alone and unadvised.

"Your future is at your feet," Nina said. "Your poor old feet! And all you've got to do is step out into it. What a prospect, Delia!"

We stopped for gas, and Nina told the attendant, as she

always did, "Fill it with irregular, please," before she turned to me with one of her brainstorms. "You ought to divorce him, Delia, to begin with. Now that you've found the bastard, get rid of him once and for all."

I honestly hadn't thought of it. Danny and I, it seemed to me, were the sad reverse of a couple who live together in such harmony that a marriage ceremony becomes irrelevant. I felt divorced already.

"I mean, you've dropped his name—right?"

Of course I had. I'd been Delia Frontenac for so short a time that Delia Miller had returned to me naturally when I was cast adrift. I'd welcomed it as I would have an old childhood toy. But an actual divorce . . .

I pondered the idea while the gas pump clicked. It seemed pointless. It sounded expensive. It would bring me into contact with Danny again. And I really had no idea where he was.

Nina broke into my speculations. "You ought to drop Miller, too," she said, starting the car. As she spoke, there in the Exxon station, so far from my father's house, I missed my parents all of a sudden—an emotion so strange it took me a few seconds to identify it. "I mean, you've given up your father's whole shtick. If you don't play the game, why keep the name? We could think up something really fitting for you."

My sweet, unaccustomed, daughterly nostalgia made me stubborn, and I muttered, "I'll stick with Miller, thanks, Nina." I felt the way I had when Ray Royal laughed at my father's beard.

"Well, it *was* your critical-formative name," Nina said peaceably as we drove away—a journalist's refusal to have a point of view. We drove with the windows open and the radio on, eating our sandwiches and planning my future. Nina devised a string of her wild scenarios: "Little did our heroine know . . ." but now they thrilled me. I didn't know when I'd been so happy, as if Route 7 were made of yellow brick, as if at the end of it . . .

Well, after all, Lamb House Books was at the end of it:

take a right turn at the intersection in the town of Gresham
and then a left at the dairy farm. Gresham—all white houses
and black shutters and bright red front doors—got Nina off
the subject of me and back on her hatred of the country. She
said Gresham was no better than a housing development,
everything the same. "And no *stores*. Where do they go?
Where do they eat? What do they *do?*"

After the town, we barely missed having to stop while
the dairy herd crossed the road. They'd just gone by, and
went patiently into the barn, flicking their tails in each other's
faces, their udders swaying.

"Ugh—a barn made of concrete blocks," Nina said. "I wish
you could interview cows—ask them how they like concrete
and steel tubing and bright lights."

"Cows don't care," I said. You could hear faint, happy moos
all the way up the road.

"Sez you," Nina replied, but I could tell she had already
forgotten the cows. She was getting nervous and bitchy, as
she always did before she had to interview strangers. "This
damn road is hell on my shocks," she said.

On a small hill, up the road, was the old red cowbarn, and
beyond it a white farmhouse, and then a creek and some trees,
and then a huge yellow house with a sign in front that read:

LAMB HOUSE BOOKS
P. Lamberti, Prop.

Nina pulled into the driveway and stopped the car, still
bitching. "Picturesque Connecticut. Do you know what it
costs to keep up a place like this? To make it look like 1827
or whatever? Plenty of big seventies bucks. *P. Lamberti, Prop.*
God, the phoniness! And it'll be all antiques inside, all the
chairs will be uncomfortable, and in some back room they've
got a huge color TV hidden away behind an eighteenth-cen-
tury armoire."

"It's a pretty house, though," I ventured. It was huge,

gabled, freshly painted, with a shine to it. The sun, getting
low in the sky, glanced off the house and hung over the barns
down the road. "Come on, Nina," I said. I felt a weird pos-
sessiveness about the place, and I didn't want to hear it
criticized. "You wouldn't mind living this way yourself if it
were in town." Among the junk in her back room was an old
Hoosier cupboard that would be perfect for a color TV.
"Brush yourself off and quit getting hostile. You'll write a
better story if you like the place."

"You're right. And the guy sounded nice on the phone, for
a hick."

"I doubt if a rare-book dealer would be exactly a hick,
Nina."

But she ignored me, got out of the car, and brushed bits
of salami and bread from her wide lap onto the clean gravel.
"Anything you notice," she said to me, tucking her notebook
under her arm and then her wild, brilliant hair behind her
ears. "Anything *interesting*."

"I know," I said, but I thought that maybe, after Nina got
going on the interview, I would wander down the road and
look at the cows—just a quick look. I'd never actually seen
one of those vast milking operations in action. I liked cows.
Maybe I could get taken on there as a milkmaid or a cow-
hand. I was thinking this as we went up the walk, but before
we'd gone far two dogs, exactly alike except that one was huge
and one was just big, came bounding around the house and
leaped (with fine instinct, sensing Nina's fear of dogs) on me.

"I'm going to stay out here and play with the dogs for a
while, Nina," I said, hearing in my voice that inexplicable delight I always feel around animals.

"Well, keep your eyes open," she said nervously, and went
up to the door. "And your ears." She pulled the old brass
bell, looking around at me. "Any little thing might be useful.
Local-color stuff."

"I know, I know." I knelt in the grass hugging the dogs. I
suspected they were a mama dog and her puppy. A tag that

hung from the mama's leather collar said "Victoria." The puppy wouldn't sit still long enough to show me his tag. He brought me an old yellow tennis ball and waited, rump in the air, until I threw it for him, while his mother sat by salivating approvingly.

A short man with curly, graying hair opened the door for Nina. She introduced herself, and then she said, "That's my friend Delia Miller. She wants to play with your dogs."

"Well, come in for some iced tea when they get too much for you," he called, waving his pipe at me. I said okay and waved back politely, but I had no intention of going in. I wasn't keen on hearing Nina and P. Lamberti talk about rare books, or any kind of books. Booksellers appealed to me about as much as book writers, or book readers. I stayed on the lawn with the dogs; the longer I stayed, the less inclined I was to go in. It was cooler there, under two vast maples. The sun got lower and lower. The dogs were some whiskery, impish breed I'd never seen before. I threw the sloppy tennis ball for the pup, and watching him romp with it filled me with satisfaction. The dogs and the falling sun, and the red barn down the road and the yellow house behind me, and the trees . . . I suppose it was corny, a calendar picture, but it had the kind of peaceful beauty that makes you homesick for a home you've never had. I sat down in the dry grass and thought of absolutely nothing except how nice it all was, hugging Victoria around the neck. She whined and licked my ear, and I giggled with a kind of generalized happiness that didn't exclude the mysterious future which, whatever it might be, was at my feet.

"Do you prefer dogs to people?"

The bookshop man had sneaked up on me. The gray-haired *Prop.* "No," I said, letting go of Victoria. "But I prefer them to books."

"Ah." He nodded. "Well. There *are* a lot of books inside, but I keep them out back in the shop. We're through with them. In fact, we're just sitting in the living room drinking iced tea. Or maybe you'd like a Coke."

I got up then. I saw I was being rude. "I'm sorry," I said. "I meant to come right in. I just have a thing about books— about rooms full of them, especially. I thought they'd be all over the place. They give me the creeps."

I expected him to look at me oddly, and he did, but he smiled, too. "Well, I'm not much of a reader myself. I just buy them and sell them."

I looked at him with interest. "You don't read them?"

"Well." He shrugged. The gray in his hair was more of a silver; when the sun hit it, it looked lit up. "Most of the books I deal with aren't the kind of thing you read. People buy them because they're old and rare or the bindings are beautiful. Or simply because they have a passion for it." He put his pipe into his mouth and puffed on it loudly a couple of times, not the way Englishmen do in movies but as an old peasant might, with a pipe made from a goat's horn or a seed pod. "Don't you collect anything?"

"Coins," I said, watching what he did with his pipe.

"Well then," he puffed. "You know all about that particular passion."

It hadn't occurred to me that I, a practical person, could be categorized as someone with a passion. I looked at the idea for a moment, thinking of my lovely silver and gold coins locked in my father's attic, and I missed them fervently, as earlier I'd missed my parents.

"And of course rare books are a good investment, like coins," he said, and then—perhaps realizing how boring the conversation had become—he sighed deeply, removed the pipe, and gave a great stretch in the setting sun.

The dogs frisked around us, and P. (for Paul) Lamberti threw the ball a couple of times for the puppy. Then he said, "This is the last time, Albert." The dog caught it in midair and took off around the side of the house, as if he understood. "Go on, Vicky," Paul said to the mother dog, and she too disappeared down the dirt dog path that had been worn in the lawn—maybe it's a kid path, I thought, hoping not, though without understanding why, but then I spotted a swing set off in the back yard. Of course.

"Now will you come in for a cold drink?" he asked with another smile.

I said I would, but we lingered outside. Paul Lamberti wore wire glasses, and he took them off and squeezed his eyes shut and rubbed them, as if he was tired. I tried to figure out how old he was, and thought about forty. Thirty-eight.

"Nina and my wife are talking antiques. Antiques are Martha's great passion," he said. His eyes were small and brown—they looked brown in that light, anyway—like mine and my father's. He had a sort of buttery-looking skin, very tanned. When he said that about his wife's passion for antiques, I knew with certainty that his marriage was no good—not from his words, but from the way he put his glasses back on quickly all of a sudden, almost jammed them on. From the first, I could read all his moves. I thought: he's unhappy with his wife, he is very attractive, he likes me, that's why he came outside. If the sun had already set, who knows what I might have done? Hugged him as I'd hugged the dog, there in the dusk under the maples. But it was a lingering summer sunset, gentle and rosy. I remembered the flashy city sunset I'd watched from the Ferris wheel with Danny, and it seemed to me that this sunset was just as important to me as that one had been, though I couldn't yet say how.

We stood, close together, looking at it for a few more minutes, talking about the dogs (German wirehair pointers), about the dairy farm down the road, about all kinds of things. I told him about Nina's peculiar journalistic methods.

"She talks to you for half an hour about rare books, and to your wife for an hour about antiques, takes a look around, skims through a price list or something—"

"I gave her a catalogue."

"See? And then she sits down and writes the definitive story on you."

"And I thought I was just too dull to interview."

"Oh, no!" I said, and blushed, but I don't think he saw. He was looking down into his pipe, and frowning slightly.

"We have two children," he said, taking the pipe out of his mouth and speaking very formally. "Megan is six, and Ian is four. My wife's last name was Lambert, mine is Lamberti. We met at a party and were so struck by the coincidence we got married."

"It was that simple?"

"No—no, it wasn't very simple at all, really."

We began to walk side by side down to the creek, and he dropped the subject. Why did he bring it up at all? I thought, though I was getting an inkling.

The lights in the dairy barn, off a little in the distance, were on, and behind us the windows of the house shone with a pale light, but the sky was still pinky-gray, and we could see each other's faces well enough. We looked at each other sidelong, not directly, and when our eyes met by accident, we smiled and turned away.

We talked about living in the country, and I asked him why he had chosen this rural pocket of the state, this tiny town, this isolated road. We were standing in the small grove of birches by the creek at that moment—I remember it so well: the black water almost invisible except for silvery flashes as it moved, and the light sky behind Paul's dark head, and how near we were to each other. I watched him ponder my question, and I saw him come to a decision: to trust me.

"Do you want to know the real reason I live out here?" he asked. "I have a lot of fake reasons I usually give people when they ask. But I'll tell you the truth if you want to hear it."

I said I did, and thought: with all my heart.

"I had a bad experience driving down Orchard Street in New Haven one day," he said. His voice was very low, but he spoke slowly and each word was distinct, as if he'd rehearsed it many times. "Do you know Orchard Street?"

"Where the Black Panthers used to have their headquarters."

"That's right." He sounded pleased, as if I'd just taken a huge step toward understanding what he was going to say. "We lived in New Haven then, in a house on Canner Street. I don't remember what I was doing on Orchard—some errand. This was four years ago. Ian was a baby. Well, I was coming down Orchard, alone, right at dusk, when three men suddenly appeared before my car, holding guns. Rifles. Two black men and one white, lined up across the road like a firing squad. Just standing there, pointing."

"What did you do?" I whispered when he stopped.

"What could I do?" he asked, sounding so elaborately nonchalant that I sensed it couldn't have been an act of heroism. "I put the car into reverse, backed up to Chapel Street, and drove like hell out of there."

"I think that was a very smart thing to do."

"Thank you," he said, with a sigh.

"And they didn't shoot?"

"Just stood there."

"Did you tell the police?"

"No. I mean, nothing had happened, really. And—" Again he hesitated, reluctant to confess. It was as if he was giving himself some sort of test. "I was afraid they'd track me down from my license plate and retaliate. And all for nothing. Nobody did anything. It was just . . ." He inhaled deeply. "I suppose I overreacted. I think now it was just some guys fooling around, acting tough. But it got to me." He paused again, and repeated, "It got to me."

"So you moved here."

"Yes. I had been working in a bookshop, running my own business on the side, and I decided to go into rare books full time. Martha, of course . . ."

I looked at him in the gloom. He puffed on his pipe.

"Did she want to move, too?"

"Martha thought I imagined it. The guns."

"You mean, made it up?"

"No. Imagined it," he said shortly, and started walking

slowly back toward the house as a way of closing off that phase of the conversation. "Anyway, we moved out here, and it's one decision I've never regretted."

Tell me about the ones you do regret, I begged silently, but the dogs leaped on us as we left the grove of trees, and the subject was dropped.

"They like you," Paul said as the dogs romped joyfully around me—an acknowledgment that he had been right to trust me.

The path to the house was made of bricks, in an intricate pattern, and as we walked up it to the front door I had the odd conviction that there was more to tell, and more I had to listen to.

Before we went in, we looked at each other—that was all, just looked. Not since sixth grade, when I used to study, furtively, Danny's arms and hands across the aisle, had I liked the look of a man so much. He was short, compact, and dark—again like me—and his face was strong and sensible and good. The silver threads of his hair shone. I noticed all this while we gazed at each other, the way you might notice the greeny-gray of the water as you were swept out to sea by the tide. Then he smiled a little and opened the door for me to pass in, and I did so, trembling with an indefinable and altogether strange emotion.

Inside, the house was as Nina had predicted, full of the kind of antiques that don't look, at first glance, much different from any beat-up old furniture. There were plants, a bowl of apples (early Macs) on the coffee table, brass candlesticks on the mantel. It was lovely. When I stepped inside with Paul, into the dimness of the entrance hall and then, just beyond, into the living room, where Nina was inspecting a faded sampler in a frame on the wall, I got the old cozy feeling. I don't know why certain places have this magnetism for me, the power to draw me to them as if they're enchanted castles and I the princess in distress, wandering the forest. The Lambertis' yellow house had this power. I could have moved in right then, eaten up all the apples in the bowl, searched out, deep in the house's bowels, the armoire with its color TV, and then curled up in the Lincoln rocker and gone to sleep there.

Then Paul's wife entered from the kitchen with a fresh pitcher of iced tea, and it all disappeared—not the house, just the sense that it welcomed me and was mine. The attraction was still there, I still found the house cozy and beautiful, but it wasn't mine; it was hers. She fitted into that house as neatly as Humphrey fitted his kitchen. Take her out of it and it wouldn't be the same house nor she the same woman. I'd say her pride in the place shone all around her, but *pride* doesn't begin to express it. Neither does ownership, or even love. Who was the old French king who said, "I am the state"? That's the way it was.

Martha Lamberti was fairly unremarkable to look at, just as the old furniture, taken separately, was unremarkable. But it all went together, Martha included, to the point where the rest of us seemed out of place. I must have looked as uneasy as I suddenly felt, a superfluous person in my faded sun dress, perched not on the Lincoln rocker but on the edge of a hard wooden bench painted dark red centuries ago. Nina looked blowsy; her curly red hair, frizzed from the heat, had flown all over the place, and the low-necked pink jersey, showing the substantial curved line where her breasts began, seemed in this setting like something meant for a whorehouse porch. Even Paul, who lived there, had the air of a visitor who should never have come. He seemed, in fact, aggressively ill at ease; there was something in the way he stood by the mantel, with both hands laced around his glass (pipe discarded) and his feet, in worn sneakers, turned in at the toes, that said: on my honor, I will do my best to be as unsuitable as possible.

Martha was the cause of all this, I'm not sure how. Her looks were part of it. She had a vaguely attractive upper-class face, blue eyes, neat eyebrows, short nose, good skin, thin lips. She was wearing a little tennis dress, with *MBL* stitched on the chest. She had a reddish tan, legs that were thin below

the knee and fleshy above, and thick hair pulled into a neat
blond bun like the one John Dean's wife wore at the Watergate hearings. One look at her and you knew everyone in her
family had strong chins, good backhands, and superb dentists.
Her middle name would be a last name, like Bromwich, or
Bentley. (It was, in fact, Broughton.) But it was more than
her looks that turned the rest of us into misfits; it was her
manner: she was on top of things, in a way even Nina, for all
her talent, her counterculture experience, and her city so-
phistication, would never be. Martha was utterly unshakable.
I decided that five minutes after I met her, and she never
proved me wrong, she never flagged. Some extra organ that in
other people had been phased out revved up in her, reshuffled
the heap when necessary, and put Martha back at the top of it,
neat and smiling and saying the right thing.

The first thing she said to me after "Hello" and "Have
some of this lovely cold iced tea" was—since I hate iced tea
and asked for a Coke instead—"Luckily, we do keep Coke
on hand." It was typical, with its implication that I was somehow outside the normal run of things in her house—that I
was a special case—but that her graciousness (and the bounty
of her house) would envelop even that, even Delia Miller and
her bizarre desire for a Coke in the face of lovely cold iced
tea. I've never known anyone who wanted so to be liked and
approved of, and who was so good, having attained that love
and approval, at throwing it back at you as an unworthy gift.

But it took me months to reach these subtleties. At the
time—my first evening inside Martha's yellow house—all I
knew was that Martha made me uncomfortable. I thought of
how she'd dismissed Paul's terrifying experience as a delusion.
How could she? I fumed to myself, and felt pools of sympathy
fill up inside me.

Paul went for my Coke. When he handed it to me, a spark
of electricity shot between us through the cold glass.

I suppose we stayed another fifteen minutes. Nina, her
interview done, was mostly silent and looked restless. I could

sense the wheels turning, the articles she would write getting into gear in her head. Paul didn't say much, either. From his place by the mantel, I could feel his gaze on me. I became aware of my thin brown arms and my bare legs and my short, heavy brown hair, wondering how they looked to him. I tucked in the corners of my lips, as if reflectively, to show my dimples—a trick I learned in seventh grade from Sandy Schutz and hadn't practiced since—and I angled my profile in Paul's direction to show off what I fancied were its neat lines.

Now and then I was able unobtrusively to turn and study him, particularly his mouth, which interested me. It was almost pretty—the corners turned up, and under his lower lip a deep bite was chiseled out—and contrasted nicely with the rest of his face, which wasn't pretty at all but rather harsh (short blunt nose, hollow cheeks, and those narrow nut-brown eyes behind the glasses). In short takes, I tried to print his face on my mind forever. I may never see him again, I thought. It made me panicky, though I didn't really believe it for a minute.

Martha and I did most of the talking. She drew me out in a way I hated, asking me questions because there was time to fill, not because she wanted to hear the answers. But of course I had to answer them. I told her about my job, my sore feet, Nina's article on Grand'mère, my sister's work at Yale and her impending trip to Greece, and my desire to become a first-class cook, maybe open my own restaurant someday. As I said this last, in response to "What do you want to do with your life, Delia? Or are you too young to feel you have to answer that?", I realized I'd never told it to anyone before, not even to myself. At some point in the recent past (When Danny returned? When I heard Malcolm was dead? When Paul and I looked at each other out on the brick path?), order and purpose had begun to flutter inside me. I had the sense that *this* was why I had to throw off Grand' mère and Juliet's apartment and the memory of Danny's dirty hands on me—because with these burdens weighing me down I'd never be light enough to fly where I had to go.

Nina glanced over in surprise at my confession, though she said nothing, and Martha looked at me with an interest that was momentarily real. I immediately regretted what I'd said. It seemed a bad omen to confide my ambition to a being as alien as Martha, and I drained my glass with an abrupt show of haste and said, "We really should be going, Nina. I promised my sister I'd get in kind of early." (It wasn't really a fib; my life had become so separate from Juliet's that she no longer took much interest in my comings and goings, but she still bugged me if I got in late, as if I were fourteen. I assumed it was on my mother's orders.)

"So when your sister leaves New Haven, will you stay on?" Martha asked me as we all stood up. "Take cooking lessons or something?"

"I don't know," I said at the door, matching her smile, though I could never match, can't even adequately describe, the combination of maternal concern and hostessy goodwill contained in the faint frown that accompanied it. "I'm open to possibilities."

When the door closed on her good wishes for Nina's article and my future, and a lovely, fierce look at me from Paul accompanying his brusque good-bye, I regretted that we'd left so soon.

"Well, they were really nice," Nina said when we were in the car. I said I thought so, too. "You and the husband sure stayed outside a long time," she added.

"I liked him."

"I saw that. So did the wife, I think." She started the engine and backed efficiently out of the driveway. I looked up at the lighted windows of the yellow house, with their tiny wavery panes. No one was looking out that I could see. "But they're very married," Nina went on, in a big-sisterly way, as we drove down the road past the dairy farm. "A real *couple*. Even partners in the business. They travel to these rare-book shows all the time together. And did you hear the story about their last names? Isn't that wild? Though I gather their families are incredibly opposite. Apparently she comes from top-drawer New England stock, and his parents are immigrant Italians, big on character and savings accounts and going into business for yourself. Interesting, anyway. What kind of dogs were those two bruisers?"

I told her, and I also told her Paul wasn't much of a reader. "He just buys them and sells them. Never opens them."

"Oh, thanks," Nina said. "I like that. That's cute."

"Did you get the kids?"

"I met them just before they were hustled off to bed. They shook my hand. Little *beasts*."

"Nice furniture, though," I said, with a smile over at her. I was glad to hear the kids were beasts. "But I didn't see any flannel shirts or cornmeal mush."

"Well, this isn't the country after all," Nina said as we passed the darkened cow barn. "This is *fake* country."

We were silent after that, Nina worrying about driving at night, me thinking about Paul. I tried to recall the moment when he'd taken off his glasses and then put them back on again and I'd known he and his wife weren't a *real couple* at all and my heart had lifted. In the car, as we sped down Route 7, the moment got away from me, and I thought to myself: I must be crazy. And then, just before we hit New Haven, it all came back, the precise look of his face, his eyes, his gesture, and I was filled with overwhelming happiness. I'm in love with that man, I thought, and with equal sureness knew he was in love with me.

It should have been a staggering thought, but it didn't stagger me. It seemed delightful and appropriate that, after Danny and my long, gradual, doomed courtship, this love should come so suddenly—practically at first sight. I'm in love with a forty-year-old gray-haired bookseller, I thought. With a wife and kids. Still it didn't stagger me. It seemed absolutely right. We'll work it out, I thought with serene vagueness, and when Nina dropped me off I smiled at her gratefully, benevolently.

"I can't wait to read your article, Nina." I thought of how I would clip it, treasure it, keep it always.

"Did you say German short-hair pointers?"

"Wirehair."

"Right," she said, and sped away with a wave. I watched her IM NINA license plate turn the corner, thinking *Good old Nina* in a bemused way, as if I were drunk.

"Cordelia?"

Professor Oliver came toward me from the apartment house courtyard and stood in front of me with his hands in his pockets. I said hi, and he said, "I've just been dropping some books off for Juliet, Cordelia, and I'd like to talk to you about her, if you have a minute."

I said I did, of course, though I wanted badly to go upstairs and get into bed and think of Paul. "Do you want to walk around the block?"

"Maybe we could find a coffee shop . . ."

"There's a bar at the corner," I told him. "I could buy you a beer." That appealed to me, having a beer with my sister's professor of Greek.

"Are you old enough to drink?"

"I'm twenty-two," I said indignantly, thinking: I'm in love with a forty-year-old man.

"Then I'll buy *you* a beer," he said, and took my arm in a courtly way.

I smiled up at Mr. Oliver, and he gave me a paternal smile and said, in his Pakistani accent, "You look happy. Were you coming from a date?"

"Sort of."

"I suppose that question makes me old-fashioned," he said in his regular voice. "I suppose young people do things differently nowadays, and dating as we used to know it is quite passé."

I looked closely at him as we passed into Dutch's Shamrock Tavern and tried to imagine him out on a date, younger, necking at a drive-in or something. I failed. He must be about Paul's age, maybe even less. Was the gap between forty and twenty-two that huge? Was it just that Mr. Oliver was a stodgy professor of Greek? I imagined him in some grimy, book-cluttered office downtown in one of those massive Yale buildings, poring over his books and losing touch with the real world. Then I remembered that Paul must spend a lot of his time doing the same thing, and I began to get depressed. Would books forever blight my life in some way? He's too old for me, I thought. I don't even know him. He has a wife and two kids. I resolved to forget the sunlit moments on the lawn with the dogs, the spark that leaped through my Coke glass, his last fierce stare at me in the doorway . . . and while I resolved all this, I knew it was nonsense, I knew I loved him and he loved me, and our ages and our tastes didn't matter a bit.

"What did you want to talk to me about?" I asked, since Mr. Oliver simply continued to look at me, a little mournfully, stroking his goat beard. The waitress came with our beers, and when she was gone he said, "I think you should get your sister out of here."

"What do you mean? Out of where? She and Alan are going to Greece." I thought he meant she'd been working too hard and needed a vacation.

"I don't mean to Greece, and I think you should get her away from Alan. I think you should call your parents and make them come get her. I'd call them myself—I met your father once when he was at Yale—but I don't want to interfere directly. And you seem a sensible girl, Cordelia. Call your parents. Call your mother, and get her to come take a look at Juliet. In my opinion, Alan is crazy, and Juliet is seriously ill."

Nonsense, was my first thought. I tried to get a mental picture of Juliet. I hadn't seen her much since I started eating all my meals out. I hadn't, in fact, seen her at all that day. I'd left while she and Alan were out jogging, as usual, and hadn't been home since. But except for her chronic bowel troubles and her thinness, she seemed healthy. She'd always been healthy. No one in our family was ever sick; our parents had taught us to despise illness.

"Ill with what?"

"Mentally ill, Cordelia."

I was filled all of a sudden with foreboding. Mentally ill: that was a different cut of meat entirely. I thought of the glint in her eyes, and Alan's. I always told funny food stories at work about Juliet and Alan. "Juliet, my nutty sister." You'd have to be nuts, I'd often thought, to live on tofu and seaweed; what if it was true? I remembered how I'd suspected it, and had put it out of my mind. I was seized with a need to see her, to look at her up close and test Mr. Oliver's opinion.

"Excuse me for a minute," I said to him. I got up and walked quickly through the bar and out the door. I ran around the corner to our apartment building and up the four flights. I burst panting into 5-B and there was Juliet, sitting in a rocking chair by the window—just sitting there. The apartment seemed curiously bare; the bookcases were empty. Juliet stood out with peculiar distinctness against the stark walls, and I remembered that she and Alan had been going to pack up their stuff that day and farm it out to friends in preparation for their trip to Greece. "I don't know when we'll be back—if ever," Juliet always said dramatically when asked about their plans. It was a well-known fact that Greece was her spiritual home.

I looked at Juliet, trying to get a fast, objective view. She had a book in her hand, but it was closed. She was emaciated, I realized with a shock. Her body was like a child's, or an old woman's. Her face was ravaged. She took up hardly any room on the chair, and on that hot night (I had to go and get a towel to wipe the sweat off my face) she looked cool—chilled.

"I've just come to get something," I said to her, throwing down my towel, and went to the phone for the address book, not yet packed, which contained my parents' California phone number. "Where's Alan?" I asked, hoping I sounded casual. Juliet just sat there rocking and looking out the window down into the filthy courtyard; it came to me suddenly that she had been doing that a lot lately. I wondered if she had watched Mr.

Oliver leave, seen him stop me and talk. It wouldn't be good for her, probably, to feel spied on.

"Alan's gone to bed," Juliet said, and her voice sounded sepulchral, like a voice coming through a tiny window in a padded cell. Why hadn't I noticed all this? How could I have dismissed her eccentricities as harmless? *Joked* about her? I was filled with dismay at my summer of self-absorption.

"Oh, Juliet!" I said, and knelt next to her chair. I took one of her cool little hands. "Are you okay?"

She looked down calmly into my face and gave my hand a slight squeeze. I could feel all her bones; even her palm felt bony. Then she let me go and opened her book. "Of course I'm okay, dopey. Don't be out too late."

I could have cried. I don't know when she'd spoken to me with such affection. I took one more look at her, said good night, and ran out and down the stairs again.

Mr. Oliver was just as I'd left him, but he'd drunk most of his beer. "You're right," I said grabbing his hand on the tabletop. I seemed to need to clutch somebody's hand. He clutched mine back; we sat looking anxiously at each other. "I'm going to call my mother. Is there a pay phone in here?"

"In front, I believe," he said, "near the door."

"What's wrong with her?" I asked him. "What should I tell my mother?"

"I don't know what it is, Cordelia. Alan, for one thing." We let go our hands; they were soggy with sweat. He fingered his little beard, I played with my scallop ear, both of us uneasy, neither wanting—out of loyalty to poor Juliet—to speak ill of Alan. "He seems a little fanatical to me," Mr. Oliver said finally.

"You said you think he's crazy." I wouldn't let him off. I had to know these things.

"Yes," he said, looking me straight in the eye. His face was rosy with his quickly downed beer. "Don't let her go all the way to Greece with him. I don't think she eats at all, Cordelia. I believe she needs professional help."

"I'd better call right now," I said, before he was through—

hoping that, on some cosmic balance sheet, my urgency would make up for the months of neglect.

I called collect, and had an irrational fear that whichever parent answered wouldn't accept the charges, but it was my mother, and she did.

"Cordelia! Such a surprise! How are you, honey?"

Her voice was strange, it was so long since I'd heard it, and at the same time it was the most familiar thing in my life. I broke down into shaky little sobs. The people at the bar turned and looked at me, and I turned my back to them, leaning my head against the greasy wall, and said, "I's not me, it's Juliet, Mom, she's sick."

I told her what Mr. Oliver had said, and I asked her to come and get Juliet and take her away.

She didn't speak for a moment, then she said, "She's supposed to go to Greece."

"Mr. Oliver says not to let her go. He says to get her away from Alan."

Another pause. "I never liked Alan," she said finally. Another pause, a sniff—I realized the pauses signified tears. Juliet was my mother's favorite, we all knew that. "I'll get a plane out as soon as I can. We were coming home next week anyway."

"Is Daddy there?" I had such a hunger to hear my father's voice as well as my mother's that I sobbed again as I asked, like a little kid in trouble.

"He's at a reading."

"At this hour?"

"It's earlier here," she said, and then, as if she'd been thinking throughout this exchange, "I'll call the airlines and call you right back."

"I'm not at the apartment," I said. "I'm at a pay phone."

"Well, what's the number?" she asked impatiently, not giving me any credit for my cleverness in sneaking out to make the call in secret. "Don't move, I'll call right back," she said when I gave her the number, and hung up, cutting off my good-bye.

Mr. Oliver stood beside me. "She's going to call back after she calls the airlines," I said, the tears still spilling down my cheeks. Mr. Oliver put one arm around me. I wept on the shoulder of his limp white shirt. The TV was on in the bar, and I listened to the local news, which was reporting an armed robbery in New Haven. I raised my head, thinking of Malcolm Madox, and saw the police pushing two handcuffed black men into a patrol car. Everyone at the bar was watching me, not the television. I looked fixedly at the screen, at a fire in Meriden (two children dead of smoke inhalation) and the sports scores.

"The Yankees lost a doubleheader," I said to Mr. Oliver. He patted my shoulder.

The phone rang during the weather, and I picked it up. "I'll be there tomorrow about noon, Cordelia," said my mother, her tears cleared away and her voice quick and efficient. "I don't think Daddy can come with me, he still has obligations here. But I'll come and take Juliet out to the house. Can you come with us, honey?"

"I have to work."

Her voice sharpened just a bit. "You still have that job?" I admitted it. "Well." The old exasperation. "I'll get Phoebe to come out and help. I have to open up the house, all that."

"I'll come on my day off, Mom. Besides, I may be quitting soon."

"Ah. Good," she said vaguely, already—I could tell—focusing on clean sheets, mail delivery, groceries. "Is it hot there?"

I wanted to say: Oh, Mom, I miss you, but I said, "Very hot."

"Does she still look like a convict? With that haircut?"

"Yes."

"Well." Another pause. "I'll be flying into Hartford and from there I can link up with that little shuttle plane to New Haven, and then I'll get a cab."

I realized that, California time, she'd have to be up at dawn to accomplish all this. "I'll get off work early," I said.

"Cordelia, it would really help if you could take the day off tomorrow and *be there* till I come. Can't you do that? Just this one time? Call in sick?" I said I would, and she sighed. "Well, that's something anyway. Keep an eye on her. All right?"

"All right."

"I'll see you tomorrow, honey," she said, and we said good-bye, but her last words before she hung up were "Try to get her to eat something."

Mr. Oliver walked me back to Juliet's and said something as we parted that I didn't catch. It may have been Greek or some other foreign language, or maybe just a form of "good-bye" in his singsong Pakistani voice. We pressed each other's sweaty hands again, and then I ran up the four flights to see if Juliet was okay.

She seemed to be. She and Alan were both asleep, breathing in harmony. I wandered into the stripped living room and sat in Juliet's chair by the window with a handful of the peanut butter crackers (not, technically, on my list of forbidden foods) I kept hidden in my room. The apartment was a mess again, the corners full of dust-kittens and the windows filthy— all my hard work undone. The only rooms I bothered to clean any more were my bedroom and the bathroom. Once, I'd come upon a used Tampax, Juliet's, in the unflushed toilet, the blood a dark, purply-brown, wrong-looking color. Was that a sign of something? Should I have known? I went and got my List Notebook, and wrote:

Things Bothering Me

Juliet
Monarky of Humph
Paul?
Thret of Danny coming back
        "   " parents   "   "
How will I learn to cook?
Juliet

The crackers made me thirsty, and I got a drink of water in the kitchen. I considered calling Nina, but I knew she'd be at her typewriter and crabby about interruptions. I thought I ought to call Humphrey and tell him I was sick. With what? I asked myself, and could think of nothing except Juliet's ailment, whatever it was, so I put off the call until morning. I had been thinking of giving Humphrey my notice tomorrow; now I wouldn't be able to. The resentment, and the Oh-poor-me feeling that had leaped to the edge of my mind while I talked to my mother, came back in a flash. I beat it down— I was used to beating it down, had done it instinctively as a kid, over and over when it threatened, knowing it wasn't good for me. But the effort got me depressed and tired, and I went to bed.

But first I looked in at Juliet again. Her breathing sounded the same. Alan was a dark lump, way over on his side of the bed. All safe, I thought, looking at Juliet's dimly lit face. My heart lurched. I remembered Jake the dog. I imagined myself—something I'd never done, hardly ever—with a child, looking in on it, never being able to rest until I knew it was safe, asleep. Then I got into bed, and in the drowning moments just before sleep I had a quick vision of Paul, and briefly, furiously, persuasively, the conviction returned to me in force—and secret, like a golden egg I was hatching—that he would be the love of my life.

I forgot to set my alarm, and I was awakened by the sound of the apartment door slamming: Juliet and Alan gone jogging. I got up and showered and rummaged in the kitchen for something to eat. There was some sesame butter. I spread it on a piece of stale brown bread and washed it down with apple cider. Then I had a few more peanut butter crackers from my cache.

It was already very hot. I imagined Juliet out running. She and Alan did two miles a day before breakfast. I pictured her in her red shorts with her bony knees going up and down and her tiny claw-hands clenched, and wondered how she did it, why she did it—Juliet, who'd always hated physical exertion, who thought sports were stupid, who made fun of Miranda, the basketball player. In high school, Juliet managed to get herself excused permanently from gym simply because she was so smart. "I told the nuns I was too intelligent for volleyball," I remember her saying to my parents. I remember their delighted faces as they looked pridefully at each other and back at Juliet. And my disgust—I recall that, too. I loved volleyball.

Before they returned, I called Humphrey and told him I wouldn't be in because of family troubles. "My sister is cracking up," I said. I couldn't lie. Since my last encounter with Danny, I felt impelled to honesty. I would not be like him, I would not be dragged down to that level again, where you steal and tell lies. "My mother's coming from California to get her, but I have to stay until she comes."

"Oh, man, that's awful," Humph said. "You stay there. Don't you let that girl out of your sight. This is the tofu sister? You stay right by her side, hear? It's a crazy world, Delia. I can get Archie to help with the salads. I can cut down the menu. It's a crazy world. Get her to eat. Lay a croissant or something on her. You got any croissants stashed away? Let me send Archie up later with a couple croissants."

I told him Juliet wouldn't eat a croissant unless you sat on her and forced it between her teeth, and then, because he was being so kind, I said, "Humph, there's something else I wanted to talk about. I'm going to leave the restaurant. Can I give you two weeks notice? Is that enough? I want to move on—take some cooking lessons or something. I know you don't agree, but I think I could be a really good cook, and I want to learn how."

His warm, fat voice broke in; Humphrey Ebbets was never at a loss for words. "Honey, you gotta do what you gotta do. I'm gonna hate to lose a salad maker with your kind of skills, you are A-1 terrific, Delia, left-handed or not left-handed. I'd give you a reference anywhere. I really think you've found your gift. I like the way you fit in at the restaurant, I like having you in my kitchen, and I'm gonna miss hell out of you, but I know where you're coming from, I've been there myself, you're an ambitious kid, it's written all over you, and smart as a whip, that's you."

I waited for him to offer to teach me, but he didn't, of course. He said, "You're probably thinking of going up to the Culinary Institute upstate, and I'm not saying they don't turn out a decent chef up there. Decent—you know what I mean." I'd never heard of the Culinary Institute. "But my advice is to latch on to some lessons from somebody really good." *You*, Humphrey, I pleaded silently, but to no avail. "I could make a few suggestions. You might even want to go to New York to take some lessons. And then get yourself a place with a nice little kitchen—I'm talking apartments now—and just cook, just keep the old stove going. And then, see, you get yourself a *sous-chef* job. Now, this operation is too small for more than one chef, but maybe I could help you there, I know a lot of people in this business."

He wasn't through, but I quit listening closely. It sounded hopeless, hopeless. It would take more money than I had. I imagined asking my parents for some cash for cooking lessons. Maybe my mother, distracted over Juliet, would write me out a fat check, but I doubted it.

"Two weeks will be fine, Delia, I'll put out my sign and I'll spread the word. But I'm gonna miss you, honey. Now take care of that sister of yours, and I'll see you to-morrow."

I thanked him and hung up, just as Juliet and Alan came in. Juliet looked like death and headed for the shower. Alan poured himself a glass of cider, drank it, poured another, and drank it while I watched his Adam's apple go up and down. Alan was pretty thin himself, but healthily thin. As I watched him in the kitchen, it came to me who he reminded me of: Anthony Perkins in *Psycho*.

"How come Juliet's so skinny, Alan?" I asked him.

"You can never be too thin or too rich," he said with a smirk.

"Yes, you can. She looks like a famine victim."

"Bullshit."

"She looks like she's going to die. You shouldn't have her out jogging, Alan."

"Listen," he said, slamming down his juice glass. "She feels good, right? She feels good and she looks great and she's happy, so you can stop worrying about her. Basically, she's a strong, healthy girl."

"She's not happy, and she doesn't look good."

"Well, *I* think she looks good," he said, but he wouldn't look at me. He looked guiltily at his empty glass, and his voice became edgy. "Isn't that what counts? I think she is one gorgeous hunk of woman."

I hated him then, his long dumb face and furry hair and pointed ears. I knew that he did good deeds at the clinic where he rescued addicts from the skids. But isn't it true that psychiatrists always have screwed-up private lives? Seeing what Juliet had become, I decided Alan was either a dope or a devil or crazy, and whichever one it was, I hated him and his false bravado.

"She looks like hell," I persisted. "My mother is flying in from California today. She'll be here any minute." (Not really a lie—an exaggeration.) "Juliet is sick. She needs help."

Alan's response to this astonished me. He collapsed suddenly on a chair, squeezed his eyes shut, and began to cry. "I know," he said. He covered his eyes with the fingers of one hand, but the tears slipped past them and down his cheeks. "I know she's sick, Cordelia. I've tried to help her, but I can't." He looked up at me—his face was red and wet—and then covered up his eyes again. "I've failed with her, she's gone beyond me. I don't know what to do with her."

I didn't know what to say. I looked at the scraggly hair peeking around the corners of his running shirt and thought how hard it was, for some reason, to sympathize with him, even when he cried. "Well, I guess you don't have to do anything with her any more, Alan," I said.

He stood up. "You were right to call your parents. Let them have a try. I give up. I've failed—failed—failed." With each "failed" he banged his fist against the refrigerator, and then he turned his fierce, red face to me and said, "There's only one thing for me to do. I'm splitting."

He headed for the door, remembered he was in running clothes, and went toward the bedroom.

"What do you mean, you're splitting?" I followed him down the hall. "You can't just leave, Alan. What about Greece?" I knew Greece was off, but I wanted to hear what he had to say. "You and Juliet have plane tickets. What about Juliet?"

"You and I both know she's not capable of going to Greece. Fuck Greece. Fuck everything," he said, and I knew he meant Juliet, too. I went and banged on the bathroom door.

"Juliet! Come on out of there."

Juliet yelled, "What?"

"Open up, Jule. Come on out here, quick!"

She emerged from the bathroom wrapped in a robe, with her hair wet. Plastered to her head, it looked like a bathing cap. Her face was dead white, and her fingers, clutching the robe around her, were translucent and skeletal.

She squinted at us, confused. "What?"

"He's leaving," I said. "He's going to desert you. He's walking out."

"Alan?"

Alan was sitting on the bed, looking beaten. "Juliet, I can't take it," he said. "I can't write, I can't do anything. I haven't been able to help you. You need more than I can give you, Juliet. I've failed. I've tried, but . . ." His eyes clouded up again. "I make you worse. I don't know why. I admit it, Cordelia," he said, looking wearily at me.

Big deal, I thought. We were all silent for a moment. Juliet still seemed bewildered. She put her hand to her head and frowned. I was beginning to see just how much her morning jog took out of her.

"Mom is on her way in from California," I told her.

She didn't look at me. "But you're leaving, Alan?" she asked. "Just like that?"

"I can't take it, you've gone beyond me," Alan said, standing up and looking around the room as if he might pack a bag or change his clothes. "We just aren't good for each other, Juliet. I can't take it any longer."

I screamed at him, "If you say that once more, Alan, I'll kill you with my bare hands. *You* can't take it! You did it to her, you know you did." I had a strange impulse to stand in front of Juliet and shield her, like a mother bear with her cub.

"You don't know one damn thing about it, Cordelia," Alan said in a hateful, controlled voice. "Would you mind getting out of this room so I can talk to Juliet alone?"

I looked at Juliet, and she nodded bleakly, still looking at Alan. "Yes, go, Cordelia. I need to understand this." She touched her forehead again.

I slammed the door on them and sat in the living room in Juliet's rocking chair, cursing silently. I wished my mother would come early, and catch Alan in his cowardly retreat. I wished Mr. Oliver were there. I tried to think of something horrible to do to Alan, to punish him for turning Juliet into a wreck, blaming her for his troubles, and then walking out on her.

I could hear his voice behind the bedroom door, talking in short fits, but I couldn't tell what he said. There was no sound from Juliet. Then I heard drawers opening and shutting, and Alan came out in jeans, a suitcase and a tennis racket. He kicked at a pile of paperback books on the floor. "Fuck these," he said, looking anxious but trying to sound casual, even jaunty. "I've got most of my stuff—fuck the rest. I'm traveling light."

"I see that," I said sarcastically.

He regarded me directly for just a moment; there was panic in his eyes. "I can't handle this, Cordelia." He dug into his pocket for his door key and threw it at me. It landed on the floor. "Keep the apartment. I won't be back."

"But you love her, Alan. She loves you," I protested. "She'll go crazy for sure if you leave her." He didn't answer. "Besides, you did this to her! She wasn't like this before!"

"I haven't done it to her, Cordelia, whatever *it* is. I don't even know. But if Juliet has troubles, they're her own troubles. I've tried to help her—"

"Help!" I cried indignantly, but he wouldn't say anything else. He headed for the door. There was no noise from the bedroom. I peeked in. Juliet was still sitting on the bed, blank-faced.

"What are you afraid of, Alan?" I asked him. "Why won't you wait for my mother? Face the consequences?"

He went out the door and shut it gently behind him. I heard him going down the stairs, fast, with a ratlike scurrying sound.

From the window, I saw him emerge from the building and walk down the sidewalk to the car. He threw the suitcase into the back seat. I yelled out the window, "Where are you going, Alan?"

He shouted something I couldn't hear, but I'm reasonably sure it was "Mind your own business." The car door slammed, and he drove away. It had all happened in perhaps twenty minutes—maybe fifteen. I sat in the rocking chair, trying to think what I should do. I had a vague idea that Alan should be forced to confront my mother and confess his crimes—to bear the brunt of her grief and anger at Juliet's condition. *He did it*, I was still repeating to myself when Juliet walked, zombie-like, out of the bedroom, shivering, still wrapped in her bathrobe.

"Well, he's gone," I said grimly.

She sat quietly on the sofa, looking around the room as if checking out the dust, and then all of a sudden she began making an "aaah" noise, part scream, part wail, and looking at me with her hair all wet and her mouth stretched in anguish.

I leaped up and knelt beside her. "Mom is coming. We know you're sick, Juliet. She's going to be here any minute." I exaggerated so that she wouldn't think to leap up and run out after Alan. But she didn't move, except to rock back and forth on the sofa and moan. I thought she'd blame me, at least, for letting him go. I thought she'd ask me how Mom found out. But she said nothing, just moaned. I wondered if she'd gone mad. I didn't know what to do. She looked like a prematurely aged child. Her tiny face came to a sharp point at her chin, her cheeks were gaunt, and her eyes were huge and dull and tragic.

"Juliet?" I said, and she stopped making her noise and collapsed on the sofa in a fetal position, crying. The bottoms of her feet were cracked and white; even they looked ill and tired. "Alan was crazy!" I yelled, suddenly angry all over again at his flight. "Look what he's done to you." She cried harder, denying nothing. I don't know if she heard me. "I'll make some tea. A nice cup of ginseng?"

She didn't answer, but I made a cup and set it beside her, and then I cleaned the apartment, furiously, eradicating the summer's accumulated dirt. I dusted everything and ran the vacuum, and I hung up all Juliet's clothes or put them in the hamper. Then I washed the kitchen floor and wiped off all the counters and cupboards and washed the accumulation of dishes. During all this, Juliet lay quiet or sobbed or moaned, hardly moving. She didn't drink the tea.

"Jule, do you want a peanut butter cracker?" I asked her when I was done. I was hot and sweating, and I spoke irritably, but the offer was made in good faith. I thought maybe some real food would snap her out of it. I thought maybe she didn't eat because she was sick of Alan-food but didn't want to admit it. "I have Triscuits, too," I said. But she didn't answer, just moaned.

I didn't even know if she was lucid until, I guess around

eleven (I was doing my best to make bean soup out of navy beans and water and herbs), she raised her head and called, "When did you say Mom is coming?"

I rushed into the living room. "Noon," I said, and, quickly, to take advantage of her return to life, asked, "Want some bean soup, Jule?" She just laid her head down again. "Tea? Some hot tea?"

"I want to die," she said, but I didn't believe her. If she really wanted to die she'd be in the bathroom slashing her wrists or at the window ready to leap. I brought in more tea. When I checked a few minutes later, it was still untouched. I sat down beside her and said, "I know how you feel, you know. Partly, I mean. Danny walked out on me, remember."

I didn't expect her to answer, and she didn't, though she moaned again—perhaps in sympathy. While we were sitting there, my mother knocked at the door. Juliet gave a little scream and ran with unexpected energy to open it. She collapsed into sobs all over my mother, as if she hadn't just been crying for three and a half hours.

My mother's light hair was frizzed all around her face from the heat, and she looked haggard, but she stayed dry-eyed. She set down her bag, which had a *New Yorker* sticking out of its side pocket, and she and I led Juliet back to the sofa and made her lie down. My mother sat beside her, held her hand, and smoothed Juliet's forehead with her fingertips. I could tell she was shocked at Juliet's appearance—she gave me a look which said so, and she picked up Juliet's hand and looked at it as if it were something she had found on the beach, some old fish skeleton.

"Is she packed?" she said to me.

I hadn't thought of that. I went to pack up Juliet's stuff, leaving my mother murmuring, "I'm taking you home, to your own room, Juliet. We're going to get some good food into you. You're going to rest. You're going to see a doctor." Juliet said, but weakly, "No, no," and my mother started over: "I'm taking you home. Daddy will be here day after tomorrow. We're going to make you well. You're not a worthless person, Juliet. You're not going to die, because we love you and we won't let you. You're going to eat some good food and get well."

Juliet protested again, but my mother's voice went on and on. It scared me that Juliet had to be spoken to that way, in that special, placating voice, as if her mind really was breakable and had to be treated gingerly. If that were so, how precarious the whole summer had been, how close we all had been to disaster.

I packed her things neatly, finickingly, the clean clothes in suitcases, the dirty ones from the hamper in a plastic bag. Some of the clothes in the hamper were Alan's; I put them, with a pair of his slippers I found in the bathroom, his toothbrush and razor, and the books he told me to fuck, into another bag and took it out to the incinerator.

"Alan walked out when I told him you were coming," I told my mother. "He left as if the cops were after him. He says she did this to herself."

My mother's lips tightened, and Juliet sobbed afresh. I brought out her suitcases and sat down again. "Anybody want bean soup?" I asked, but nobody did. Juliet got dressed in a T-shirt dress I'd left out. It hung on her in loose folds. My mother stared at Juliet's naked knobby knees. "You should let your hair grow, Jule," she said. Juliet reached up her hands to her hair and pulled at it, hard, until my mother took her hands away and said, "That's enough of that."

I called a taxi and we all piled in with the suitcases and drove out to my parents' house, the three of us together on the seat, my mother and I sweating on the ends and Juliet cold in the middle. She wasn't crying any more. She stared stone-faced at the little card with the driver's ID: GABRIEL MARQUEZ.

"That can't be Marquez," she whispered after a while. "Driving a cab in Connecticut."

"It's just a coincidence, Juliet," said my mother, and explained to me, "There's a writer by that name," which I thought was nice of her. Juliet kept staring at the name as if she remained unconvinced.

"What about you, Cordelia?" my mother asked me when the silence had gone on long enough. She turned to me for diversion, as she might have picked up her *New Yorker*. "What do you plan to do now?"

"I have to go to work tomorrow," I said. "So I can't stay overnight at the house. I'll keep the apartment, I guess, for a while. Until I find a place to stay that I can afford."

My mother sighed. "But what are you going to *do?* You said you were quitting your job."

I shrugged and said, deliberately vague, "Look for a new job, I suppose."

My mother looked at me over Juliet, disapprovingly, narrowing her tired blue eyes. "Cordelia, I wish you'd consider college. Junior college. Community college. No, listen," she said when I began my automatic protest. "Not because I want you to become a scholar, or do anything in the academic line. I know that's not your . . . thing," she said, in a voice that put no stock in my having a *thing* she could take seriously. "But just so you could meet some people, get out and see the world. These little dead-end jobs in shops and diners, Cordelia—"

"I don't work in a diner!"

"You know what I mean. You've got to do something with your life. You're too old to just drift along."

I said nothing. I knew I wasn't drifting, knew I never had been drifting, but I had no words to convince her of that.

"There are some nice little colleges in California, Cordelia. Not demanding places, but colleges I think you could profit from. They have all sorts of innovative programs—"

"You despise those places!" I burst out. "I've heard you and Daddy make fun of them. California colleges where you can major in surfing and TM!"

"With a degree you could at least get a better job," my mother said implacably. "And you wouldn't have to study."

"I never said I didn't want to study!" I shouted indignantly.

Gabriel Marquez turned his head around to look, and Juliet put her hands over her ears. "I just want to study what interests me."

"Which is . . . ?"

I clammed up, as I always did. "You'll see," I said, and looked out the window, stonier than Juliet.

The rest of the ride we were silent. My mother blew her nose twice. Juliet sighed and moaned once, and my mother put an arm around her and Juliet sank her head down on my mother's lap. I edged as close to the window as I could and watched Route 95 speed by, wondering how I was going to get back to New Haven. I didn't relish paying a cab to go all that distance—my mother was paying the cab driver twenty-five dollars for the trip. I'd take the bus back, I decided. I'd take the bus to downtown New Haven and treat myself to a nice dinner, and then walk back to the apartment and get some groceries and throw out all the Alan-food and read the want ads and maybe arrange to rent a television for a couple of weeks.

My mother had the cabbie stop at the supermarket on Route 1 outside the village and sent me inside with a list: pumpernickel bread, sweet butter, olives and pickles, English wholemeal biscuits, herring snacks, tea, lemons, and Brie—the essentials of life, according to my mother. Then we drove out to the house.

I expected to be thrilled and moved by this homecoming with my mother and sister. I wanted to feel that way. Instead, the house looked shabby and neglected, too large, too closed-up. Inevitably, I recalled how it used to oppress me, how I had always been a foreigner there, just as out of it as if I'd been among one of the obscure tribes whose language my mother had mastered. If the house alone hadn't brought it all back, my mother, in her well-meaning way, would have when, as we went up the front walk, she put a hand on my arm, and said, "Think about what I said, Cordelia. I promise I won't nag. But think about it. For Daddy and me."

If that's not nagging, I don't know what is, I said to myself, perhaps unreasonably. To my mother, I said, "I have other things to think about," which I know was rude, but I didn't want to give her any false hope. Wild bulls couldn't drag me off to college in California.

I stayed long enough to get the beds made and Juliet into one of them, and to have some bread and herring and tea. I pulled down the screens and swept the porch and put out towels and dusted furniture, munching on wholemeal biscuits. I worked hard for two hours while my mother hovered around Juliet, trying to tempt her to eat (and failing), and then I took a shower, put on a clean old dress (too short) I found in my old room, and left to get the bus.

"If you wait, Phoebe or I could drive you home," my mother said. "She'll be here any time now."

Juliet had gone to sleep, and my mother was drinking tea on the porch. She looked extremely tired, my old mother—still pretty and delicate-looking, with no hint of a California tan, but with signs of strain in her face and little dry, crinkly pouches under her eyes. I felt sorry for her, with a daughter like Juliet on her hands. I knew I should stay and help. I would have liked to see my aunt. But I wanted to start arranging my unsettled life.

"I've got to get back and get organized."

She smiled at me timidly. "You could start in a week, Cordelia."

"I've only got two weeks," I protested, misunderstanding.

"I mean school. You could be on a plane next week and on your way to California. You'd love it out there, honey. So warm all winter, and such a breeze in summer, and the ocean. And it's just swarming with young people."

I pride myself on my control. I stood up and said, "I'd better get going. There used to be a four o'clock bus, there probably still is."

"Oh, Cordelia, your father will be so disappointed."

"He should be used to it," I said, but I hugged my mother

anyway, even though in my anger I could have broken all the windows and knocked over the woodpile. I suppose that was dishonest, the hug was a lie, but my passion for honesty doesn't mean honesty at all costs—not really. I couldn't hurt my mother any worse than I was already doing, and she knew the hug didn't mean capitulation, or even apology. It meant I loved her. I did love her, but I couldn't wait to get out of there. I was sick of seeing all the pampered understanding dished out to Juliet.

I walked to the bus stop, lugging my coin collection, retrieved from the attic, in a shopping bag. I couldn't wait to dive into it again and see how everything looked after all this time and figure out how much the coins had appreciated.

The bag was heavy—I had two large cardboard albums full of coins—and the day was hot. I must have been crazy not to wait for a ride, but I trudged along to the village Green, where the bus stops. It wasn't until I was actually there, in front of it, that I remembered Hector's Market.

It was a shock. I knew, of course, that George and Claire had sold it to the Uncle Jody's Country Crackerbarrel chain, but I had never visualized the change, the way that the dark, pleasantly smelly inside would be lit with a garish light and infested with the stink of scented candles. I had time, and I went in, out of the same fascination with which, I suppose, you'd spy on an old lover with his new wife, if you got the chance. I knew it would be horrible in there, but what surprised me was that the horribleness passed off almost right away, and the transformation took me over completely. The rough-hewn barrels full of kitchen gadgets, bins of soap in the shape of fruits, penny candy for two cents in glass jars, cheap wooden toys, racks of cat cards, and a suspicious storekeeper in a striped apron and collarless shirt—it all looked *right* in there. Within a minute or two, I hardly remembered the old Hector's. I've heard people say, when someone dies, that they don't want to see them dead, they're afraid they'll forget them as they were when they were alive. That's just how it was.

I didn't linger. I bought some penny candy and a little note pad with a village scene (not our village, but similar) on the cover. The bus came then, and I just got a quick look up at the diamond-paned windows before we took off: they were exactly as I remembered, glittering in the sun. I sucked on a jawbreaker that tasted of soap and made a frantic list of everything I could remember about Hector's as I knew it: crowded aisles, dim light, magic . . . I tucked it safely away to transcribe into my List Notebook. (I've used it in writing this, to recall the old Hector's. The list brought it all back—and here I must admit that words do have some power, though photographs would have been even better.) But I felt real panic that afternoon when Hector's as I had loved it receded from me.

Back in New Haven, I lugged all my stuff, as if by an instinct for solace, straight to Grand'mère. I went in the front door, sat down at my favorite table, settled my shopping bag on the floor beside me, looked up, and there was Paul.

"May I sit down?" he asked me. I nodded, of course, and he continued, parking himself across from me, "I came to catch you as you got out of work, but the waitress told me you hadn't been in today. I was just about to get your number and find a pay phone and call you."

He was the same—the little glasses, the beautiful mouth, the graying hair. It was too good to be true that he was sitting across from me, in a blue shirt, at Grand'mère, with the yellow light from one of the brass lanterns falling on his glasses. He looked like a god, an angel, a movie star. Seeing him was so wonderful, after Juliet and Alan and my mother and Hector's —and the crazy fear that I'd made him up—that I just sat and looked at him while he talked.

"I had to see you," he said, knotting his hands together on the table between us. I studied his hands, small and strong like himself, with fine black hairs on the backs, and suppressed a desire to cover them with my own. "For one thing, I've been deputized by my wife—by Martha . . ." Here his hands became still, flattened out on the tabletop. I couldn't imagine what he was going to say. "To offer you a job."

"A job?"

I don't know what I expected—I suppose for him to declare a passion for me as powerful as mine for him. I had no doubt he felt it, even as he sat there sober-faced and spoke on behalf of his wife. I remembered how it had shimmered around us on the lawn; it was there now, buried beneath his anxiety. But a job?

He explained that Martha had decided she wanted to hire a mother's helper, and when my face fell he said, "What she really wants is a cook. Martha is a first-class cook, but she . . ." He paused while I waited, looking from his face to his spread-out hands on the checked tablecloth, wondering at the unexpected turns our conversation was taking. Why are we talking about Martha? I thought.

"She doesn't feel she has time to cook, she has so many other activities. So she wants to teach you to cook. She thinks it would be fun for both of you. And then you could take it over."

I suppose I still looked dubious and let down. I said, "But nobody has a cook!" Of all the possible replies I could have made, it was the first that I got out.

"Martha's parents do," Paul said. "So does her grandmother. A cook-housekeeper. Her parents have a cook and a maid. Martha feels she needs one, too—a cook, not a maid," he added hastily. "Though I should explain that she also wants help with the kids. She has a cleaning woman for the house, but she says it's the cooking and the kids that take up all her time. She has her own money—I mean from her family. She—we can well afford a cook."

"Does Martha work?" I asked hesitantly. I couldn't help wondering what Paul's wife did with her time.

"Officially, we're partners in the business," Paul said. "She helps me catalogue and price." I could tell he was trying to be fair and honest, both at once, and he was having trouble. "And then she also—well, she runs. And she takes weaving lessons. She's a very good weaver. Also, she goes antique hunting, she does a little buying and selling. I don't mean to say she doesn't need to get away from the house and the kids. I don't mean she should be a drudge." He didn't say what he did mean. He stopped there, and Crystal, who had been hovering, came over and asked me if we wanted dinner. "Eventually," I told her, Paul confirming this with a nod, and we ordered a carafe of the house Chablis. Crystal raised her eyebrows at Paul and gave me a quizzical look, but I didn't respond, and she raised her eyebrows again and went to get our wine and report to Cynthia, behind the bar.

"I'm sorry," I said finally to Paul. I don't know what I was feeling, I had never felt so many different ways at once: disappointed, hurt, insulted, frustrated, in love. But I knew I didn't feel wild elation at the prospect of being cook and baby-sitter for Martha Lamberti. I'd had enough of drudging for other people living with Juliet and Alan. "I don't think it's the job for me. But I thank you for thinking of me. I thank Martha, I mean." I must have sounded cold, though I didn't mean to—or maybe I did mean to. What a day it had been, after all. I've been through the wringer, I thought—something Danny's mother used to say after a busy Friday in the store.

Paul looked stricken at my words, and then I did put my hands over his. But before I could speak again, he said, "Let me just tell you everything before you decide." I realized he was pleading with me, and the knowledge that he did love me—that strange, impossible, secure fact—caused me to smile at him. He didn't smile back, but he turned his hands up and held mine. He was so earnest I could have kissed him. I had a great longing to kiss him.

"The kids are both in school," he said. "Megan is in first grade, Ian goes to nursery school all day. They usually hang around the shop with me after school, but in the evenings I have people coming in a lot of the time—clients. Martha wants someone to give the kids their baths and all that. They go to bed at eight-thirty . . ."

His voice trailed away. He must have seen that these domestic details were not winning me over, and he looked apologetic. I unlinked our hands and ceased to smile. I wanted to know *him*. I wanted his wife and kids to remain invisible. His recital forced me to look at them—the dear little children in their sleepers, the jolly clients streaming in to buy Daddy's books, Paul and Martha walled in behind all their years together, the romping dogs . . . Ozzie and Harriet and the kids. I felt left out, as usual, the outsider looking in.

Paul and I stared at each other. He took off his glasses and rubbed his eyes, as he had on the lawn. I remembered how he'd looked then, like a picture we'd had in school of Jesus ascending to heaven in a sunset just like the one we'd shared. There he was, all rosy and glowing and lovable, going up, out of reach.

"Forgive me," he said. "It's not for you. Of course it isn't. You can do better."

He kept his hands over his eyes. His glasses, on the tabletop, were dusty and spotted. I picked them up tenderly, breathed on each lens, and wiped them on the edge of the tablecloth.

"There." He looked up at me and at the cleaned glasses I offered him. "Tell me about the cooking part," I said, smiling.

He began to laugh. It was the first time I'd ever heard him laugh. He has a wonderful, abandoned way of collapsing into it; his face softens, his eyes half close, and he lets out good, strong "Ha ha's"—it's the laugh of a much larger person.

I waited for him to finish. I didn't know what was so funny, but I sensed that something important was happening, something was snapping in him and something else tightening up. Finally he stopped—it wasn't that long, maybe half a minute of his laughing and our looking at each other—and drew a deep breath and put on his glasses again.

"Well," he resumed. "The cooking." His hilarity was gone, but so was his anxiety. "There's not that much, really. Mainly dinner. We wouldn't expect you to fix breakfast, and Martha isn't usually home for lunch. You'd have to pack a lunch for Ian, and then weekends . . ." He kept pausing, to see the effect of his recital on me. I was fine; the specter of Ozzie and Harriet had disappeared with his laughter. "Sometimes I have a client in around lunchtime. I suppose you might make us some sandwiches or something. Martha usually does if she's around, if she has time." I pictured him among his books eating a peanut butter sandwich supplied by a grudging Martha in a running suit.

Crystal brought the wine, and we clasped hands again as we drank. "What else?" I asked him. I wanted to know again—everything—because I knew it no longer mattered.

"Well," he said, and stopped—wondering, I suppose, what to tell out of the welter of detail he'd left behind. "Well, Martha went to cooking school in Paris, at Le Cercle de Cuisine." I'd never heard of it, but I realized I should have, so when he looked sharply at me as he pronounced the French words, I tried to look impressed. I'd ask Humph about it. "She's a fantastic cook," Paul said. "It used to be one of her passions, but she's gotten tired of it lately." How odd, to master these housewifely arts—cooking, weaving—to no purpose, I thought, my distaste for the princessy Martha growing. The pointless, aristocratic life she led seemed wrong to me, as I saw it did to Paul. "She really likes the idea of teaching, though," Paul said, with a kind of dogged, dutiful loyalty. "So when you said you wanted to learn, she said a bell rang in her head. It all fit together."

"Then why didn't *she* come and offer me the job?"

Because I'm in love with you, Delia dearest, I wanted him to say. "We didn't know how to reach you," he said instead. I hated the word *we*. He used it sparingly, but every time he did I felt stabbed. "And I had business in New Haven today, so I said I'd stop in here." He looked down into his wineglass. "No," he said after a minute of silence. "I wanted to ask you myself. I thought you'd probably say no and I wanted to persuade you. I thought I could present the case better than she could."

"Yes," I said without comment, and the current passed through our hands.

"I should say the pay will be pretty good," he went on evenly. "Martha suggested a hundred fifty a week. As I said, she has plenty of money of her own." I sensed bitterness in his voice, but also a kind of pride, or satisfaction. "Plus room and board, of course. And I forgot to say you'd have one day a week completely to yourself."

"Where would I sleep?" I was wavering, of course; I was halfway there. Was it the money? I could save most of it. In a year I'd have several thousand in the bank, plus what I already had. And I wouldn't have to dip into my savings, after all, to support myself while I learned to cook. If only Martha was really good, would really teach me, wouldn't get sick of it . . .

"There are two rooms over the bookshop," Paul was saying. "There's a bathroom there, sort of antiquated. And it's not insulated very well, so it's cold in the winter. We'd fix that, of course." Hope made his voice boyish, again on the verge of laughter. "We don't use the rooms at the moment, I store things up there, but they'd be all fixed up by the time you came—"

"All right," I said abruptly. What decided me—the lure of the yellow house? of two cozy rooms in it, over Paul's shop, where I'd sleep buoyed up by his books? a vision of Paul's arms around me through the cold winter? Maybe it was the practicality of the scheme: I would learn to cook, I would save money, I wouldn't be alone, and I needn't stay forever. I don't think it was the mere fact of Paul's pleading. I don't think it was only that I loved him. I hope I'm too hardheaded to take a crummy menial job to be near the man I love. Well, I don't know, but after a glass of wine and all those words, the thrill of excitement I'd felt in my talks with Nina about my limitless future began to race through me, and I saw that the job had its virtues.

"All right," I said. "Let me come and talk to Martha about it. I want to find out more about the cooking part. But it might be okay. It sounds better than it did at first."

He didn't smile or look pleased or do anything but stare at me, and I stared back. I had never seen a face I liked so well, a face I wanted so much to know. He squeezed my hand tight, tighter. Our knees met under the table, and we each slid one foot forward to link ankles. The closer we became, the more it seemed to me that we were joining ourselves together for the start of a great journey. "That day before the firing squad, Delia," he said. "I didn't want to die because I realized I'd never even lived." He spoke passionately, in a tone I'd hardly ever heard in any man but my father, and then he did smile again, his brilliant smile.

"I've fallen in love with you, Cordelia," he whispered, and Crystal came to take our order.

We had cold broccoli soup and *tournedos* of beef Ebbets and sorbet (lemon for me, raspberry for him) and coffee and a couple of brandies. I was glad Paul could still eat under the influence of strong emotion. I've never had any sympathy with people who are too much in love to eat. We talked about how miraculous it was that we'd fallen in love in the sunset like that, simultaneously. We kept laughing, happily, as little kids laugh when they're having fun. We didn't talk at all about Martha or Danny, though I told Paul I was separated from my husband. He looked just slightly relieved, and I knew without his saying so that this fact subtracted some of the falseness of his own position with Martha—and I think it made me seem older. He was forty-two.

"You could be my daughter," he said with chagrin.

"I'm awfully glad I'm not," I said, taking his hand again.

I wanted to ask him why he didn't leave Martha, but— this will sound odd—I felt I didn't know him well enough, and it wasn't yet any of my business. We had a long road to go down, I saw—a lot of words would have to pass between us.

Our talk, over dinner, was sparse. We ordered more wine. I kept remembering the eating scene in the movie *Tom Jones*. We held hands from time to time, our knees rubbed together under the table, and when we traded bits of our fruit sorbets, licking from each other's spoons, I thought I might slide off my chair from the ecstasy of it.

We did talk some, if only for appearances. I was vividly

aware that I was under the surveillance of the entire Grand' mère staff. I told Paul about Juliet and Alan and my mother's return, and the fact of the empty apartment sat before us like dessert. When we finished eating, he said he'd drive me home.

"You could come up and see my coin collection," I said, indicating the bag on the floor.

"I'd like that very much," he said seriously.

I told Crystal to tell Humphrey I'd see him in the morning— there was his bald head, peeping out through the pane in the kitchen door, and I waved tipsily. Paul and I left with his astonished eyes upon us. We drove out Whalley Avenue, my coin albums separating us on the seat, and we didn't talk any more, except that Paul swore softly at each red light. When we got to Juliet's, we lugged my stuff up the four flights to the strangely silent, empty, clean 5-B and, once inside, dropped everything and rushed panting into each other's arms. We kissed frantically. I felt we had waited years to kiss each other instead of exactly one day, and until the moment I die—probably on my deathbed it will be my last impression of this wonderful world—I will remember the way it was, kissing Paul.

"I want to make love to you," he said after a while, but at that point I made us stop. We sat on the sofa, holding hands. The speed of it all had exhilarated me; now it scared me a little. "I'm not ready," I said. I had put clean sheets on Juliet and Alan's double bed, intending to move myself into their room for as long as I stayed on. (Since Danny's invasion of my bed, my own room had lost its appeal.) Now the big bed awaited us, clean and cool and ready, but I held on to Paul's hands tightly as if to keep us fastened down together, decorously, on the sofa. "I'm a slow sort of person," I told him, wishing I weren't. "I need to digest this much first."

He accepted it, though I don't think he understood. It was one of the great differences between us, that his instinct was to grab fast and hard and impulsively, while I was cautious, looking ahead. Part of the reason I wouldn't take him to bed was that I didn't want to reminisce someday about the start of our love affair and remember that we made love before we ever got to know each other. I don't know why—it made the feeling between us less like love, I suppose. When he put his glasses back on and left, later than he plausibly should have, I was glad that the bed was still clean and cool and neatly tucked—and yet I lay there sleepless for hours, wanting him. Maybe it was twelve years at St. Agatha's School that gave logic to such behavior.

Paul picked me up the next day after work (SALAD PERSON WANTED, Humph's sign read once again) and drove me out to the yellow house to have dinner and talk to Martha. We held hands all the way and kissed at stoplights. We were very carefree. I knew I would take the job, and we loved each other. Wives, husbands, children—none of it mattered.

I was daunted, though, by Martha. I had forgotten, totally, that she was daunting. She was in a silk dress, and she exclaimed, "Delia, dear, you're like the answer to a prayer!"

There it all was, the gleaming house, the dogs, the antiques, the same bowl of apples, even the low sun—just the same, but completely, indescribably changed. I was no longer a casual visitor: I was a hired domestic fooling around with the master of the house.

Martha had set the table on a screened-in porch off the big old kitchen, and the table setting—which was arty, with a centerpiece of exotic seashells and flowers, and the napkins folded into birds—daunted me almost as thoroughly as Martha had.

Then there was the kitchen itself. It was nothing like the kitchen I had reveled in at Colonial Towers, where I used to thaw and heat up and blend the goodies Danny and I loved. That had been a tiny place, all Formica and chrome and plastic with everything within reach. This was all brick and wood and copper, bigger than the kitchen at Grand'mère, but very obviously done by a decorator. A stage set, I thought.

Martha showed me the gadgets; she had more, many more, than even Humphrey had. I felt defeated already, looking around that room. It was too big, too complicated, too elaborate and classy. I began to doubt my ability to learn to cook in a place like that.

The two rooms over the bookshop were promising, though. Martha and I took our glasses of sherry there—up a stairway off the laundry room, near the back door and handy to the kitchen. There was a large room and a smaller one and a toilet and a sink.

"We'll enclose the bathroom part and put in a fiberglass shower stall," Martha said, kicking aside some empty cartons and not seeming to notice that a visible layer of dust settled over one of her elegant shoes. "We're having insulation blown in—been meaning to do that for years, actually. We also have a little heater for you to use in cold weather. You could have a hot plate, too, if you wanted. To make coffee on? And here—do you like this wallpaper?" She showed me a sample, flower-sprigged and old-fashioned. "I thought paper on the walls would be cozy. You'll have a bedroom, you see, and this would be a sitting room. We have a nice old spool bed up in the attic, I'll have Paul bring it down . . ."

These details cheered me. They made it real, for one thing. The last few days of my life had been dreamlike in their swiftness and fullness. The rooms over the bookshop gave me a stopping place, an anchor to attach my thoughts to. But when Paul's name came up in that casual, wifely way, I saw that it was going to be difficult, too, living in those rooms—living at Lamb House Books. It would be better to be in love with Paul at a distance. "Something different"—that's what I'd giddily decided I wanted. Well, I would have it. I couldn't imagine how it would end, and I kept myself from trying. I thought instead of the pretty wallpaper and the nice old spool bed and coffee made on the hot plate, and I smiled as hard as I could at Martha.

"Chez Cordelia!" she cried, looking inspired. She gestured

around the dusty space. "That's what it'll be—your own place, off limits to the rest of us. By invitation only!"

She spoke gaily, and I nodded with approval. *Chez Cordelia*: I liked it, it sounded like a restaurant.

We went back to the main house and sat down to eat, Martha and I flanking Paul at the square table. I wondered, humbly, if I would eat with them, or alone in the kitchen, or with the kids. When I asked, Martha said, looking hurt, "Why, we'll all eat together, Delia! Good Lord, you don't think we'd let you eat *alone!* Sweetie, you're not a *servant* here!" She shot a distressed look at Paul, who was hunched over his plate and didn't notice, but the look was meant for me, anyway, to underline her words.

Martha had prepared, for dinner, a veal pâté, and sole grenobloise, and marinated cauliflower, and a very light mousse. The meal compared favorably with Humphrey's best, except for the pâté: hers was better—though I said to myself, critically, that hers *should* be better, all she had to do all day was jog and weave, while Humph had to run a business and get out over a hundred dinners a night. But I decided that was a petty, prejudiced way to think, and I gave Martha my honest opinion of her pâté.

She was pleased. The meal had been designed to win me over, but the guilty thought that what I liked best about it was Paul's knee comfortably against mine under the tablecloth made the food, delicious as it was, go down tastelessly, over a lump of dismay. Each bite was one more knot binding me there where I shouldn't be: sitting at their table, eating their food, giggling at the antics of their dogs out in the yard, listening to Martha's tales of her cooking-school days in Paris. The elaborate, beautifully arranged and garnished food, the careful mix of tastes and textures, the pale-green wine in old, etched glasses—it all seemed silly, frivolous.

"We do look forward to having you here, Delia," Martha said to me over espresso—just as I'd been trying to come up with a plausible reason for backing out. She patted my arm as she spoke. I have trouble resisting these affectionate physical gestures, however casual, and I gushed out something appropriate. Martha announced that I'd better meet the children, and Paul went to hunt them up. They were obviously well trained, and had, I gathered, eaten early and been sent up to their playroom—the usual procedure when the Lambertis had guests, I was to discover, though in the future I'd be up there with them. (Martha's democratic ideals didn't include inviting the cook to her dinner parties.)

The kids came decorously out to the porch, two blond little kids in summer pajamas, and shook hands and said they were pleased to meet me.

"And tell Miss Miller you're looking forward to having her stay with us," Martha said to them.

Ian buried his face in his stuffed dog. Megan began, "We're looking forward to—"

"Oh, please!" I interrupted. "Couldn't they just call me Delia?"

Martha frowned. I shouldn't have proposed this variation on standard etiquette in front of the children, I realized. But she was gracious about it, smoothed out her frown, and said, "Would you like to call Miss Miller Delia, Megan?"

I could tell Megan didn't care much one way or the other, but she said, "Oh yes."

"Delia is short for Cordelia, Megan," her mother said. "Isn't that a pretty name?"

Megan said it was. Paul's brown eyes stared out of Martha's family's face.

"Ian? Would you like to tell Cordelia that you're looking forward to having her stay with us?"

Ian didn't speak, and I said, "We'll have a lot of fun, Ian," but he looked dubiously at his dog as if he didn't believe it. And why should he? Megan, prompted by a look from her mother, said, "We're looking forward to having you to stay with us, Delia." She gave a meaningful, longing look to the mousse, but Martha hustled them back upstairs.

"They're cute," I said inanely to Paul.

He shrugged and said, "This may sound terrible, but they're her children. All hers."

We were silent, staring at each other. This is a mistake, I kept saying to myself. A mistake, a mistake, a mistake.

"Well!" Martha said briskly, coming in. "It's true, Cordelia. We just can't wait for you to come!" She beamed at me. "All settled? You'll come as soon as they get a replacement for you at the restaurant?"

I said I would, trying not to look miserable. "You'll be one of us," Martha said. "Just one more member of our slightly wacky family," and she laughed and pecked me on the cheek.

As soon as Paul and I got into the car, I told him it was a mistake. "I can't do this! She's so nice. I can't do this to her! Think of all the lies, Paul!"

He said nothing. We drove down the road past the darkened barns, to Gresham. At the stoplight there he kissed me, but I felt no better, and I drew away.

"We can't!" I said, keeping my voice under tight control. I didn't want to cry in front of him. I hate women who cry all the time in front of men. Why should women have to break down in tears, when men don't? Then I looked over at Paul and saw tears slipping down his face.

I made him pull over into the empty parking lot of a supermarket, and I held him in my arms. "I've been thinking all during dinner, Delia," he said. "We have to talk. We have to get this straight." He sat up, and we held hands. "I know how you're feeling," he said. "But don't." His voice was stern, though he looked at me tenderly. "Don't feel that way. You're not stealing someone else's husband. Martha and I hate each other. She despises me, I despise her. We loathe each other. We're enemies, total enemies, but we don't even fight because we don't care enough." His grip on my hands got tighter and tighter. "We stay together for the kids and the business, and because of our incredibly complicated economics, and because it's the easiest thing to do. But we have nothing—nothing, I swear it. We go our own ways." I looked at him in despair, shaking my head. "There are plenty of marriages like ours, Delia," he said gently.

"I've never seen one."

"There's a lot you haven't seen."

"You should just—break up," I insisted. It was horrible, unthinkable, that two people could live like that. Was it even possible? Could it be true? It occurred to me that I knew nothing about the man who was holding my hands so tightly.

"You should leave if that's the way things are," I said.

"You have no idea—it's so complex. It seems simple to you because you're so young, Delia. But I hope that someday . . ." He left the rest unsaid, looking earnestly into my face, but it was enough for me. I could imagine Paul and me flying off somewhere alone together—like the couple in a print of a painting Miranda used to keep in her room—sweeping through the sky over cows and roofs and trees, clasping each other. "I love you, and I won't have Martha wrecking it," Paul said in a different voice, loosening his grip on my hands and pulling me toward him. His words were like music; I could have got up and danced.

We necked in the parking lot, under the lights and the ads for toilet paper and ham and tomatoes on sale, and then we drove back to my apartment.

"You love me, Delia?" he asked.

Of course I did, but I considered carefully. "I know hardly anything about you," I said, looking at his profile. His glasses lit up every time we passed under a streetlight. That was almost all I knew of him: what he looked like, the texture of his hands. Only what I could see and feel. He still had no past. His past was as mysterious to me as our future was, and as delicious, full of potential goodies.

I wanted to know about how he cried and wet his pants on the first day of kindergarten, about the death of his turtle, about the day his brother Tom threw a fastball straight at Paul's head and knocked him cold, about his mother's lasagne and his father's butcher shop and his Aunt Rosie and his Uncle Pete and his college days and his tonsillectomy— all the things I know now but didn't then, the things that made Paul *Paul*. I hungered for them. I looked at him in the intermittent light, while he waited for me to speak: profile, curly hair, glasses (His glasses! How old was he when he first got glasses? Was he nearsighted? farsighted? astigmatic?) and wished for long, free hours with him so he could turn himself inside out for me. I thought of all the years Danny and I had had to get to know each other, and yet already I knew Paul better than I would ever know Danny.

"I love you with all my heart," I told him confidently.

Ah, what a smile that man has. Even in the near-dark, I felt his smile down in the depths of my bones.

By the time I got home, I was wearier than I could ever remember being. I'd been through the wringer, all right— squeezed flat again and again like a cat in a cartoon. I needed to sleep. But after Paul left me I was suddenly starving. It was as if Martha's perfect meal had been a dream. I went into Juliet's kitchen and ate some swiss cheese and some peanut butter crackers. Then I stumbled into bed with the crumbs still on my face and dreamed of nothing.

I lived in the apartment after that as if it were a hotel, keeping the door securely locked (fearful, always, of Danny's return), knowing I would leave it soon. My parents gradually retrieved all of Juliet's books and papers and clothes. My father, jolly and unchanged by his semester in California and the illness of his middle daughter (and the new disappoint-ments of his youngest), took me out to dinner one night. We went to Grand'mère so I could show off Humphrey's cooking. But Humph had the only off night I'd ever known him to have: the soup was salty and the veal was tough. My father ate without enthusiasm, and when I told him that my new career as a cook would be beginning any day, he looked at me sadly, and said, "With your brains, Cordelia? Your background?"— adding, with heavy irony, "*Upon such sacrifices, my Cordelia, the gods themselves throw incense.*"

"It's not a sacrifice, Daddy!" All my life he'd quoted things at me when I wanted to be taken seriously. "It's what I want to do, it's what I can be good at."

He just smiled and looked resigned, as if I had announced I was entering an order of cloistered nuns, but later he said, when I told him more about the Lambertis, "They sound like nice people."

"Just because they sell books."

"No, no," he protested. "They'll take care of you, at least. You'll be in good hands."

I thought of Paul's square, tanned hands reaching under my T-shirt, and I smiled at my father.

My mother came to see me, too, during that time. My parents never came together because someone had to stay with Juliet every minute. They were afraid she was suicidal. She hardly ever ate. The one time she had gorged—actually gorged—on crackers and cheese, my mother had found her in the bathroom trying to make herself throw up. They had begun taking her once a week to a doctor in New York who specialized in her condition.

"It's called anorexia," my mother said. I was astonished that Juliet's oddities had a name, and specialists. "She and I might need to live in Manhattan during the week for a while so she can see this doctor more often. He's awfully good." She sighed.

"Poor Mom," I murmured.

She actually said, then, near tears of tiredness, "You're my comfort, Cordelia."

But she didn't approve of my plans. "Cooking," she said in a wan, despairing voice. "You could study cooking in college. That's the kind of thing I *meant*, honey. They have all sorts of nonacademic courses like that."

"Why should I spend good money to learn to cook in college when I can get paid to learn at the Lambertis? Besides, if you mean those cooking schools, Humphrey told me they aren't that good."

"Oh—Humphrey," my mother said, waving her hand in dismissal at the very idea of my fat friend in the white hat. My father had told her about the veal and the soup.

We dropped the subject before we both got mad. She knew my mind was made up, and she wanted to stay on good terms with me. I knew what my mother meant when she called me her comfort. It was only by comparison. Juliet was ill. Miranda, she told me—it was my first inkling of this; it had been kept top secret in the hope that it could be remedied— had left her husband, Gilbert, and was living with three other women in a commune near Boston. And Horatio—my mother looked grieved whenever his name came up. My father had jokingly called him "the international playboy," my mother spoke sorrowfully about waste. At the moment, with my culinary ambitions, my bank account, my common sense, my stodgy (for all they knew) lifestyle, I was not a bad specimen of a daughter, and my mother's recognition—however circumstantial—of that fact touched me profoundly.

I didn't tell either of them about Danny's return; they seemed to have forgotten his existence. I certainly didn't tell them about Paul, or about why I had left Madox Hardware. I told my mother plenty about Juliet's eating habits, and I told my father about Mr. Oliver's Pakistani accent and his concern for Juliet.

"Remember Professor Bhaer and Jo March?" my father said with a twinkle in his eye. "In *Little Women*?"

I'd seen the movie on TV, twice. "But Mr. Oliver already has a wife, Daddy. And Juliet is—you know." Not much like Katherine Hepburn at the moment, I didn't say.

"Well," he said, refusing to relinquish his lovely idea. "You never know."

My parents told me, each in turn, about California, my father emphasizing the inspiring beauties of the scenery, my mother the vital and delightful young people the place was packed with. They showed me photographs of beaches, orange groves, Berkeley. The more they said, the less I wanted to go out there.

"What makes you such a homebody, Cordelia?" my mother asked in half-mock exasperation. "Are you going to stay in Connecticut all your life? I'd suggest sending you to Paris, to learn to cook there yourself, at that school, but I know what you'd say."

"I don't speak French."

"Honey, you could *learn*."

She never gave up, my mother. "I don't want to learn French," I said. "Except for the food names. Humphrey taught them to me." I picked them up effortlessly: all the *pâtés* and *salades* and *potages* and *cassoulets* and *patisseries* and *gateaux* I'd learned about at Grand'mère. I began reeling them off to impress my mother. I hoped she would at least compliment me on my accent, but I suppose that was like trying to impress a duck with your backstroke.

"Man cannot live by bread alone, Cordelia," my mother said with a sigh, getting up. She had Juliet's last load of stuff piled by the door, ready to go.

"*Pain*," I said, trying to get her to laugh. "*Pain de ménage, petits pains, ficelles, brioches, croissants . . .*"

She smiled, but then she sighed again, kissed me, and left. I'll make them a meal, I vowed. When I've learned to cook. A meal that'll knock them on their ears.

When I'd been in the apartment, alone, for a week, during which Paul made two more decorous visits, Humphrey hired a new salad person, a skinny little guy named Nelson.

"He may not have salad hands," Humph said, holding mine, "but he's got it *up here*. Salad brains! Not the instinct, but the capacity. Second best," he hissed so Nelson wouldn't hear, and treated me to a dinner on the house. When he kissed me good-bye, smelling of fines herbes, we both wept a little.

I had a last meal with Nina, too. She had quit her job with the *Nickel* and was going to New York with Archie. Some connection of hers had wangled him an audition with a prestigious piano teacher, and Nina had plans to worm her way into a job on the *Village Voice*.

"But for the moment," she said, with a light in her eye, "my job is to keep him psyched up. This is his big chance. I want to see him at Carnegie Hall. I want him making records, and giving concert tours."

We wished each other luck. She gave me a number in New York where she could be reached. "Call me any time, Delia," she urged. "To get things off your chest, to complain, to gossip—you know. Whatever." I said I would, and she gave me her reporter's sharp look. "Are you sure you know what you're getting into out at that bookshop?" She'd heard, then, from Humphrey or Crystal, about Paul and me holding hands and trading bits of sorbet.

"No," I said. "I don't know at all."

"I think you're crazy, to be frank, Delia. This sort of thing isn't like you."

"It must be," I said. "Because I'm doing it."

I hugged her when we parted, but I felt distanced from Nina. I had thought that my great love for Paul would bind me to her, because of hers for Archie, but I suppose being in love is an isolating state; it makes other people's emotions, however similar, seem unreal.

I cleaned the apartment for the last time and packed my meager goods. On my last day there I made a new list in my List Notebook:

Reasons Why I'm Going There

1. cooking lessens
2. save money
3. dogs, cows, etc.
4. chez Cordelia
5. Paul
     Paul
          Paul
               Paul . . .

until it went off the page.

I stared at his name for a long time, and then, for some reason, I turned the page and printed, all by itself, with curlicues, my own name: CORDELIA MILLER. I'm looking at it now, precise and grandiose, with a coffee stain beside it, and I'm remembering the state of mind I was in when I wrote it. I was excited, I know—eager to begin my new life, eager (despite what my mother thought) to learn something. I couldn't wait to get my hands into dough, to turn out a hollandaise as smooth as cream, to bone chickens with my bare hands.

I was feeling cautious, too. I wasn't completely without misgivings about barging in on someone's marriage, however rotten it had become. It was sturdy enough to hang on all these years, I thought in my rare cynical moments. But I was in love—I have only to turn back a page and look at Paul's name, scribbled over and over in what I can only describe as an ecstasy, to remember how in love I was.

And so when Paul came to pick me up, I took his hand and led him into the bedroom, where we made love on the bare striped mattress.

Then, in yet another rosy sunset, we drove out to the yellow house.

Chapter Seven

LAMB HOUSE BOOKS

I would have liked to stop right there, and catch my breath—
to spend, maybe, three days on that drive up Route 7 in Paul's
green Volvo, or eight hours snuggled up with him on Juliet's
bare bed while he slept and I thought, or a solitary week in my
two rooms above the bookshop for the purpose of taking stock
of my recent past and charting my immediate future. I felt
the urge to make another list, though I didn't know what the
items on it might be. I needed time to figure that out.

But I had no time for reflection. Life ran on quickly, like
a movie. The yellow house plucked and chewed and swallowed
me at top speed. Within three days it was as if I had been
there forever. I knew Ian needed two stuffed bears, a donkey,
and Kermit the Frog in bed with him at night or he would cry.
I knew Paul couldn't stand curried food. I knew Albert the
dog chased cars if they were going fast enough. I knew
Megan's teacher's cat's name. I knew that the cleaning
woman's new car was a lemon. I even learned, after painful
confrontation, that when you go toward the cupboard in the
kitchen where the wineglasses are kept you have to watch out

you don't get banged in the hip by a corner of the table. And that you have to jiggle the handle on the toilet in the downstairs powder room.

Also, that moments alone with the master of the house were going to be rare indeed.

Mostly, those first few ovewhelming weeks, I cooked. In her first bloom of enthusiasm, Martha tucked me under her wing and barely let me out of her sight. The night I arrived, flushed and happy from my hour on Juliet's mattress with Paul, she gave me a volume of Julia Child to look at before bed. I think *Mastering the Art of French Cooking*, Volume I, is the only book I've ever stayed up reading until dawn. It was a revelation. There it all was: the brain of Humphrey Ebbets, laid out in black and white. I felt the way I know I was supposed to feel, back in school, when I read poetry—inspired, uplifted, joyful, with a sense of new worlds opening up before me—all that. I even had a vision, one that seemed related to my vision in the Frontenacs' kitchen that day with Snowball years ago. This is it, the vision said to me: this is the way you want it to be. I thought of Humph, white-hatted behind his stove, and the vision said: you could do that, you could have that authority, you could wear that hat. There were those few seconds of complete certainty before the vision faded, leaving me in the middle of my sitting-room floor, on the old rag rug from Martha's mother's attic, with Julia Child's recipe for Apple Charlotte open on my lap and the sun rising out my window.

In the morning, yawning and bleary, I met Martha in that cavernous, inhospitable kitchen. She handed me a big white apron and said, dubiously, "You don't look rested, Cordelia." I could sense her thinking: temperamental hippie nut, stays up all night doing God knows what . . .

When I explained about Julia Child, she gave me one of her genuine (as opposed to polite) smiles, studied me the way Humph had when he decided I had salad hands, and pronounced, "I think I can do something with you." I realized

ultimate pointlessness of the extra time and trouble and expense that go into a really gorgeous meal. I can see the transience of it. And still I love it, the whole routine, from chopping and sautéing and whisking to watching people wolf it down. I should be able to say I cooked for Paul, knowing it was his beloved self I was learning to nourish, but this wouldn't be quite true. I cooked for the sake of cooking, and I took to it the way Juliet took to Greek.

Martha and I talked while we cooked. I told her about my family; her estimation of me went up visibly when she found out I was Jeremiah Miller's daughter. In turn, she reminisced about her childhood on her parents' Greenwich estate. Her life since then, however plush, had apparently been one long downhill slide. She liked to talk about her mother's cooks. There had been a Frenchwoman who was so thrifty she devised a dish out of steamed carrot tops and potato peelings. Another had enclosed everything in a pastry crust. "Even our breakfasts," Martha said. "We had poached eggs in little pastry nests, with sausages en croûte on the side. We kept expecting Wheatena in puff pastry. But she didn't last long. Mother was always firing her cooks. The odd thing is, she was a terrific cook herself, but she felt that a lady just didn't *do* her own cooking. But that's her generation—nowadays there are other reasons," she added, looking momentarily defensive.

But Martha was a lady in a sense of the word I hadn't realized existed outside of those old movies where the footman aspires to love above his station. She didn't have servants—at least, she never would have called Mrs. Frutchey and me her servants. We were "my cleaning woman" and "my mother's helper" (or, as I heard her refer to me on the phone once, "the girl who boards with us"). But we were servants, of course, and so were the endless procession of carpenters, handymen, plumbers, and gardeners who came at Martha's call, in their little vans, with their ladders and toolboxes. She ran her house the way God must run heaven. She was the big enchilada, and for all her graciousness and goodness, none of us was allowed to forget it.

It didn't take long for me to see that Paul was under her jurisdiction just as much as Joe Larkin, the gardener, or Mrs. Frutchey or me. He couldn't make a decision without her help. He couldn't pay the paperboy or have the hedges pruned or buy a shirt without consulting her. Neither of them seemed to consider this odd.

During those September weeks, when Paul and I were separated by Martha's dedication to shaping me into her *chef de cuisine*, I was able to look at the two of them with some objectivity. The short history of my romance with Paul (sunset/Grand'mère/sofa/Juliet's bed) was like a dream; what was real was the yellow house, and the marriage that lived in it.

It interested me to see Paul and Martha together. They were—what's a good word?—*chummy*. Comfy. Familiar with each other. I noted this with a sort of detached loneliness. They bickered a little, and in the course of these polite squabbles I sometimes saw hints of unexpressed furies—enough to make me believe that, deep down in their souls, they did hate each other. But I could see these tiny rips in the seams only because I was always looking for them. To an observer with less of a stake in it, I don't doubt that they seemed an ideal couple, as they had to Nina. They did, after all, live together, and had for fifteen years, in what looked like, not passionate commitment, perhaps, but peaceful friendship, anyway. I suppose that, most of the time, the hate got shelved behind the rest—books, house, kids, groceries, cars, the old photographs and jokes. I suppose it's the same when you live with someone you love for a long, long time. It's not on your mind all day, any more than hate is. It's too wearing, I suppose, and it takes time.

At first, watching the relationship between Paul and Martha was my chief interest, besides the cooking. And then, as September matured into October, I became distracted from it by the resumption of my affair with Paul.

Martha began to trust me in the kitchen. I had demonstrated, if nothing else, my ability to follow recipes, so she went back, gradually, to her old schedule of weaving classes and running and antique hunts and lunches in Hartford with her friends. She seemed glad to leave me there with a grocery list and a menu.

"You were her new toy," Paul said, in the ironic voice he reserved for talk of Martha. "The glamour is wearing off."

She was gone for longer and longer periods, and Paul and I were able to stop clutching each other for brief moments in the shop and stealing kisses while Martha was in the bathroom. We began making love, wherever we could, whenever Martha was out, and we became almost gruesomely efficient, adept at doing it in our clothes, on the floor, in haste—even when we weren't really in the mood. Once Paul had the flu when Martha was scheduled to be gone all afternoon, and we spent the hours in my bed, Paul feverish and lustful, leaping up to gulp water and returning to fling himself on me again.

Once we ran upstairs while the plumber banged on pipes in the cellar. Another time, we had our clothes half off and our legs wrapped around each other halfway up my steep, narrow staircase before we realized, laughing, the impossibility of making love there and dragged each other to the top and did it on the floor. When the opportunity came, we took it. I won't say the urgency that always hung over us spoiled our lovemaking. Sometimes it was part of the fun. We were perfectly happy together, every time—at least, that's how I remember it. But the shadow of Martha was there. We were like prisoners given time off for recreation—for the time was given to us, it wasn't ours to take. If Martha hadn't gone out lunching or running, we couldn't have met. The amount of time we had, whether we would be able to lie in bed and talk or be forced to rush into our clothes and get back to work—the quality, duration, and frequency of our lovemaking—all depended on Martha.

He talked about her, too, more and more. "Did you ever think she might have a lover?" I asked Paul once, hesitantly, when Martha had gone out, all dressed up, for a day in Hartford.

"I wish she did, but she doesn't."

"How do you know?"

"Martha wouldn't want a lover."

I didn't press him to explain. I didn't want to seem nosy about his private life with Martha. Eventually, I learned that this discretion was a mistake: he longed to talk about it. As soon as I caught on to this, I listened. I even probed. I can't say I didn't want to know; I did, and though I dreaded his revelations, I ached to hear them. I had to know what I was up against.

"Martha thinks sex is messy," he told me during one of these confessional sessions. "She's told me that plenty of times. She says even taking a shower afterward doesn't make her feel clean. The stuff pours out of her for two days—that's what she said."

It was impossible to imagine the immaculate Martha reveling in sex the way Paul and I did, and I couldn't help feeling superior to her because of this, though I could easily imagine what a slut she would have thought me for enjoying it so easily and so gladly. I poured out my soul for Paul in our lovemaking, to make it up to him for all those cold years with Martha, and part of the joy I felt in the happiness I brought him was my triumph over her.

Paul told me I was his savior. I asked him what I'd saved him from.

"A living death," he said dramatically. "I wish I could tell you how I felt, Delia, when I looked out my front door and saw you on the grass with the dogs, and the sunset behind you. You looked—you looked—"

"Like Jesus?" I laughed, remembering my image of him.

"Don't laugh," he said.

Sometimes, in the evenings, Martha would be weaving (whuffle, *wham*, whuffle, *wham*—I'd hear the faint beat of her loom), and Paul would be working down in the shop, and upstairs from him, in my sitting room, where I pored over my coin albums or re-read Julia Child, I could sense the force of his feeling mounting up through the floorboards with the heat from his little wood stove.

"You're like a loaf of fresh-baked bread," he told me once. He used to push back my bangs from my face and hold my head between his hands or stroke my skin with his fingertips while he came up with his outrageous similes. "You're like the luscious little grapes that used to grow in our back yard when I was a kid."

"You're like a truffle," I teased him. I told him how my father used to compare me to trees and things.

"I wish I were a poet," he said, with his beautiful, sly smile.

"God forbid!" I exclaimed, as he knew I would.

I was happy with him, always, but in a suspended, temporary kind of way. I never believed for a minute that what we were living was real life. That would come eventually, and I had no trouble seeing it: the big bed we would share, the rack with both our toothbrushes on it, his kids visiting on weekends, the memories and snapshots. I had vague dreams of a restaurant/bookshop combo.

I could hardly wait.

And yet the waiting had its own excitements. I loved, for example, to take him his lunch at the shop when he was working, and watch him turn over fragile old pages with his strong fingers, or go reverently through the cartons of junk people were always bringing him. I never knew how profitable Paul's business was, and whether it was more of a money-making proposition or a hobby, but he did know his stuff. This impressed me, as competence always does. I used to sit (on his lap, if Martha and the kids were safely out) and listen to him talk on the phone to his endless, avid list of book fanciers, snuggling into his shoulder while he amorously, absently caressed my thigh. Learning as I was how Martha commanded him, every masterful deal, every brilliant and lucrative find was a relief to me as well as a pleasure to him.

I got to like the bookshop. Paul's shelves of books didn't

weigh me down as my parents' houseful did. I didn't consider
them my persecutors. They were merely scenery, a backdrop
for my beloved Paul, who opened them only to make a living,
and whose chosen recreation was the same as mine: a TV
set, someone to watch it with, and a platter of cheese and
crackers.

The three of us, in fact, used to watch television together
in the evenings if there was nothing else to do. Nina was
wrong about the armoire—the set was placed quite openly on
a pine chest—but she was right about the back room, a little
nook off the dining room where the TV, the newspapers, the
Monopoly game, and Martha's basket of needlework were
kept. Martha was snobbish about what we watched; she preferred BBC imports on public TV. I have no objection to
them myself, but they often didn't come in very well, and it
was one of Paul and Martha's running arguments: would you
rather watch a dim and hazy *Masterpiece Theater* or a crystal-
clear *Kojak?* Paul preferred clarity, Martha culture. Culture
usually won, and we watched thirteen episodes of *Upstairs/
Downstairs* without ever being sure who in the large, fuzzy
cast was who.

Paul and I sat, invariably, on the small and aptly named
loveseat together, tingling with the forbidden nearness, while
Martha embroidered in the wing chair, her wools and canvas
a statement of her superiority to mere TV. It was a seating
arrangement she herself dictated. I wondered sometimes, I
wonder still, how much she knew. It seems impossible to me
that the heat Paul and I generated wasn't perceptible to as
seasoned an observer as a wife, but she never gave a sign.
That was Martha's strength, though—her ability not to let on.
(It was also, I believe, her weakness.) It seemed at times that
she threw us together. I occasionally had the unsavory notion
that she had hired me as Paul's mistress first and cook second.
And yet she seemed, genuinely, to like me. Flashes of real
comradeship penetrated that Amy Vanderbilt personality. I
could swear she liked me—*almost* swear it . . . no, I would

never swear it, or anything about Martha. I just don't know. Somewhere inside Martha was a closed-up little nut of truth that no one will ever get at, and inside it is—among other things—the real reason why she chose the wing chair, leaving the loveseat to Paul and me.

I think Mrs. Frutchey, the cleaning woman, knew about us. She and I used to have a cup of coffee together most mornings while she told me about her car troubles, husband troubles, sister-in-law troubles, stomach troubles. Mrs. Frutchey seemed to sail her whole life on a sea of troubles, and they never rocked her. She told them to me always in the same competent, unperturbable way, whether they involved her husband's drinking or the muffler on her Valiant. She had lovely, mild brown eyes and a thin face without wrinkles, and she always put six heaping spoonfuls of sugar in her coffee.

We usually talked about her concerns—my life, God knows, compared with hers, was like a cup of chicken broth compared to a six-course meal at Troisgros. But one day she looked me straight in the eye and said, "Delia, there's a lot going on in this house, isn't there?" I looked as vacant as I could. "You know what I mean," she said. I felt a blush coming on, and I gave an ill-at-ease, deprecating snicker. "I'm not here to approve or disapprove," Mrs. Frutchey said. "But I warn you, she's not a woman I'd want to tangle with, myself."

She never said any more about it, but every time I saw her after that, I wondered: how did she know? I wished I had asked her, but to ask would have been to admit. But what did we do or leave undone, I asked myself, that Mrs. Frutchey cottoned to? I had to conclude, finally, that because Mrs. Frutchey was black, and poor, and genuine, she picked up vibes that were closed to anyone as white and rich and phony as Martha.

I've said very little about the children or the dogs, and yet Megan and Ian, Albert and Victoria were large presences in my life. Megan and Ian were graceless, nervous children, accustomed to their mother's formal semi-neglect but not well adjusted to it, by which I mean that they didn't complain but they weren't happy. Megan was prone to sullenness, Ian to fits of temper, and both of them could be vicious when they thought they were unobserved—kicking each other, snatching toys, teasing. Once I caught Megan making a horrible face at me when I told her it was hair-washing night (Megan had long, thick, snarly hair), and twice she bit me. Ian had a tendency to wet the bed. I was with the children a lot, though my duties with them didn't actually amount to much—just the baths, really, and rounding up Ian's various stuffed animals before bed.

And telling Megan stories. I tried reading to her at first because that's what Martha told me to do, but I found out quickly that she hated being read to as much as I hated reading. The books, she said—indicating with disdain her full shelves—were too full of people. She liked books about *only children*, she told me, with a disgusted look toward Ian's room, where we could hear the *Sesame Street* records he preferred to fall asleep to. Megan also liked concocting her own ingredients for stories; like her mother, she needed to run things.

"I wish there was a book about a beautiful princess who lives all by herself on a desert island with only her puppy," she said to me one night after our usual halfhearted tussle with Mrs. Piggle-Wiggle. So I told her a story about a beautiful shipwrecked princess and her puppy. It became a ritual with us: she gave me the recipe and I cooked up the tale. I feel silly admitting what a pleasure these stories were to me, and that I grew fond of Megan the way an actress is fond of her audience—the way my father loves his public. I never much liked Ian; he struck me as a mean, solitary little boy, and he didn't like me, either. But I was flattered by Megan's respect for my storytelling, and it formed a good-enough basis for our friendship.

"Delia tells the best stories," she said smugly to her mother one day.

"Delia does?" Martha asked in undisguised surprise. I

shrugged and tried to look modest. "Stories about what?" She seemed really to want to know—I suppose to be sure I wasn't corrupting Megan or teaching her bad manners.

"Everything," Megan said with her know-it-all air that I found so irritating when it was directed at me. "Beautiful princesses, and witches, and creepy monsters."

"My goodness," Martha murmured, visibly losing interest. She was separating eggs. Megan gave her a look that would have meant no dessert and an early bedtime if Martha had seen it.

Actually, all our stories gradually fell into one pattern: the beautiful, persecuted princess is forced by her cruel tormentors into solitude of one sort or another, where—though she is sad and lonely at first—she gets to like her banishment and meets up with an animal who becomes her loyal friend. The persecutors ranged from witches and creepy monsters to cruel queens and mean stepmothers, and she was driven to a series of isolated castles, humble huts, desert islands, and enchanted woods, where she found happiness with (in order of preference) puppies, cats, cows, ponies, and butterflies. My stories were brisk and simple, each about fifteen minutes long. I would wind up at 8:30 sharp, tuck in the covers, and say good night—deliberately not kissing her. She never asked me to, merely said, "Good night, Delia—don't let the bedbugs bite" (a line she found ceaselessly, quietly humorous). I would say we had a strange but mutually satisfying relationship. Will she grow up to think of me, I wonder, as a sort of Mary Poppins? More likely, she won't remember me at all.

Megan and I both liked Jay Block's dairy farm down the road. If I had dinner under control, we often took a walk there in the late afternoon at milking time, past the little woods, over the creek, up the Blocks' driveway to the old red barn (now used as a garage) and beyond it to the new concrete structure Nina had objected to. There we could watch Mr. Block's beautiful Holsteins hooked up to the milking machines—and Mr. Block himself, along with his two thug-

gish, restless sons, supervising the operation and talking, endlessly, milk yields and feed prices.

Mr. Block used to say things like: "There was a time when
a cow could get by producing two thousand quarts a year—
say twenty-five hundred. Back when I first got into this business, after the war. Now she's got to produce fifteen, eighteen
thousand."

Mr. Block was a tall, bald, weathered man who loved cows.
He knew every one of his herd by name, and he claimed every
cow he'd ever owned had a unique personality.

"There's a cow out in Nebraska," Mr. Block told us once.
"She produces over twenty thousand quarts a year, regular.
Now *there's* a cow. You see," he said to Megan, "the whole
point is fewer cows making more milk. That way you get
fewer farmers. You understand that?"

Megan nodded sagely.

"Well, I'm damned if I do!" he cried, slapping the nearest
cow on the rump. The cow turned and looked at him—fondly
or balefully, it was hard to tell. "But I'm not getting out of
this business," he said with decision. "Knock wood"—but
there was none to knock. "You won't find a nicer animal than
a cow." His sons stood by with dubious, embarrassed looks
on their faces. Mr. Block looked me in the eye challengingly.
"They'll have to carry me out of here with my toes turned
up."

All around us, as he talked, was the steamy straw-and-ferti-
lizer smell of cows, the sound of their gentle chewing, and the
noise of the milking machines. I loved it there. I also liked
the meadow, where, while the autumn weather held, the
cows wandered all day at their eternal munching—scrubby
rolling acres bisected by the stream, a cow's paradise. I took the
dogs down sometimes after lunch. They were unexpectedly
wonderful with the cows. Even excitable Albert became calm
and docile, lapping water and then flinging himself into a nap
at my feet. The cows paid no attention to any of us, and on
warm Indian summer days we all went to sleep there—dogs

and me—lulled by the cows' *crunch-slobber-crunch* and the *flop-flop* of manure deposits and the occasional gentle moos. As a cook, I was enchanted by their need to keep eating.

"Their business is to eat," Mr. Block said once, proudly. "Fifty pounds a day of high-protein grain, fifty pounds of alfalfa, and all the grass they can handle."

"They're born with a hunger that's never satisfied," one of the sons surprised me by saying—surprised his father, too.

"Well, that's a real nice way to put it, Ralphie," he said, obviously wondering if there wasn't more to his boy than he'd suspected.

Ralphie Block waylaid me once in the meadow and asked me to go to the movies with him. He was stringy and blond, already balding on top, and he looked like he belonged in black leather, on a motorcycle—though as far as I know he was a devoted dairyman, with regular habits and a shelf-full of 4-H trophies. He took my refusal as if he'd expected it, beginning to nod understandingly before I'd finished my lame excuse— so that I wondered if he knew about me and Paul. Maybe he'd seen us through a window, and the movie invitation was the beginning of blackmail. (The slimy phantom of Malcolm Madox hovered in the air before me.) Or maybe he was going to go right home and work on his anonymous communication to Martha, clipping letters of the alphabet out of *Farm Journal* to form his accusations with.

As the weeks went by, I had thoughts like that more and more. During my long afternoons alone in the kitchen preparing our elaborate dinners, I wondered about such things. Did anyone know? Did Martha know? And, like a bubble that's getting bigger and bigger but hasn't yet broken, the question: why doesn't Paul tell her? What was he waiting for?

The bubble broke on Thanksgiving Day. But first the dogs. I have to tell about the dogs, Victoria and Albert, and what a continual joy they were to me.

I had always wanted a dog, but my sisters' allergies had prevented it. Now I had two, and whenever I was bored or lonely or just plain full of beans, I went outside with them and romped. They were wonderful dogs, amiable and smart and generous; in return for a small investment (two minutes of stick throwing, say, or a dog biscuit, or a couple of pats on the flank) they were your slaves for life, and no questions asked.

Everyone in the family, I think, depended on the dogs for this ungrudging love. That peaceful country house was full of tensions (I suppose every house is), and the dogs were one release from them. Martha took them on her runs; Megan romped with them first thing off the school bus; Ian would roll around the yard with them after one of his terrible tantrums, and come in soothed. And Paul loved them. Until I came, they were all he had, he told me. I never really understood Paul's distance from his children, or what he meant when he said Megan and Ian were all Martha's. He was stern with them, with a confused affection that he seemed to be able to demonstrate only by tickling: his tickling of the children was a solemn and important ritual, regularly insisted on by both the kids. But his relationship with the dogs was deeper and more meaningful to him.

"They never judge," he said one day when we had taken them for a run. We were standing, panting a little, in the grove of trees by the creek, and Paul hugged me (riskily) and said, "Neither do you, Delia. I'm so grateful for that. You accept, you just accept." I felt bad, because it wasn't really true—I was beginning to judge and to question and to be dissatisfied. When I kissed him and clung to him, in love and remorse, he pulled away and said, "Let's go upstairs"— thinking of the Blocks down the road, the gardener due any minute. Resentment filled me. When will it end? How will it end? Don't we love each other? Why don't you do something about this? The judgmental questions beat in my head as we trudged back to the house and the dogs frisked loyally around us. Well, I can't help it, I said to myself, watching Paul fondle them. I'm not a dog.

"I love you," I said, and he turned from the dogs and—

drawing me inside—began to fondle me instead. But the questions didn't go away.

Martha's mother was invited for Thanksgiving dinner. I was looking forward to meeting her, and to showing off my skills. With Martha's help, I had boned a whole turkey and was serving it stuffed with chestnuts and raisins and crumbs.

"Cordelia has taken to all this incredibly quickly, Mother," I had heard Martha say on the phone. "She's a natural cook." I grinned to myself with pride until I figured out that, of course, she knew I could hear her and was psyching me up for the big feast. But maybe she meant it.

On the morning of Thanksgiving I was in the kitchen when I heard a car horn honk and the squeal of tires and loud barking. I ran for the door—I knew Ian was outside somewhere—and was just in time to see a car speed away down the road, and a woolly heap in the gravel: Albert, with his skull crushed and his long nose covered with blood.

Paul and Martha weren't far behind me, and then the kids. I tried to motion them back. "Don't—don't," I said. "He's dead, he's done for." I didn't want the kids to see, or Paul, and I was untying my apron to put over the body, but Paul ran up and knelt beside it. He put his hand on Albert's still flank, and then he looked up and down the road for the car that had done it, and then he went to pieces.

He stood up and staggered, weeping, his face distorted. I hardly knew his face, it looked like an old man's. He went blindly to Martha, and she put her arms around him, motioning to me to take the kids inside. I stood stunned, watching Paul's shoulders shake and hearing him sob. Megan and Ian turned and ran, crying, toward the house—horrified more by their father's grief than by the dead dog by the road.

I knelt by Albert and put my apron over him—the blood was already drying on his muzzle, and had settled in clotting pools in the hollows of his broken skull—and then I followed the children. No one paid any attention to Vicky, but her frantic barking, with a little question at the end of each yelp, was all around us.

Inside, I cuddled Megan. I had never before so much as hugged her, and I was astonished at how fragile a bundle she was—a butterfly of a child. "Albert liked me, didn't he, Delia?" she kept asking, and I kept saying yes. Ian had gone upstairs, after yelling at me to get away from him. After a while, Martha came in.

"Paul's gone to get a shovel. He's going to bury him out by the creek," she said, her face red from holding back tears. I told Martha she'd better see to Ian. There was a crash from above, and she ran to the stairs, wiping her nose on her sleeve.

Megan pulled away from me, and climbed slowly after her mother, and I went back outside. Victoria was still barking beside the body of her puppy. She had nosed the apron off his crushed head. I tried to pull her away and she growled, but when I knelt to pick Albert up she let me; that was what she'd been wanting. He was a big, heavy dog, but, dead, he seemed very light—as if death was nothing, living was all. I carried him easily across the brown grass to the creek, where I could see Paul digging, and Vicky trotted behind. Across the road, in the distance, were the cows as usual. I thought of Albert's docility with them, and of all the stories I'd told Megan in which a good-hearted puppy was a pivotal character, and tears came to my eyes, blurring the scene.

I set Albert down on the dead leaves by the creek and pulled Vicky to me. "It's okay, Vic, it's okay," I whispered to her. But she sat rigidly, paying no attention, watching Paul.

Paul didn't look at me until the hole was finished. He started out in a wool jacket, a sweater, and a shirt, but by the time he was done he'd shed everything but the shirt. It took him a while, though the ground wasn't frozen yet and was particularly soft down by the water. But he dug deep, and I could see that from time to time he was still crying. Vicky and I sat beside Albert's body and waited. I noticed closely—perhaps Vicky did, too—that the sun coming through the leafless trees made the icy water sparkle, and that the deep, mucky hole looked cold. Finally, Paul scooped out the last shovelful and turned to me.

"Do you want to put him in?"

I hesitated. "Don't you?"

"Don't you see I can't touch him?" His glasses were all wet, but he didn't bother to dry them, just looked at me hopelessly through his tears.

I gathered Albert up and carried him to his grave, wrapping the bloody apron closer around him. I tried to be gentle, but it was a long way down, and I had to let him drop the last couple of inches. I reached in and smoothed the apron and then, without a word, took the shovel and filled in the hole. It occurred to me that there should have been a ceremony, a velvet-lined box, a hymn, but there was only Vicky whimpering beside me, and Paul turned away with his hands in his pockets, and the mucky dirt.

When I finished, I leaned on the shovel and said, "He must have been chasing it. Damn those people—didn't even stop."

Paul had dried off his glasses on his flapping shirttail. "Poor old Albert," he said unsteadily, and we started back to the house. Vicky hesitated, and began to paw at the grave—just tentatively, as if waiting for instructions—and Paul went over to her. "Come on, old girl," he said gently. He put out his hand, and she licked it and followed us. As we came out of the trees into the bright, cold sunshine, Paul stopped. "I'm sorry," he said, and his voice was stretched thin. "I'm sorry to carry on like this. But I loved that dog." I began an understanding murmur, but he raised a hand to stop me. "And I'm sorry I—I had to hold someone, and I obviously couldn't go to you."

"Don't even think about it, Paul," I said. "It doesn't matter." But the memory of Martha's arms around him was as strong as the memory of Albert's dead body, and I think my voice must have lacked conviction, because Paul said, "These things take time, Delia."

His words were like something out of a movie about some pampered, philandering husband who wants everything and doesn't have the guts to make choices. They made our relationship look cheap and ordinary, especially after the shock of

Albert's accident, and the tears, and the burial. I hated his excuses. I hated him for talking about it like that—for talking about it at all—and I felt briefly lit up and glowing with rage. I said, "I don't have all that much time."

A little snort of bitter laughter out of the same movie. "Delia, you're twenty-two!"

"There's a lot I want to do, Paul. I'll be gone from here eventually," I said brutally. "I can't stay around forever, taking cooking lessons and being nanny to your kids."

"Nobody's talking about forever, Delia."

"Well, how long, then, Paul?" I immediately realized the question wasn't fair, but I didn't take it back.

"I don't know, I don't know, I don't know," he said in a low, miserable mumble, staring at the ground. The sun lit up, as always, the silver in his hair. I remember how elderly he had looked to me earlier. Now he looked like himself. If we hadn't been in full view of the house, and if little lights of rage hadn't still been flickering inside me, I would have put my arms around him, dragged him down on the hard brown earth . . .

"I wish I were in that grave with Albert," he said.

It didn't soften me. "Stop it, Paul!" I snapped at him. His words struck me as self-indulgent and babyish. I wondered, with a shock, if I could really love him after all, thinking those things about him. "Don't talk like that," I said, trying not to sound merely irritable.

"I don't deserve you, Delia. It's that simple."

"Stop it, please. Let's not talk about it. This is no time. Let's get this damned day over with, Paul. We can talk another time." My voice died out wearily. I just didn't have the energy. I thought: I've got that huge dinner ahead of me to cook and serve and clean up after. I thought of all the potatoes I still had to peel, and the limp turkey to stuff, and the green beans to snap, and the artichokes to wrestle with. I started toward the house. Vicky ran ahead, and Paul trailed behind me. We were like some dreary tail end of a parade.

That was a horrible day, that Thanksgiving. The sun went

behind a cloud, and a cold wind sprang up and found its way through every crack in that old house. The kids were alternately weepy and rowdy and sulky. Vicky whined and whined, and got underfoot. Martha and I kept crying furtively, at odd moments. Paul seemed all cried out, but he was touchy and withdrawn, watching football games on TV and yelling at the kids to pipe down. By the time Martha's mother showed up in her Mercedes at 4:00, all anyone wanted was to crawl off somewhere alone and sleep.

But Mrs. Lambert wanted to drink sherry with us—me included, insisting that I sit down, take a break, have a drink. In fact, she paid more attention to me than she did to Paul, whom she treated as a sort of trusted, valuable underfootman, sending false, sparkly smiles in his direction when he took her coat and brought her drink, but hardly ever looking at him directly or speaking to him.

She wanted to talk about "our tragedy," as she called it. "Have you discussed it with the children, Martha?" she asked, throwing off her mink and patting her snow-white upsweep. She looked exactly like Martha—same eyes, nose, chin, but all slipped down a notch. She wore rings on four out of ten fingers, and she had an expensive, powdery, little-old-lady smell. "Have you had a good, thorough talk about it?"

When Martha said no, they hadn't really discussed it much, the children hadn't seemed to want to quite yet Mrs. Lambert said, "Well, don't you think you should, darling? You can't just *encourage* them to repress their feelings."

It was somehow obvious, from the loud deliberateness of her voice and the tense set of Martha's shoulders, that this kind of talk was new to Mrs. Lambert, and had been adopted as a harmless way to make herself seem younger and modern. Martha had obviously been brought up to repress her feelings. It also became clear to me why Martha had married the son of an Italian butcher instead of the lawyer or stockbroker her mother would certainly have preferred. (Martha's long-dead father had, I knew, been a stockbroker, and both her sisters were married to corporation lawyers.) When I met Mrs. Lambert, I felt an immediate increase in sympathy with Martha. In her own way, she had defied her parents just as I had defied mine. Paul was her Danny.

Mrs. Lambert got Megan on her lap and began to talk about what a good dog Albert had been, and how much they would all miss him. She talked about the death of her old dog Roger, a golden retriever, when she had been just Megan's age, and how she had cried. Megan listened miserably, overflowing with silent tears, and, when she could, she slipped down and ran upstairs. "There," her grandmother said, resuming the sipping of her sherry. She had apparently given up on Ian, who was in his room listening to records. "I do think it's better to bring these things out in the open."

Martha just sat there, tight-lipped, smoothing the skirt of her beige wool dress and tapping her matching shoes together, until Mrs. Lambert changed the subject to the vagaries of her gardener, and Martha joined in gladly, with relief that she could stop disapproving. She liked her mother, I could tell, and would rather please her than fight. At sixty, she would be her exact replica.

I excused myself—though I would have liked to hear their discussion—and returned to the kitchen. The turkey wasn't getting done fast enough, and I kept basting it and checking the thermometer, and then worrying that all the opening of the oven door was slowing it down. Paul wandered in and out, from football games to family. He had to pass through the kitchen to do so.

"I *am* sorry, Delia," he said to me a couple of times, and once he came close to me and whispered, "I need to be alone with you. I need to put my arms around you." I don't know if this was part of his apology for crying on Martha. "We've got to talk."

"Well, I don't really know how we're going to manage that!" I said in a voice that was probably too loud and certainly too snappish. But I was frazzled. Martha's elaborate menu had me insecurely tackling things I'd never attempted before. While Martha was sipping sherry and talking about the servant problem with her mother, I was trying to get everything to be done at the same time, and worrying about unmolding the oeufs en gelée—my first aspic—without melting the top and ruining the turkey design I'd made with egg yolk and truffles and pimento and carrot strips. I kept feeling like crying; my head hurt; I thought I might be coming down with something; and I was afraid everything was over between Paul and me.

He retreated from me, looking hurt. I brooded about him, and our conversation that morning, through the rest of my dinner preparations. "These things take time," he had said. But he had also said it wouldn't take forever. Where, between *time* and *forever*, was the point at which he would leave Martha? I considered giving him an ultimatum. I considered giving Martha notice. I even considered just giving up, and made a short mental list of the two ways of giving up that were open to me:

1. calling off our affair
2. leaving things exactly as they were

At it turned out, I didn't do any of these things. But all during that dreadful day, I thought I would have to choose one of them, and they whirled in my head. If I could, I would have abandoned the aspic and turkey and potatoes and green beans and artichoke hearts and tarte normande and gone up to Chez Cordelia and made feverish lists. I headed them mentally:

What's Wrong with This Situation?
What Did I Ever See in Him?
Where Can I Go from Here?

All questions, all uncertainty. And poor Albert dead and in his grave.

Vicky stayed with Paul, following him from room to room and, at dinner, by special dispensation, lying under his chair. Her occasional human-sounding whinnies of pain punctuated our meal—always with that pathetic question mark at the end, as if she hadn't quite grasped it yet, or still had hope that Albert would return. Every time she did it I had to blink back tears.

The meal, in spite of everything, came out pretty well. The pommes Anna were browned a little too much on top. One corner of the aspic stuck to the mold, but the children clapped their hands at the turkey decoration on top; it seemed to cheer them up. Mrs. Lambert was full of enthusiasm for the food. For a fashionably thin woman, she had an enormous appetite—or perhaps she was trying to set us all a healthy-minded example. Paul was silent, but he ate a lot, endearing himself to me all over again, but not enough for me to send him a smile or a word. Martha and her mother did all the talking, discussing in detail this dinner, past dinners, restaurants they'd been to, and restaurants they planned to go to. I heard more stories about Mrs. Lambert's cooks, and she asked me polite questions about my illustrious parents. She had all my father's books.

"They must be missing you on a family holiday like Thanksgiving," Mrs. Lambert said. She had a large smile that always looked ready for the photographer, and her teeth were either false or fabulous.

"Well, I wanted to do the dinner," I said.

"It's her midterm exam, Mother," Martha laughed. "A-minus, Cordelia. You did very nicely." She had left a little pile of overbrowned potato on her plate, I noticed when I cleaned up.

Over dessert and coffee, the conversation turned to my restaurant ambitions.

"Your own little place, Cordelia!" cried Mrs. Lambert. "Why, what a delightful idea. You remember Elsa Rolfe, Martha. She opened up that place in New York. Oh, it was a

fast skittering of Vicky's big paws. I felt my cheeks burn hot—
or had they been burning all the time? I hid my notebook
under the bed, and when Paul came in, I held out my arms
to him.

He got into bed with me and we held each other. Vicky lay
with a sigh across the bed at our feet.

"I'm going to leave her, Delia," Paul said. "Soon. This can't
go on. I can't stand it, I want to be with you, I don't want to
lose you, I love you . . ."

The words clicked neatly into my brain. I felt I could
support myself on their strong webbing, I felt that if I were
falling they would hold me up, I imagined myself falling . . .

"Delia, you're burning up with fever," Paul said, releasing
me. He sat beside me and put his cool hand on my forehead.
I smiled drowsily at him, and then I leaned over the side of
the bed and threw up my Thanksgiving dinner.

It was flu, of course—some bug that was chic just then in
the New England area. I lay in a hot, dry haze of happiness
for two days. My knees ached, and I couldn't eat, and my
skin felt bruised and ticklish all over. After the fever broke, I
sweated for the next two days; Martha and Paul brought me
ginger ale and bendable straws, and laid cold, wet cloths on
my head. I was so happy the whole time that I was almost
sorry when, on the fifth day, I woke up feeling recovered.

But the happiness remained. I threw myself into my cooking, into my love for Paul, into life itself. Paul and I didn't
refer to his leaving Martha. We didn't need to. I knew it
would come, that he was plotting his way, and I waited with
a new, confident, loving patience that found its way into our
lovemaking: it became slow and secure and lazy, and we spent
huge chunks of time entwined on my bed, smiling into each
other's eyes.

Winter came, harsher than it had been down on the shore,
and the stretch of snow out the kitchen window, sloping back
to the silvery woods, seemed to me magnificently beautiful.
And, with a space heater installed to take the chill off, my

two rooms were a ceaseless pleasure. I felt pleasantly enclosed up there, and safe. I didn't need to dread Danny's return. He would never find me, never think to look for me in such a setting. (*Cordelia* in a *bookshop?*) I was happy in Chez Cordelia—happiest when I had Paul to warm my bed, but happy on my own, too. I had my old shop bookcase back again; I'd missed it, and had my mother bring it to me. It sat beside my bed, with cookbooks piled on top. I read them at night before sleep, the way I know some people read their Bibles.

I saw my parents off and on. They drove up to visit, crossing the state south to north to check up on their youngest— always separately because one had to stay home with Juliet, and always with a strange shyness in their manner that I found endearing. It meant they were both beginning to comprehend my apartness from them after all these years. With comprehension would come, I hoped, acceptance. For the moment, at least, they stopped nagging me.

Usually, my mother took me out somewhere for lunch if she came on my day off, but on one of her visits she and I had tea up in my sitting room. She looked in a bewildered way at the tray when I set it down (china pot, two delicate cups, silver spoons, a little plate of cookies), and then she looked at me. "I never would have expected this of you, Cordelia," she said, and, trying to elaborate, she became oddly incoherent: "Linen napkins, tea leaves, this wallpaper, that nice shop downstairs . . ."

"Oh, it's all the Lambertis', Mom," I said cheerfully. I knew she was contrasting this tea-serving Cordelia with the one who drank beer and entertained poker players in a tacky high rise. "It's not really *me*."

"Well, what *is* you, Cordelia?" she asked me. It was a sincere question. I suppose it was partly Juliet's illness and Miranda's commune and Horatio's irresponsibility; I could see her wondering if she had ever really known any of her children. "What *is* really you?" she repeated, and the confused look on her face meant that she knew she was starting from nothing, and that whatever I said would be something she didn't expect.

"I can get along anywhere," I said, trying to give her something solid and true to latch on to. It wasn't easy. I like to figure other people out, but I'm not really an expert on myself. Also, I felt the basic untruth behind my words: the one place I hadn't been able to get along very well was at home. But I went ahead, doing my best. "It doesn't really have a lot to do with *me*, where I settle in. I was happy eating canned beans with Danny, and I'm happy doing French cooking here. Not that I could ever go back to canned beans," I added hastily. Or Danny, I thought but didn't say. "I mean, I've learned to make a really good cassoulet—actually, it's my own version, crossed with Boston baked beans. I put in just a hint of molasses and I leave out the sausage—" I saw my mother getting irritated, so I went back to the subject, but it was difficult for me.

"I guess I've just been searching around," I said lamely, and then revised. "What I mean is that I think I'm progressing all the time, toward—" I got my vision again, and I put down my teacup and caught my mother's two hands in my hands. If it was time to be frank, I would be frank. "I want to have my own restaurant, Mom. Own it, and be the chef. Not now, not even soon—maybe when I'm thirty or so. When I've learned more. I want a place, a very small place, where everything I serve is perfect, just perfect, but not, you know, the kind of food that scares people. Not a lot of fancy stuff. Good, nourishing, delicious, sensible, gorgeous food. The kind of place where people go on their lunch hour but where they go at night, too, if they want a special meal. And I'd set up my kitchen just the way I like it, maybe I'd have just one helper, and I'd cook in small quantities, and every day have something really interesting, really special on the menu—"

My mother had been listening patiently, nodding and smiling, but finally she interrupted. "That's a very nice ambition," she said. "A little restaurant. Maybe unrealistic—well, who knows? But, Cordelia, who you are isn't what you *do*. You can't define yourself by what you decide to cook for dinner."

"No, but . . ." I let go her hands and thought for a minute while my mother picked up a cookie and munched on it.

"Did you make these?"

"No. I haven't gotten to pastry yet, really."

She seemed willing to drop the subject of Cordelia, but I wanted to finish. "I thought I could. I mean, I thought Cordelia the chef would be enough."

"Oh, Cordelia."

"Well, I mean, the part that shows, the part you can talk about. I'm all right inside, I've just had to get my outside straight."

She gave a sigh, and smiled fondly at me. "Honey, let's drop it." Then the smile faded, though the fondness remained. "Oh, Cordelia, I wish you read more. There are so many areas we can't communicate about." She was really distressed. I thought what a shame it was, her dependence on books. I suppose she was thinking of some poem or something about finding the real you, and that if she could only quote it to me, and I recognized it, all would be well.

"I read cookbooks," I said.

Her eyes brightened. "You do?" she said, with such hope that I had to laugh, seeing behind her question a sort of domino theory: first cookbooks, then . . . ? ? ? . . . until I was slumped in a chair like Juliet, reading Greek.

To give her credit, she laughed, too, and we began to talk about something else—Juliet. In fact, my mother had an astonishing piece of news. My father's prophetic wish had come true: Juliet was seeing a lot of Professor Oliver—Ivan, my mother called him.

"But he's married!" I said. I was shocked, but my mother explained that he had left his wife—or his wife had left him, she wasn't sure. A divorce was in the works. I was still shocked. Every dissolved marriage I hear about grieves me, the way news of any upheaval—war, earthquake, death—grieves me. And at the same time, somewhere in my head was the flip side of that grief: I imagined myself telling Paul about Mr. Oliver and his wife. I would drop it casually, drawing no moral, but it would be another assault on the wall of his marriage, and a hefty one.

"It's so wonderful," my mother said. "We can trust her with Ivan—such a good man. He takes her to the movies, they go to concerts at Yale. Being with him seems to calm her. Of course, she has a long way to go," my mother added cautiously, as if too much confidence would break the spell. She also told me that she'd seen in the *Times* that Alan was having a play produced off-Broadway. "I don't want Juliet to know," my mother said. "I don't want her ever to think about that awful man again."

I thought how unfair it was, that awful Alan had managed not only to finish his play after walking out on Juliet, but to get someone to put it on. "Just like him," I said to my mother. "To write plays. So he can push people around and get away with it."

"Why, that's a good point," she said warmly, and looked at me the same way she did when I said I read cookbooks, as if there might be hope for me after all.

On an impulse, I invited the whole crew of them to Christmas dinner. It was Martha's idea, really. She and Paul and the kids were going to Greenwich for the holidays. Her mother put on an awesome spread at Christmas that included not only roast goose and a case of champagne and three kinds of pie, but a huge tree lit with candles, and presents for the grandchildren that tended toward life-size rocking horses and eight-room dollhouses with electric lights. She expected her three daughters and their families to be on hand.

"Why don't you invite your family here for the day?" Martha suggested. "Show them what you can do. Or a friend? Whatever you like, Cordelia. I'd love to see you have a little social life." She was beginning to worry about me, just as Juliet and Alan had. No girlfriends, no boyfriends, solitary Cordelia . . .

There was no question of my going to Greenwich with them, however.

I invited the whole family, and in a few days it was all arranged. On Christmas Day, the family would assemble at Lamb House Books: my parents and Juliet, Miranda, Horatio, and Aunt Phoebe. Gradually, the list expanded to include Mr. Oliver, Miranda's friend Annamay, and my aunt's new beau, whose name was Preston Maguire.

I had missed Aunt Phoebe. Recently, we had taken to telephoning each other, both of us determined to ease the mild estrangement that had grown up when Danny abandoned me and my aunt kept trying to fix me up. Every time I heard her soft, precise, sympathetic voice on the phone, I felt like telling her about Paul, but I controlled the impulse, seeing it as a childish ploy to get my aunt to mother me—to pour all my troubles into her narrow but receptive lap.

But I also resisted it because the situation between Paul and me was still so half-baked. I knew the triangular setup at Lamb House Books would sound bizarre and unhealthy, even to my liberal aunt, and I wanted to be able to say something like "His divorce will be final April thirteenth . . ."

Failing that, I talked to my aunt about apples, about Juliet and Miranda, about resuming our moviegoing, about cooking.

"Are you still skinny, Cordelia?" she asked me. "Or is all that French cuisine going straight to your hips?"

"Still a skinny little runt," I told her. "And it's not cuisine, Aunt Phoebe. It's just good home cooking."

I had had an idea one day, while I was concocting my own version of Julia Child's soupe au pistou, with grated zucchini and a purée of garbanzo beans. I had imagined my little restaurant (humble but fabulous: that's how I described it to myself) and the lit-up sign over the door:

CHEZ CORDELIA
HOME COOKING

That really appealed to me, and when I told it to my aunt, she liked it, too.

"You don't think it's a dumb idea?" I asked. her. "Me opening a restaurant?"

"Frankly, Cordelia, I've never tasted your cooking, except for the tuna salad sandwiches you used to make me. And I think you fried me an egg once or twice. But I hear you're pretty good."

"I *am*," I assured her fervently. "I'm very good, and I'm getting better every minute. Wait till you taste my Christmas dinner."

"Humble but fabulous?"

"Well, for Christmas we'll skip humble."

We reminisced about past Christmas dinners at my mother's. She served Rock Cornish game hens every year, stuffed with wild rice, garnished with mandarin orange segments, and served with an odd, orange-and-sherry flavored sauce—a sauce so time-honored and invariable that the taste of sherry always means Christmas to me. The hens were usually overcooked, because my mother would become engrossed in one of the new books she got for Christmas, and she always forgot vegetables. Once we had canned water chestnuts and a big bowl of prunes with dinner.

"But there was always plum pudding for dessert. Imported from England and flaming."

"We won't be having plum pudding, Aunt Phoebe," I warned her. "And I promise not to overcook anything."

"Oh, drat," she said cheerfully. "All these family traditions going down the drain."

The Lambertis left for Greenwich the day before Christmas. It looked as if Paul wouldn't be able to kiss me good-bye, but after breakfast Martha took the children out to cut holly boughs to take to Grandma, and Paul and I met in Chez Cordelia.

He pressed a tiny, wrapped-up box into my hands. "I'll miss you, Delia," he said after he kissed me, and there was real pain in his voice. We had been separated before, of course. He and Martha had gone away for a weekend to an anti- quarian book fair (leaving me with the kids and with tortured visions of him and Martha alone in a hotel room). And once he went to Boston, by himself, on a buying trip; Martha and the kids spent that weekend in Greenwich, and I had two blissful days of experimentation in the kitchen. (It was then that Cordelia's Apple Cider Pie came into being.) When Paul returned from these trips, he had been almost incoherent with the joy of our reunion.

"I can't get along without you, Delia," he said, holding me tight. "I need to see you every day. Just *see* you." It was one of the things I loved about him, that intensity—the deter- mination to grab and hold, to *experience* things. His love for me was an active, vital part of his life; he felt it, he said, every second—making me ashamed of the long hours in the kitchen when I forgot him.

It also made me ashamed of the fact that I really wasn't sorry to see them all, with Vicky and the holly, pile into the green Volvo and drive away. When they were at Martha's mother's, I knew I didn't need to worry about Paul and Martha renewing their old bonds of affection. It wasn't like being in a hotel room in New York. If nothing else, I knew his mother-in-law's company put Paul in a state of self-ab- sorbed, unaffectionate irritation. (I gathered that Martha's sisters affected him similarly, though all he could tell me about them was that Jeanne was always trying to get all of them to roll up the rugs and dance, and Cassie pronounced "Paul" as "Pole.")

So I could enjoy, with some guilt but no jealousy, my short respite from the responsibility of feeding the Lamberti family (I sometimes felt like Jay Block with his cows) and from the kids' small bedtime tyrannies and from the strain of my double life—of having Martha, after an especially good dinner, squeeze my hand and say, "You're so *dear*, Cordelia," and the next day getting down on the floor of the shop with Paul.

There were going to be ten of us for Christmas dinner. I boned another turkey—child's play, after you've done it once—and rolled it up with a mushroom-sausage filling. On the side, buttered green beans, an onion tarte, and a cranberry-pear relish I invented, plus two desserts: Cordelia's Apple Cider Pie and a cold lemon soufflé.

Christmas began with a fresh snowfall. I shoveled the front walk and the driveway, and the plow rumbled past around noon. I was glad the roads were clear and the family would be able to get there, but after that I must admit I thought a lot more about the meal to come—the preparations, the timing, and the spookiness of being hostess in Martha's house—than the family who would eat it. I changed out of my moccasins and ragged jeans into stockings, heels, perfume, and a gray dress with a white collar and cuffs (about which Juliet would comment, from out of the depths of her depression, "Oh God, another one of Cordelia's artless little neutrals"). I was putting on Paul's present—tiny star-shaped gold earrings— when I looked out the window, and there was Miranda coming up the path with her friend Annamay. As I ran down to let them in, apprehension and excitement mingled in me like a potent before-dinner drink, making me stumble on the stairs.

Miranda and I greeted each other with screams. We hadn't met in a year. Miranda seemed to have grown, and had to bend way over to hug me. Her long, biscuit-colored hair was caught at the top of her head into a bun, and she wore a purple leotard and a wool skirt. She looked like a dancer, and had, in fact, taken up ballet.

"Too late, of course, like Zelda Fitzgerald," she laughed. "But it gives me enormous personal satisfaction, Cordelia." She beamed at me and then at Annamay. Annamay was nearly as tall as Miranda, but more solid; her legs were tight with muscles, where Miranda's tended to be twiggy. She was exotic-looking, with long, fish-shaped eyes and heavy lids. She was dressed like Miranda, except that her leotard was black.

"Annamay is a professional," Miranda said, and took her friend's hand and squeezed it. Annamay looked modest, and explained that she danced with a small troupe in Cambridge.

"Small but superb," Miranda said, and squeezed Annamay's hand again. I realized that they must be lovers; this registered in me with a surprisingly small jolt.

"You look terrific, Miranda," I told her, and it was true. I remembered the change in Aunt Phoebe after her divorce; something like the same process seemed to have taken place in Miranda. I was glad to see how becoming divorce could be.

My parents and Horatio and Juliet and Mr. Oliver came next, crowded into my father's beat-up Dodge. Horatio was visiting my parents down on the shore for a week. "Between orgies," he said, kissing my cheek and snorting out his old, evil chuckle: *hn, hn, hn,* through his nose. Horatio is tall and fair like the rest of them; he had grown a beard which, except for its color, was exactly like my father's. It seemed too big and bushy for his small features, and made him look younger, as if he'd put it on for a joke. He had brought six bottles of wine and a Bloomingdale's shopping bag crammed with gifts.

"Cordelia, this house smells like Lutèce," he said. "Who's your caterer?" He took off his snowy cowboy boots, exposing bright red socks, recited some lines in French, and, looking pleased with himself, went over to the china cupboard to inspect Martha's collection of spongeware.

Juliet was frail and hungry-looking in black. Her hair was growing out messily. She seemed just as glum but less petulant than she had been when I saw her last, and no fatter. She gave me her thin, thin fingers to squeeze; her nails were bitten to the quick, exposing plump cushions of fingertips, the only fat on her. Mr. Oliver got down on his knees to pull her boots off, and she sat passively while he did so, like a doll being undressed. Mr. Oliver had changed, too, since his divorce. His hair was growing, like Juliet's—it fell softly from his bald spot to his collar—and he was wearing a spiffy-looking suit. I assumed this was Juliet's influence, although it was hard to imagine her throwing her weight around, there was so little of it.

Mr. Oliver gave me one of his black-dot cartoons: myself in a chef's hat on a rare 1913 Liberty Head nickel. Juliet handed me a package wrapped in silver paper, made her remark about my dress, and melted into a chair, leaning on Mr. Oliver, whom everyone was calling Ivan with a nonchalance I admired; I couldn't bring myself to do it. "Meg and Beth didn't call Professor Bhaer Fritz," I said to Miranda.

"But isn't he sweet?" Miranda asked, and hugged me, her goodwill spilling all over the place. *Sweet*, I thought, severely understated Mr. Oliver's virtue in the face of Juliet's formidable problems. I wondered if he ever longed for his drab, chubby, emotionally stable ex-wife.

Aunt Phoebe and Preston Maguire arrived while my father, wearing a knitted vest sent him by one of his admirers, was still standing in the doorway booming out a poem he had written for the occasion. My aunt and I hugged each other a little tearfully; she sniffled when she introduced Preston. He was a large, youngish man with melting brown eyes and a stutter, and he played the trombone with the New Haven Symphony. He turned out to be very silent, maybe because of the stutter, but he had a huge, toothy grin that made you want to grin back. He handed me a bottle of brandy. My aunt gave me a present, unwrapped—a wooden plaque that read:

> No matter where I serve my guests,
> They always like my kitchen best.

"Oh God, Auntie P.," said Horatio.

"I love it," I said. "I'm going to hang it over my bed."

"André Soltner has his over the stove," said Horatio.

I imagined Martha's reaction if I hung my plaque on the Delft tiles over her stove. "I'll have to wait till I get my own kitchen."

We all exchanged presents. I gave my aunt a pottery bank that was just like her hound dog, Bounce, and I gave Juliet and Miranda matching silver-plated ring caddies shaped like cats—you slip your rings over their tails. For my father, I got a sweatshirt with a picture of Shakespeare on the front, and one for Horatio with Sherlock Holmes. I gave my mother a teapot, painted with violets. It played "Tea for Two" when you poured; I demonstrated it for her, and she was delighted.

My father gave me a copy of *Tristram Shandy,* but everyone else gave me practical gifts—down booties and cookbooks and copper pans. Martha had left a gift for me, my own copy of *Mastering the Art of French Cooking.* Inside Volume One, it said, in Martha's handwriting, "To Cordelia, with our best love, Martha and Paul Lamberti." (The final *i* in Lamberti, as always in Martha's signature, trailed off in a wobble, significantly undotted.) Megan had drawn—at Martha's instigation, I suspected—a picture of Vicky and herself, both smiling, with "We love Cordeelea" printed at the bottom.

"How do you like it here, Cordelia?" Miranda asked me, eyeing these tokens of affection. "Being the beloved *au pair?*"

"I'm a cook," I said firmly. "And I like it fine."

"But don't you miss the sea?" Juliet asked with sudden intensity. She always called it the sea—all of them did—never the Sound. "Way up here in the corner of the state?"

I said no, I really didn't, but as the conversation went on around me I pondered it: to me, the sea meant fishing with Danny off Billy Arp's dock, and when I thought of that gray-green shimmer of water it wasn't the sea I missed, it was a whole complex of outdated emotions that brought a lump into my throat.

My siblings and I sat together, the three of them—even, languidly, Juliet—talking in the special, facetious, allusive language that had been going over my head for years. They were talking about what failures they all were as writers and academics, and how the family gifts hadn't held up in their generation. There was a shrill anxiety in their laughter at themselves. I sat and studied each of their faces in turn: Horatio with his beard, Miranda blooming, Juliet like an elf. How young they all look, I thought, and then, immediately after: how irresponsible they all are—a judgment that may seem obvious but which to me came as a shock. I was used to looking up to them as older, smarter, more confident people than I, and when they forced me to perceive them, over the sherry and cheese and crackers, as slightly pathetic children— whiz kids whose promise had come to nothing—I was over-come with a sentimental love for them. I gravitate toward people like that, I realized. Their weaknesses touch my heart. And then I thought, almost for the first time that day, *Paul* . . .

A lot of sherry was drunk before dinner—by everyone except Juliet, who had brought a six-pack of Perrier. My ruddy-faced father became ruddier, and aggressively paternal, and made Juliet and Miranda and me stand together by the fire so he could snap our picture. "These are my jewels," he intoned, kissing us each in turn. In the picture, Miranda and I flank Juliet, looking like her healthy keepers.

My aunt accompanied me to the kitchen when I went to check the turkey, and told me Preston Maguire wanted to marry her.

"Do you want to marry him?"

She looked at me in surprise. "I don't want to marry anyone. Delia, I thought you knew that."

"But he seems so nice."

"Well, he *is* nice. But that's no reason to marry him."

She asked me, hesitantly, about my own status. When was I going to divorce Danny? What was I doing with myself? I was almost twenty-three years old, saddled with a useless mar-riage to a— She hesitated, not wanting, after our past conflicts about it, to call Danny a rotter, a cad, a rat. She could have called him any of those things, of course, and I'd no longer be able to defend him.

"To a man who deserted you," she finished lamely, and when I said nothing she persisted, "Are you seeing anyone else?

I hate to pry, Delia, but I have such a special affection for you, and I want you to be happy."

"Yes, I'm seeing someone," I said reluctantly.

"And are you happy?"

"I'm ninety-nine point nine percent happy," I replied with a smile. I wondered if I should allot to Martha more than one tenth of one percent.

"Such precision!" my aunt exclaimed. "Well, I'm glad to hear it, and I promise I'll drop the subject. Let's talk about dinner."

She told me everything looked delicious. "Perfectly simple, simply perfect," she crooned, bending over the turkey. It did look good, like a nice plump baby, but I was a little worried, now that we were actually going to sit down and eat. I wasn't very experienced at devising menus. I didn't know if onion tarte would be overpowered by the turkey's sausage stuffing. Was the tarte really necessary? Were green beans enough of a vegetable? Should I have searched out some baby carrots? Or done artichoke hearts again?

"Don't be so nervous," my aunt said to me. "That's your family in there, honey, not Craig and Julia."

"That's the trouble," I said, but as it turned out I needn't have worried. Most of them were slightly tipsy, and it was Christmas; they would have forgiven anything, eaten anything. They raved about the dinner, and the only problem with the beans and the tarte was that there wasn't enough of either. Miranda said, "Cordelia, I haven't had a bean like this since I was in Paris."

Preston said, "I've never had food like this, Cordelia," stumbling on the C and smiling.

Their faces looked like the faces of the people I used to observe dining at Grand'mère: satisfied, contented, good-humored. This is the way people should look, I thought. This is why I want to cook.

We drank every drop of Horatio's rare white Burgundy, and the conversation at the table became jolly. Even when the talk turned to Horatio's abandoned career, and Miranda's, the old anxieties and rivalries smoothed out, and everyone was mellow and loving.

"I may move to California," Horatio said over coffee and Preston's brandy. "Maybe to Monterey. Or the south of France. I want to enjoy life for a while. Fleet the time carelessly and all that." No one pointed out that he'd been doing just that for a couple of years now. My parents looked at him benignly, just as if, a week ago, they hadn't been complaining to me about Horatio's waste of his gifts. "I'm all dried up," he said, almost with pride, scraping at the label on the brandy bottle with his thumbnail. "All written out."

"Typical child prodigy," Miranda said. "Over the hill at thirty." But she smiled at Horatio and added, "Just like me, kiddo. I'd hate to tell you what a mess my new novel is." The sympathetic gazes swiveled down the table to Miranda. She shrugged. "I can write, that's no problem. But I have nothing to say."

"Oh, Miranda," said Annamay, putting her head on Miranda's shoulder. Miranda laid her cheek against it, and everyone smiled at them, the way they might smile at kittens.

"Well, Dad's still got plenty to say," Horatio said, and they began to talk about my father's new book, *East from the Sea*. It was a very melancholy book, my aunt had told me—an old man's book.

"What did you think of it, Cordelia?" Miranda asked me, with a small gleam of mischief but no malice.

"Well," I said, and stopped. A chorus of "You haven't read it" echoed down the table, and they all grinned and hooted. It took me by surprise, this fond, playful tolerance.

"You don't need to read my poems, Cordelia," my father said. "You inspire them." He raised his glass of brandy to me.

"Oh, Daddy," I protested. "You hardly ever even see me."

"I have my memories," he said, suddenly serious. "I have wonderful children," he added, turning to Preston. "Couldn't ask for a better bunch of kids."

I looked at the faces around the table, over the coffee cups

and dirty plates, and I recalled how I used to feel crowded out
by them, and by the vast numbers of words they generated.
In my winy haze, all that ancient resentment seemed pointless,
and I felt truly kin to my family, maybe for the first time ever.

"Then there's Cordelia," said Horatio. He had drunk more
wine than anyone, and I became wary again, half expecting
belligerence, but he spoke my name affectionately.

"Oh, Cordelia's the real writer in the family," Aunt Phoebe
said. "I've always maintained that. She's the observer, the one
with the sharp eye who stands back and watches."

"The writer who doesn't write," Horatio said smartly.

"She may," my father said, with more goodwill than conviction. "Sometime."

"No, thanks," I said, and began briskly to stir sugar into my
coffee. "Unless I write a cookbook."

There were various encouraging noises, more compliments
on the meal, a discreet belch from Horatio. Juliet had become
more and more silent, regarding the scanty plate of food Mr.
Oliver had fixed for her as if it were swarming with maggots.
The plate was still there, and she hadn't eaten one crumb that
I could see. All of a sudden she sat up in her chair and began
to talk, and everyone else stopped to listen; it was as if the
pewter coffeepot had come to life.

"Ivan and I saw Luciano Pavarotti being interviewed on
television," she said, with compelling irrelevance. Her voice
was small and cold, but oddly husky, perhaps from disuse. "He
said, 'I was blessed by God with the ability to enjoy life, and
I thank Him for that every day.' He said it so simply, with such
serenity in his face, I began to cry and cry, I felt so left out and
lost, because I was born with just the opposite, the inability to
enjoy anything, the ability—the fantastic ability—to hate myself and my life and everything in it. I hate this food and I hate
this table and these plates, and I hate turkey and horrible
stuffing and beans and pie. I hate forks and spoons and coffee
cups, and I hate you all."

She began throwing her silverware around, and I think she

would have begun on her pristine plate of food if Mr. Oliver hadn't taken her by the shoulders and held her. She collapsed into long, gasping, helpless sobs. The rest of us sat stunned and unmoving, as if she had put us under a spell, but what had really happened was that she had broken the spell. We were no longer a contented, bantering family group, bemused by food and wine and love. We broke up into a bunch of separate worriers, burdened with our private cares, gazing at Juliet in horror.

I was overtaken by a primitive rage at her. I hadn't realized how much I'd wanted to impress my family, and she had spoiled everything, cooling the warmth my dinner had created with her bratty explosion. I didn't forget, either, that she was the Miller with the dramatic gift; I admired her timing—the way she put in her two cents right at the end, so we'd be left with the taste of her troubles instead of my cooking.

Mr. Oliver said, apologetically, as if she were his wife or his daughter, or as if her behavior were his personal failure, "I'll just—let me—" He led her into the living room.

There was a depressed silence. "Poor old Jule," Miranda said, and Annamay shook her head, looking tragic, but inwardly thankful, I imagined, that she didn't have a sister like Juliet.

Horatio said, in his old cynical voice, "You can't help but wonder how many people secretly feel the same way but would never admit it."

I stood up, tottering slightly. I had to speak; a statement had been building up in me all day, and Juliet's speech had made it imperative. "Well, I don't feel that way," I said. Their faces all turned up at me, but their expressions were various: surprise, amusement, brow-furrowing concern, apprehension. I was too angry to feel foolish, and I plunged on. "I love turkey and pie and wine and everything, I love you all." I began, horribly, to cry before I could stop myself. "I love every person in this house," I blubbered—something like that. I can't imagine now what it was I said, but when I stopped and sat back down, abruptly, everyone murmured in support.

My father nodded approvingly at me. Miranda said, "Aw, Cordelia." My aunt got up and knelt beside me and stroked my hair. Horatio reached over to clap me on the shoulder.

"Tiny Tim Cratchit," he said.

My mother looked down the table at me with tears in her eyes. "Don't mind Juliet, honey," she said. "She didn't mean it. It's a good sign. Energy and resistance. It's an improvement, believe me. I'm just sorry—" She made a gesture of helplessness.

From the other room, I could hear Juliet sobbing more quietly, and Mr. Oliver's low, reasonable voice. I felt bad, now that I had everyone fussing over me, that my sister was in such a state, but I felt a certain triumph, too. It was good to be loved and petted by my family. Maybe, years earlier, I should have cried and poured out my soul. Maybe they wouldn't have scoffed, maybe they would have put down their books and listened to me.

Along with my exultation and the remnants of my anger (will my feelings toward my family ever be simple?), I couldn't help feeling some relief. If Juliet's outburst meant she was getting better, then I had to welcome it. I thought: I can exchange my own pride for my sister's health—but it wasn't a completely ungrudging transaction.

I won't say the spell was restored by my little speech. In fact, we were restless at the table after that, conversation was fitful. I knew that pretty soon people would begin looking at their watches and talking about the long drive home. But we were considerate with each other. There were small displays of affection, warm smiles, plans for future reunions.

We all kept our ears half tuned to the living room; after a long silence, we heard the astonishing sound of Juliet's laugh. I got up and peeked in, at the risk of alienating my sister, but she didn't notice. She was looking at Mr. Oliver. He was cracking walnuts for her, and she was giggling and eating them from his hand.

I reported this in a discreet whisper to my mother, and a low

murmur was passed around the table: "Juliet's eating nuts."
It restored a little more of the spell, and by the time everyone
stood up and asked for their coats, there was an easier feeling
among us.

"It was a lovely, lovely meal," said my mother.

"A wonderful dinner, Cordelia," my father echoed.

When Juliet came up to me and apologized, I hugged her
out of real affection for her poor bony self. She seemed to
flinch at the contact—something hurt, the strength of either
my squeeze or my affection—but she forced herself to squeeze
back, and we leaned on each other in a sisterly way—I half
drunk, she genuinely needing support. Then she went slowly
down the path on Mr. Oliver's arm.

The rest of us hugged, kissed, called good-bye. I would have
begged them to stay, but I wanted to keep my dignity, and my
edge of victory over Juliet. I'd exposed myself enough. I was
half ashamed of these calculations, especially because I really
would have liked for some of them to linger on, but it was late,
and I don't suppose I could have persuaded them. I went outside shivering, and saw them off in the blue December night,
and when I returned to the house it still seemed, not un-
pleasantly, full of their complicated presences.

The next morning, I had a slight hangover and a bad case of
loneliness. The Lambertis would be gone another two days.
There had been snow during the night, and the house was
spookily quiet under its blanket. I shoveled the paths, but when
I finished that I was without duties, without occupation. It
began to snow again, hard. I tried to settle down with a murder
mystery—Martha had a collection of them on a bookshelf in
the TV room—but I couldn't concentrate. What I needed
was a good gossip, the hashing over of yesterday's dinner—
Juliet's behavior and my behavior—with a sympathetic soul.

Calling Nina in New York would have been perfect, but
Nina was unavailable. I had had a disturbing Christmas card
from her. The card itself was all in German ("*Fröhliche
Weihnachten*"), and it was postmarked Vienna, where Nina

and Archie were living. The eminent piano teacher in New York had rejected Archie as a student. "She said he's got an immense talent," Nina wrote, "but he'd gone too far in the wrong direction on his own and with mediocre teachers, and she didn't have the guts to take him on." The teacher had, however, recommended him to a conservatory in Vienna she was connected with. Nina and Archie had flown there for his audition, he'd been accepted, and they had stayed. They'd found an apartment, and Archie was working hard.

The thing that bothered me about Nina's note, besides the fact that she was thousands of miles away, was its cheerfulness. "Vienna is all cafés and pastry shops and beautiful music," she wrote. "Of course, I had to turn down the *Voice* job, after all, but I'm sure to find something here, once I learn German."

I pictured her there, with her Brenda Starr hair pinned up, eating pastry and getting fatter, putting all her energies into wangling good breaks for Archie, Nina, whose business was words, in a place where all the words were closed to her. It would take years, I imagined, for anyone—except possibly my mother and Juliet—to become good enough at a new language to write it for a living.

There had been a time when I'd envied Nina's single-minded passion for Archie. Now, looking at her German Christmas card, with its saccharine nativity scene and its incomprehensible greeting, I was disgusted by it.

So, Ninaless, friendless, locked in by the blizzard, bored, still unsettled by the Christmas dinner with my family, I wandered around the house. I straightened the kids' rooms. Megan had taken with her to her grandmother's the beautiful-princess hand puppet I gave her for Christmas, but the Cookie Monster I'd given Ian was shoved under his bed. For the first time, it saddened me that Ian disliked me so thoroughly. I wondered if he sensed I was a threat to the stability of his life—a very different kind of monster from the furry fellows on *Sesame Street*.

I stopped at the door of the room where Paul and Martha

slept, and looked in: four-poster hung with old crocheting, twin highboys, a worn and valuable Oriental carpet. I had done this many times—just peeked. I had never crossed the threshold. The beautiful room was enemy territory, full of hidden dangers. Even to stand there and look into it was bad for my morale—it looked so completely impregnable.

That bedroom fortress was bad enough. For the sake of my peace of mind, I shouldn't have looked through the Lambertis' pile of Christmas cards (kept in a basket on the coffee table), wondering who Al and Nan were, and David Lawrence who wrote, "Thanx again to you both—hope I can do the same for you sometime," and the Northrup family, and Aunt Loretta and Uncle Pete . . . But I did look through them, season's greetings from the long chain of relatives and friends and clients and acquaintances coiled up on the side of Paul's marriage—and, on the other side, me. They haunted me all day, those ghostly well-wishers, who, when they heard Paul and Martha were getting a divorce, would cry, "The Lambertis! Why, they're such an ideal couple!"

For lunch, I polished off the plate of food Juliet had scorned the day before. I hadn't the heart to cook. But even straight from the refrigerator, the food was delicious, and that proof of my powers cheered me up. For dinner, I planned, I would make a perfect omelette—something I'd been practicing.

I was watching an old movie on TV (*The Spanish Main*, with Maureen O'Hara, who reminded me of Nina) when my mother called. I expected a little gossip, a few more compliments on the previous day's dinner, but she said, without preamble, "Cordelia, the police are on their way up to see you."

I gripped the receiver with both hands and dropped into a chair. My knees were actually weak, and I felt, briefly, faint. The police. This was what I had been dreading all these months since I left Madox Hardware: the footsteps on the stairs, the knock at the door, the flashing of the badge, and the accusations.

"Cordelia?"

"What do they want to see me about?" I managed to ask. To me, I sounded sick and stunned, as if I'd just been punched in the stomach, but my mother didn't seem to notice.

"It's the murder of that Madox boy, where you used to work. Someone broke in and robbed the store last summer and shot him, and they've caught someone but they can't identify him; apparently, he won't cooperate at all. They've been investigating this for months, and now they're questioning all former employees. I don't know, it sounds vaguely incompetent to me, I should think the FBI has all kinds of methods these local police ought to know about. When Horatio was researching this sort of thing for his books it seemed to be a fairly simple matter, just identifying someone. After all, they *have* the man right there."

As she talked, I began to relax. It wasn't me they wanted. It wasn't the trivet, or Mr. Madox's revenge, that was leading them to my door. And yet I wondered: wasn't it, really? What if they'd told my mother this story to spare her? What if they had a warrant with them for my arrest?

I didn't really believe this, but it worried itself into my brain while I waited, looking out the window at the colorless view. It had stopped snowing, but the road was still unplowed and looked slippery. Would they drive all the way up here in this weather to put a few routine questions to a former employee? I tried to think. Who knew about my shoplifting, besides Mr. Madox and me? Malcolm, but he was dead. Juliet and Alan. Alan was gone, in New York with his play, but Juliet . . . had Juliet talked to the police? I almost called my mother back to ask, but I saw how odd it would look and stopped myself. I could only hope Juliet, so sunk into herself, had forgotten the circumstances of my flight to her and Alan in New Haven. Mr. Madox, though—I imagined him nursing his grudge, being distracted from it by the death of his son, then returning to it, getting comfort out of it, mulling it over, and going to the phone, his knotty old hands shaking with rage as he dialed the police . . .

About three o'clock, a car pulled up. I had expected the

flashing blue light, but there was none, and the two men who came up the path wore topcoats over suits. They could have been insurance agents, or a team of doctors making a house call. They introduced themselves as Detective Sherman and Detective Toscano. Sherman had light hair and sideburns, Toscano dark hair and a moustache. They smiled at me and called me "Miss Miller," and said they were sorry to bother me. Keeping very calm, I asked them to sit down, and they perched side by side on the edge of the sofa, keeping their coats on. When Sherman reached into his inside pocket, I thought it was for handcuffs, but what he took out was a large photograph. He handed it to me and said, "Have you ever seen this man?"

It was Danny, of course, and as I took it and looked at it, everything became clear. Danny had robbed the store and killed Malcolm Madox. I felt sick and faint all over again; it was another punch in the stomach. Danny, I thought, you idiot, you stupid jerk.

"He's my husband," I said. "Danny Frontenac."

The two looked at each other, just briefly, with flickers of surprise, and then they concentrated on me. "We've been holding this man up at Connecticut Valley for almost four months," Sherman said, while Toscano took out a notebook and a Bic pen. "He's refused to cooperate, won't identify himself, won't talk at all, even though it's been explained to him over and over that it's to his advantage to tell us who he is. And now—" He spread out his hands on his knees and sighed. "You tell us he's your husband and his name is Danny Frontenac."

"Would you mind spelling that last name?" Toscano asked.

I spelled it for him, and said, "He's my estranged husband."

Sherman sat back again and crossed his legs. He probably didn't realize it, but he was smiling, and so was Toscano. "And when did you see him last, Miss Miller? Or should I say Mrs. Frontenec?"

"Miss Miller," I said, and frowned, pretending to think about it. They waited patiently while I worked out my position. I saw immediately that it was dangerous. Danny had robbed the store I was fired from. If I said I had seen him back at the beginning of September—it was just before the murder, I was pretty sure, that I'd run into him at the fair—if I admitted that, it would look like collaboration. And if I lied about it and they found out—if Danny told them he'd been with me . . .

I felt sicker and sicker, but I had to say something. "I'm trying to recall the exact date," I said, smiling wanly. "It was in October, year before last. What's that? Fifteen months ago? I can't remember what the date was."

"The date doesn't matter, Miss Miller," said Sherman. Toscano wrote in his notebook, scribbling without looking. His eyes were on me. Sherman asked, "You haven't seen him in fifteen months?"

"No. He walked out on me. Just left, without a word." I would dazzle them with my sorrows. "I never knew why. I have no idea where he went. I have no desire to see him again."

They asked for more details: where Danny had worked, who his parents were, how long we'd been married. I gave them the address of George and Claire in Florida and told them about Danny's job at the shirt factory.

"Would you say your husband was . . ." Sherman screwed up his face as if trying to find an inoffensive word. "An unstable individual, Miss Miller?" he finished.

I remembered Danny when I saw him last, not fifteen months ago but last fall. I remembered his scraggly beard, and how he smelled, and his torn sweatshirt, and the look of a wild horse in his eyes. But I couldn't tell them that. "Oh, no," I said. "Until he up and left me, he was completely stable. Mr. Average."

Toscano turned over a page, and Sherman cleared his throat and pulled at his tie. "Okay. Good. Now. About you. I should tell you that this all looks, kind of, a little funny. Okay? I mean, you used to work at this hardware store—"

"I know," I said quickly, to get it over. "It looks like I might have put him up to it. Is that right?"

"Well—" Sherman shrugged. I looked at Toscano, and he shrugged, too.

I compressed my lips in a firm line, and shook my head. "It's odd, I admit that. I see that it looks a little funny. But I don't know what to say. I didn't put him up to it. I haven't seen him. I don't know anything about it." They'll go back to Danny in the mental hospital, I thought as I said this. They'll confront him with his name and the statement of his wife, and he'll tell them we were together not four months ago—a day or two before the murder, in fact. "She told me all about the place," he'll say. "She was fired from there for shoplifting. She told me all about it." I wondered how extensive his mental disturbance was. And how much would he hate me—for blowing his cover, for lying about our last meeting, on general principles . . . ? Enough to say, "We planned it together, Delia and I"?

I sat looking at the detectives, shaking my head and saying, "I don't know anything about it. I heard about Malcolm's murder, a friend of mine saw it in the paper and told me. But I never connected it with Danny. There was no reason to." I thought of something. "But it said brown hair in the paper. Danny has red hair—bright red hair!" I thought it would save me; they had the wrong man, there'd been a mistake.

"He seems to have dyed his hair," Sherman said. I tried to imagine Danny pouring brown dye on his scraggly mop. And the beard? He must have shaved it off before the robbery. I would have liked to know, but of course I couldn't ask. "Dyed it brown," Sherman went on, looking covertly amused. "It's grown out since he's been—ah—confined, of course. It certainly looks to be a very brilliant red."

"It is. I mean, it always was. I see." I paused and tried to look sincere and perplexed, with just a hint of impatience. "Well. I wish I could be more helpful."

Sherman scratched his head. He seemed to have an endless repertoire of nervous habits. "I'm not so sure you can't, Miss Miller. Maybe you could tell us—ah—where you were on the

day of the murder. That would be September four of last year.
For our records. This is all routine."

That's what they always said on TV—just routine—and
two days later you found yourself hiring Perry Mason for your
defense. "Well, I remember that I was at work when I heard
about it. A friend of mine called and told me."

They wanted Humphrey's name and address—Nina's, too,
but I told them she was in Vienna, and they just nodded.
Setbacks were part of the routine, too.

"And the day before that? That would have been a Friday—
the third of September."

"Well, I worked. I can't really remember. I'd have to think
back."

"You weren't . . . seeing anyone? A man? Maybe you had a
date that night."

Toscano held his pencil ready, waiting to note down the
name of a boyfriend, but I said, "No," glad I could be truthful,
for once. "I might have gone to the movies with Nina, or over
to Humphrey's with some of the people from the restaurant.
I just don't remember." I was damned if I'd tell them about
the fair, but I had to tell them I'd been living with Juliet, because they asked me, and that opened another door of panic:
they would interview Juliet, and she'd tell them I was fired for
shoplifting. "My sister is ill, though," I said. "She's home
with my parents, undergoing treatment. You might have seen
her there today?"

Sherman shook his head, and said he doubted if they'd have
to bother her. "We'll check with this Mr. Ebbets at the restaurant. We may be getting in touch with you again." He stood
up, and so did Toscano, pocketing his notebook.

I saw them to the door. I had to hang on tight to the doorknob as we stood there, my knees were so weak. Would you
believe we lingered there for another five minutes, talking about
the weather? About Toscano's ski trip to Vermont? About the
prospect of a New Year's Eve blizzard?

Before he left, Sherman said, "I should tell you that your
husband's lawyer may latch on to you at some point. He'll be

trying to prove insanity, of course, and he may want you as a witness."

My knees got weaker, but I'd seen enough TV to know my rights. "I don't have to testify, though, do I? I don't have to tell him anything."

"You can tell him to go away and leave you alone, if you want to, Miss Miller," said Sherman. "And you don't even have to put it that politely." Toscano snickered. "He can't force you to testify on behalf of his client."

And can you force me? I asked silently, wondering if it was true, that old murder-mystery cliché that a wife can't be made to testify against her husband. I didn't want to ask, so I said nothing, and when they were gone, wishing me a happy new year, I collapsed into a heap, right there on the bare floor by the front door. I wished Paul and Martha had left Vicky with me. I would have been immeasurably comforted if I could have put my arms around her neck and hugged her tight and taken heart from her doggy love.

It was fitting, I trought, that the Lambertis should be away and the house empty. I had never felt so alone. I didn't even long for Paul. I couldn't confide in Paul or in anyone, so what use would any human being on earth be to me?

It wasn't until I'd spent several hours feeling sorry for myself that I thought of Danny—Danny as a real person, that is, instead of an abstract force that could bring trouble on my head. I was eating my omelette (and it turned out, after all, pretty well) when I pictured, suddenly, the murder—the scene inside the hardware store: Malcolm confronting Danny, snarling something at him, Danny pulling the trigger (in panic? in rage?), and Malcolm crumpling to the floor. Or would there have been a struggle, a fight? Malcolm knocking the gun from Danny's hand and pinning him down, the gun just out of reach of his scrabbling fingers, and then the sudden overturn, the gun grasped, Malcolm lunging toward Danny, and Danny shooting—Malcolm clutching his chest and staggering, and . . .

I had no acquaintance with violence, only this TV stuff. My most fearsome memories were of my father's friend, Theodore Low, The Dentist Poet, smashing whiskey bottles. That, and scenes of Vietnam on the news. Danny, I thought, who couldn't kill in a war, had killed in a hardware store for petty cash. How like him to bungle the robbery, to lose his nerve and get caught. How like him to *fail*: I could say that, finally, of a boy who was once my hero, my dreamboat, my sweetheart. Now he was a Macbeth, who killed for gain and let himself get caught.

And then, almost immediately, I thought: I'm *glad* he failed. Who wouldn't lose their nerve after such an event—the taking of a life—except a hardened soul? A Malcolm Madox, for example. Sympathy for Danny overwhelmed me—my poor, weak Danny, who couldn't kill in cold blood without falling apart. He's a good boy, I insisted silently to the absent police: he was driven to it.

I would have called someone—my aunt, my mother, Miranda—but whom could I tell it to? That I had loved and married a murderer? And that the police might be coming for me any minute as an accomplice?

By the time the Lambertis got home next day, my self-pitying panic had calmed to a cold, sick dread—like a recurrence of flu. I had spent some agonized time wondering whether to tell Paul and Martha, and decided I'd better. Not the whole truth, of course; my life, I decided, would be forever clouded by that gap in the whole truth, but I couldn't help it. I had never wanted anything so passionately as I wanted to remain uninvolved in that murder.

"I think I should tell you that my husband is suspected of killing a man," I said to them that evening after the kids were in bed. "He's locked up in a mental hospital. He was found at the scene of the crime with a gun in his hand. The police were here yesterday to question me." I managed to keep my voice as unemotional as if I was reporting a visit from the dry-cleaner's van. "They'll probably be back," I said. "There's a

funny sort of coincidence involved." And I explained that I
had once worked at Madox Hardware.

Martha was startlingly sympathetic, but Paul didn't like it,
I could tell—any of it, from the police at his house to my taste
in husbands to the funny sort of coincidence.

"How upsetting for you, Cordelia, the day after Christmas,"
Martha said with indignation. "They have a nerve, I think.
Why do they have to drag you into this?"

"Well, it *is* odd," I said uncomfortably. "That he would rob
a place where I used to work. They wanted to know if I'd seen
him. I suppose they thought he and I might be working together."

"But that's disgusting!" said Martha. Her complete, automatic faith in my honesty touched me, it was so unexpected.
I was glad I'd never gone farther than the threshold of her
bedroom. "They should be able to take one look at you and
see that you couldn't be involved in anything so horrible. Aren't
they trained to read character?" She threw down the needle-
point canvas she'd been working on and drummed her fingers
on the arm of the wing chair. "They are so *stupid!*" She sat
shaking her head. It was the sordidness that bothered her, I
realized: murder coming so close. She was rejecting it.

"Let me get this straight," said Paul. "You knew this guy
who was murdered?"

"Vaguely. I used to work for his father."

"But you never mentioned this place to your husband?"

"I haven't even seen him in over a year!" You know that, I
said to myself. He was looking at me as if he knew nothing, as
if I was a stranger.

Paul picked up his pipe and began to fill it, something he
normally did only for book business—it gave him confidence,
he said. I didn't know what to make of his lighting it now.
"It is an incredible coincidence," he said slowly, sucking in
smoke.

"I can't help that," I said. The thought glanced against my
mind: *sometimes you have to tell lies on behalf of the truth,*

and recoiled from it. It sounded like Watergate talk, or something Malcolm Madox would say. Was that what I'd come to? "He walked out on me a year ago October. I haven't seen him since, and I don't want to. I don't know what else to say."

Martha slapped the chair arm suddenly with the flat of her hand. "I don't see that it's such a coincidence," she said. "This hardware store is in Hoskins, didn't you say? That's not that far from your home town—Danny's home town—is it, Cordelia? It's the same general area, isn't it? It's natural he should stick to familiar territory. They'll probably find other robberies down there that he was responsible for. Or he could even have been watching you, Cordelia. He could have spied on you and on the store. The man's irrational, obviously. Who knows what he's capable of?"

I tried to make my mind work as if it were ignorant of the truth. Were Martha's ideas plausible? Yes—marginally—I decided, and stored them away for the police.

We talked it over a little longer, until the lies I had to keep telling ganged up on me and gave me a splitting headache. I kept wanting to confess, and I feared that if I was ever put on the witness stand I would blurt out everything. The trivet, the back room with Malcolm Madox, the marital wrongs Danny had accused me of, my affair with Paul—it would all come rushing out, no one would be able to shut me up, they'd carry me out shouting and raving, confessing to everything, anything . . .

"I guess I'll go to bed," I said. I looked pleadingly at Paul, but he gazed intently into his pipe.

"Have some hot milk, Cordelia," Martha said in her maternal voice—the one she doled out so sparingly to the kids—and she shook her head again in disgust. "The stupidity of these people! And on the day after Christmas."

The same two detectives came back two days later—silent Toscano, nervous Sherman. I felt I knew them intimately. I noticed Toscano had on a new tie, though Sherman's seemed to be the same as before. They gave me, in a nice way, a

thorough grilling, right out of the movies. But, strangely, as
they questioned me, I became a little more confident. Miraculously, no one—not Danny, or Juliet—had told about my
shoplifting, and my being fired for it. If anyone had, the
police wouldn't be putting me through it so pleasantly.

I had to give them a complete account of my movements
since Danny left: where I'd lived, where I'd worked, who my
friends were, where I hung out. I did so gladly—there wasn't
much to tell, and none of it could connect me with Danny.
No one but Nina knew I had seen him at the fair in New
Haven, and Nina was in Vienna.

As they were leaving, I asked them a question that had been
bothering me all these months. "How's Mr. Madox? Does he
still have the store, or . . . ?" I didn't know how to express what
I feared—that he had lapsed into depression or madness or
senility after Malcolm's death. "Is he all right?"

Sherman said, "The old man passed away, a month or so
after the murder. Heart attack. The store was bought by one
of the big chains, I forget which one. They're remodeling it
now, I believe. Gonna have a spring opening. But the old man
was just wiped out by the murder."

It was that statement, I think, that made me break down
later that night. I thought about it all afternoon—harmless
old Mr. Madox, dead of grief—and, if you followed his death
back, around all the corners of the maze, there I was at the
beginning, with a trivet in my hand. By evening, I all of a
sudden couldn't stand the weight of it any more, and I began
to cry, right in the middle of telling Megan her story. It was
a story about a beautiful princess cast away to a snowy waste-
land. After many struggles, she carves herself a snow house
out of a huge drift and settles down there, eating snow ice
cream flavored with the delicious red berries that grow outside
her front door. I was trying to decide whether a seal would
befriend her there, or a penguin, or a lost husky from a dog-
sled team, when I felt the tears begin to come. I couldn't stop
them. I sat on the edge of Megan's bed and sank my head

down on my knees and wept—mostly for Mr. Madox but partly for me.

"Cordelia, it's not *sad*?" Megan said tentatively, and then she yelled, "Mommy! Cordelia's crying!"

Martha came upstairs, and I was led away, with Megan wailing behind me, "It's not a *sad* story, Cordelia! It's not fair, you didn't finish!"

The last person I would have chosen to collapse on—except maybe for Detectives Sherman and Toscano—was Martha, but I did. I sat with her on the sofa downstairs and broke down thoroughly, Juliettishly, while she rocked me in her arms. Paul was in the shop with a client—thank God, because I told her everything. I couldn't control myself. It all poured out, the whole story of Danny and Malcolm and Mr. Madox and me, a tale of theft and blackmail and perversion and lies and guilt and death that probably shocked her to the marrow of her fine bones, but she never let on, she just kept her arms around me and let me cry and rant, and never said a word, except words of comfort. She was so nice about it, I wanted to go on—I had a mad impulse to go on—and tell her about Paul and me, as if I were a penitent Catholic and she a ladylike priest in a neat blond bun. I was really going to do it (I'll pack my stuff and get out of here in the morning, I thought, I'll go home to my parents the way Juliet did) when Paul came in, smoking his pipe and smiling. I could tell he'd just made a fat deal, and when I saw him there, looking pleased and then surprised and then concerned and then, almost invisibly, antagonistic, the urge to tell left me, and so, in fact, did my tears. I wiped my eyes and blew my nose while Martha explained to Paul, with a reassuring look at me, that Cordelia was upset by the police visit. I apologized to Martha for my loss of control.

"We all have to break down sometimes," she said—it was a truism she believed in theoretically but which was not, in her case, true. I was grateful to her, though, for her sympathy. I knew she would keep mum about what I'd told her, and would defend me to the death, because I was her cook, she had chosen me, I was part of the world of the yellow house. I trudged up to my room, without looking directly at Paul, feeling enormous double relief: that I'd gotten so much off my chest, and that I hadn't said anything to Martha about Paul and me. I had a clear intimation that our love for each other was nearly used up, that there weren't many drops left in the bottle—not nearly enough to carry us through. I cried myself to sleep.

The police left me alone after that. Detective Sherman called up once to thank me, and to reassure me that I wouldn't be called as a witness. I asked him what the probable sentence would be if Danny was found guilty, and he said twenty-five years to life for felony murder, but in practice—his disapproval echoed loudly around his words—he might be eligible for parole after eighteen years. "But he could get off," Sherman said. "There's gonna be a lot of medical testimony, and these psychiatrists never agree."

"What happens if they prove he's insane?"

"He goes to the state hospital until he's—what do you call it, cured? Sometimes these guys are out in ninety days."

I asked Sherman when the trial would be, and he said probably not until summer, maybe fall. He told me about motions and counter-motions, but I lost him. I kept wondering how Danny, formerly my adored husband, had changed into one of "these guys," a murderer who might or might not be insane.

The defense never got in touch with me, and I had to conclude that Danny hadn't mentioned me to his lawyer. I wished I could thank him, and it occurred to me that I might do so by voluntarily testifying for the defense that I had seen him before the murder and had thought him unbalanced. But I was unwilling to climb to those heights of altruism. I imagined the prosecuting attorney and me.

"In what way did he act irrational, Mrs. Frontenac? Can't you do better than that? Can we really take it as proof of insanity that your husband took a few dollars from your wallet? If we could, I'm afraid many of us would have to declare our wives insane." (Laughter.) That's the way they do it on television.

And I had to admit, along with the prosecuting attorney, that it did look as if Danny was sane at the time of the murder: he had picked out Madox Hardware because he knew the proprietor was a defenseless old man. He hadn't counted on Malcolm Madox being there. He had gone to Hoskins, armed, in a stolen car. (I could see, now, the string of crimes stretching out behind him north from the point where May and her boyfriend had dropped him off.) And he had shot Malcolm Madox, point-blank, through the heart. If his mind had given way, that was when it happened, when he saw what he had done.

I phoned Humphrey a few weeks later, and he said the police had been in to see him. "I gave them an earful, you better believe. I told them they'd be better off going after the Pope than my little Delia," he chuckled, and then we talked about cooking. "You learn all you can up there," he advised me, "and then you move on. If you want to open your own place, you've got to rev up to cooking for a crowd. That's a whole new can of tomatoes."

I began to think, all that winter and early spring, about getting a real job as a cook. I wouldn't have, quite so soon, if all had been well between Paul and me. Before Christmas, we'd been talking, aimlessly but with excitement, of what we might do. He had a book-dealer friend out in Portland, Oregon, whom he thought of going into partnership with. Paul had been to Oregon and liked it; the crime rate, and the pollution levels, and the apathy quotient were among the lowest in the nation.

"What's an apathy quotient?" I asked him.

"It's a measure of whether anybody would come to help you if you got mugged on the street."

"I thought there weren't any muggers in Portland, Oregon," I said, but it wasn't a subject he could joke about. He held on to my shoulders and looked at me and said, "Delia, will you go with me? Leave your family and everything, and go to Oregon with me to live?"

I didn't want to move to Oregon, but I wanted to be with Paul, so I answered, "Let's get our lives straightened out first, Paul, so we can be together, and then we can decide where to live."

"You're right, you're right," he said. "First things first." But his gaze went over my head, far away. He was thinking of the safe streets and clean air of Oregon, while I wasn't thinking any further than the divorce court.

But that was before Christmas. After the police visits, things changed between Paul and me—subtly changed. It wasn't that he believed I was guilty of anything. He knew me better than to think I could really be implicated in murder and armed robbery. The trouble was that he knew I was keeping something back. I suppose he assumed it was something that affected *us*—some clandestine contact with Danny, or a lingering affection for him that was making me shield him from the police—but he knew, at any rate, that I wasn't telling him the whole truth. I kept wondering why I didn't, and I remembered seeing him, the night we met, make a conscious decision to trust me, and to tell me about the firing-squad incident. I couldn't do the same. I didn't know why I held back the truth from the man I loved, but I did, and it altered our relationship, and as spring came we both knew the stuffing had been knocked out of our love, and that our time left together was short.

There had never been any desperation in our affair when it had only Paul's marriage to Martha to blight it; we rose above that joyfully because we loved each other. But when we saw that our love wasn't, after all, limitless, a kind of troubled frenzy became part of our lovemaking. There wasn't much lazy talking, even when we had the time. We pounded our bodies together, and scratched and bit each other, and sometimes the sounds we made were more sorrowful than ecstatic. It was, in a way, horrible, and yet we kept seeking each other out. We couldn't get enough of each other.

I made a list, one day when an unexpected late snowstorm pushed spring back a week or two. I was up in my room, the snow struck sharp against the windows, and in a mood that was half misery, half anticipation, I wrote:

List of Regrets

1. marriage
2. love
3. honesty
4. small expectations

I studied that list for a while, especially the last item. Before me, in my bookcase, was the copy of *Great Expectations* my father had given me years ago—dark green, with the title in gold on the spine. That's the ticket, I said to myself. Maybe I should read it—knowing I wouldn't. But I'd make my expectations great.

Bits of another list drifted through my head, but I wasn't yet ready to write it down. I looked again at the "List of Regrets"; it was also, I knew, a "Good-bye List."

When the snow began to melt, Paul took me out for driving lessons. Martha thought I should learn; it was inconvenient that I always had to be driven to the market for groceries. Besides, she said, if I intended someday to be a successful chef with my own place, I should know how to drive a car—I couldn't very well hire a chauffeur to drive me to the fish market every morning. I thought this was a good point, and though I'd never much thought about it before, I became eager to learn to drive.

I took to it as readily as I took to cooking. Behind the wheel of the Volvo, with the world spread out before me, I felt as if I could do anything. The gears made perfect sense to me, and changed easily under my hand. Instinctively, I knew you watch the road and not the front of the car—the thing both Paul and Martha had told me was the hardest part for them to catch on to. It wasn't until I learned to drive that I saw how deprived I'd been all those years, how you're almost an amputee without a car. Even short trips, places in Gresham I used to walk to, I drove to in the Volvo, for the sheer exhilaration of it, the glamor of leaning your elbow on the windowsill and putting the radio on loud and feeling your hair blow in your face. I loved making turns, the way I'd lean to one side and the car would follow me. And the special satisfaction of successful parallel parking could put me in a good mood all day. I think I must have got out of driving what I used to get out of loving Paul—speed, excitement, risk—but in the car I had the extra advantage of control.

Once, while we were out in the car, Paul and I were over-taken by the desperate lust that was always in the air between us, and we parked the Volvo by a stretch of state forest. We walked deep into the woods and made love in a clearing full of soft early grass and saxifrage. It was a warm day, the sun beat down on us, Paul's sweat dripped in my face, and when we stood up we were both grimy from the April mud. At one time, this encounter would have made us happy—the craziness of it, and the mud, and the eerie beauty of the silent woods in the middle of the afternoon. But we drove home almost without speaking and went to our separate showers.

Although we no longer talked much together, certain things became clear to me, and I know they did to Paul, too. He wasn't ready to leave Martha, for one. And I didn't love him enough to push it, for another. These two facts were intimately connected. If he had been more independent, more of a doer, less of a dreamer—*less weak* was how I tried not to put it—I would have encouraged him more. And if I had encouraged him more, he would have left her. And if all these ifs had been realities, I would have loved him enough to trust him with the facts about Danny's killing of Malcolm Madox. And all would have been well. Chez Cordelia and Lamb House Books would have merged into some lovely, unique conglomeration of good smells and rare bindings.

This did not, of course, happen, and as spring thrived and mellowed it became obvious that it wouldn't, and I thought about leaving. Martha surprised me by announcing that she had been offered a job teaching some cooking courses that summer at the arts worshop where she had her weaving lessons, and she thought she might take it.

"I've never had a real job," she confessed, as if the fact surprised her.

"You're a great teacher, Martha," I said. "Take it." And then, reluctantly—because I knew she was about to say how much more she'd have to depend on me to keep her house running if she went to work—I told her I was going to look for a job myself.

She wasn't happy about it. "I've learned so much from you, Martha," I said. "But now I've got to see if I can do it for a living." When she protested, I quoted Humphrey. "He says I've got to learn to cook in quantity—restaurant cooking." Martha had a great respect for Humph since she'd traveled down to New Haven to check out the food at Grand'mère, but his views didn't impress her.

"You're rushing it, Cordelia," she said. "You've only been here, what, seven months? That's hardly an adequate apprenticeship." I didn't point out that I'd been doing most of my learning from cookbooks since she had abandoned me for weaving and lunching and antiquing, but she seemed to realize it herself, because her voice got a shade less frosty and she said, "If nothing else, you've got me here to give you a critique on your cooking every night. Cordelia, I really don't think you're ready to face the great world."

I thought I was, though, and I began, furtively, to read the help-wanted ads every day in the Hartford *Courant*. If Martha caught me at it, she said, "Oh, Cordelia, for heaven's *sake*." She felt, I think, that I had in some way betrayed her. (If she only knew, I thought, that this was the end of my betrayal of her, not the beginning.) She said once, "I didn't spend all that time training you so you could walk out on me."

"We agreed it would be temporary, Martha," I said. "You couldn't expect me to be a mother's helper forever."

"Nobody's talking about forever, Cordelia," she said—just as Paul had, under similar circumstances. "But this is so *soon*," she complained.

"Don't let her push you around," Mrs. Frutchey said to me one morning while she cleaned the oven. She wore a scarf tied around her nose and mouth to keep out the ammonia fumes, and the words came out muffled but firm. "She's just a spoiled brat. She's had her money's worth out of you, don't you worry."

Paul didn't comment one way or another about my proposal to leave. He was pretending to be unaware of it, averting his eyes if he saw me with the *Courant*, and concentrating fiercely on the television if Martha or I mentioned it in the evenings. He and I hardly ever spoke. I got my driver's license at the beginning of May, so the car no longer drew us together. Even our sexual encounters were becoming less frequent, though when we did meet it was more explosive and strange than ever. After lovemaking, we used to stare in anguish at each other, just for a second or two, and then one of us would mumble an excuse—bread in the oven, school bus expected—and make a speedy exit. The rest of the time, we avoided each other.

As the weeks went by, this bothered me more and more. I became driven by the need to talk to him, but I didn't know how to go about it. I was desperately unhappy, and I knew he was, too, though all around us that May there was a feeling of great joy. Megan had a best friend from school named Jennifer. They were constantly at each other's houses, and the friendship made Megan blossom. Even Ian was getting on better without Megan's teasing. And it also made Martha happy. "It's such a relief," I heard her confess to Mrs. Lambert on the phone. "I thought she was on her way to being *odd*." Megan became, in a matter of weeks, a vastly more pleasant child; in awe, I watched this happen and rejoiced in the power of love, for that was what it was—Megan's first great love. I missed our beautiful-princess stories, though; she lost interest in them. Now, Megan told me, what she and Jennifer liked to do was go up to her room after school, shut the door, and act the stories out. "I play the princess," she explained. "And Jennifer is the wicked queen, and Vicky is the puppy." I could hear them up there, after school, while I cooked in the kitchen, and I felt oddly jealous. "Aren't they just dear?" Martha would say if she was home.

In the midst of the family bliss, Paul and I generated moroseness the way we had, before, generated passionate rapture. One afternoon, when we were in my bed, I decided I'd had enough of the silence between us. I pinned him down on the mattress and said, "Paul, we're just not going to end up together, are we? Let's admit it to each other. It's just not going to work out, is it?"

"You don't seem to think so," he said. He had his glasses off, and his eyes were larger and wet-looking without them. "You're planning to leave here, aren't you?"

Nobody's talking about forever—both of them said it, but neither one meant it, and I began to feel locked into a prison just as surely as Danny was. "What does my leaving here have to do with it, Paul? The point is for *you* to leave here."

He was silent. I could tell he wished he had his pipe, but he was too cautious ever to smoke it up in Chez Cordelia. He lay there on my bed looking pensive and miserable and so beautiful to me I could have gathered him into my arms and held him there forever. But I just sat and waited.

"Delia," he said at last, in a whisper. He closed his eyes.

"What, Paul?" I said gently.

"I don't know if I can ever leave here," he said, nearly inaudibly. "She owns me—this place—it's all her money, it's all hers. I don't know if I could manage any other life but this one."

"What do you mean, she owns you?"

His voice rose. "I was a nothing when I met Martha. All I knew was I didn't want to be a butcher. I was a wanderer, I didn't know where I was going. What I was doing. The money changed all that. I can't tell you how important it is."

"The money."

"I know it's wrong, I know it's weak and disgusting. She bought all this for me, when I decided I had to get out of the city. But it's hers, all of it."

"What about moving to Portland, Oregon?" I persisted. "What about going into business with that guy out there?"

"I don't have a business to contribute, Delia," Paul said. "The business belongs to Martha, along with everything else. I told you, she owns me. I can't leave. I can't give it up, I'd have nothing. You wanted me to tell you the truth. That's the truth. I thought I could do it, when I met you. But I can't, I can't, I can't."

We got out of my bed and got dressed, with our backs to each other, and I knew we'd never get in it again together. What he told me seemed so horrible that I tried to think of a way to get out of believing it, but I couldn't. I even saw glimmers of further truths: I felt sure that it had happened before, Paul had had a previous affair, and that to preserve her respectability Martha had topped her rival's bid as she had topped mine. The more I examined the idea the more it convinced me. Of course there had been another Cordelia, maybe more than one, and Martha had outbid them all.

I began to watch Martha. The knowledge of her limitless strength astonished me; I was impressed by it, but I couldn't see it as a virtue. It was more like a dread disease; her background and upbringing were in her like an inoperable tumor, and she suffered from it. She suffered from the necessity of keeping her shaky, rotting marriage propped up by her iron will and her money. The maintenance of the illusion of harmonious family life was the eternal, painful task of her life. What made it, I suppose, unimaginably worse was the fact that she'd been raised on old-fashioned Yankee honesty—to tell the truth, admit her mistakes, and rectify them if possible. And her whole life was a lie.

During my last weeks at Lamb House Books, when I studied the situation there and looked for a new job and cooked furiously, an interesting fact pushed itself up before me: I could have succeeded with Paul. We could be together now, with the kids visiting every other weekend and Martha remarried to a nice corporation lawyer and Paul sitting beside me as I write. If I had only insisted a little harder. If I had been more like Martha—more like her than she was herself, for it would have been my will opposing hers (and all the Lamberts behind her, pushing) and winning. Paul was there for the taking, available to the toughest customer. But I couldn't welcome it, that tumor of deceit that Martha seemed to thrive on, I had had too much of it, and I dropped out of the contest.

I was there from September to May, long enough to have had a baby if I'd been inclined to. Long enough, anyway, to learn to drive a car, to have a birthday, to spend a memorable Christmas and begin a new year. I fell passionately in love and then climbed, painfully, out. There was time for all that, and for three seasons to pass, and for Albert to die, and for my puff pastry to become as light as a butterfly wing. I look at those nine months from here and it's like remembering a long and vivid dream; they have no reality for me. All I have to show for them is my competence in the kitchen. For nine months, Lamb House Books was my life—now, it's nothing, just ten million memories, as if that space of time was a person, or a dog, and it died.

Chapter Eight

ST. DUNSTAN'S

I found St. Dunstan's Retreat House through my aunt. She heard from Preston Maguire, who was a Catholic, that they needed a cook. Preston had seen the ad in a Catholic weekly magazine, and my aunt sent it to me:

> Skilled, experienced cook wanted for small private institution. Beautiful setting. Live-in. Reliable, stable, intelligent individual preferred.

"You're reliable, stable, and intelligent," my aunt said. "And you can certainly cook. If you need a reference, Preston could write six pages on your apple-cider pie alone."

I wrote to the address given and got a prompt letter back from St. Dunstan's, asking me to come for an interview. At the head of the sheet of notepaper was a cross entwined with flowers, and it was signed "Sister Rita Ann, Director." I studied it for a long time, the black cross and the yellow flowers, the heavy engraved paper and Sister Rita Ann's florid capitals and winged commas. Her handwriting was large and fluent, the writing, I imagined, of someone who liked to eat.

I stared at the paper, trying to read a future for myself in it, until the cross blurred out and I could see only the flowers—primroses, they appeared to be, or buttercups. I decided to go for the interview.

I made a batch of cheese-and-mushroom tartelettes, and then some fresh-strawberry ones (I was proud of my pastry), and a fish mousse, and a nice ratatouille, and a batch of oatmeal-raisin cookies. I packed them into a basket, with a linen cloth, and I set the basket inside a styrofoam picnic cooler. With a sigh, Martha said I could take the car—she was already interviewing possible cook-housekeepers—and I drove the thirty-five miles northeast on a beautiful early June day.

On the way, I tried to imagine the place, and as it turned out, I was pretty accurate. St. Dunstan's was a massive house on a hill, with a long drive in front and the hill sloping down in back to a lake, the lake bordered by flower beds. Off in the distance I could see a large vegetable garden. The house and the grounds and the nuns were peaceful and immaculate.

They had set a table outside for tea, with cookies on a flowered plate, and we sat in the sun by the lake, Sister Rita Ann, Sister Carmelita, and I. They belonged to a conservative order that still wore habits—long black skirts, full sleeves, and complicated white headdresses that covered their heads closely and then sailed into the air like birds.

"St. Dunstan is the patron saint of naughty children," Sister Rita Ann told me, with a twinkle in her eye. She was just like her handwriting, large and handsome. "From the tenth century. Schoolchildren used to pray to him as their masters approached to give them a flogging. St. Dunstan put the teachers into a trance, and their canes fell to the floor. He lived in a room that was only the length of his body when he curled up to sleep, and as wide as his outstretched arms."

"About four by five?" I asked.

The two nuns inspected me sharply for flippancy, but I didn't intend any, and, seeing this, they smiled. "You have a sincere desire, Cordelia, to know the truth of all things," Sister Rita Ann observed. "Is that right?"

"I suppose it is," I said with humility.

St. Dunstan's Retreat House, they explained, was a place where Roman Catholics could get away from it all and confront their souls. "We believe in the total experience, however," said Sister Rita Ann. "We feel that this pastoral setting is a part of the peace one can find here. We also have chamber music in the evenings—several of the nuns are gifted musicians. And now and then we have a guest who is well known in the world as an artist." She smiled. "A number of singers come to us regularly, for instance—particularly coloratura sopranos, I don't know why—perhaps the demands on the voice also put extraordinary demands on the soul . . . You don't sing, by any chance, Cordelia? Or play an instrument? Well. Our greatest need is for a cook. We believe in feeding the body as well as the soul."

The nuns ate several tartelettes each, both kinds, and they spooned ratatouille onto their saucers and finished it up. They smacked their lips over the fish mousse. "We must save a bit of this for Sister Norma," they said. They ate slowly and steadily, not forgetting to offer me more tea and one of the butterscotch cookies they had provided.

"Eat one," Sister Carmelita urged. "Just to see what dire straits we're in." Sister Norma had been doing the job—and none too well, was the delicate implication. The cookies were made from a mix, they admitted, looking in distress at each other as I bit into one. They tasted like the ones I used to make for Danny and me—Slice 'n' Bake.

"Fortunately, it has been hot," said Sister Rita Ann. Her large, calm hand lingered over the oatmeal cookies, shamelessly seeking the biggest. "We have been able to get by with chops and cold platters and simple salads. But our guests have come to expect the extraordinary." She chose a cookie and raised it to her lips, paused. "Not the exotic, I don't mean that. But care, and judgment, and attention to detail. An attitude toward work we might adopt from the Shakers." She took a bite, nodded, and smiled.

A bell rang, and Sister Carmelita—a tiny, frog-faced nun

with teeth stained yellow as if she chewed tobacco—excused herself and tripped toward the house, holding her long skirts off the ground; something was about to go on in the chapel. "We feel very fortunate here," Sister Rita Ann told me. "We have every heavenly blessing and most earthly ones. All we lack is a cook."

Their last cook, a fine man but a drinker (she told me frankly), had fallen into the lake and drowned. "Not on our property," she hastened to add as I looked toward the lake. "At the south end, in the village. He fell over a rail. We hope he didn't die by his own hand. We're having a month of masses said for his soul." Her uneasy face smoothed out a little, but she remained silent for a few moments while we both looked at the lake. The water was brilliant with reflected sun, and a flock of ducks was swimming across, leaving intersecting triangular wakes. Sister Rita Ann shook her head and crossed herself.

(A few months later Jimmie Nolan, the bartender in the village, told me more about the cook. They were drinking buddies. Michael, the cook, had been a small, dapper man who made up limericks about the nuns and who had a passion for fine wines, though he would settle for whiskey—or, indeed, for anything. He had left a tab of fifty-five dollars at the Green Horseshoe Café when he died, and Jimmie paid it. Jimmie is quite sure that Michael fell drunk into the lake by accident, though he pretended to insist, for a long time, that Sister Rita Ann pushed him.)

Sister Rita Ann explained the rule of silence—lifted in the common room and in the kitchen, so that was all right. She assured me I needn't go to services, and that my free time was my own. We discussed salary requirements, and she smilingly offered a pittance over the minimum wage. "And of course you'll have all this as well," she said as we turned back, before going inside, to look at the lake again. (*And*, she said—not *but*. I admired her assurance.) The ducks were gone, and the lake was smooth as aspic.

I took the job. I was charmed by the nuns, the lake, the house—and the kitchen, which was as sane and streamlined as

a wire whisk. Martha found a cook within a week, a niece of
Mrs. Frutchey, and hired her on a trial basis.

"I'm going to keep an eye on that girl, let me tell *you*," Mrs.
Frutchey said to me during our last coffee break. "Time the
master of this house settled himself down." She gave me a
meaningful look, and I blushed. We hugged each other and
exchanged little gifts—identical calico-cat planters. We'd both
bought them at the Gresham Gift Shoppe, and we laughed at
the coincidence.

I wish my leave-taking from Paul could have been as un-
complicated. My aunt came to pick me up, to drive me to
St. Dunstan's. Paul and I had said good-bye the day before
while Martha was out.

"I suppose it's for the best," he said, in a voice that had
all the emotion frozen out of it. "I hope you'll be happy,
Delia. I hope things work out for you."

I was almost glad of the impersonality of it—that that was
how I would remember him, as the stiff, passionless Paul instead of my warm and impetuous lover. But then, as I was
leaving, and he and Martha stood on the front step saying
formal farewells, he suddenly caught me in his arms, in front
of everyone, and held me as if he could never let me go. When
he did, there were tears in his eyes. I thought of how often I'd
seen Paul cry, and how lovable he was, after all.

I got in the car with my aunt and looked back at the yellow
house. I knew I would dream about that place—the cows,
Albert, the beautiful furniture, the ribbon of wood smoke that
coiled in winter from the bookshop chimney, Paul's kisses . . .
Paul had gone inside, but Martha stood there waving and
smiling, a grand and terrible woman, as my aunt and I drove
away.

Here at St. Dunstan's, it's not only the devout and wealthy
guests who find peace. For me, it's a haven of solace from
the confusion of the last few years—order out of chaos. I have
a room on the third floor which isn't much bigger than the
fabled cell of St. Dunstan. It contains a skinny bed, a desk,
a dresser, my coin collection, and my battered bookcase—to

which I have given a fresh coat of white paint. My little TV
sits on it, as ever. On my bed is a crocheted afghan made for
me by Sister Norma (grateful to be freed forever from the
cooking). Outside my window is a giant copper beech, and
beyond it the blue lake.

The regularity of the life suits me. I was afraid, at first, that
it would be too much—I'm not cut out to live like a nun—but
the restrictions on me are very light. The rule of silence and
the rule against having men in my room are the only ones I
can think of. I am allowed the use of the nuns' station wagon
(the ashtray filled with nickels and dimes for tolls). They welcome me into their private common room, where I play poker
sometimes (for dried beans) with Sister Carmelita and Sister
Evelyn Margaret. I am permitted wine in my bedroom, in
spite of the tendencies of my predecessor.

I spend my days off with Jimmie Nolan, the poet, who lives
upstairs from the Green Horseshoe Café, where he tends bar.
He cooks for me up there, hearty feasts on a double hot plate,
and rubs my back in his big, sagging bed. I get tired. I work
hard at St. Dunstan's, keeping to the nuns' high standards. But
in return I'm gifted with sound and renewing sleep.

It may seem odd that the man in my life is a poet, but he
never talks about it, and he doesn't write about me. I suspect
Jimmie's poems aren't very good. They never get published.
He writes about his dog Woolly—a mongrel with a heart of
gold—and about the village and the bar and its patrons. I
like to hear him read his poems. On the page, his strings of
words have a way of sliding out of my grasp, just as my father's
do, or Shakespeare's. But when they're read aloud, it's Jimmie
I see, not those painful rows of letters, and it's Jimmie's strong,
lilting voice I hear, not the beating of the blood in my own
brain.

In the evenings, Jimmie and I sit on his bed and watch TV.
Jimmie never laughs with the laugh track—it's always odd
things he finds funny, and his unexpected laugh is always a
comfort. So is our lovemaking in the dark.

In September, Danny was tried in the New Haven County

Court House and convicted of felony murder. He was sentenced to life at Sommers State Prison. A month or two later, I began receiving letters from him—atrociously spelled, strange, almost mystical at times. He works in the garden at Sommers, and he seems to have a profound relationship with the plants he tends that I'd never have expected from him. In one letter he called them his children, and he was deeply sad when winter came and he was moved indoors to laundry duty.

I write back to him, of course. I don't suppose Danny wants to hear what I have to say. I think he's lost interest in me as Cordelia. I think I'm mostly an address (Lord knows how he got it) where he can direct his letters. I see how odd it is, though I've never pointed it out to him, that he and I communicate now only via the written word, and I think back to the grade-school remedial reading class that brought us together.

His letters are mostly about his life in prison, the daily round. It sounds like a rough place. The prison isn't, in fact, far from here, but Danny has never suggested I visit him, and I know I never will. He writes mostly about his chances for parole, and about the appeal his lawyer is working on, on the grounds that Danny was never fit to stand trial in the first place. Now and then, when his letters veer off into incomprehensibility, I am forced to wonder if he was fit—ever. I almost included in one of my letters an apology for not standing by him, not coming forward and testifying in his defense; that failure continues to haunt and confuse me. But I realized the unwisdom of admitting this in print. And I doubt if it would mean anything to Danny. I don't know if he even reads my letters. I doubt it, and so I write him everything. I send him my lists, and I tell him about the nuns. I even copy out Jimmie's poems for him (the one about the fishing trip to Canada, the one about Dutch Collins, the town drunk, and all the dog poems) because I hope they'll brighten his gray prison days.

These letters Danny and I exchange are important to me—possibly more so than they are to him. I need to keep my connection to Danny, to remind myself of the Cordelia I once was, and of the infinite, unpatterned strangeness of life. Danny's letters prevent me from becoming too sure of things—or of myself, and the power I fancy I have over my life.

And I need to keep tabs on him, too. I don't think anyone else does. His parents, I heard, have remained in Florida through all this, refusing to acknowledge a killer as their son; and to my family he is merely an embarrassing, invisible no-body—Cordelia's youthful folly, best forgotten. But he's still my legal husband, and I won't abandon him entirely. I think of him as a debt to be paid, and I keep his letters in a bundle in my desk, like bills. For Christmas, I sent him a large supply of good stationery, but he doesn't use it. He writes to me on the cheap, gray prison paper—his way of making clear to me, I think, how unconnected we really are. And yet the letters keep stitching between us, and his watch is still on my wrist. I check the punctual St. Dunstan's bells by it; it proclaims that I was once, at any rate, Delia, his beloved wife.

My family likes coming here to visit. My father sees St. Dunstan's as a new, fertile source of poems; he's written one called "The Lady of the Lake," which he says is about me but which I don't understand at all. When he was interviewed on *Sixty Minutes* not long ago ("everyone's troubadour," they called him) he referred to me as "my youngest daughter, Cordelia, who saves souls through her cooking," and when Harry Reasoner tried to get him to elaborate he just looked enigmatic and changed the subject to Horatio, who is touring Italy to collect material for a new book he's working on, called *Murders from the Portuguese*, starring Elizabeth Barrett Browning.

Preston Maguire and my Aunt Phoebe spent a weekend here, on retreat, at the end of apple season. Preston played the trumpet after dinner, and when the weekend was over Aunt Phoebe announced that she had searched her soul and was going to marry Preston after all. "I'm so glad I can still surprise myself," she said gleefully to me.

Juliet and Mr. Oliver—Ivan—were married at New Year's. They had a quiet wedding in the chapel at Yale, and then astonished me by throwing a huge, no-holds-barred reception where everyone drank champagne and did Greek dances. Miranda was there, with flowers in her hair; Annamay had moved out of her life, and her ballet instructor had moved in, a muscular young man named Charles. When they danced together, people stopped to watch them, and when the music stopped Charles lifted Miranda effortlessly to his shoulder. They stood there, posed like beautiful statues, while everyone applauded.

"Where do you fit into this family, Delia?" Jimmie asked me, clapping lustily.

"I don't," I said. "Never did."

"That can't be true," he said, after a little thought. "Or you wouldn't be so fond of them."

"They're my family, I can't help it."

"It's more than that," he said, and smiled. "I've got it— they're the melba toast and caviar dip, and you're a corned beef sandwich and a beer."

"Is that the best you can do, Jimmie?"

"I think I might get a poem out of it."

"Your metaphors are as crazy as my father's," I told him, and he accused me of not understanding the poetic mind; that, at any rate, is true.

I find myself, lately, growing fatter—a little blowsy, Jimmie says. He says I look like a cook. Sometimes he and I make plans to someday buy the Green Horseshoe Café from Art Hodges, Jimmie's boss, and open our restaurant there, with the sign in lights:

CHEZ CORDELIA

HOME COOKING

But for the moment, I'm contented here. In the mornings I am in the cold, clean kitchen by seven to get things going, and when the others emerge from the chapel at a quarter to eight, the trusty smell of my hot coffee greets them. Lunch is at one o'clock; after a break, I work on dinner most of the afternoon, with one of the nuns by my side to help with chopping and beating. Dinner is at six, and it's the gastronomical high point of the day—maybe the spiritual high point, too—who knows? Aunt Phoebe is in the process of rejoining the Church, and she speculates that the loaves and fishes may have been the Galilean equivalent of filets de poisson Bercy aux champignons served with a good crisp-crusted bread and a chilled white. And Sister Rita Ann called my watercress soup a miracle.

The food is what the retreatants pay for here. I don't mean to belittle the service, but that you can get at any retreat house: masses, sermons, confessions, peace and quiet, nuns, a library full of devotional reading matter, and the group sessions they've started adding to the program. Of course, that's what they come for, but it's my cooking they pay for: the spinach-stuffed crêpes, the baby beef liver soaked in milk and gently sautéed, the goulash and homemade noodles, the avocado soup, the mousses and sorbets and madeleines and coffee cakes. I'm a good cook—not a fancy cook, though I can bone a whole chicken and assemble it again around a duxelles inside of half an hour—but a good, inspired, hard-working cook. Over the stove the plaque from my aunt hangs:

> No matter where I serve my guests,
> They always like my kitchen best.

I still make lists. The other day, a beautiful windless Sunday (my afternoon off), I sat by the lake with my List Notebook and wrote:

Things I Need

1. to cook for people
2. to love someone
3. to have money in the bank
4. to be boss of my life
5. Chez Cordelia

I put a star after that last one, and doodled curlicues around the words. I liked the way it sounded, and all the things it meant to me. The list made me happy—it still makes me happy. I read it over often, as the nuns read their prayer books, to remind myself of where I'm going.

In my spare time, I work on this narrative, the story of my life. I do it to make sense out of things, so I can stand back and get a look at them. And I have done this. But I wrote it for another reason, too, and in that I've failed: I wanted to get at the whole truth, but the whole truth isn't available to me, only my little bit of it. Danny's story, or Malcolm's, or Paul's, or Juliet's, or my father's—they'd all be different, just as Alan said. They'd all be true, as true as mine, and as false. Even if they were all put together, in a book as long and complex as life itself, there would still be something missing, some mystery words can't convey. I don't know what this is—I can only call it *the real truth*—but I know when it's not there.

Well. I sit here at this desk in my tiny room, looking out at the lake, with a glass of Burgundy before me. I survey my corner of life as captured in the unreliable stack of words I've managed to put down, and the only sense I can make out of it is this: direction is laid out in front of me, and though I consider myself a prudent and sensible person, I know I'm never going to get there as the crow flies, in a straight zoom. I'm going to keep being fooled by blind alleys and going down dead ends and crashing into doors and fences. But I've got to do it my own way. That's the stone I've been kicking ahead of me all my life, and I can't stop now.